T0165277

Gary Levey

The Golden Rule

Book 1 of The Joad Cycle

He who has the gold, makes the rules.

iUniverse, Inc.
New York Bloomington

The Golden Rule
Book 1 of The Joad Cycle

Copyright © 2010 Gary Levey

All rights reserved. No part of this book may be used or reproduced by any means, graphic, electronic, or mechanical, including photocopying, recording, taping or by any information storage retrieval system without the written permission of the publisher except in the case of brief quotations embodied in critical articles and reviews.

This is a work of fiction. All of the characters, names, incidents, organizations, and dialogue in this novel are either the products of the author's imagination or are used fictitiously.

iUniverse books may be ordered through booksellers or by contacting:

iUniverse
1663 Liberty Drive
Bloomington, IN 47403
www.iuniverse.com
1-800-Authors (1-800-288-4677)

Because of the dynamic nature of the Internet, any Web addresses or links contained in this book may have changed since publication and may no longer be valid. The views expressed in this work are solely those of the author and do not necessarily reflect the views of the publisher, and the publisher hereby disclaims any responsibility for them.

ISBN: 978-1-4502-3754-3 (pbk)
ISBN: 978-1-4502-3756-7 (cloth)
ISBN: 978-1-4502-3755-0 (ebk)

Printed in the United States of America

iUniverse rev. date: 7/22/2010

For June,
My life and this book are better because of you.

I thank my sister, Dale, the English teacher, who helped make this book readable and my friends, mostly conservatives, who allowed me to see the vicissitudes of modern American life through their eyes and who endured the debates.

Novels of the Joad Cycle

Book 1: The Golden Rule

Book 2: Profit (Due: Autumn, 2010)

Book 3: Circle of Life (Due: Winter, 2011)

Book 4: The Rightness of Things (Due: Spring, 2011)

The world is too much with us; late and soon,
Getting and spending, we lay waste our powers:
Little we see in Nature that is ours;
We have given our hearts away, a sordid boon!
This Sea that bares her bosom to the moon;
The winds that will be howling at all hours,
And are up-gathered now like sleeping flowers;
For this, for everything, we are out of tune;
It moves us not—Great God! I'd rather be
A Pagan suckled in a creed outworn;
So might I, standing on this pleasant lea,
Have glimpses that would make me less forlorn;
Have sight of Proteus rising from the sea;
Or hear old Triton blow his wreathed horn.

—Circa 1802: William Wordsworth, "The World Is Too Much with Us; Late and Soon"

Prologue

Angel Falls, Maine—2084

Discarded and forgotten, the small community of Angel Falls, located in north-central Maine, had been a quaint, peaceful, out-of-the-way village, a community of families sharing common good, caring for neighbors with hope and kindness—a sin that proved unforgivable. Avarice and self-interest might have saved Angel Falls, but the community was too far from mainstream American enterprise and suffered for it. With its burnt-out cottages and storefronts and its streets pockmarked with bomb craters, Angel Falls died, a monument to American greed and aggression, a caring community only Mother Nature could love now.

A young couple walked down what had once been Main Street, gripping each other's hands. They avoided the spent American ordnance, the scorched craters, and the detritus of this place that had once been a haven of happy memories. Though this was home, on this cool northern-Maine February day, it was more. It was hard reality. The couple stopped at familiar buildings but moved on quickly; it hurt too much to linger. Here was American injustice incarnate. Here was proof that legal wasn't moral. Here, a national government facing a choice had rationalized the destruction of life, liberty, and the pursuit of happiness.

The couple didn't talk because their grief was so intense it couldn't be swallowed away, and shared guilt only made comfort futile. All that the young man and woman could bring to this reunion were tears, so in quiet desperation and their emotions overloaded, they traipsed beyond the town into the blackened and blistered hills seared with perversity.

Years ago as teens, they had hiked these hills, those happy times lost to them now. Like the town below, their joyous hills had been abused by power and greed. Where great evergreens once shaded the sun, they now stood brown, bent, and defeated, drooping like sick old cousins communing at a funeral.

When their lake came into view, the young woman doubled over and retched. The man cursed and knelt to comfort her. They sought each other in an embrace and closed their eyes, refusing to accept this corruption, as each desperately searched for something that might soothe their soul. But guilt, however innocently generated, had its price, and their pain could never be assuaged.

When they opened their eyes, the view hadn't changed. Stunned, they stared at the hollow of cracked, brown earth that once had been an emerald green lake. Now it was insubstantial pools of murky, brackish water that barely contained the bones of the small, innocent creatures that died for the sins of humanity. At the far end, where a beautiful waterfall once replenished the lake and gave the town its heavenly name, there was a rock formation covered in dead brown moss, its hidden cave exposed.

Her hand trembled as she pointed and her voice broke as she spoke for the first time. "I… I hid there." He nodded.

She sobbed and kissed his neck. "How did it come to this?" she whimpered.

"It wasn't our fault, it wasn't," he said, trying hard to believe it himself. Truly, it wasn't their fault, but that was no help. Doing *nothing* wasn't a good enough defense. It had been their fault because it was everyone's fault. He swallowed hard and began …

Chapter 1

Aeden, Indiana—2065

Economics defines, enables, inhibits, and prohibits. It provides a complex explanation for a simple thing. But taken too seriously, it is life and death—in the long run and short run and in the macro and the micro. What had gone wrong? Economics became the fulcrum on which lives had been lost.

A young teenage boy entered his backyard and searched for anyone or anything that might be watching him. Remembering that to keep his task a secret he had to watch everywhere, he even scanned the skies. Comforted that he was free from obvious surveillance; he made his way beyond the shadows of his home and into the twilight world of his father's garden.

Careful not to be seen, he followed the garden path and knelt in the safety of the tall bushes his father, Howard, had planted to protect his cherished Dionysus flowers from prying, competitive eyes. The boy felt his way as he trimmed the largest leaves from each flower's stalk. In his mind's eye he pictured the deep blue leaves falling away from cabernet flowers onto the strange orange mulch that Howard hoped would enhance his creation (and thus his professional career). Driven by his father's admonition, do not get caught, the boy went about completing his task.

Howard relentlessly cautioned him not to let anyone see what he was doing. When Gil asked why, Howard explained, as he often did, that Gil was too young to understand economics and the politics of the Executives was unfathomable. All Gil needed to know was the renegade leaves were a threat to Howard's career and his ambition to live as an Executive in the hills above.

"Gil, what thc fuck are you doing?"

Caught. Gil shoved the cut leaves away from the flowers they so recently adorned and looked up at the silhouette of his friend, Tommy Ward, peering down at him.

"Hi, Tommy," he whispered as he smoothed the dirt where the telltale leaves had recently rested. "What, what are you doing here? Do you have permission to be out?"

Tommy laughed. "Entrepreneurs don't ask permission, you know that. Why are you hiding down there?"

Gil didn't respond until he was sure the leaves were out of view. Then he stood and moved away from the flowers. "I'm on my own property, Tommy, I'm not hiding. I don't need permission to be outside as long as I stay within my home coordinates. Even so, don't tell anyone, okay? Don't. Howard would opt out if anyone found out."

"What is it with parents? Opt out? Who ends life because a stupid bush needs trimming?"

"How did you know?"

Tommy ignored the question. "Kessler would opt out too."

The comment about Tommy's father surprised Gil. "Kessler has these problems, too?"

Tommy nodded and recited from the homeowner's covenants. "Appreciation of Personal Property is regulated by the Interstate Commerce Commission. It is illegal to improve personal property by means outside the covenants, and any resident guilty of that crime is subject to negative net worth adjustment up to and including total divestiture as determined by the Homeowner's Association and approved by the Executive."

Gil nodded. He had been drilled on the covenants by his Archive avatar. "Do others break the covenants, Tommy, besides Howard and Kessler?"

"Sure, I suppose."

"That's reckless." He considered it. "Or very brave."

"I hadn't thought of it as brave, Gil but you're right. If you're willing to risk the loss of worth—and maybe even disappearance—for a chance to move up to the hill, that's brave."

"Howard and Kessler can't be the only brave ones."

Tommy looked at his home across the street. "I'll let you in on a secret," he whispered. "Kessler's in our yard, right now, spraying his Renaissance trees. He discovered a new strain that's attacking them so now he spends each night spraying them with this Genetic Aid stuff that's advertised on the Mesh. He thinks someone in the community is turning bugs loose on his trees to screw up his net worth and career so there's less competition to get promoted to Avalon."

"Why are people so malicious? Why do they try to screw up each other's careers?"

"I don't know about malicious, Kessler says its business. Everyone works so hard to get ahead, and the competition is so intense and the rewards are so terrific, that hard work isn't enough. Besides, it's not easy to attract the attention of the Executives; they're busy people." Tommy stared over Gil's roof to the hills above where the Executives lived in their palatial mansions. "Kessler keeps bitching at me that if our net worth declines, we won't be able to support our lifestyle, and we'll have to move to a poorer community. He says it to scare me because he knows how much I use Virtuoso." Tommy paused and smiled a little sheepishly. "Actually, it is scary. Imagine not having Virtuoso."

Gil considered it. "I wouldn't like it. Kessler's right about worth, though. Howard calls it "destructive creation" or "creative destruction," or something like that. It's when someone fails and it creates an opportunity for someone else to succeed. Adults have it real scary. I'll bet Howard would like to know he's not alone. Can I tell him about Kessler?"

"No way. They're competitors so let's keep it between us. I don't know about Howard's flowers, and you don't know about Kessler's trees."

"Why can't they just talk to each other? We live close enough."

"When was the last time you saw one of our neighbors talk to another? Besides, Kessler doesn't like Howard because your father refuses to contract for partners and without two incomes, you can't afford to have as nice a place as the rest of the neighborhood. It keeps home prices down. Re-partnering is a great economic advantage, but Kessler says Howard rejects every offer. Why does he refuse partners all the time?"

Gil was uncomfortable. "I don't know. He really liked my mother ..."

"Yuck, like? That's an economic perversity. Well, whatever, we'll keep this secret." They touched fists on it. Tommy smiled and pointed. "The Executives must be partying. Look how bright the lights are on the hill tonight."

Gil followed Tommy's gaze. "Someday, I'm going up there, and when I do, I'll visit the Chairman's mansion."

"Sure you will. You'll get a personal invitation from the Chairman himself. Take me with you, okay? I want to offer him some advice. I'm sure with you there, he'll listen."

"You can come, if you want."

Tommy pretended to knock on Gil's skull with his knuckles. "Chip to brain, anyone home? Remember the statute. No clones are allowed so unless you're escorted, you can't go."

Gil's smile faded. "I'm just as good as you are."

"What can I say? Apparently not. I don't make the rules. It's not fair, you having a second chance and all."

"How's that not fair?" Tommy just shrugged.

"Maybe you'll get there before me, Tommy, but I'll be the first clone. Just you wait."

"We'll see. Say, have you considered my offer?"

"I can't. My Archive avatar keeps me too busy, and I have hobbies. I don't have time."

"You're making a big mistake. I found this cloaking program that beats security most of the time. Now I can get out whenever I want without registering. I'm working with a few other kids to develop a really great business model. We'll be rich before our time."

"We're too young for business deals."

"The hell we are. Fourteen is plenty old enough and I'm tired of being a liability. It's creepy how my debts keep accumulating. I need to do something to become an asset and if I'm going to outperform all the other kids, I need to take shortcuts like all great entrepreneurs. Kessler is supportive; he's given me the names of some dealers where I can invest once I free up the capital. I'm going to have the highest net worth in the neighborhood, just you watch. That's how I'm reaching the hill. I'm doing it honorably. I'll cut deals until I really understand how to screw people. I won't be like Kessler, hoarding all the time and too scared to deal. That's so last generation. Join me, Gil, it's a little dangerous—but my cloaker will mitigate the risk. What do you say?"

"Tommy, I can't. I don't have time." He couldn't tell his friend the real reason. Tommy was aggressively capitalistic and Gil didn't have that hunger.

"Okay, your loss. When I'm on the hill, you'll visit. I'll be rich and bribe someone so you can come. Money talks." With that, Tommy bolted across the street that separated their homes, jumping the metallic green MAG lines that guided cars down Gateway Lane. As he ran in the moonlight, Gil admired his friend's freedom. Then he returned to his task. He felt around for all the leaves he'd cut and put them in the bag he'd stuffed in his pocket. "Don't leave even one," were Howard's instructions. As he left, he stared at the lights on the hill again—the lights of Avalon, where the Executives luxuriated and evaluated.

He tried to imagine what his home in Aeden looked like to the Executives on this early spring evening, as the full moon cast long shadows across the even rows of homes set on the precise street grid. The shadows sliced across the manicured, multicolored lawns and serene pools, not quite obscuring the luminescence that appeared as varying shades of gray in the moonlight. This was man's nature, not nature's nature, under the watchful eyes of the Executives on the hill.

Unique and immaculate landscaping surrounded houses that were identical outside down to the smallest detail. The Executives were thorough.

They required a constant as a framework for evaluation. Gil wondered if the Executives identified neighbors by their landscaping instead of their names, like he and Howard did.

There were other communities like Aeden in Indianapolis, and throughout America. He learned this from his avatar, his virtual instructor in Archive. But Aeden owned the advantageous position as the northernmost point of the city, just below the Executive mansions of Avalon.

He heard approaching sirens in the distance. What would the Cleaners be doing in the neighborhood? He looked up from between the bushes in time to see a MAG car speeding on its track through town. Tommy was standing on the track, but he wasn't looking. Gil started to yell but too late. He watched, horrified, as the MAG collided with Tommy and careened off its track. Tommy's body flew to one side and flopped, lifeless in a widening pool of blood.

Gil realized what had happened. Tommy's cloaker hid his presence so he wasn't monitored. This allowed the MAG to drive into him.

His instinct was to help, but he knew better, so he made sure no one was watching and inched closer. In the uneven light, Tommy's lifeless face seemed serene as it stared up toward Avalon. So this is death, Gil thought, twisted, grotesque, and unnatural. A chill ran down his spine.

A man emerged unharmed from the car. He stared briefly at the body in the street, and then at the damage to the right-front of the MAG. Before he could call for help, the Cleaners arrived and the man left when another MAG appeared, but he never once acknowledged Tommy's lack of existence. From his hiding place, Gil stared at his friend as something unfamiliar and unidentifiable fluttered like a moth inside his chest.

Tearing himself away to avoid being spotted by the Cleaners, he went inside and incinerated the recently removed blue leaves. After he was done, he sat down to his usual late supper alone. While catching up on the latest sports news on Archive, Howard's avatar appeared on his monitor.

"Howard," said Gil, Tommy Kessler was hit by a MAG tonight and killed. I saw it."

Howard's avatar registered concern. "Did anyone see you out there?"

"No."

"And you did what I asked?"

"Yes."

"Good," Howard's avatar said. "Sorry about Tommy. What happened?"

"He was playing in the street when a MAG hit him."

"He was out without authorization again, wasn't he?"

"Probably, sir."

Howard's avatar looked at him, thoughtfully. "Let this be a lesson to you. Life asks you to make difficult choices, and you must always do what's right. Have the Cleaners arrived?" Standard procedure called for HomeSec, Homeland Security, to summon the Cleaners to eliminate issues and sanitize so that nothing untoward is left for neighbors to be concerned about.

"That's the odd thing, Howard. The Cleaners were headed here before the accident."

"They probably had other work. Still, it was very adult and responsible of you not to get involved. I'm proud of you, Gil. Kessler's a real tightwad, but he has adequate net worth so I'm sure he's backed Tommy up. Even with the age difference, you can still be friends with his clone, someday."

"I guess neither of us will get to the hill now," Gil mumbled under his breath. But Howard's avatar had lost interest. "Should we say something to Kessler?"

"What?" The avatar's eyes returned to him. "No. There's no need. He's such a busybody, he'll want to know how you know, and we don't want that."

"Howard," he hesitated to ask. "Why flowers?"

"Flowers?"

"Yes, why do you work so hard on them?"

"Because flowers are everything to us. When they're noticed, I'm noticed, and I can get that promotion I've been working for so hard and so long."

"I know, but why flowers?"

"That's how it's done. It's immature and unprofessional to waste your life trying to do something you value if no one else values it. We've talked about this before. Without a market, there's no purpose. Commerce is everything. You're growing up, Gil. It's imperative you learn that. You have to realize that your worth is dependent on what other people value. Don't ever forget that. It's the most important lesson an adult can learn. It's the difference between a long, prosperous, and happy life and a sad life and early death. Understand?"

"Not really, but if it's so important, I'm sure I'll understand it eventually."

"You will." The image of Howard's avatar flickered briefly. "I have an errand for you tomorrow. I've been called to headquarters, and I need you to do something for me."

"Sure. Leave me a message. I'll do it in the morning. I've got some studying, tonight."

"Okay, goodnight."

"Night."

After Gil completed his studies, he signed off Archive. He was tired, but after the events of the evening, he didn't feel like sleeping. To occupy himself, he signed onto Virtuoso, entered the changing room of his Virtuoso unit, removed his clothes, and waited for the HomeSec Personal Identification Device or PID that was implanted in his tailbone to register access. When the green light went on, he opened a compartment next to the operating chamber, removed a small plastic box, took out two contact lenses, and placed them in his eyes. The silver-like disks caused his eyesight to dim but he could still see well enough to step into the chamber.

"Ready for circuit overlay," he spoke, raising his arms over his head and closing his eyes to protect the silvery lenses. A slight vibration reminded him to keep his eyes closed but he could sense his body being bathed in the light that mapped him into Virtuoso. With a second vibration, he opened his eyes and was ready.

"Scenario Andrea," he spoke and, almost immediately, he was standing on a hilly meadow on a pleasantly cool, starry summer night. As Virtuoso completed the requested scenario he felt a gentle breeze cool his skin. "Now," he said, "Andrea."

He inhaled the familiar vanilla scent and turned. A teenage girl with wavy, dark blonde hair blowing in the breeze ran to join him. He extended his arms to receive her. In the cool air, her body was warm and calming. He stared into her large brown eyes and felt something akin to what he'd felt when Tommy died, but wonderfully better—so much better.

"Where have you been?" she asked petulantly. She looked down below his waist. "I see you missed me." She pointed to his burgeoning erection and laughed. She kissed him hard and pressed her body to his. He wrapped his arms around her. She felt so right, even though inside the chamber he held nothing but air.

Two years ago, at Howard's urging, he created her. He diligently reviewed the inventory of Virtuoso models and rejected each in favor of creating an original girlfriend. It was difficult but rewarding work and before she was generated he knew everything about her—her eyes, her hair, her voice, and even the small constellation of freckles in the shape of Orion on her chest above her heart. For a boy coming of age she was the dream girlfriend—at least for this boy. Each time she came to him, she came with her own memories of them together, of their experiences, their conversations, and a history they made up along the way, and she never forgot.

He bent to kiss her, her eyes closing solemnly and she emitted a sexy, almost silent, growl as she returned his kiss. Her mouth was soft and yielding, and she nipped his lips with her teeth. He backed away, but she grabbed his head in her hands and planted her softest, wettest, and warmest kiss. He felt her tongue brush his lips and her hard nipples press against his thin shirt.

"Is it too cold?" he asked. "We could go somewhere else, or change the temperature."

"As long as I am with you, I am warm," she said as she embraced him tightly.

Just then, a tall, black, Asian man walked toward them. "Hola, Gil," the man shouted cheerfully. I am Wu Tung Johnson, the designer of the BeyondLife Sports series for Virtuoso."

Gil stepped back, at first enthralled, and then embarrassed by his erection. "Wu Tung, wow, I'm a big fan. Your games are kicking. I'm huge into them. What are you doing here?"

"I am here for you, big guy," the designer said smiling. "Stubaru, maker of the world's most efficient off-road vehicles, and StarMesh Motels, the motels that treat you like you are an Executive, want you and your date to enjoy tonight on them." He pointed to a car at the base of the meadow about fifty feet away. "That is our cool new Stubaru GPS ATV. It is the car I use to get to my competitions because it is fully integrated into the Stubaru All World satellite Mesh network. Wherever I want to go outside our public MAG system, Stubaru will get me there and back again. Like all Stuburus, it has climate control, all-weather traction, and a state-of-the-art entertainment system programmed to provide you with hours of your favorite diversions while the car does all the heavy lifting. You and your date will enjoy the car on your way to the StarMesh Hotel, the hotel favored by the chairman and his executive staff. When you arrive, you will be treated to an executive-level suite and chairman-level service."

Andrea squealed with excitement. "But I don't have worth yet," Gil said, concerned.

The avatar laughed. "You won't need any tonight. All of this is on us."

"Wow, thanks, I researched this car in Archive. It's cool, but so expensive. I can't believe I'm going to get a chance to use it."

"We are aware of the research, Gil. That is why I am here. You are coming of age, and you will have worth someday. This is your opportunity to experience and enjoy what your economic future will be like."

"You're certain Howard's account won't be charged? He told me not to accept Mesh gifts from strangers, because they're not really gifts."

Wu Tung laughed again. "Your father is a wise man, but maybe a bit overly cautious. What he said comes perilously close to anti-commerce talk." Gil was concerned by the comment, but Wu Tung laughed it off. "It is okay. I have no desire to report him. Tonight is for you and everything is free. If you are not familiar with the term 'free,' Archive can define it for you."

It was Gil's turn to laugh. "I know what 'free' means. Thanks."

"Just remember, whenever you or Howard are in the market for a real all-terrain vehicle, consider Stubaru, or if you are traveling and need a room, the convenient StarMesh Hotels." With that, Wu Tung Johnson disappeared, leaving Gil and Andrea with a car and a destination.

She smiled admiringly. "Do you know what just happened?" he asked. She nodded. "I was pitched by a world-class adventure gamer! I'm growing up, and they recognize that soon I'll be economically viable. Wow, look at this car. It's a real beauty. Someday, I'm going to have the worth to lease one of these babies for real. Are you ready to test it out, Andrea?"

"Whatever my man wants," she said, proudly.

They settled into the back seat as the car headed to its destination. She cuddled and kissed him lightly on the lips. He wrapped his arm around her shoulder. "What are you thinking?" she cooed.

"Is this how it is for everyone?"

"What do you mean?"

"You know, the way I feel about you."

"How do you feel about me?"

"You know."

"It is wonderful, isn't it?"

"Was it like this for Howard and my mother?"

She gave him a quizzical look. "You never talk about your mother."

"I never knew her. She died when I was born."

She hugged him. "That's a shame. How did she die?"

"It's embarrassing. She was involved in civil disobedience and was executed as a traitor."

Andrea held him tighter. "Oh my poor baby, is that why you never talk about her?" Gil nodded. "Everyone needs a woman in his life."

"I would sure like to find one," he joked.

She pinched him and he yelped. "You will know exactly how many is the right number when you try to have more than me."

He looked into her adoring eyes. He could tell her anything. His thoughts drifted to Tommy. "Andrea, why don't people cry? Not me, but people."

"That is a funny question. I guess nobody is unhappy, so there is nothing to cry about. People live forever and there is no sickness. Everyone works. There are no wars. No poverty. No envy or jealousy. People live well and have access to Virtuoso to simulate and stimulate. With Archive, Virtuoso, and cloning, why would people cry?"

"I don't think that's true, the part about envy."

"Why?"

"Howard wants to become an Executive and move to Avalon. He wants it bad. When a co-worker got promoted, I think Howard envied him. He never talks about it, but I think he did."

"It is silly to envy anyone."

"Silly?" He gave her a squeeze.

She smiled and tickled him. "With all knowledge available in Archive, no one has an advantage over anyone else. Everything is there for everyone; it just depends how you use it. And with Virtuoso, anyone can be whatever they want and experience whatever they want, so no one can say they have been excluded from anything; so no envy."

"You're right. Still, it doesn't feel like I fit in all this."

She kissed him. "Trust me, you fit. It makes me sad that you feel that way. You have this one long life and with all the opportunities available, shouldn't it be the life of your choosing? Shouldn't it be the life you know is uniquely yours and not one you settled for? Gil, don't settle. That would be sad." As she spoke her hands tried gamely to change the subject. Her fingers worked their special magic, and soon he set the vehicle to autopilot, stopped thinking, and followed her lead. Both the car and their hands moved through uncharted territory toward their respective destinations. The car arrived first, but until a valet interrupted them, they were too involved to notice.

"Good day to you, sir," the avatar-valet said, smirking at Gil's arousal. To hide his embarrassment, Gil used Andrea as a shield as the valet continued, "My, you are a handsome couple. I see why Mr. Johnson referred you. We've assigned you to our second-most popular suite, the Presidential Suite. Everything you experience with us," the avatar valet paused … well, everything the hotel provides is exactly like real so in the future, when you travel, we trust you will consider our StarMesh Hotels first."

They were pleased with their suite. "Oh, my," Andrea gushed as she entered. "This the best place in the entire world! The huge aquarium with the dolphins, it is amazing." Her head swiveled to take in the beauty. "And oh, look, the Milky Way; it is so close. Oh, Gil, I'll never forget this. It is so romantic."

He shared her wonder. The opulence and finery were far beyond anything he had ever seen. He began to understand wealth. It was access to places like this that motivated Howard to do everything he could to improve his net worth.

Gil pointed to the large bed floating beside a picture window with a view of a great waterfall that plunged from the mountains to the valley far below. They stared out at the scenery before jumping onto the bed, laughing. He put his arm around her and together they stared out. He followed the waterfall as it blasted from snowcapped mountains and cascaded down an immense ravine in what looked like a dollar-sign like spray before pouring into the river below and flowing peacefully past the lights of a small fishing village. He stared up into the clear night at the infinitely greater lights above. She rested her head on his shoulder and smiled a smile he could never resist.

"So what else do you think we're not supposed to feel?" he asked, continuing their previous discussion.

"What is with you? With all this beauty, you are asking weird questions." Her smile morphed into something more seductive. "I can show you things you should feel."

Not exactly understanding, he laughed, and then took a chance and began to caress her body.

She kissed him passionately. "No one will kiss you like I can," she murmured. "No one knows you like I do or loves you like I do. I promise, you will never know anyone who wants to be what I want to be for you."

He needed little convincing. In their two years together, she was already everything to him. Under her watchful eye, he had matured and become more confident. Now she was edging him toward something different, something new—something beyond.

He felt her hands between his legs. Her touch excited him and made him want to reciprocate. As he grew in her hands, a small and diminishing part of him remembered that the experience wasn't real, and he was alone. But they were speeding toward the unknown, and the unexpected intensity of it kept him focusing on his mounting passion until he was totally engaged. They were naked, and she was on top of him. He felt her guide him into her, and he gasped at the sensation, at the warmth. Her hair fell around her face and tickled his chest. Her lips locked onto his as she undulated, writhed, and squeezed until he couldn't tell if the sounds he heard were hers or his.

She was a motivated teacher, and he reacted to her every cue as she provided just the right incentives to turn him into a fast and willing learner. He pulled her more tightly to him and responded with greater ardor to her guttural noises, sounds from wherever her soul lived, sounds that inflamed his excitement. He was making love to the girl who loved him, loved him in the most intimate way, beyond what anything real could offer. There were screams, hers and maybe his, and as they breathed heavily, she rested limp on top, grinding slowly, sensually.

"I love you," she gasped.

The words expanded, filling an unnamed need in his mind, no, in his heart. He knew the words, but had never heard them spoken like this before and they hung in his thoughts, a defining statement at an essential moment. He never considered the effect words might have and never thought of this act and those words. He gave himself up to the moment. Briefly and far too feebly, his mind tried to reengage, but before it could it was absorbed back into the moment as his body fired off signals that stopped thought itself.

Feeling her shudder, he wondered whether there could be anything better in life to feel. And then it got better as he drained into her, and his mind's eye flashed blinding light. Weak, with body glistening, she fell forward, her mouth rasping air against his sweaty throat.

After a stunned silence he offered his judgment, proudly. "I love you, too," he said. She raised her head, and something tapped gently on his face. Something wet. A tear? Andrea was crying.

He held her close and gently rolled her onto her back. She looked up with moist, dark, eager eyes; no one had ever looked at him like that. Not anyone, ever. The passion in her kisses was his forever. Gently, he wiped her tears away, first from his cheek, and then from hers.

"Why are you crying?"

She looked up at him, through glistening eyes. "I was thinking about who you are and who you will be, and it made me cry."

He didn't know what that meant but he kissed her again. "Please don't be sad."

Swimming against an incredibly strong current, an unwanted thought surfaced. This isn't real, it said. Even the tears aren't real. But this thought, having fought heroically to gain his attention, briefly cooling his ardor, faded quickly into the afterglow. Still, the thought hadn't lost or disappeared entirely.

"What is wrong?" She asked.

He stared into her eyes. "I have to go." He kissed her gently.

"Please, no," she said as tears rolled down her cheeks, again. "I love you so much."

"I know. It's not that. I'll be back. I always come back."

He kissed her and told her once again that he loved her. She kissed him and, somehow, sooner became later—a second and third lovemaking later, before he signed off.

Drained, he sat alone in the Virtuoso chamber, the smell of lovemaking and the scent of her vanished, and his stomach was covered with semen. A wave of sadness hit him as he cleaned himself and removed his lenses.

Chapter 2

Aeden, Indiana—2065

Gil awakened in the morning to an empty house. He lay in bed for a few minutes as a feeling of emptiness worried its way into the happy memories of Andrea and last night. Maybe it was Tommy. Finally, he stirred to face the day.

He peered out the window and saw the Cleaners had done their work. There were no signs of last night's accident. The neighborhood was undisturbed, oblivious to Tommy's change of status.

He showered in a soft, scented, waterless mist, and stood before the mirror checking the few curly hairs that had begun to sprout on his chin. "Information," he spoke aloud and waited as a news broadcast appeared in the mirror next to his image. As usual, most of the morning's news was about business. The stock report lauded the performance of Howard's company, American Natural Grain Stuffs, or ANGS. Then he noticed a small red light flashing on the mirror and remembered his promise to run Howard's errand.

"Messages?" he asked the mirror.

Howard's image appeared. "Sorry I was so busy last night. When you get up, I'll be at work. That vice president's slot is on the line and my efforts are finally paying off. I need you to do something important for me. There's a family member who's elected to opt out and unless it's handled correctly, it'll adversely affect my net worth—our net worth. We can't let that happen."

The image stopped talking as Howard drew his upper lip over his teeth and tilted his head back, looking for stray nose hairs to manicure. "The family member is Bernard Rosenthal," Howard continued. "I think we've talked about him. Anyway, he's your great-grandfather, my side, of course. I don't know anything about him, but it turns out he's been in hiding."

Hiding? Gil wondered. Why would someone hide? How? And from who?

"The hospice requested a family member be present to handle his exit interview and the paperwork. They want to be sure of the financial implications and we're the only family they could find. I'd do it, but I'm stuck at the office. You're old enough to be responsible so ..."

He waited as Howard ran a comb through his hair. "This vice presidency is important. If he elects to opt out, it'll make it harder for us, for me, so I'm counting on you to convince him to reconsider. Visit the hospice and talk to him. I've cleared it so you have a MAG available. He's very old, even by today's standards—well over a hundred—so if he's not thinking clearly, sign the renewal order for him. If that isn't possible, it's up to you to persuade him of the damage he'll do to your career and mine if he opts out. Gil, do whatever you think will work, but make him decide to live. He mustn't opt out. I know you won't let me down." The image disappeared.

"No more messages," the avatar in the mirror said.

He dressed and went downstairs to another terminal where he accessed his school requirements and rescheduled them.

"Archive?"

The pleasing feminine voice he selected long ago answered, "Archive."

"Information on Bernard Rosenthal?"

"Working ... Bernard George Rosenthal. Currently resides in Hospice Unit Seven, Indianapolis, Indiana. Born March 5, 1946 in Indianapolis, Indiana. Educated at Indiana University; graduated in 1969 with degrees in Accounting and Economics."

"Are there other living Rosenthals?"

"There are no other family members with the name Rosenthal."

"Give me his genealogy."

"Married Jane Gallagher in 1998. Their son, Mark David Rosenthal, was born September 11, 2002. Bernard and Jane also had a daughter, Frances, born in 2014. In February 2033, Mark Rosenthal changed his surname from Rosenthal to Rose. Subsequent generations have used this surname. Mark Rose became a visionary social and economic architect and was the last president of the United States. His son, Howard, was born May 21, 2033. Your trueborn self was born to Howard and Henrietta January 1, 2051."

"Why did Mark Rosenthal change his name?"

"No reason was given on his petition."

"Bernard Rosenthal was in hiding. Where's he been?"

"Unknown. He was an employee of ANGS Corporation in 2031. He was there for thirty-five years. His last official document was filed with the Internal Revenue Service in 2032."

"What's the Internal Revenue Service?"

"A long-defunct federal agency that collected funds from productive citizens and redistributed them to the less-productive and non-productive indolent. The agency was eliminated with the passage of the Omnibus Freedom from Taxation Act of 2039."

"I see," he said, not seeing at all. "What else do you have on Bernard Rosenthal?"

"Personnel reports at ANGS indicate he was dismissed for sub-par performance. In 2032, ANGS filed charges against him for theft of proprietary corporate information and information system sabotage. Two years later, the Department of Homeland Security officially catalogued him as a terrorist. He was tried and convicted, in absentia, for crimes against ANGS and the country and sentencing was delayed until his capture. No other records exist."

"He's a terrorist?" Gil pondered that. "Has HOMESEC been informed?"

"HOMESEC communication is not available to you."

"Did he express a reason for coming to the hospice?"

"He wishes to exercise his exit option."

"Is he aware there are other options?"

"There is no record that he registered his preferences with the Secretary of Life Management."

"What about HOMESEC?"

"HOMESEC responses are not available to you."

"Shouldn't I notify them?"

"Have you been given such instructions?"

"No." His relative was a terrorist. He must have done something terrible if his son, Mark, had to change his name. Gil wondered if he could do what Howard asked. "Thank you, Archive. That's all. End inquiry."

The screen reverted to a wave of slowly undulating underwater grasses that then faded into the mirror. Why would someone disappear and then re-emerge, knowing the authorities wanted him? Why would someone return just to die? There must be a thousand silent exits this man could have taken, and no one would have been the wiser, and he must know what this will do to Howard's career. Maybe he returned for revenge against Howard.

Just maybe Gil could fix it.

Chapter 3

Hospice Unit Seven—2065

Hospice Unit Seven was on the south side of town. To get there, Gil used the private transportation system by himself for the first time in his life. But because of yesterday's incident with Tommy, even though merely a passenger, he found himself staring out the windows of his MAG anticipating potential accidents.

Then a video began. Gil watched as pictures of old businesses morphed into newer and more dynamic, current businesses, overlaid with pictures of death and dying. "Hello fellow traveler," a deep voice intoned. "Have you ever wondered why businesses are ongoing concerns yet we, the people who run them, are not? Have you ever thought of death, your death and the end of wonderful things, and wondered why that is your only reward for a prosperous life? Of course you have, everyone has; everyone but the followers of the Morgan Church of the Almighty Dollar, where death isn't in your future prospectus. We at Morgan are intimate with a more accretive God. Through rigorous use of medicine and technology, hard work and capital appreciation, death has no power over a Morgan soul. Join us, today, and live forever, prosper seeking God's true rewards, here on earth, as it once was only in heaven." The video ended with scenes of people living in wondrous splendor in palaces on the coast of some large body of water. The images faded to reveal the holy symbol of the Morgan Church of the Almighty Dollar, the gold dollar sign imbedded in a silver and green lemniscate, like wings, the sign of infinity. "This is a message from Tom Morgan, chief spiritual officer of the United States of America and I approve this ad."

Gil arrived at a three-story brick building located downtown, near

Democracy Boulevard. The MAG stopped automatically by the gate. "Gil Rose to see ..."

"Bernard Rosenthal," a very old, large, black guard finished for him. The MAG must have transmitted his personal information ahead of him. Cool. Wherever you go, you're expected.

"Morning, Mr. Rose. Disembark here. The car will park and return here when you are ready to leave."

"Thanks and good morning," Gil replied, cheerfully, trying to sound adult. The guard directed him through glass doors to a Personal Identification scanner. With his identification validated, he walked into the lobby and located an Archive interface on the wall.

"Archive," he said.

"Information?" recognizing his voice, his own personal avatar's voice responded. It was comforting knowing that in this new place, he was recognized.

"What room is Bernard Rosenthal in?"

"Room 313. Follow the blue lights, please." He thanked his avatar and followed the lights to an elevator. When he stepped out of the elevator, he continued to follow the blue dots until he neared the room. An attractive, older nurse was leaving. Though old, she was the prettiest real woman Gil had ever seen. He looked at her badge: Tara Peyton.

She smiled. "You're staring. Are you performing Mr. Rosenthal's EI?"

He blushed and quickly looked away. "Sorry, his EI?"

She laughed at his embarrassment. It seemed a kind laugh. "His exit interview."

"Oh yeah, right."

The nurse pointed to the door. "You're young for this. Do you understand his options?" Gil nodded. "Our policy is to keep him comfortable until his EI is complete. When you're done, if he still wishes to opt out, we'll provide the gentle means. That's how it works."

"Okay," he said. "What happens if he doesn't want to opt out?"

"Then he's all yours, Mr. Rose," she said. With that the nurse turned and walked away. He took a deep breath and entered the room.

The old man was lying on a bed by the room's only window, his hair white, thin, and wispy, his eyes bulging, and his pale face lined with deep furrows and covered with a growth of white beard, days old, making him look even more decrepit. He reminded Gil of the unproductive homeless people he'd learned about when he studied twentieth-century social history in Archive. Yes, he thought, that was how the old man looked—like one of those homeless people before the chairman solved America's social problems. He'd learned that most homeless people had been mentally ill, physically debilitated, emotionally shattered, or just plain lazy, and all were incapable of coping with economic opportunity. It worried him that the old man's condition would preclude him from grasping his options.

"Come to close my account, son?" The old man's voice was rough yet fragile, and rather than staring at Gil, he gazed forlornly out his window; staring at something only he could see.

"No, sir," Gil responded. "I'd prefer that you renew and stay with us. Did you know you can do that? You won't have to die for a long, long time?"

"I'm aware that except for murders and executions, death is elective, and the current school of thought has it that murders and executions are ultimately elective."

"Why would anyone elect death?"

Bernie tried to concentrate. After years of anticipation, this moment sent his tired, sad heart thumping, making him feel almost alive, fearfully alive. He waited. When the boy just stood there, unsure, he spoke. "Come to close my account, son?" Was the boy ready?

"Why would anyone elect death?"

The question was naïve, but he'd expected it and his purpose was to change that. "Why?" Bernie responded. "I can only speak for myself. I elect death with a free will, a clear mind, and boundless cynicism." He awaited the boy's response.

"Mr. …" Gil began.

"Please call me Bernie."

"Bernie." He paused. "I'm …"

"I know. Gil Rose."

"How?"

"You have your Archive and I have mine," Bernie said dismissively.

"Did my avatar tell you I was coming?" Good, the boy was confused.

"Gil, my boy, I'm ready to go so I won't take up much of your time. The quicker we do this, the quicker you can get back to your father's garden to snip at his secret horticultural failures."

Bernie smiled at the stunned expression on the boy's face, a face that brought back memories, a face that looked more like the boy's mother than that of a Rosenthal. "How did you …?" the boy asked. "Who are you?" What little confidence Gil had when he arrived was gone. "How do know about Howard's flowers?"

"I'm old, not senile."

"I … but …"

"If old and senile makes this easier for you, I'm sorry to disappoint you."

"How did you know about Howard's flowers?"

"It isn't prudent to fall out of touch. That's why I'm opting out. I've seen enough. I've lost the desire to be any longer. I just wanted to tell a family member before I go."

"But Howard wants you to renew. Do you understand what renewal means? Look at how old you are. No offense." Bernie smiled as the boy tried to convince him. "Medicine can almost halt aging; even reverse some of it, so you could live decades longer, maybe even forever. If it's the money, I'm sure Howard wouldn't charge you market interest on a loan—you're family. Anyway, something can be worked out and you can be productive again. Besides, if you die, you'll miss tomorrow."

It was an acceptable argument. "Son, you're very young. You expect tomorrow to be more glorious than today. Good for you, even though you'll most likely be disappointed." He felt that the boy might be different, but hope could be warping his judgment. "I've taken age-suppression medications to get this far, but I don't care for them, and I'm afraid you're naïve about the wonders long life has for me. If I don't opt out, it's likely I'll be arrested. Then, if I'm lucky, I'll become a perpetual guest of your government at some prison facility appropriate for someone of my stature. Prison is a depressing prospect if you're planning to live forever, so, if it's okay with you, I'll just solve this last mystery of life and be done."

"No, you've got it wrong. People don't go to prison anymore. If you commit a crime, there are chemical preventative behavioral treatments, and once you're employable, you can repay society and begin contributing to your own worth."

"Ah, yes, cerebral chiropractics: a clever little tweak and you're, somehow, more productive. Unfortunately, forever isn't enough time to repay all that's owed me."

"What are chiropractics?"

"It's not important," Bernie said, waving it off. "I won't have my ingredients re-mixed. I'm rather miserable enough, thank you. Besides, that's not why I want to opt out."

"Why then?"

"Because I've failed."

"But living longer gives you a chance to recover from that."

"Or fail for even longer."

"That's not possible. There's always something you can make good money doing."

"I failed because you believe that crap."

The boy looked confused. "I know things aren't perfect but we live in the best, freest, and most productive country on earth, in the history of earth.

Yes, Howard's flowers need trimming to correct a flaw with the petals, and some of my neighbors sneak around trying to hide imperfections in their landscaping from the Executives and maybe they try to hurt other neighbors, economically, but other than that, everyone's free, prosperous, healthy, and productive, and no one dies too young." Briefly, Gil considered Tommy's death but thought it best not to mention him. He continued, quietly, more to himself than to Bernie, "there really isn't anything more to want in life than that."

Realizing how difficult this was going to be, Bernie shook his head and sighed. "My view of the world was once as naïve as yours. Unfortunately, it took me too long to see it and by then it was too late. I can never forgive myself for that. You have no idea how many levels of power are working against you, and how many angles they're doing it from. If you ignore even one, even for a moment, they suck you into their reality."

"Wow, that's really paranoid."

"You seem like a nice kid. Maybe this isn't going to work. Call the administrators." Gil began to protest, but Bernie motioned for him to stop. "It's too late for me, and maybe for you, too. I shouldn't have expected more. All you know is what that God-forsaken Archive has taught you. I don't know what I was thinking. It's all instant gratification today. No one searches for what they don't know. That's the great crime and it's why I want out." Bernie caught himself mid-rant. His emotion surprised him. Feeling his heart hammering in his chest, he took a deep breath and tried to speak calmly. "I want the injection. Tell the nurse to shove it in here." He rolled to his side, pulled his pajama bottoms down, and pointed to his bluish-white, veined and bony ass. "It's my last and only right, so goddamn it, I'm exercising it. Go and tell her."

Gil tried to quell his panic and responded angrily, "Yeah, I'll tell her. I'll tell her you're a coward who can't live in a world made for productive people. I'm embarrassed I'm related to you because you're a failure and because of it, Howard and I will be devalued. How does that make you feel? You're killing Howard's dreams—I mean our dreams. Why are you doing this? What horrible thing did Howard do to you?"

Bernie rolled over, fluffed his pillow, and watched the flush leave Gil's face. "If your world is so free, why does what I do have any effect on Howard, you, or anyone else?"

Gil's response was quick but unsure. "Your flaws could be ours, too."

"That's crazy. And what flaws are we talking about?"

"You talk way too fast. In Archive and Virtuoso I can regulate the conversation. I can't concentrate if you bombard me with words."

Bernie waited. After a few awkward moments, Gil spoke again. "Our scientists have ways to control or wipe out disease and extend life to almost forever. They have therapies, too, that eliminate crime and poverty. If you think that's bad, you're the crazy one."

Bernie closed his eyes and dropped his head to the pillow. "I guess it depends on your perspective. If I renew, somehow, your genes get a clean bill of health. Howard, maybe, gets his promotion to vice president and you move up to Avalon, where every dream becomes reality. From your perspective, eternity is a much more pleasing proposition than from mine. Consider my perspective. I'll be caught, imprisoned, and probably executed or if they choose to invest in an old man, I'll go through so much chemical behavior modification that I won't recognize myself and at my age, that's not a good thing. You'll have to excuse me if I choose not to sacrifice to benefit your father's career.

"And let's consider what happens if I opt out. At a minimum, my pain and disappointment end and, at best, I ascend to the infinite hereafter to join my loved ones while here on earth you're left with my besmirched name and the ramifications of an unfortunate indiscretion by a long-lost relative. If you're resourceful, you'll get by, and you'll live quite nicely in Aeden or in the next community below in this perversity you call economic status. You'll continue to crawl around at night faking your way to perfect flowers so Howard can overcome his family tree and receive the promotion he so desperately needs so he can acquire more stuff. Excuse me if this nice, perfect world isn't my cup of tea."

"No, yes, wait, you're purposely trying to confuse me," Gil complained.

"Are these the choices of a free people?"

"Yes, I mean yes, we are free." The boy was uncertain. Good.

"Way back in my world, freedom meant succeeding or failing on your own. If success or failure occurs when someone else declares it, it isn't freedom, not even in your perfect world."

"There are trade-offs. We don't talk about them, but we understand. We're not stupid."

"You shouldn't rule that out. You could be stupid. You don't seek information on your own and Archive and Virtuoso are your only source of knowledge. They provide every input and every sensation. You know what they want you to know but little of what you need to understand. You're like everyone else in the country; you've been willingly seduced. When was the last time you sought an answer outside the system?"

"Where else would I go to ask a question?"

"So, you can be a fast learner." Bernie waited, as slowly the boy understood and smiled.

"I do have a question," Gil said. "A long time ago you were convicted of something, and they've been searching for you since. Why isn't HomeSec here guarding your room? Why isn't Angs prosecuting you? And what would you do if I called them?"

Bernie laughed, at both the questions and the look of satisfaction on the teen's face after asking them. "First, please don't call. I'm here without their knowledge. If they knew, they'd arrest me, sentence me, and probably opt me out in a most painful way. Dying now, here, this way, it is the only option."

"But it's impossible to keep information from Angs and HomeSec."

"Your definition of impossible must be different from mine."

"Only the chairman controls Archive."

"Let's say, for now, I have a friend with privileges."

Intrigued, the boy pulled his chair closer to the head of the bed and leaned forward. "Did your friend tell you I was coming?"

"No, I told her to get you."

"That's a lie. Howard sent me here."

"The message in your mirror wasn't from Howard. My friend sent it. She's very persuasive. Howard doesn't know you're here, and it would be a mistake to tell him. But on the way home, he does want you to pick up Genetic Aid, whatever the hell that is."

"Genetic Aid is…"

"I don't care. I needed you here. This is about you and me. I need your help."

The boy sat for a moment in uncomfortable silence. "What do you want?"

Bernie feared this moment. He turned and stared out into the distance, silent as he swallowed back his emotions. He began, embarrassed by the sound of his sad, broken voice. "If I could only have what I want …" He slumped back onto the bed, exhausted, slowly blinking tears from his eyes. "You know what? Continue to live your illusion—there's less chance of getting hurt." This was harder than he'd thought. "I'm tired and I just want this done." The sorrow hurt too much to continue.

Gil broke the silence. "You brought me here to tell me something, Bernie, so tell me. You could have died wherever you were but you took the risk to get me to listen. You're this far, talk to me. Tell me about your failure, if that's it. Go ahead. Or tell me about Howard's, or mine. You know you want to. You know you will. You didn't bring me here so you could die quietly."

"I came to ask you to be part of a revolution, but you're not ready."

"A revolution?" A laugh escaped. "A revolution in these great times. You're crazy."

"It's no joke. You have no idea how much I've lost, and how much you've lost already."

The boy waited in silence until, reluctantly, he stood. "Okay, if there's nothing else, I'll tell the nurse of your decision." He started toward the door.

When he reached the door, Bernie asked. "Do you know what a familiar is?"

Frozen for a moment, Gil turned. "They're, they're clones—redundants incubated at Life Farms to restore trueborns who've died or to replace their malfunctioning organs."

"Why?"

"Why? I don't know. They're grown with the permission of the government if the recipient has the worth to fund replacement."

"So it's death for everyone without wealth. Don't you find that interesting in a free country? What happened to your friend, Tommy, after the Cleaners finished with him?"

"How did you …? Howard said Kessler, that's Tommy's father, has enough worth to replicate Tommy, so he'll become a familiar."

"And what do you think that really is?" He asked, patiently.

"It's a clone that takes on your identity."

"Okay. So what happens to your friend?"

"I guess … I hope he'll be regenerated. He'll be younger and we won't be friends right away but because we live so long, eventually, we could be friends again, just like we would have been if Tommy hadn't … you know."

"Do you remember how you felt when he died?"

"I don't know, maybe a little disappointed. But my avatar taught me about Morgan. In Morgan, death is the hell that awaits lazy people but if you create enough wealth, you will live forever. Tommy's family has wealth, so Tommy will be back."

"So your father has raised you to be a practicing Morgan. That's unfortunate. Morgan has a great marketing gimmick with its living forever and heaven on earth through capital accumulation brand, but what it's done to people is one of the reasons I want to leave this world. The existence of Morgan makes my failure worse. Explain how watching your best friend die can, in any way, make you feel hopeful. Shouldn't life be too vital for death to feel that insignificant?"

"But …"

"Gil, you must realize that your friend's death isn't conceptual; he's truly gone and the real sorrow is you don't feel grief at the loss. You've bought into this world where immortality is sold as the reward for economic productivity. You're young and you have much to learn. I hope someday you'll realize that life doesn't change; only our feelings about it do and your feelings are based on a well-crafted lie."

"How can you say that? You don't know our technology and our medical breakthroughs."

"You believe in wealth-based immortality, that's all I need to know."

"It's more than a belief."

"Really? Then explain this. Why is Tommy so important to your world that it's willing to divert vast sums to perpetuate him? Why would it do that?"

"What you're saying is crazy. Value, worth, wealth is what makes you important. America is free and in a free market, this is how people live."

"I thought America was a republic?"

"Maybe once, but a republic isn't needed anymore. There's a market for everything so why not Congress? They take care of the details. And if there's profit in it, why not perpetuate Tommy?"

"You're how old, fourteen? And you believe that crap?"

"It's not crap. I'm fourteen and an excellent student, by the way, so good I earn extra Virtuoso time. Everyone works hard to build their worth so they can insulate themselves from things that once brought grief. As long as you can afford it, we're a free country."

"So happiness and freedom are privileges to be purchased."

"There's nothing wrong with that if you work hard, save, and create opportunities."

"When I was young, millions couldn't afford basic medical care or minimal nutrition, and they died while others wasted far more wealth than they could ever use."

"Your world wasn't perfect either." Gil said, gloating.

"No, it wasn't. But times haven't changed much. People still value their own lives too much while allowing others to struggle and die."

"Everyone has the same chance to succeed if they work hard."

"That's fine. But why doom those who aren't succeeding to death?"

"We live in an interrelated economy, so if you help the lazy unproductive, it hurts everyone."

"Even if that were true, it doesn't change anything. Innocent people are killed. Instead of trying to solve that problem, we invested in medical technologies like cloning so people of worth can live forever. The worst part is there is no one left who feels the outrage."

"Whatever, the government isn't evil."

"If you think that you are totally unaware of the world you live in."

"The country is a lot like Aeden. We're a bit luckier because we're closer to where the Executives live, but each community has its own set of Executives who evaluate and reward."

"Where the hell did you learn that?"

"In Archive."

"Help me out. What exactly were you taught?"

"I learned about the epidemics of the 2030s and '40s when antibiotics stopped working and the population declined. To rebuild, Chairman Crelli created private economic communities, like Aeden, where economic performance became the basis for life."

"What happens to those here who don't provide value?"

"Everyone provides value."

"Son, there are places in this great country where people live or die on the scraps and garbage they find. It has always been that way. The only reason Crelli allows them to live is it costs more to eliminate them than to ignore them."

"That's not true." Gil seemed angry at that allegation.

"You could find out for yourself."

"That's crazy. You know I can't do that."

"Or won't."

"Why are you picking on me? I came here to help. You're talking crazy, and you think I'm crazy for not believing you."

"Before you were born, laws were passed requiring all babies to receive special treatments that altered their personality. The treatments suppressed certain enzymes or proteins and affected behavioral characteristics deemed to be cost prohibitive, high-maintenance by the government. Among those unwanted traits were empathy and compassion."

"Stop it. Stop talking like that. Who would do that?"

"The United States government."

"Why?"

"Revolutions are cost prohibitive for the government but they require commitment to pull off. If nobody gives a damn, there's no chance for revolution. To achieve that state, the government and private industry funded research into addictive entertainment and leisure technologies that cause people to focus on fun and games rather than on the real everyday issues that truly affect their lives. At about that time, the reporting on events, it was called "news," disappeared; there was no one to tell of the insidious inner workings of government and private industry because there was no profit in it. The indifference of the population and their attention deficit provided the opportunity for leaders to consolidate power so they could run America any damn way they wanted. That's why we no longer have a republic and we have Morgan, Archive, and Virtuoso, and why productivity and worth are so overwhelmingly important to our way of life. It all works in concert to divert attention and interest to the harmless and mundane, like landscaping, gossip, sports, gaming, everlasting life, or whatever serves the leaders best and turns citizens away from more critical issues."

"Why are you so angry? Was everyone like you back then? Were you ever even productive? Howard and I have a good life. He creates value and we live well and no one gets hurt. I don't see what you see. What we have is a good life and that's not a crime."

"You don't see the crime."

"Boy, you are paranoid."

"You said that before. Just because I'm paranoid doesn't mean they're not after me." Bernie paused, choking back sadness. "Once, I had a conversation like this with my son, Mark."

"The president." Bernie nodded. "You didn't convince him either, did you?"

"Sadly, no."

"Did this friend tell you all the stuff you're telling me?"

"She and others, yes. They got my attention."

"And now you're trying to get mine." He nodded. "Even if what you're saying is true, why do I care? And if I cared, what could I do?"

There was hope. "There's revolution."

"Why that?"

"That's what I'm here to explain."

"You can't if you die."

"That's true."

"Suppose I listen, but I don't believe you?"

"If you listen, truly listen, I promise I'll do whatever you want afterward."

The boy was quiet, thinking. "You know … I'm a clone." Gil seemed embarrassed but at the same time relieved. "My trueborn self was a baby when I died."

"Gil, listen carefully. I have powerful enemies in the government who never forget and never forgive. Yes, because of me, your trueborn self was to be executed by the government."

"So it's the chairman again." The boy was mocking him. "Why would he kill a baby because of you?"

"You're not as insignificant as you think, and he's killed so many. He wanted you dead because of me. But there's something more. This will be difficult for you, but please believe me—they failed. They didn't kill your trueborn. What I'm saying is, you're not a familiar. They wanted you dead, but they failed. Before the execution, we switched you with another, and they killed him thinking it was you."

Gil stared at him in horror. "That's horrible. Do I thank you for rescuing me that way? What did you do to cause that? Why would they kill a baby, any baby, because of you? I bet it's a great story, but bet you can't prove it. I'll bet even Howard doesn't know, right? And there's no record of it in Archive."

"Everyone, including Howard, believes you're a familiar and for your safety it has to be that way. Crelli wanted you executed because you weren't provided with behavior modification treatments like all the other newborns. When he found out, he knew I caused it and you had to die. The only obstacle was you are Mark Rose's grandson. He couldn't save your life, but as president, he negotiated with Chairman Crelli to have you cloned. We intervened and the clone baby died in your place. For now, you must remain a clone or your life will be in danger. But never forget you are trueborn and untreated."

"And Howard doesn't know?"

"No one knows and please don't tell him or anyone else."

Silence hung heavily in the room. The boy looked bewildered but mostly sad. Bernie should have expected it. "Let me get this straight." Gil said, "You did something so horrible that they wanted to kill me, but instead you had them kill an innocent baby."

"But you were innocent, too. What I did is a heavy burden. I live with it and worse."

"And now you're asking *me* to accept it." Gil paused. "I always felt something wasn't right. I mean I hoped, who wouldn't, but I don't want to be trueborn if someone innocent had to die. How can I accept that? How can you? Still, I felt normal, but I never said anything. How could I? How did I know what normal felt like? They said I was familiar, so I accepted it. I don't understand. Why would they do it? What did you do that was so terrible they wanted to kill me?"

Bernie took Gil's hand. "This is all I want. Listen to what I have to say, and when you believe, help me. What I need you to do could be dangerous so I won't lie to you. After you hear it, it's up to you but I know you'll help. Nothing is as it seems, and nothing ever will be again." Bernie waited anxiously. Finally, the boy nodded.

"Listening is a talent that'll serve you the rest of your life. To truly listen, you must believe what you're hearing, whether you actually believe it or not. You must picture yourself living in the story. Try to become comfortable in it. This is difficult but it's the only way you will invest enough to believe it or not. This is essential because regardless how convincing I am, the only way you will know the truth is by feeling it. I read somewhere that a friend is nature's true masterpiece. When you listen, be my friend. When I'm done, trust your heart."

Gil nodded.

"It all began with my son, Mark, your grandfather, his engagement party."

Chapter 4

Indianapolis—2025

Thanks to a guest list of impressive business players drawn from the neighboring decks along the Geist Lake shoreline (as well as from New York, Chicago, Boston and Philadelphia), it was going to be a grand party. Bernie's hard-earned network of contacts, Mark's dazzling college performance, and a large budget, insured that Mark's engagement party was going to be every bit as impressive as required.

Bernie moved through his lakeside mansion observing the hired help and guests through the panoramic windows that overlooked the lake. The party had spread from his house to the lawn and then down landscaped steps onto the deck and gazebo perched on his man-made lakefront beach. He motioned to the caterer, who moved quickly to him.

"Make sure to empty each bottle of champagne, nothing goes to waste, it's expensive."

The caterer nodded. "Very good, sir."

"Tell the workers to ration the sturgeon, caviar, and carpaccio; they need to last all day."

The caterer nodded again. "Of course, sir."

"Security is stationed around the house checking for invitations?"

"Yes sir, we assigned the best from our private army, sir."

"And their weapons are hidden."

"Of course sir, we want everyone safe and we want you to enjoy this momentous occasion."

"Yes, of course, that's why you get the big dollars. See to it and, at the end of the day, there will be a big tip for your team."

"That is very kind, sir."

Bernie was excited. This was the moment when the fruits of his successful business career overshadowed all he had endured to get here. He was chief financial officer, an important, highly paid—yet unloved—accountant. In a world of engineers and marketers, he'd been forced to swim upstream through the shark-infested waters of corporate politics until the owners had no choice but to grudgingly recognize his value to their business. Bernie had parlayed the ten years since his promotion to CFO of American Natural Grain Stuffs, Inc., into a lifestyle that would have met with even his father's approval. He wasn't rich, not yet, not relative to the truly moneyed whom he admired—but he was comfortable, and that meant he was winning. Just that morning he'd said to his wife, Jane, "I think we've made it. We live better than 99 percent of Americans and 99.9 percent of the rest of the world." He laughed when she pointed out how insensitive that was, even though it was true.

Because he represented the top 0.1 percent of the world, he had no choice but to make this a social event of note, one that perpetuated relationships among the wealthy and powerful, generation after connected generation. He had the wherewithal, and today was going to be a monumental day for his son, Mark, and Mark's fiancée, Terry.

Like Bernie, Mark had graduated with a bachelor's degree in business. But where Bernie had been a hard-working, above-average student, Mark was truly a star, earning his degree in macro econometric engineering, magna cum laude, in three years from Indiana University's School of Business. He had been accepted for graduate studies at Harvard and the University of Pennsylvania and Bernie urged Mark to go, but so far, he had declined. In truth, Bernie was proud when Mark informed him why. "Dad, there'll be time for graduate school. You always said the classroom isn't where the action is."

Bernie entered the living room and shaded his eyes from the bright, late-spring sun shining through the windows. Jane was holding court near their massive, white brick fireplace. He edged into the group smiling proudly at her natural ability to schmooze.

"Am I interrupting?"

"I hope you don't mind, Bernie," said a marketing executive who was recruiting Mark. "I want to run off with your wife. I'm sorry, it's not business." The man smiled as he lifted a champagne flute to toast. "Really, you don't deserve this woman."

"Darling," Bernie said smiling, "before you do anything you regret, I hope you've made it absolutely clear about the suspicious demise of the other men you've run away with."

"Now, sweetheart," Jane added quickly, "you promised me you'd keep that quiet so you won't disappear too." Everyone laughed.

He embraced her. "Have you seen Mark and his bride-to-be?"

"I saw him earlier. He was talking to two men I didn't recognize but then I don't recognize a lot of these people. Afterward, he and Terry went outside. I haven't seen them since."

"If you see him, tell him I'm looking for him." Bernie excused himself and walked outside where the breeze blowing off the lake cooled the warm afternoon. His attention was drawn to the colorful triangles of sailboats skimming the white-capped water.

"Daddy?" He turned to his young daughter, Franki, sunk deeply into a cushioned lawn chair on the deck.

"Hey, sweetheart, how's the party?"

"It's a crummy party." She pouted. "It's just adults."

He squatted beside her and put his hands on hers. "Honey, this is for Mark and Terry, but for me and mom, too. There are things every parent wishes for. They want to know that their kids are safe, loved and free to pursue their dreams. This party is the beginning of that for Mark and Terry so it's a big deal. You'll find your Prince Charming and have your party soon enough. Because of that, do you think you can fake a smile? For them?"

"I'm not a child, Dad. I can fake a smile."

"Atta girl," he said.

"You owe me a party next," she said in her best negotiator's voice.

"Absolutely," he promised, "with just your friends and no boring adults." She was right, he did owe her. He never seemed to have time for her anymore.

"Cool," she said, giving him a hug.

He winked at her and then made his way slowly through the crowd, exchanging handshakes and hugs with the men and hugs and kisses with the women. Near the lake, he located his son talking solemnly with friends.

"Mark, it's time for the speeches. Grab Terry and come on down to the gazebo so we can thank everyone." Without waiting for a reply, Bernie continued to the beach.

"Dad," his son shouted, "We need to talk ..."

Bernie waved back at his son as his gaze caught thickening clouds in the distance. He hustled to the gazebo terrace below to get the guests', attention.

"Everyone, listen up," he yelled. When no one paid attention, he shouted, "hey, everyone! I've got a speech to make."

Someone shouted from above. "If you're making a speech, I'll need more liquor." Everyone laughed. Bernie nodded and smiled.

When Jane arrived, the guests moved closer and he began. "Just our luck," he said, pointing to the threatening clouds. "All week the weather forecast predicted a beautiful day. Now it looks like we'll have to get a move on or we're going to get drenched. The Rosenthal family has been looking forward to this occasion for some time. Jane, Mark, Franki, Terry, and I are very grateful that everyone found time in their busy schedules to share this joyous moment with us.

"For those who don't know, let me explain why Jane and I are such proud parents. Mark was valedictorian at his Indiana University's School of Financial Engineering. He was president of the Indiana Collegiate Management Council and a three-year officer of the Future Entrepreneurs of America Society. Last spring, he led a team from the university that developed and commercialized a collaborative, interactive business software game and we hope someday the royalties will comfort Jane and me in our retirement—and possibly will pay back our tuition investment." There was laughter from sympathetic parents. "Mark has won numerous awards including the Millennial Entrepreneur trophy given to the most promising graduate of the year.

"But most of all, Mark has been a phenomenal son and friend. Now, after years of boating, fishing, and breaking bread together, Terry, who we love like a daughter, has consented to join our family." As the crowd applauded and cheered, Bernie shaded his eyes and scanned the crowd for his son. "Mark, come up here and say something."

There was applause but no sign of Mark. Bernie continued to look but couldn't find him. Finally, Mark emerged at the top of the hill and slowly made his way down to the gazebo. Immediately, Bernie sensed something was wrong. Mark looked uncomfortable, something rare for his son. When Mark stepped onto the gazebo deck and waited awkwardly for the good-natured applause to die down, Bernie looked questioningly at his son, but Mark just shrugged.

Jane put her hand in his, and together they hugged Mark. Once the applause died down, Mark spoke quietly. He was uncharacteristically brief and off point.

"I … I want to echo my father's sentiments and thank you for coming today. I'm very grateful. My best memories as a child are of Mom and Dad and their wonderful, easy relationship. I hope to have a relationship like theirs someday. Thank you all for coming."

Although there was applause, there was also murmuring in the crowd. Bernie hugged Mark, but let go when he felt Jane tugging on his arm.

"Where's Terry?" Jane whispered.

"I don't know," Bernie answered, and together they turned to their son. "Mark?"

"Where's Terry, honey?" Jane whispered.

"Mom, I've been trying to talk to you and Dad all day."

"We've been here, honey. You didn't try very hard. What is it?"

"You're not going to like this, but I ... I accepted a job offer."

Bernie beamed. "That's great, son. Congratulations. What's the lucky company?"

Something in Mark's comment concerned Jane. "Where's Terry? Something's wrong."

Before Mark could answer, two men approached. Instead of responding to his mother's question, Mark began the introductions. "Mom, Dad, this is my new boss, Andy Crelli." Bernie shook his hand.

Crelli was young, looking to Bernie to be in his early thirties. He was vibrantly good-looking in the way rich young men often are, with a confident, almost cocky demeanor. He had prematurely gray hair brushed back and oiled in place and was wearing an expensive suit, perfectly tailored, with a perfect Windsor knot in a perfect silk tie. His olive skin accentuated his light hazel eyes—intense, penetrating, and inexpressive—like an engaged cobra.

Bernie glanced at Jane, who was usually friendly and much more adept than he at first meetings. She stared blankly at the man.

Bernie welcomed the stranger, but even though Crelli was the much younger man, the veiled intensity of his stare made maintaining eye contact difficult.

"Mr. and Mrs. Rosenthal, Mark has said so many good things about you; it's nice to finally meet you. Your son is extraordinary, a tribute to you both." Crelli's voice was pleasant but businesslike. Pleased by that, Bernie and Jane smiled.

Mark pointed to Crelli's companion. "This is Andy's personal assistant, Reno Soren. Reno, this is my mother, Jane, and my father, Bernie."

Soren offered his hand. The handshake was much different from his boss's, his grip too uncomfortably firm for Bernie's taste. Soren looked like a mauler, a rugby player in a business suit. It would've been difficult to guess what executive program he was recruited from.

"Mr. Rosenthal. Mark's a great kid." The muscles in his face were visible as he spoke.

"Yes, I know, thank you."

"I'm sorry my wife couldn't attend," Crelli continued, "but we'll get together at our first opportunity," Crelli added in a strong, confident voice. "Your son will fit perfectly in my organization. We have a unique model. I, that is my company Crelli Enterprises, seek out focused, well-educated, and talented young professionals who exhibit exemplary passion, people like your son who have the vision, energy, intelligence, and drive to make things happen. When we hire young people like Mark, on-the-job training is the only way to go, so we provide them high-exposure, high-yield situations with unparalleled opportunity and mentor them in real time."

"What young person could ask for more, Mr. Crelli?" Bernie responded, somehow disappointed he wasn't young enough to qualify.

"Please, call me Andy."

"Okay, Andy, we're pleased you think so highly of our son."

Crelli smiled. It was a well-trained, magnetic smile. "I'm pleased to have him. Bernie, you may not know this but your boss, Tom Gorman, is on my board."

"Mr. Gorman is a great businessman," Bernie said noncommittally.

"Tom is that. Frankly, with all that's going on, we need all the dedicated businessmen we can find. To buy the love of any citizen willing to trade their vote for handouts, President Parrington has vowed to raise taxes on us, the entrepreneurs, so it's time, once again, to retighten our belts. In America, it keeps getting harder to earn a profit."

"Certainly it won't be that bad, Mr. Crelli," Jane interjected.

Crelli's brow furrowed a little. "I see we have a democrat here, I should have suspected as much with Mark's views on social issues. Anyway, we'll find a way to overcome Parrington. He'll come to realize that business owners drive America. It is the great American entrepreneur who fights the good fight against relentless, international competitive pressures that threaten to undercut us in every market. We fight the fight while Parrington's higher taxes and more rigorous regulations drive up the cost of doing business. Parrington is just another democrat who lacks faith in free-enterprise capitalism, but someday, he'll learn our religion. There are better ways to get elected than to con voters by using taxes on the productive that drive us to oblivion."

"I own a business, too, Mr. Crelli, and I don't see it that way," Jane said.

"How do you see it, Mrs. Rosenthal?"

"I see a country that allows the wealthiest among us—Bernie and I included—to prosper, while people like my employees, the old, sick, and indigent barely survive."

"But, Mrs. Rosenthal, Jane, surely your customers expect high quality at low cost, and higher taxes and needless regulations threaten your ability to deliver. If you can't keep your customers, what happens to your employees can't be good."

"Andy, I hear those arguments all the time. It's funny how businesses blame the government for their failures. Taxes aren't bad. They make things safer and better for everyone. The services provided increase employment and that's more people to buy more things from entrepreneurs like you and me. I don't know you, but I assume you and your executives are compensated quite handsomely. A little less of that could go a long way."

"Mother," Mark yelled, embarrassed.

"No, its okay, Mark," Crelli said, smiling. "Your mother makes a good point. Jane, at Crelli Enterprises, executive compensation is based on how effectively we deliver our plans. If we don't show dynamic, bottom-line growth, our stockholders take their money elsewhere, strengthening the competition."

Crelli turned from Jane to Bernie. "I can see where Mark gets his passion and business savvy." Crelli then addressed Jane. "I couldn't disagree with you more; Jane, but I appreciate your point of view. Ultimately, America succeeds or fails based on which of us is right."

"Andy, what does Crelli Enterprises provide?" Jane asked.

"We enable companies to prosper by offering them integrated, diversified technologies including nanotechnology, biopharmacology, telecommunications, integrated business applications, and related consulting services. Our primary revenue is generated through consulting in the field of artificial intelligence with applications that continuously and proactively monitor and manage every process in an enterprise and are capable of making effective real-time operating decisions in collaborative harmony, horizontally and vertically, across a global operation, even going so far as to learn and correct mistakes."

"Really?" Jane laughed. "Was that an answer or are you trying to sell me something?" Crelli smiled again. Bernie was about to apologize for her, but Jane held up a hand to stop him. "Whatever it is, it sounds too expensive for what I do. Why is Mark right for your business?"

"Crelli Enterprises is my life, and I believe my employees should feel the same, so we reward them accordingly. The world continues to be a very dangerous and unfriendly place. The economic and natural resource crises we've been living with since the turn of the century have made it absolutely critical that we employ the best people in the right positions. Mark is one of those people who will enable Crelli Enterprises to redeem our economy. Mark will make a difference in our future. He feels it too. That's why he accepted."

"Mom, Dad, I'm sorry this seems sudden. I didn't intend to make a decision until the end of the summer, but Andy offered a once-in-a-lifetime opportunity."

"Where are your headquarters?" Bernie asked.

"We're in Kentucky, near Cincinnati. Once Mark joins, he'll lead his own team, in effect his own business group, and he'll pursue some of the socio-economic concepts he developed in school and, of course, we'll finance everything."

"Why would you do that?" Jane asked.

"America is desperate for a better future and we're going to provide it."

Mark interrupted. "Mom, there's no way I can pass up what Andy's offering. I'll be doing what no one else would ever permit a recruit like me to do and I'll even have a small ownership stake right out of the box. Dad, it's a dream come true."

"I believe you believe that, Mark. It's just so sudden. I thought you'd consider your options. This is just … unexpected."

"Carpe diem, Dad." Bernie knew later that evening he would endure Jane's withering stare over his favorite platitude. "How many times have you said that to me?"

"I know. You're right." Bernie conceded.

"All this is fine," Jane asked, "but where is Terry? What about her?"

Bernie had forgotten about Terry. "Mark, when was this decided, and why didn't you tell us? And Mom has a point. Where's Terry?"

"We discussed it earlier today."

Jane looked concerned. "What about Terry?" she persisted.

Mark glanced at Crelli, and then at Reno Soren. Their expressions were unchanged. He returned his mother's gaze then looked down like a little boy. "We broke up."

"What? No!" Jane and Bernie yelled in unison. Nearby guests turned to stare, but Bernie turned to address them. "Everything's okay, enjoy the champagne," he said, feebly.

"Mark!" His mother admonished. "How could you?"

"It wouldn't have worked, not right now," Mark whispered.

Bernie was angry but surrounded by guests; he tried to remain calm. "What have you done?" he whispered. "This is your engagement party. Nobody breaks up at his own engagement party. Do you know what this event cost? Do you know how much embarrassment you're causing mom and me?" He grabbed his son's arm. "Find her now. I don't care what you say, but make this right. You're not breaking up with her, not after all these years and all this expense just to accept what appears today to be a good job offer. There are plenty of those around for someone with your talents, Mark. It's not right and it's foolish and selfish. I … you're better than this. Find her and make this go away or …"

"Or what, Dad? As soon as I start the job, I won't have any time. Look at how long your days are. You're never home. It'll be the same for me. I'll be traveling all the time. I won't have a family life. It wouldn't be fair to Terry."

Tears rolling down her cheeks, Jane looked away but reached for her son's hand. "Oh, Mark," she said, choking away the tears, "don't let go of your dreams for a job. I've never questioned your judgment before. You love Terry.

You can't put your career in front of that. What does that make you? What are you thinking?"

Crelli offered his hand to Mark's parents. "Excuse us, Jane, Bernie. I have an appointment elsewhere. I apologize for any difficulties this may have caused but I assure you, what Mark accomplishes with us will more than make up for how you feel right now."

Before shaking hands, Bernie moved closer to Crelli. "Why are you doing this?"

"Bernie, we're both businessmen. My needs are so great that it's critical I assess the loyalty of my staff. Mark passed this first test. Don't be pissed, Bernie, I know for a fact you've done similar things for your career. It's the way of the world. We're professionals; we know. Mark is one of us now."

Livid but unable to answer, Bernie shook Crelli's hand and watched as he and Soren climbed the stairs and disappeared into the crowd.

Furious, he turned his attention back to Mark. He wanted to yell, but wouldn't make a scene. "Why didn't you tell us? Terry is family, too."

"I didn't think I'd get the offer Dad, and when I did, there wasn't time. That's how Andy operates. If I can't match his intensity, he won't want me. Don't get the wrong idea; Andy is a caring man who runs an exemplary business—all his employees look up to him. This is an extraordinary opportunity. I know I've hurt everyone but I had no choice. The decision was hard but I'll live with it, and you'll see it's the right one."

A chill went through Bernie. "Mark, nothing is worth what you've just done."

Jane was angry. "Crelli is just a young hustler. Poor Terry, you gave her up for him?"

"Mom, it's not like that. Once you get to know him, you'll see. He's brilliant and intense. I've never met anyone like him. I can't pass this up."

"We need to take this somewhere private," Bernie whispered. "Call Terry."

"She's gone," Mark said glumly.

"I don't understand." Jane sounded like she was going to cry. "I don't care what you say; I'm going to call her and make sure she's okay. I won't blame her if she won't talk to me after what you've done, but I have to try."

Mark looked helpless. "Andy offered me everything I wanted and more and sealed it with stock options that, if his company continues to do well, which I know it will, will make me rich. You heard him, Mom. Once I get my feet wet, he promised me the freedom to implement my own ideas. Please don't be down on him. You don't know him. Andy has the vision and the passion of truth. He will make the world a better place. That's why I want to work for him. For all that, he's completely supportive of marriage and family and committed relationships, but if I'm going to make a difference, I have to commit to other things first. I explained it to Terry and told her that wherever I ended up, I wanted her to join me, eventually, if she still wants me."

"You said that?" Jane asked dryly.

He nodded, glumly. "She cried and then just said goodbye. It was her call."

Jane was upset. "Oh, Mark. God bless her, Terry did the right thing, even if you didn't."

Mark was hurt and turned to Bernie. "Dad, I know I'm too analytical and that makes me appear uncaring, but this is tearing me up. I really love her."

Before Bernie could stop her, Jane added, "honey, I don't want to be mean but I'm not sure your understanding of love is the same as your dad's and mine."

"Jane, that's enough." Bernie scolded. "It's his life." She looked at him angrily, but before he could say more, the rain began to fall in earnest. They had been so involved with Mark that they were unable to say their goodbyes. As servers ran frantically to clean up, guests fled to their cars, leaving their drinks on the railings outside to fill with rain.

As the house and grounds emptied, the unhappy family moved into the gazebo. "Mark, your father and I love you. That'll never change. But this, you're testing our limits. Is there any way we can change your mind?"

"Mom, it's done. I'll live with my decision."

"Then you owe me something," Jane said.

"What?"

"Tell your boss if he treats you wrong, he'll answer to me."

It was later when Bernie lay in bed beside Jane, an unopened bottle of Merlot on the nightstand. Thunder rumbled and flashes of lightning projected the silhouettes of tree limbs on the window treatments. At this stage of their life, for an evening of lovemaking, planning was essential. They had anticipated capping off the glorious engagement party, but when the time came, Bernie climbed sullenly into bed and stared silently at the slowly revolving ceiling fan.

"Penny for your thoughts," Jane said softly. "A dollar if I'm in them."

"You're always in them. I was thinking about … well, you know."

"It won't do any good to brood."

"I'm not brooding. I'm angry."

"Really? I couldn't tell when we were talking to Mark. About what specifically?"

"What do we know about this Crelli guy and Crelli Enterprises?"

"Why are you angry about that?"

"It's not that. Mark's always shown good judgment before. He's an adult and his own man. I'm angry, no, more disappointed, I guess, that he didn't tell us about Terry and the job."

"He should have." Thunder cracked loudly, causing her to flinch. "But obviously he made up his mind and didn't want our opinion."

"But the responsible thing to do would have been to tell us before the party. The cost, the embarrassment."

"That's not the most important thing."

"Of course not, but we spent a fortune, and we look stupid. If he's old enough to make stupid decisions, he's old enough to act responsibly once he's made them."

"If it makes you feel better, bill him for the cost of the party."

"I can't ..."

Jane smiled. "Cut him some slack. We don't know what he and Terry talked about but we can be sure he won't make the decisions we'd like him to make. Remember when you told your dad you were marrying a much younger divorced Catholic?"

Bernie smiled at the thought. "I was in my forties."

"And yet he still made our life hell until I won him over. Give Mark a chance to win us back. If that stubborn man—God rest his soul—finally accepted me, even conditionally, into the high and mighty Rosenthal tribe, anything's possible. I feel bad for Terry. She wouldn't answer my calls, the poor thing."

"She'll talk to you. You're all she has."

"I know." They were silent for a while before Jane spoke again. "What about us? Is this going to happen tonight or are you just going to obsess?"

"Is what going to happen?"

"Don't be coy," she said.

"I thought you were tired."

"I'm clearly not. Are we negotiating?"

He stared at her face against the white pillow. Her deep green eyes never failed to excite him. He struggled his way toward a romantic notion, but it danced just out of reach. He yearned for the magic of their early days when he could summon inspiration from thin air. But the pressures of work and age and family made conjuring that magic too exotic tonight.

"Is it me?" she asked.

He wanted so much to behave like a nineteen-year-old testosterone grenade and go off whenever she pulled the pin. "It's never you." He offered. "It's, I don't know. Maybe talking about my father isn't the best foreplay. Besides, I'm tired and disappointed. Youth has its advantages. I didn't need jumpstarting back then."

"I wish I'd known you then."

"Very funny."

"I find you incredibly sexy when you're impotent," she joked.

"Ouch. I find you beautiful all the time."

"Do you mean that?"

"Of course I do. I will never forget that beautiful young woman at my business parties who changed everyone's opinion of this boring financial guy."

"That's nice to hear, Bernie. It's a long, downhill slog from being noticed by everyone to being invisible to strangers—and even entire generations. I'm just an old lady now."

"But you're my old lady."

"I know, Bernie, but ..."

"Have I been so inattentive that you're looking to strangers for acceptance now?"

"I'm just feeling sorry for myself—post-party depression, sorry."

"You're beautiful and sexy and I'm lucky you chose to share your life with me."

She smiled. "That's a great start." She snuggled to him and rubbed his cheek gently with the back of her hand. He cherished her—friend and lover—one of God's great creations. Absently, he stroked the small of her back as the habits of seduction slowly kicked in, and he worked his way to the upturn of her tailbone, massaging the flesh of her buttocks. Distractions dissipated, and there was only her. He put his head on her pillow and kissed her. After all the pressures, there was finally only her in his head.

He kissed her neck and the fold of her elbow. He brushed his mouth over her breasts. She rolled her head back, closing her eyes, her mouth against his ear, tongue exploring.

Before momentum could build, an image, unbidden, wedged its way into his mind—Crelli. It chased a chill down his spine and opened a pathway for unwanted thoughts to re-emerge, successfully defeating his desire. He died away from her, receding into another set of distractions that ruined the evening's purpose. She sensed it immediately and pulled back.

"I'm sorry, Jane, maybe later. Can I wake you?"

"You should finish what you start." She kissed his lips. "Don't forget me or I'll ..." instead of completing the thought, she turned away and covered herself with blankets.

He wondered if, in some way, Mark's decision had something to do with not inflicting this frustration on Terry. He lay back, silently berating himself for bad partnering and parenting until, eventually, like the storm, his mood passed, and in the early hours of a new day, he woke her and fulfilled his promise.

Chapter 5

Indianapolis—2031

The years passed quickly. Bernie awoke to an unusually warm first day of spring. He noticed the light green shadows of new growth on the tree branches offering hints of the coming heat. He turned forlornly to the mirror to gaze at his close-cropped, receding, salt-and-pepper hair that was rapidly losing its pepper.

Jane was fixing her hair at the bathroom sink. "Honey, I read an article on Senator Crelli yesterday at the hairdressers."

"What did it say?"

"Ever since the e-Rot trials, he's become more than just a media celebrity. He is getting respect as a serious-minded senator."

He laughed. "That's e-RATS—electronic revolutionaries and terrorists."

"Whatever, the article explained how his campaign for more aggressive policing and harsher penalties for hacker-terrorist crimes got him elected. Our community has such good security that I didn't realize how many terrorists there were and how many he's put away. I still hate what he did to Terry, but from a career standpoint Mark's decision wasn't wrong. Crelli is a hero, which is unusual for a politician these days. By the way, the article called Mark the acting CEO of Crelli Enterprises. I'll bet that makes him angry."

Bernie scowled. "I still hate the bastard, too, and I wish the media would give Mark more recognition. He deserves it. He's young but he's doing a great job. And it's not temporary—even Senator Crelli says that. I'm so proud of Mark. It's because of him that Crelli felt confident enough to leave Crelli Enterprises and became a senator. Now they're both patriots. Remember when ANGST was targeted by cyber-terrorists?"

"The pressure and the hours you worked. You were so exhausted and stressed."

"They would have destroyed us if it wasn't for Crelli and his task force. Hell, without Crelli, everyone would have lost faith in our economy and its ability to transact business. When e-RATS target you, it's terrifying. I learned the hard way."

"You aged five years that year."

"And ANGST was lucky. We would've lost hundreds of millions of dollars if Crelli's e-SWAT team hadn't been able to track down those e-RATS. Even as big as ANGST is, I didn't think we'd make it. But thanks to my Technology Director, Crelli's federal e-SWAT task force, and your love, we beat them, and I survived." Bernie checked his watch and straightened his tie.

"Honey, when you leave, check on what they're doing to the entrance."

"That's our Homeowner's Association. They've finally put that special assessment to work and started on the security wall. Walls like it haven't helped with mobs of unemployed who've ransacked homes closer to the city, but out here the wall should protect home values."

"Why can't the government find jobs for these people or provide handouts? It's pretty scary driving around. Every time I stop, I'm not sure what the pedestrians will do. A few of my friends have been robbed. I heard a driver was killed and his car stolen."

"The chaos is driving taxes higher but we should be getting more police for the money we're paying. The Toms were forced to approve a private security army to keep headquarters safe. It's so bad that I invested some of our retirement money in stocks of companies that rent out private armies, providing security that municipalities who are going broke can't provide. Jane, maybe you should start working out of the house."

"Bernie, I run nursing facilities, you know I can't do that from here."

"Then you should travel during normal rush hour. Even so …"

"I have to work, Bernie. I hope the design for the security wall doesn't detract from our neighborhood."

"I've seen sketches. It'll be fine. They've contracted with a company owned by a German Muslim fellow, Smith something. I've seen completed walls from the same contractor all over town." Bernie looked at his watch again. "Is it seven already? I gotta run, Jane, my love to Franki." With that, he bolted from the bedroom.

Jane yelled after him. "Call me if you're not going to be late." He smiled.

After an over-long drive through heavy traffic, he entered through ANGST's new security gate into the parking lot. Once he parked, he watched as other ANGST employees began the dreaded hike to the office. The path from the parking lot was called the "death march" because, for no apparent reason, it wound with serpentine turns with random concrete steps placed at awkward angles and heights. Although the main entrance was no more than fifty yards away from the lot, it was nearly impossible to walk there with a normal human gait.

Before he took to the path, Bernie stared up at the window on the third floor, his corner office. It was easy to pick out because the window beside it had been bricked-up. After his promotion to chief financial officer, corporate regulations required that he occupy a larger office. To comply, the ANGST Maintenance Department had moved an existing wall in his office out the required distance, but unfortunately, it intersected with a window. Ignoring his protest, they bricked up the offending window. Now, from the outside it looked like there might be a prisoner housed inside. To Bernie it made the building look like it was wearing a pirate's eye patch.

He climbed the stairs to his office and was settling in when his secretary entered. "Have you scanned the news?"

"No, Carolyn, I'm preparing for the executive committee meeting. What's up?"

"Remember Jim Bonsack?"

"Sure. His company installed some of our business intelligence software a few years ago. As I remember, he was a heck of a salesman. What's he up to?"

"He's dead."

"What? How?"

"I forwarded you the article. Check it out."

Curious, Bernie found the article.

Murder Suspected In Death of Bonsack, DSS Executive

Indianapolis – Authorities confirmed that yesterday's golf course explosion that killed James R. Bonsack, the chairman of Bonsack DSS, Inc., a Chicago-based technology company, was intentional, setting the stage for a multistate murder investigation. Early speculation had centered on the possibility that Bonsack had inadvertently set off an abandoned explosive charge left by the land developers who built the new Brandy Dale course. Authorities now say a military-style explosive was used in the murder at the upscale golf club.

Bonsack's playing partner, Buchanan "Bucky" Duke, president of Indianapolis-based Applied Intelligence (AI), was stunned. "I don't know why anyone would want to murder a great business leader, technologist, and humanitarian like Jim Bonsack," said Duke. "It makes no sense."

Duke declined to comment on rumors that his company is looking to sell and that Bonsack was a potential suitor. "We were friends and golfing partners," was all he would say. Sources indicate a sale was nearly finalized.

The Indianapolis Police Department released lab reports that indicate the golf ball Bonsack struck was, in fact, a bomb made from a powerful explosive, similar to those used by e-RATS. "Trace particles removed from remnants of Mr. Bonsack's skin and clothing, and a club head found a distance away, clearly show residue of an explosive compound coated with a glossy white veneer," said IPD Homicide Detective Lieutenant Earl Conger. "Our view is the compound was molded into a golf ball. It detonated when Bonsack struck it."

Asked how someone could replace Bonsack's ball, Conger replied, "Brandy Dale is a heavily wooded course with deep rough. Where Bonsack played his last ball was very isolated. Someone stalking him could easily have stayed up-course and waited until he hit into trouble, exchanging the golf ball and disappearing without being seen." It is Conger's belief that whoever committed the crime knew enough about Mr. Bonsack to know what kind of golf ball he was playing. The lieutenant added there were no suspects and no motive for the slaying. e-RAT violence has escalated recently so that is looked upon as the direction the investigation will take.

"So, what do you think?" Carolyn asked.

Bernie was speechless. He was shocked to hear that someone he knew had died, particularly someone as young and dynamic as Jim Bonsack, the epitome of an aggressive, personable salesman. And to be murdered! "I'm amazed. Murder? What's the world coming to?"

Carolyn nodded sympathetically. "I'm scared. So is everyone in my neighborhood. And Mr. Bonsack was so good-looking. I didn't mean to keep you from your meeting, but I thought you'd be interested."

"Thanks, Carolyn."

Late, he rushed into the already darkened boardroom. The dim, soft light and deep, dark noise-absorbing carpet gave the room the desired eerie feeling of an inner sanctum. He nodded to his bosses and sat to their withering stare. Tom Gorman, the CEO, was a small, heavy-set, leprechaun of a man, gray-haired, with a pleasant smile and a mean disposition. His partner, another Tom, tall, lanky Tom Morgan, was President and just as mean, but this Tom had the look of a college history professor. They were a matched set, the Toms. Long ago, when Bernie was just an accounting manager, they joined forces to buy a controlling interest in the company; Morgan was the thinker and Gorman, the no-holds-barred executive implementer. Gorman savored his reputation, even commissioning a chalk outline of a dead body sewn into the carpet in front of his executive desk in order to intimidate underlings. At Bernie's first meeting in Gorman's office, he was grilled while standing on the chalk silhouette. He'd felt like he'd be fired on the spot and was so intimidated that after that, he tried to avoid Gorman's office. He often wondered what about that meeting had qualified him for the promotion he received shortly afterward.

The meeting began poorly. Without clarifying, Morgan began calmly. "Nice of you to come, Bernie. I'd like to make a point, if I may? As God is my witness, I'm so sick and fucking tired of our people calling my company, ANGST. The fucking name is ANGS got that? Ay-en-gee-es. With no tee. Am I spelling it slowly enough? It's bad enough the workers use it, but when an executive mouths it, it reinforces unacceptable behavior. Starting today, I vow, there will be hell to pay if I find anyone unwilling to meet this simple requirement. I'll start with you, Bernie—you know I will. This is the last time that term is used. The next time it happens someone gets klaatued."

Embarrassed by being late and surprised by Morgan's tirade, Bernie was appalled by the term "klaatued." Years earlier, at Gorman's recommendation, Bernie hired Arlene Klaatu, an expert consultant, to work on a corporate information project. She and the Toms didn't work well together and there were numerous arguments until one day, she just vanished—absolutely and completely. Her leased car was parked in its spot in the company parking lot; her clothes were still at her hotel along with an airline ticket home. But Ms. Klaatu, herself, disappeared, never to be seen again. No wrongdoing was ever discovered, and the case remained unsolved.

From that incident, a legend was born. Anyone arguing with or disobeying an executive directive was said to be at risk of being "klaatued." But to Bernie's knowledge, this was the first time he'd ever heard a Tom invoke the legend. It made him uncomfortable.

"Tom, I'll get a memo out to alert everyone as to the proper pronunciation."

The next item of business was the Angel Falls project.

Gorman opened the discussion. "As we know, America is becoming a smaller portion of the global economic pie, and it will take generations to fully repurpose our population to accommodate that fact. For us, it is time to readdress economic decisions made nearly a century ago, when America became the preeminent economic power in the world. We've wrestled with what to do with our Maine facility for years and having heard everyone's views; we've decided to close it. We have a substantial offer from a business conglomerate in Kazakhstan, so we're selling the Angel Falls equipment and moving on."

"Tom?"

"Yes, Bernie?" Gorman said, obviously annoyed.

"I've reviewed the economics and I'm concerned. We haven't appropriated nearly enough separation funds for our employees there or for the community. Closing will be hard on them. Angel Falls is isolated near the Canadian border and it will lose its primary revenue source. A hundred families live there, and most are dependent on us. The small businesses, restaurants, and shops need us to survive. When we're gone … hell, there are no businesses within commuting distance, so families will have to relocate. Angel Falls is a beautiful town. A small river runs through and there's a lake with a picturesque waterfall that freezes in the winter. It's incredibly beautiful. We've been doing business there for over a century, and I believe we have a responsibility to do more. That's why I rechecked the numbers. We can provide additional funds to the families and still net a significant return. The funds we provide will help loyal workers through what will be a frighteningly lean period."

Gorman stared at him and sighed. Then Gorman looked at Morgan, one nodded and the other spoke. "We're pleased you've enjoyed your visits, but this is purely an economic decision …"

"But, it has nothing …Tom, the plant is profitable; all the studies show it."

"Don't interrupt me, Rosenthal. When did your limited accounting mind start questioning my engineering discipline? We aren't going to invest more capital there, the logistics are too costly. We've identified buyers for the damn equipment and when we move production here to Indianapolis, our cost to manufacture will decline, increasing profits and that's what we're in the business for, unless you have a better reason, Rosenthal. This will happen. If you must think of Angel Falls, think of it as no longer existing. What happens to the people or the community is not my problem. End of discussion. Thanks for your insight, though."

"Tom, I know I'm a financial guy, but just because we can get a better return overseas is no reason to decimate a community. Companies all over the country have been doing it for years and towns like Angel Falls—and even larger ones—have ceased to exist because there's no work. Think about what this is doing to our country. Someone has to pay for out of work people."

"As long as that someone isn't me, I could give a fuck. Who says businesses always have to pay? Times are changing, and America can't afford to punish stakeholders for making correct decisions. My job is to keep my business competitive. If I must do it without Americans, so be it."

"But the people …"

Morgan interrupted. "People? You're not listening, Rosenthal. Who cares about the fucking people? We can't depreciate them, and most are more trouble than they're worth."

"Then what about the country? We're all patriots here. Unemployment and reduced tax revenues are getting really scary. What about that? If we keep people employed, there's more tax revenue and more consumer spending and more consumers spending means more profit for us."

Now Gorman was angry. "I don't want a lesson in economics. We will not suffer just so some hicks can buy groceries? Angel Falls is dragging ANGS performance down. Hell, if it wasn't for us, they wouldn't have jobs in the first place. If they don't like it, tell them to picket Washington and force the government to stop taxing us like it does. If it keeps it up, I'll ship the whole enterprise overseas. You know I will. I'll move everything to a tax-free zone, and I'll move from Indianapolis to the Caymans and run it from there. In the meantime, we're reducing our tax burden one facility at a time and increasing profits by moving to countries where labor is cheap and beholden to management, as it should be. Now I have one further item." Gorman's face was beet red.

Morgan leaned over to Bernie, and using some papers to hide his mouth from the rest of the group, whispered loudly enough for everyone to hear. "See what you did? Shut the fuck up."

Gorman took a breath and added, "forget Angel Falls. It's gone. I'll hear nothing further on it. However, I need the original Angel Falls acquisition work papers for a special meeting. Bring them to my office at one today. We have other business so we're moving along. Bernie, you can leave."

Embarrassed and chastened, Bernie got up to leave. Embarrassed, the other executives avoided making eye contact with him or with the Toms. Before leaving, he tried to salvage something.

"Tom, Tom, did you read where Jim Bonsack was murdered in town yesterday?"

Morgan and Gorman looked at each other without saying anything. Bernie looked from one to the other. Had he said something wrong again? "You remember Jim Bonsack? His company installed our business analytics systems a few years back. We paid him enough."

The Toms again glanced briefly at each other. Finally, Gorman replied tersely. "Bonsack was a careless, greedy businessman."

"Maybe so, but murdered?"

Without replying, Gorman abruptly continued with his agenda, leaving Bernie by the door. Humiliated, he left the boardroom. Thoroughly confused and demoralized, he went back to his office, shut the door, and tried to recover. Almost immediately, Carolyn stuck her head in.

"Want a Scotch?" she asked.

"How does what happened in a private meeting travel so fast? What can I drink to recover my sanity?"

She shrugged. "Arsenic is the current fashion. But I refuse to be party to a professional suicide. Is there something else I can do for you?"

"I need some files from Building Two."

"I hate that place. It's dark and full of spiders and rodents. But for you . . ."

"You know what, Carolyn? I need some air. You can draft a strongly worded memo to our employees advising them to stop calling the place ANGST. Morgan's up in arms again."

"But it's so exquisitely appropriate," she said.

"Yeah, but jobs are hard to find, so it's ANGS from now on, for everybody."

"Gotcha. I'll run the errand. I don't mind. Besides, you don't look so good."

He didn't feel so good, either. "No, I'll go. I'm okay. It was just another meeting."

"Bastards," she said conspiratorially. She smiled, closed the door, and left.

It was a long walk to Building Two. He unbolted the metal door and once inside he hoped the plumbing was still working. When he opened the men's room door, he was surprised by muffled sounds coming from inside one of the stalls. He hadn't expected anyone to be here so he hesitated, but need drove him. He relieved himself, embarrassed by the groaning and moaning sounds of someone toiling mightily nearby.

"Are you all right?" he asked finally. There was no response, so he repeated his question.

A voice responded. "Please, this is embarrassing. I need help."

He heard the door unlock so he walked to the stall.

"Don't tell anyone about this," the voice inside begged, "or I won't open up."

Fearing a drug addict, Bernie hesitated. "Are you doing anything illegal?"

"No." The plea was barely enough for him to decide to help.

"If you're being honest, I won't mention anything about this, whatever it is."

The door opened revealing a massive man sitting wedged between the narrow walls with his pants down and an electronic book in his lap. His face was a scary purplish red.

Driven by the sight and odor, Bernie stepped back. He paused to recover and then asked, "Are you having a heart attack? I'll call our first responders."

The man looked worried. "No, no, I'm okay, really," he wheezed. "It's just my legs fell asleep, that's all, and I can't stand."

"Your legs are asleep? How long have you been here?" The man looked at his watch. Squatting on the toilet, he was almost Bernie's height and must have weighed over three hundred pounds.

"A couple of hours, I guess. You promised you wouldn't tell," the man pleaded, perspiration dripping freely down his face, rolling over the folds of fat at his neck and soaking his collar.

"I promised." Bernie reassured him. "Does this happen often?"

The answer surprised Bernie. "More than I'd like," the man replied.

"What do you usually do?"

"People don't come in here so usually I massage my legs until the blood flows back. Then I pull myself up. I sure wish they'd make these things larger."

"They are small. But, then again, they're not made for recreation. Your boss permits you to read for hours at a time in the men's room?"

"Well, that's hard to say. Reading helps me get through the day, so I got into the habit of bringing material with me." Bernie stared curiously at him. "You have me at a disadvantage," the man continued. "Help me and we can talk later."

He grabbed the man's massive arms and strained to lift him. The man finally burst from the stall with a grunt, hitched up his oversized trousers and, with Bernie steadying him, slowly lumbered around the lavatory until the blood flowed back into his legs. While helping, Bernie kept checking his watch. He needed to find the Angel Falls files soon.

Finally, when the man was capable of supporting himself, Bernie moved to the sink to wash his hands and straighten his clothes.

"My name is Bernie Rosenthal. And you would be?"

"Ennis Parker."

"I don't know that I've seen you around, Ennis. Where did you say you work?"

"I'm in Systems, and you?"

"I'm the chief financial officer."

A horrified look came over Parker's face. Muttering, "Oh shit, oh shit," Parker turned and did his best impression of fleeing through the bathroom door in a panic, his pant legs making a loud swishing sound as he went.

With his hands still wet, Bernie was caught flat-footed. He didn't know what to make of Parker's flight. His first instinct was to let him go so as not to further embarrass the man, but he was too involved to let this pass. He bolted through the door and looked down both corridors. The hallways were mostly dark, with dim outside light filtering through dirty windows that created shadows on the worn, off-green tile floors. In the distance he heard the swishing pants and rapid clomping of stressed loafers. When he heard another door swing open, he chased after the sound.

Ahead, the obese man was making his best time, but a man of that bulk on wobbly legs couldn't be expected to put a lot of distance between himself and his pursuer. Still, Parker maneuvered skillfully through the corridors of the large warehouse.

Bernie chased. He turned a corner and tripped over Parker, who was just lying there. He knelt down, and seeing the prostrate Parker was only winded, let him catch his breath.

"No more running?" Parker wheezed his acceptance. For the second time, he helped the man up and waited for him to gain his composure.

Parker's face was still purple and his mouth sucked in air like a turbocharger. He had an odd look. Was he ashamed or scared?

"Please, you promised you wouldn't say anything. I didn't know you were the CFO. Please, you've gotta keep your promise. People are counting on me."

"If you're honest with me, Ennis, I'll keep my promise, unless you're doing something wrong. I'm the CFO and I have responsibilities."

Parker's head dangled and Bernie detected tears in the big man's eyes. He led the huge man to a couple of old, wooden swivel chairs, wiped the dust from them, and they sat down.

"Let's talk," he said. "Let's start with the easy stuff. Where do you work?"

"That may not be the easiest place to start."

"OK, who's your supervisor?"

"That's a tough one, too. Do you remember Rebecca Morning?"

"Becca was the Enterprise Intelligence Software project manager we brought in to replace Arlene Klaatu a while back. We let her go maybe two years ago when the project went over budget and we couldn't implement the damn software. Were you on that project?"

"Yes. I represented the Materials Management Department. When the project began, six of us were transferred permanently to it."

He recalled what he knew about the project. ANGS had spent almost a hundred million dollars to improve their old business systems and Rebecca Morning had been brought in to salvage the project. With her leadership, some of the systems became operational, but she couldn't get the most sophisticated applications to do what the Toms wanted. The carnage from that project was legendary. After hiring and firing three different consulting companies and transferring almost a hundred people in and out of the never-close-to-complete project, ANGS continued to hemorrhage money. Of the heads that rolled, along with Arlene Klaatu, Morning's was one of the more memorable.

"What happened after the project? Where did you go when it disbanded?"

"Disbanded?"

"Yes. When project funding stopped, the project team was broken up, and everyone was let go or reassigned to other jobs."

"No, they weren't. That's the problem. They never broke us up. At least no one ever said anything. Management assumed we were told. Most of us still hang out here in our project room."

Bernie's mind went completely blank. Of course the team had been reassigned. He remembered heated discussions in the executive committee as to where the people would go. By the time Becca was discharged, there was only a small core of employees left.

"When Becca left, there were what, fifteen people on the project. Is that right?"

"Thirteen. Two had friends who were department heads who took them back. Personnel never told the remaining eleven of us where we would be going, so we stayed here where we continue to receive our paychecks." Bernie's shocked expression registered on Ennis. "Don't look at me like that. We were never fired, and there's a recession. Without money, it's dangerous out there so with no work available, we stayed here. What could we do?"

"You and ten other employees have been hiding in Building Two for, what, two years? And getting paid to do it?" he asked incredulously.

"No, not quite. Over time, three of the guys and one of the secretaries found jobs with one of the consulting companies. A friend processed termination notices for them."

"So seven people have been here for two years."

"It is kind of amazing when you think about it. But this is ANGST, after all. It's a pretty fucked up company, no offense, so who would notice? We come and go on time. We get paid and still receive profit sharing, although I heard ANGST is reneging on our pensions." Bernie nodded. "Getting paid, that's the easy part. Killing the days, that's been tough."

"Ennis, first, I'd appreciate it if you didn't call the company ANGST. It's ANGS, okay?" Ennis nodded. "Why do you bother to come in at all? The company is paying you, and it obviously doesn't know you're here. You could easily take a second job and double dip to earn more money."

"But that would be dishonest. We're being paid, so we come to work. We only take the vacation allowed, and we try to straighten up in here when we can. When a delivery is made of archived material, we hide until the people have gone and then we file it."

"In two years, nobody's seen you?"

"No, this building wasn't in use before the project. It's too old, I guess, so nobody comes here. To pass the time, each of us has taken on a specialty, kind of like librarians or historians. For instance, I specialize in inventory and shipping information, John Roche knows accounting, and Marsha McGregor is an expert on personnel records. We're very careful. This building is supposed to be unoccupied, so if we turned on the lights it would give us away. That's why we call ourselves "moles." Say, you'd be surprised at some of the odd things stored here."

"Odd? Like what?"

Ennis drew a labored breath, wheezing out a slow exhale. "Well, we discovered checks for payments to phony organizations that support politicians."

"Are you sure?" Ennis nodded. "Holy shit."

"Yeah, and there's the computer application called 'EVA.'"

"Eva?"

"No, EVA, Economic Value-Added—it measures a person's worth."

"Oh, you mean the ANGST performance evaluation system."

Parker shook his head. "Well, yes and no. It doesn't measure work; it measures worth—economic value. As CFO, I'd think you'd know about it. Guess not. And there's something else I guess I should tell you. Somebody else is accessing ANGST's, I mean ANGS' files."

"Who?"

"We don't know. Whoever they are, they're really good, because they're like ghosts. They leave no trail." Parker shook his head, jowls swaying. "We set up our own firewall security to trap them, but whoever it is goes through it like smoke through a screen door."

"I appreciate the heads up. Thanks, I'll have my security people look into it. Ennis, about those EVA files, can I see them? Can you give me your password?"

Ennis laughed. "So you don't know anything about them? How about that? If you promise to keep us a secret, I'll give you a password."

Bernie weighed the risks. As an officer, he had a responsibility to turn these people in, but he had to know if anything illegal was going on. He rationalized his curiosity and nodded to Parker. "Agreed. Your secret is safe—for now. I won't protect you if you or your … what do you call yourselves, moles, are doing anything illegal."

"I understand. The user name is 'Rebekah' and you can use that as the password, too. It'll give you access. It's a backdoor password that allows developers to bypass security so they can fix problems."

With that, Bernie went off to retrieve the files for Gorman. On the walk back to his office he considered contacting Mark to get help if, in fact, ANGS was being targeted by e-RATS supported by foreign governments or foreign companies again. He had more to learn.

Chapter 6

Indianapolis—2031

It was late. The Toms and Carolyn had gone for the day, so he was alone in the office. With feet propped on his desk, locked at the ankles, he was deep in thought. What was going on? Was Ennis Parker important? A bunch of workers getting paychecks two years after their service was no longer required, was that important? Whatever these EVA files were, were they important? And why didn't he, as chief financial officer, know anything about them? His comfortable, sane world seemed to be rocking out of control.

Using the backdoor password Ennis Parker provided, he entered a system that shouldn't have existed. A menu appeared on the monitor. With his stomach knotted, he clicked on an item marked "Eyes-Only." A prompt appeared requiring entry of a password. He entered it but it was rejected. Had Ennis played him for a fool? He entered it again, and this time it was accepted. An alphabetized listing of ANGS's employees appeared. He browsed for "Rosenthal, Bernard G."

His profile contained information from his personnel file but when he clicked on a line that read "Net Worth," a summary of his personal net worth appeared in the way it would be presented to a financial institution—even though it shouldn't have been available to his employer. As he read, he got angry. One section contained information about his families' health and another section hyperlinked similar information about everyone in his and Jane's families.

He moved to a section that detailed information about his buying habits, his recreational choices, even his voting record and what he watched on television, and which commercials he did and did not change channels to avoid. There were detailed records of his Internet browsing habits and his phone history. Included was a psychological evaluation that was so accurate he would have sworn Jane wrote it after one of their few arguments. Then he clicked her profile. It was just as detailed and accurate. This concerned him even more; there was no reason they needed her information. This was clearly illegal. How did they get it? And why?

He flicked to a page where, under a designation called "Value-Added Quotient," there was an estimate of his contribution to ANGS's financial performance. Disturbed and angry yet fascinated with what he read, he flicked to an overall assessment of his skills:

> Advantage: Technically qualified with strong capacity for deal-structuring. Expertise in mergers, acquisitions, and divestitures has been a value generator. Malleable and non-confrontational.
>
> Disadvantage: An idealist of sorts. Not a linear thinker, annoying, and often disruptive at meetings. Talks a liberal bias not supported by action but needs watching.
>
> Prognosis: Not an insider but provides value. Never expose to strategic internal or external decision process. Remain as CFO to implement board's decisions; downgrade security clearance to general manager.
>
> Conclusion: Acceptable security risk for now. Update Next: May 21, 2032.

There was more, and it was astoundingly complete, profound, and illegal. While considering the implications of this evaluation, something more distressing bubbled to the surface. They had bought him, a thought that led first to anger and then shame. Somehow, he wanted to hurt them for this assessment, but he was too rational and too much a coward. After all, it was accurate. How do you discount the truth when confronted with it in black and white, particularly from superiors, whose dispassionate assessment considered what was best for the company. He felt sick.

Yes, he was submissive. To protect his family and his lifestyle, he needed to be. Was that wrong? No, but … he was still their bitch. He considered some pithy comments he could offer the Toms at the next meeting, but with each smile or laugh came the realization that regardless of what he said or did, in their eyes, he'd still be a loser, and not just any loser, a well-documented loser.

He wrestled with his options. They wouldn't suspect he had access to the EVA, so he returned to the main menu and searched for employees designated with what he considered unfair ratings that might cause dismissal. "They like my way with numbers," he whispered to himself. "Let's see how they like this." As he typed, the only sound was his own whistling.

He changed an employee's evaluation to something that seemed fair and saved it. The screen reflected the change but then, mysteriously, the screen blinked and reverted to the original data. He stopped whistling and hunched over to look more closely at the screen.

He changed the data again. Once more it changed back. Someone wasn't just negating his changes, but correcting them. He stood on wobbly legs and walked through the building until he was certain it was empty. He returned to his office and made the changes once again. And once again, they reverted to their original numbers.

Now he was really worried. As he collected his things to leave, to his amazement, the data changed back to what he'd entered. That was enough for him, he signed off and hustled from the building, confused and concerned with what had just happened. He wasn't sure how but he knew he was in big trouble. What kind of rabbit hole had he fallen into?

He said nothing that night to Jane because he wasn't sure what had happened. The following morning when he arrived at the office, Carolyn smiled brightly at him. "You look better today," she said. "Did you and the missus get lucky last night?"

"I won't answer that, Carolyn. It's wrong in so many ways."

"So you were a naughty boy." She grinned.

"Enough. You're watching too much media. Anyway, I could tell you but …"

"I know, but you'd have to kill me." A smile returned to her face.

"Business people don't resort to murder; we have more effective ways." He closed the door to his office before she could press him further.

He logged onto the system and pulled up his daily agenda. Gorman had inserted a nine o'clock meeting. He was concerned because it was unusual for either Tom to invite him to anything but formal discussions. They knew about last night. Before he could obsess, his worries were interrupted by a phone call. The voice on the other end brought joy.

"Mark!" he almost shouted into the phone. "My God, I thought you'd fallen off the edge of the planet. What have you been doing?"

"Just tending to business," Mark said wearily. "Senator Crelli has to keep his distance so my hands are full. But things are going well. I'm doing some real exciting stuff. Sorry I haven't made it back. I keep hoping I'm going to get a couple of days off, but you know what that's like."

"Keep your pacing, pal. Hire a firefighter or two so you can get time away. It'll help your perspective, you'll see. You don't want to burn out. Take your old man's word for it."

"I appreciate that, Dad. So did you see my article in *Enterprise Fortunes Magazine*?"

"You've published something in that e-MAG, that's great. Mom was just talking to me about an article she read about your senator. It mentioned you. Wait a second. Let me check." He searched through his in-box until the current issue of the magazine appeared on the screen. In the upper-right-hand corner was a small photo of Mark. Below was the tagline for Mark's article. "The New Republican: Profits and a Social Conscience. The Evolution is Complete."

"Sounds like a Mark Rosenthal story," he said as he scrolled through the article.

"It's about you and mom as much as me. Because of you two I have a social conscience."

"We're proud of you. In fact, you're my hero."

"Thanks, but I'm not the hero type. Anyway, Andy is sponsoring an entrepreneurs' conference in Bermuda and I'm speaking. It's kind of a big deal. I hope maybe you, Mom, and Franki can fly in and spend the weekend. We could relax for a couple of days. Do sun, sand, and blue skies with no deadlines sound alright?"

"Sounds great. Franki's in school but I'll ask her. We can get away. When is it?"

"First Thursday in April. I'm only scheduled for the keynote speech, so I'll definitely have time."

"We wouldn't miss it for the world. Mark, it's so good to hear your voice."

"Yours, too, Dad. Listen …" there was a discernible pause before he continued, "have you or mom heard from Terry?"

It wasn't the first time he'd asked. "She's doing okay, Mark. She's working hard and making good money. She visits every once in awhile."

"That's good to hear." There was a pause. "Is she seeing anybody?"

"No one seriously, as far as I know—your mother would tell me."

"Tell her I was asking about her," Mark paused. "No, don't. Never mind."

"Why don't you tell her yourself? Maybe she'd like to go to Bermuda."

There was silence. Finally, he responded, "no. I hurt her. I'm still not … I don't want to hurt her again. I just want to know how she's doing. That's all."

"Let me know if you change your mind."

"I have to go. Send my love to Mom and Franki. I'll see you guys in Bermuda. My secretary will send you the schedule."

"So your people are going to contact my people. Great."

"Knock it off, Dad. I love you. Bye."

"Bye, Mark. Love you, too."

When he hung up, he read Mark's article until his meeting with Tom Gorman.

"You're going to Angel Falls." He didn't even have a chance to sit down. He stared, somewhat perplexed.

"Tom, I gave you the information. There's no reason for me to go."

"The numbers aren't tight enough. We need you to work your magic and reassess the asset sell-off and decrease the worker and community payout fund. It needs your touch."

Bernie's face reddened. "I don't understand. I never liked this deal. At the meeting, when I tried to explain why it wouldn't give us the returns you expect, you embarrassed me and now it's the eleventh hour and you want me to squeeze out more?"

"Correct me if I'm wrong. I don't believe I've ever misled you into thinking I give a good goddamn what you think. You're our numbers man. You're good at it, and we show our appreciation by compensating you fairly. Something has changed. We need to squeeze more cash out of Angel Falls and I don't care how. I pay for your best effort, not your approval, and I want that effort now. Don't give me shit. We both know this is the best job you'll ever have."

This was where he would grow quiet, bow his head, accept defeat, and do Gorman's (or Morgan's) bidding. His EVA profile said so. He knew it, and now he knew they knew it. But what made the Toms so certain was what every ANGS employee believed in their heart: that the experience you received working for ANGS disqualified you from working for another company.

He bowed his head. "When do you want me to go?"

"As soon as you're ready. But I want another 3 to 5 percent, and I want it closed by the end of the third quarter. Are we clear?"

"Yes, Tom. But I want something too." His boss looked up, curious. "I know the people there. I've known them for over twenty years and many are friends. Don't announce it yet. Let me tell them first—as your official representative. I can't make what's going to happen better, but maybe I can make it easier. It won't cost you anything. Will you let me do it?"

Gorman arched his brow. "I don't give a fuck. Do what you want."

"Thanks, anything else?"

"Yeah. You were working late last night."

Here it comes. "I had things that needed cleaning up, so I took advantage of the quiet."

"Just make sure you keep to your area of responsibility. Now do all of us a favor and improve the payout from the Angel Falls divestiture."

He nodded as Tom left the office. "Absolutely."

He took a deep breath. He needed a break, so he stopped by his office to grab his lunch and took the stairs to the first floor. When he turned the corner, he stopped in front of an overturned pastry cart. The young man handling it had apparently lost control, tipping it, and spilling donuts and croissants everywhere. A manager burst from his office and, after quickly sizing up the situation, began berating the frightened young man.

"You ignorant son of a … look at all this waste. You don't want to keep fucking up, boy, because there are no jobs out there. You better be more careful," he screamed.

The young man cowered as he picked up the pastries. "Yes, sir," he said. "Sorry, sir."

The manager was bent on continuing to harass the boy when Bernie interrupted. "Go easy on the kid. It was just an accident."

Unwilling to cross the CFO, the manager immediately calmed down. "I just want him to be more careful next time." He turned back to the young man. "Now clean up this mess." He strode back into his office and closed the door.

Bernie knelt to help pick up the battered pastry. The young man peered at him and finally said in a soft voice, "thanks. I don't suppose you want a donut?"

He laughed, nodded, and took one that hadn't hit the ground. It was a bit misshapen, but otherwise seemed unharmed. "Thanks, fasten your seatbelt, okay?" He patted the boy reassuringly and left.

"I will. Thanks."

Carrying his lunch, which now included a battered doughnut, he exited into the courtyard where the warm spring air inspired him to take a deep, comforting breath and relax. His eyes drifted to a corner of the courtyard where the one and only tree left on Angs property provided some shade. He walked toward the great tree, remembering his early days at Angs, when it had been part of a festive grove with many white picnic tables where employees would sit in the shade and relax before or after shifts, or at meals and breaks.

After the Toms acquired control of the company, the tables had been removed along with most of the shade trees. Like the death march path, no reason was offered as to why, although it was rumored that the Toms wanted their employees working, not relaxing. Beneath the remaining oak, where there was once a white, wrought-iron antique bench that fit perfectly in the scene, an iron sign was hung: "No Loitering - Angs Management."

Bernie sat on a large exposed root beneath the tree and ate. He sensed someone near and looked up. Sirlie Turner, a heavy-set black woman was smiling a big, infectious smile at him.

He greeted her. "Hey, Sirlie, are you looking for a lunch partner?"

"You lollygag under the no-no tree, and the Toms gonna kick yo' bony ass." He loved her deep, happy voice.

"It's a stupid rule," he said, taking a defiant bite of his sandwich.

"Yeah, honey, it is, but I just hate to see one of the good guys get hurt."

"Sit down, Sirlie. Today we're going to do a little rebelling. I'm the CFO, and if I want to eat my lunch here, I will, and so can you."

She laughed a rolling laugh that began deep within her and erupted as a burst of naughty joy. She positioned her bulk beside him. "I'm gonna be in trouble for this. We both are, uh-huh."

Seeing she didn't have lunch, he tore his sandwich in half and gave half to her. "I'm buying today, dessert, too, if half a sandwich and a half, flattened donut are enough."

She smiled. "Half's alright. Gotta watch my girlish figure. If I don't, who will?" Then she became more serious. "I saw what you did in there, honey. That was nice. The boy would have been fired if you hadn't spoken up. You a good man, Charlie Brown."

"It was nothing."

"It wasn't nothing. He's always goin' too fast with dat thing. It's 'cause everybody's always screamin', 'Where's my doughnut? Where's my roll?'" Her eyes went wide as she pointed all around. He smiled. "He was just tryin' to make the rounds. He's a good boy."

"Most of the people here are good."

"Charlie Brown, you're the only one in management who treats us like ... like people. The Toms, most of the others, they look right through us. Not you. How come you dat way?"

He tore the donut in half and gave part to her. "Just the way my life happened, I guess. When I was a kid, my family had money; we lived in a large home with sports cars and all that stuff—a great life. Back then I didn't see people, you know, the way the Toms don't see them now. I took everyone for granted, they were there for me. That's all I'd known."

"What happened?"

"My mom got sick. It turned my world upside down. She began having seizures and eventually it cost her job. That was before government healthcare, so my father had to take care of us. He kind of fell apart when she died and lost his job during a recession so we barely got by. We moved to an apartment, and as soon as I was old enough, I started working after school just to make ends meet. It wasn't so different from what most kids did, but it sure was a change for me."

"Sorry dat happened to you, honey."

"The sad thing was that the only people who helped were in our new neighborhood. None of our old, rich friends gave a damn. I'll never forgive them for forgetting my mother so easily and ignoring my father. He'd sit alone wallowing in self pity long after I went to bed, because his old friends were too busy. It's strange, but people who have less seem to have more to give. I'll never understand why."

"True but sad."

"The worst thing I ever went through was my mother's suffering. It forced me to grow up. And poverty motivated me. When I was thirteen, before this happened, my father promised me a Jaguar XK when I turned sixteen. By my sixteenth, we were so poor that all I got was a bus ride to the movies. I vowed I'd do whatever it took to never be poor again, but it would be a better world if everyone was poor at some point. Then each of us would understand the good and bad of it. Now that I'm successful, I have less in common with the people in my income bracket than I have with the folks who don't associate with me because I'm too rich. Ironic, isn't it? It's sad. I miss the intimacy of poverty."

Sirlie smiled at him. "I'm all misty-eyed. A rich man like you knows the benefits of poverty. Whatever, it made you a good person."

He finished his donut. "What's a nice girl like you doing in a place like this?"

"Oh, honey, ol' Sirlie's not so nice. You don't wanna know me before breakfast," she laughed. "I just like to help out, I guess. The people here are like family. I see a lot of my brother, Eddy, in 'em. He's kinda my motivation in life."

"Where's Eddy now?"

"He's dead."

"Oh, I'm sorry."

"Shit happens, honey. Ghetto babies start life different from other kids. It's not just our mommas don't eat right, and we don't get the food we need when we's young. We never get to sleep peaceful 'cause of fights, gun shots, and sirens. It does something to ya. And there's the lead paint and tainted water and all the other pollutions all over the place dat never get cleaned up 'cause we're poor. And then there's all the stuff we hear through them thin walls, and the violence we see in our homes and the neighborhood. And the schools aint shit. I don't care what they say, dat shit changes you. People we love get hurt all the time, disappear real sudden, or die. Even the games we play are dangerous. It ain't easy being a ghetto kid, no siree. Eddy was different. That stuff didn't get to him like it did the rest of us. He was a hard worker and avoided trouble best he could. Got great grades, but the damn neighborhood grabs at you and don't let go. He fought. He'd get a leg up, and the street'd slap him right back down. He'd smile but you could see it in the sadness in his eyes. It was like the street was laughing at him. He got a good job got laid off. Got another, saved, and bought a house, couldn't make the mortgage and lost it. Dat boy had something the street wanted real bad. He even fell in love once, but the bitch was hooked and left him to work her habit. Another bitch left him a child. He raised the boy best he could, but I hate to say, dat baby was evil—died bad at eleven selling drugs to the wrong people in the wrong place. The ghetto treats good people, like Eddy, and bad ones jus' the same. Only difference is good ones don't survive. Eddy didn't."

"If you don't mind me asking, how did he die?"

"Police report says he jumped off a building."

Bernie was horrified. "God almighty, Sirlie. I'm so sorry."

"You have no idea. Police reports tell lotsa stories. Anyway, it's been a few years. Me, I'm fightin' for the Eddys out there. Way too many, you know. Way too many." She forced a wide, magnetic smile, slapped him on the thigh and, with some effort, got to her feet. "You got your wake-up call and I got mine. Most everybody gets one sooner or later. They're hard to avoid. Depends what you do with it. What about you, Charlie Brown? Will you do something?"

His eyes caught the glare from a window in Tom Gorman's office where a lone figure glowered down at them. He looked at her. "I'd sure like to change some things around here."

"You change things just by bein' here, honey. Maybe someday we'll do some changin' together, you and me. Times are tough, and jobs are scarce so don't let the Toms fire your ass for sittin' under their tree, hear? They don't like people, you know, just being people …"

"I'll stick around."

"You be good now. Maybe sometime we can get together over beers?"

"I'd like that, Sirlie."

She turned and left but he stayed for a few moments, taking in the warm day, fresh air, and peace beneath the ancient tree. He thought about Eddy, and the peace he never knew. After a few more minutes, feeling good because he'd made a friend, he stood and headed into the building. There his thoughts shifted to Angel Falls, the helpless people who lived there, and the security they were about to lose.

He worked late again that night. When he arrived home, Jane was waiting with dinner.

"A crazy day," he said. "I forget to mention ANGST is shutting the Angel Falls plant."

"Oh, no, Bernie! It's such a beautiful place."

"Yeah, I tried to get them to see reason. I can even prove it's the wrong financial decision. But you know the Toms, once they make up their minds … I'll never understand them." She shrugged. "I have to grow up, don't I?"

"At your age I'm afraid that's not possible, but at least stop fighting them. You always tell me never to try to teach a pig to sing because it wastes time and annoys the pig."

"I meant that for you, not me."

"Sorry, it doesn't work that way. Dinner?"

Afterward, she continued the discussion while they cleaned and straightened the kitchen. "Honey, if we have to move, I know what I'm happy doing, so I'll do it again. You, on the other hand, are frustrated and unhappy. You need to be somewhere else or doing something else. Find it. I'll support you. But if you stay, you've got to stop obsessing over your job at the puzzle palace. Get over it. Do the job or get another. You know I'm right."

Over the years, Bernie had advised Jane on her business, but now that he was receiving advice, he felt inadequate. "I'm too old and set in my ways. We both know I'll retire at ANGST. Jesus, I almost forgot the most important thing, Mark called."

"Bernie, you waited until now? How's he doing? What's he doing?"

"He's great. Guess what? He asked about Terry again. But before you say anything, he just wanted to know how she was doing, nothing more."

"She'll be happy he asked. What else did he say?"

"He sends his love. He has an article published in this month's *Enterprise Fortunes Magazine.* I have a printout in my briefcase. And good news, we're invited to Bermuda to hear him speak."

She gave him a hug. "Bermuda!" She exclaimed as she backed away and looked firmly into his eyes. "We are going, Bernie."

"Of course, love. As soon as I have more details, we'll talk to Franki about it."

The next morning, he arrived at ANGS unaware of the consequences of his luncheon insubordination with Sirlie. When he looked out of his office window he noticed ANGS maintenance staff cleaning up the sawdust around the dearly departed no-no tree. All that remained was a stump and a sign that read:

"No Loitering - ANGS Management".

The tree had died for his sins.

Chapter 7

Indianapolis—2031

"Mark sent the agenda for Bermuda."

Bernie watched Franki's eyes light up at the mention of her brother's name. "Is there any way he can convince his sexy senator boss to change the date?"

"I don't think so, Franki. You think Senator Crelli is sexy?"

"Oh my God, are you kidding me, yes. He's gorgeous, but there's something not right about him. It's his eyes or something. I don't trust him."

He turned to Jane. "From the mouths of babes. Really? Crelli has a great reputation and seems to genuinely want to help people. Everyone says he's a visionary."

"What do I know, Daddy? My instructor says visionaries are just people who try too hard to convince you that their view is the right one and should be yours. Because of Senator Crelli, Mark hurt Terry—and she was my best friend. That's why I don't trust him."

"What do your friends think?" Jane asked.

"Zach and his fraternity brothers and most of my teachers think he's the greatest. My girlfriends think he's dreamy. They want him to run for president. What do you think, Mom?"

"I'm withholding judgment. But he must be special if you and your friends are showing this much interest in politics. Now, back to Bermuda, we need an answer. Is there any way you can go? Dad and I are flying out next Thursday and staying through the weekend. Can you ditch school for a few days this close to finals?" Bernie listened curiously for her answer.

"I can't. My professors would let me, I'm sure, but I've got a bigger problem. Show practices are Thursday, Saturday, and Sunday, and I'm committed to them. It's my luck to get a trip to Bermuda and I can't go. You two, Mark, and Senator Crelli owe me big time."

He tried to cheer her up. "Honey, I promise, if Mark doesn't come home soon, we'll all drive down to Cincinnati to see him."

"Cincinnati is not Bermuda, but I can accept that. Before you leave, make him pick a date. I want him to meet my boyfriend, too. Got to run, that's Zack at the door. Study time, bye."

He watched with pride as she ran excitedly to her boyfriend, and then out the door. "She's a great kid, smart like Mark and beautiful like you."

"Did you just call me stupid?"

He started to laugh. "What? No, that's not what I meant. They're both smart and beautiful like you. Now, what were we talking about?"

She smiled at him. "Sex?" she replied.

"No, we weren't. Where was I?" His smile dissipated. "Oh, something else. I had lunch yesterday with Sirlie Turner. She's a shipping clerk. We ate under that big oak in the courtyard."

"I remember. That's a beautiful tree. We had fun there in the old days."

"Well it's off-limits now, but we still had lunch there. It must have pissed the Toms off, because they cut the damn thing down this morning."

Her jaw dropped. The depth of her shock and sadness surprised him. "Oh, Bernie, that beautiful tree, you're kidding? What a cruel thing to do." She wiped a tear from her eye.

He wasn't prepared for how sad telling the story made him feel, so he looked away. She was right. The deed was beyond mean, and entirely his fault. He explained it to her.

"Why? Why in God's name destroy something so innocent because of a stupid rule? If you weren't allowed there, as stupid as that is, they should have discussed it with you."

"They were making a point. If employees see the chief financial officer being chastised, they're less likely to challenge authority themselves."

"What is this, kindergarten? There's something else, isn't there?"

He paused to collect his thoughts. "They're sending me to Angel Falls to squeeze more money from the closing and they want my face to be the last ANGS face the people there see. It hurts the way they use me but if I can help the community, even a little, it'll be worth it."

"They're bastards."

Bernie nodded. "It's for the best. If the Toms went, God knows what harm they'd do."

"I'm proud of you for doing what you can."

"I'm hoping I can find a way to play both sides, give the Toms what they want but find some advantages for Angel Falls."

"Do you really think you can do that?"

He shrugged. "The Toms won't give them any break, that's for sure. I think maybe I can finagle some things the engineers didn't consider. All I know is I hate my job." He paused and shrugged again. "At least there's good news from Mark."

"Tell me about Bermuda."

"He's giving a presentation to a group of entrepreneurs and politicians. We'll go but I won't be able to tell anyone we're going. The Toms would only find some reason to keep me here." He put his head in his hands. "Jane, I think I'm jealous of my son's career. That can't be good, can it?"

"I don't know, but you're kidding yourself if you think by doing something silly like not telling Tom you're going it's the same as fighting them. They're the owners, you can't fight them. Just tell them you're going. If they make a fuss, insist—you have rights. Don't play games and give them more ammunition to hassle you with. And I'm sure it isn't jealousy. Mark's career is going great. But you're the CFO of a major company and, like your dad used to say, that's not chopped liver. Be there for Mark when he runs into trouble. You know he will, sooner or later."

"Why do they give me such a hard time? I make money for them hand over fist."

When she put her hand to his cheek, he pressed his head against it. She gently stroked his hair. "Bernie, we've talked about this. You're smart, but you're also too impulsive. You never do what they want the way they want it or say what they expect you to say. There's a cost to not playing their game so of course they will be uncomfortable with you, even though you deliver for them. You have no idea how annoying you are when you interrupt …"

"Whoa, whose side are you on?"

"When you interrupt someone while they're speaking. I know it drives me crazy, so I can only imagine what it does to the Toms."

"But I know what they're going to say."

"So? It's condescending, love. It makes people think you think they're inferior, uninteresting, or they have nothing worth listening to."

He considered it. "Maybe … I can see that. Worst part is I've begun interrupting myself. How's that for impulsivity?"

"Troubling, could be senility."

He took her hand. "Okay, I'll work on it. I'll pause before I say what's on my mind."

"That's a good start."

"Still, they don't complain when they take my efforts to the bank."

"Stop pouting. I trust you and your instincts. You should too. But it's not your instincts that get you in trouble; it's your insistence on speaking your mind. Just be more sensitive. Listen. Be who you are—just more polite. And if being you costs you your job, we'll be fine, truly."

"Sometimes I think you're the only person in the world who can get along with me."

"You do come with a steep learning curve, but if I'm the only one who understands you, I feel sorry for the rest of the world." She sat on his lap and embraced him. He returned the embrace, gratefully, and stared into her eyes.

"Why is it, do you suppose, I'm the only one who understands you?"

She was playing. She always seemed to know exactly what to do. "Obviously, you work harder at it because of my money and I suspect because of my sexual prowess."

"Are you calling me a whore? With so few admirers, Bernie, I'd be more gracious if I were you. At your age, you don't want to risk losing your trophy wife."

"What risk, I see it in your eyes how you idolize me."

"No, I don't think so. How could that be? You keep atrocious hours and have the attention span of a two-year-old. You're constantly stressed and take more joy in numbers than in people. Your hair is gray and thinning, your teeth long, and your memory short. Your best quality is you make love like a woman."

He pushed her gently from his lap. "I'm hurt. You've gone too far, this time. What the hell does making love like a woman mean? Little missy, where I come from them's fighting words."

She laughed. The sound warmed his heart.

"No, really, it's a compliment. My girlfriends wish their men had that quality."

"Your girlfriends' thoughts come second hand from the damn media. Besides that they're all old ladies who wouldn't appreciate a real buckaroo in the saddle, if you get my drift. They'd be concerned about throwing out a hip or something."

Her smile disappeared. "You don't always have to say the first thing you think of."

He persisted. "Do you really talk about our love life with your girlfriends?"

"I don't share but I'd like to. They just see the smile on my face, buckaroo."

"You're nothing but a cheap whore," he leered.

"You sure know how to make a girl feel wanted," she cooed.

"So after all these years, two children and a lifetime of shared experiences from poverty to a palace on the lake, in the end our relationship is based solely on ...?"

"Sex," she interrupted seductively.

Chapter 8

Aeden—2065

Nurse Peyton entered the room, interrupting Bernie's story. "Mr. Rosenthal, your Mesh physician has adjusted your medication. You may feel a bit light-headed. It's normal. If you have any questions, speak out loud and your avatar will respond. Refer to him as 'Herr Doctor.'"

"So the doctors aren't human anymore. I bet they're still golfing when you need them."

"Herr Doctor, remember, Mr. Rosenthal." The nurse flashed a smile before leaving.

He closed his eyes. When he opened them, Gil was staring at him.

"Are you feeling better?" Bernie nodded. "Your family life was so different from anyone's I know." Tired, Bernie gave Gil a questioning look, so Gil clarified. "Life was, maybe more open. You said what you thought or felt. Wasn't that risky?"

"I trusted my family but I was never very good at knowing who else to trust."

"Was it like that for everyone?"

"No. My marriage was blessed; most others struggled. When I was a boy, families spent their evenings together doing things. But by the time my kids were born, there were just too many distractions. In the succeeding generation, families were pulled further apart—mostly by economic demands, but often because there was only one parent to raise the children, or children moved between parents who lived in different places. Many kids never even knew at least one of their parents, and others wished they didn't know either. As economic interests began to dominate life, people became less tolerant and less patient. And they became less constant with those they should love, believing if a loved one was somehow failing there was the likelihood of a better companion or soul mate, or even child somewhere."

"What's a soul mate?"

"Someone you love and trust; it feels like your souls are joined. Jane and I are soul mates. It's one of God's great gifts. Do you have someone special?"

"I have a girlfriend and she's really special, but I don't think she's a soul mate."

"What's her name?"

"I don't want to talk about her, if that's okay. Howard works all the time so I don't see him much. She keeps me company."

"Today, money is critical for survival in a way that's very different from when I was young. Then, my mom and everyone else's mom in the neighborhood were always home. By the time I had children parents worked long hours away from home to provide financial security and a better lifestyle for their families. And unlike today, kids went to schools together, so they could be with companions and friends."

"If that was so good, why did it change?"

"Marketing, mostly. Companies realized they could increase sales by advertising all the time in the media. That generated large audiences, huge profits, and created the first Conducers—people whose entire purpose in life was to produce so they could earn enough to consume. Marketers saturated the adult population, targeting teenagers and innocent children. Business used every outlet to compete for the lion's share of every family member's time and income, and with everyone watching the media to see what they were expected to work for, over time, family relationships just evaporated." Gil seemed to have lost interest, but Bernie took a deep breath and continued anyway. "Eventually, enjoyment and enrichment came less and less from direct human interaction. As I said, for all that, I was one of the lucky ones, because of my wife and family. We talked, argued, and helped each other and were involved in each other's lives. Not only did we love each other, we enjoyed each other. You understand love, don't you?"

Gil looked embarrassed. "Why wouldn't I?"

"No reason. Nothing compares to love. It doesn't occur often enough, so once you find it, don't take it for granted." He expected Gil to respond, but Gil just stared. "Today, all communication is through Archive and Virtuoso so I can imagine how difficult it must be to find love. The magic has been kind of filtered out. How can you know a girl well enough to love her?"

"Just because it's different doesn't mean it doesn't exist."

"That's true."

"And having filters prevents a lot of hate, too."

"I hadn't thought of that."

"It's hard to imagine living like you did and you don't know how I live, you're not from now. Communication is more fun now. I know more people than you ever knew."

"Okay. You have quantity, but I'm talking quality relationships. Besides, with everything filtered through computer systems, things aren't what they appear. Once you believe *that* you'll understand everything."

Before Bernie could elaborate, Nurse Peyton's image appeared on his monitor. "Resolved anything yet Mr. Rose? Mr. Rosenthal?"

Bernie answered. "Not yet, but we're getting there."

"Whatever you decide," the nurse replied, "it'll have to wait until later. Mr. Rosenthal needs his rest, Mr. Rose. If you still want to talk, you'll have to come by later."

"I'd like to hear the rest of the story, if it's okay." Bernie nodded and reminded Gil to purchase the Genetic Aid his father requested. As Gil left, Nurse Peyton returned.

"Is he … coming around?" she whispered to Bernie.

"It's too soon. He's a good kid and clearly different. We'll see."

"For all our sakes, I hope he's ready. Now get some rest."

Gil overheard them and left wondering what, if anything, their conversation meant. How was he different? And ready for what? The MAG was waiting at the guard shack. It took him to purchase the Genetic Aid and then home. When he arrived, he initiated another Andrea sequence.

They met on a meadow high over a blue green sea, where purple and yellow dolphins tattooed with corporate logos were swimming in the breakers near the shore. Andrea sat on a white stone bench smiling as he ran to her. They embraced and the brief time apart drove him to urgent lovemaking. Afterward they sat cocooned in a blanket to ward off the cool, late-afternoon summer breezes. They watched the colorful sailboats, their sails adorned with striking company logos and advertisements, as they were propelled across the turquoise water by a warm, steady breeze.

"Andrea, I could make love to you every minute of every day. If it's like this for everyone, how do people ever get anything done?"

She reclined and put her head in his lap. Then she laughed. "Gil, because of you, I'm alive. I count every second of your day until I see you again. We're soul mates." At that, she smiled her most endearing smile and hugged him tighter.

"Andrea, I can't imagine anything better than making love to you. It's hard to believe there's more to love than sex."

"What makes you think that?"

He hesitated. Then he lied. "My friend Tommy told me." It was his first lie and he felt she could tell. He stared into her eyes, lost in a kaleidoscope of hazel brown. "Even when I'm not with you, I feel you. I don't know what to do." In response, she wrapped her legs around his waist, her arms supporting her body. She laughed at his surprise, but he followed her lead and spent the afternoon learning various ways of expressing love.

Much later, tired and sated, he cleaned up. He had promised the old man he'd return, but now he hesitated. He wanted to hear the rest of the story, but the afternoon lovemaking caused him to reconsider. He entered Archive to find something that needed doing, but when nothing presented itself, he grudgingly pulled himself away and returned to the hospice where Bernie continued the tale with his trip to Bermuda.

Chapter 9

Bermuda—2031

The day of the Bermuda trip, Jane and Bernie waited at the Indianapolis International Airport until Mark, looking thinner than the last time they'd seen him, walked out of the gate and into his mother's arms. It was obvious by the intense embraces that he'd missed them. His face was pale, not in a sickly way, but as though he hadn't seen the sun in months.

"Sorry, Dad, I won't let this much time go by again. Forgive me? When Andy ran for the Senate, I wasn't prepared; I'm just now getting everything in order. It seems like all I've been doing is fighting fires."

"Delegate."

"But you always say if you want something done right, do it yourself."

"Don't believe everything I say," he said, laughing. "And don't listen to old adages."

Jane added, smiling, "Dad means, look before you leap."

To which Mark replied, "But he who hesitates is lost."

They laughed at the old family code, to which Bernie added, "absence makes the heart grow fonder."

"True, but out of sight, out of mind," Mark volleyed as he slipped one arm around his mother's waist and the other over his father's shoulder. The ice broken, they laughed as they walked to the gate for the flight to Bermuda.

"To know you is to love you," Jane added.

"But familiarity breeds contempt."

"Come on," Mark said, relaxed now. "Let's make hay while the sun shines."

"Haste makes waste."

Jane stopped abruptly and poked both men in the ribs; they winced. "If neither of you is going to let the other have the last word, you'll both drive me crazy before the trip even begins. I declare a moratorium on unclever repartee—at least until the trip home, okay?"

On the plane, Bernie was happier than he'd been in years. Above the clouds, the sky was blue, the world below insignificant. Looking equally at peace, Jane slept, head against the window. Mark was here, and they were on their way to a business event where his son was the star. To make it better, there would be quiet moments in warm, sunny places. Life could be good.

"So, you're addressing a group of businessmen?" Bernie asked.

"Business owners, Dad, entrepreneurs mostly, a couple hundred politically active ones who want to make a difference. Andy set it up. He's a great supporter of collaboration between public and private institutions. So am I. These are tough times. When you think about how much effort, intellect, and money have been wasted because business and government won't work in concert, it's staggeringly depressing. But the timing's right. With this recession showing no signs of ending, and the poor becoming desperate, we need to take more responsibility for creating jobs. It's a sad thing, technology has eliminated the need for so many jobs but our population continues to grow. It's out of control. To survive, we must focus on public-private education and training to help more people qualify for the jobs that become available. I've developed a plan to privatize many of the government's social support systems and make them more efficient, ease the load, and reduce cost."

He admired his son's initiative but was leery of the solution. "That can only work if the right people do it for the right reasons. There are too many greedy, short-term, bottom-line business owners and government types who are only interested in protecting their turf. Everyone is out for himself, the almighty dollar, and immediate results."

"Andy will lead us into a new era. There are issues, certainly, but with his leadership we've convinced marquee entrepreneurs. There's a sense that we have to get it right this time."

"I hope so. Is that your topic?"

"It is. Higher-paying service jobs have followed heavy and light-manufacturing offshore, and as much as I want to keep the jobs at Crelli Enterprises here in the states, I have a responsibility to my stockholders so even I have been sending jobs overseas. Our economy has reached another tipping point. There are too many Americans unemployed and unemployable. If we're going to turn this around, we have to start by offering changes within communities, so we're going to give private industry the latitude as well as necessary fiscal and tax policy support. I'm proposing private industry consortiums that will take responsibility for education, from kindergarten to high school and vo-tech. We've been talking about the problems in our education system for years without doing anything while workforce capability declines. Global competition is killing us, so it's critical we upgrade before we outsource everything to places where labor is cheaper."

"Does Parrington support this? Is he willing to help an opponent like Senator Crelli?"

"Of course not, but Dad, we have so much more power in the Congress than anyone believes. We're going to fix it, fix it shortly, and fix it for good."

"If the rioting is any indication, you better act soon."

"The violence is an aberration, pockets of frustrated people, that's all."

"I've been reading. With Reverend Cavanaugh and the so-called Prophet, Omar Smith, I think it's more than pockets of frustrated people."

"We're going through a down cycle—significant, but just a cycle."

"They built a wall around our neighborhood and ANGS is like a fortress now. I hope you have the answer."

"If we don't, we'll all need a wall. Seriously, it sounds like some contractor did a good job scaring your association. Parrington's been buying off the poor and unemployed by raising taxes to support his growing welfare entitlement programs, but that's a dead end, it always has been. If it continues, he'll drain our country and make us less competitive. His way means layoffs and higher unemployment that end in an economic death spiral until we find some lower level of economic activity we can support. Christ, we could end up like some Central American country. Andy has answers. At tomorrow's presentation, you'll hear some of it."

"I hope so. I'll be interested in hearing how he plans to do it because I've never seen things this bad. I don't know if Kentucky is like Indiana, but everyone is deeply concerned and the poor seem more desperate than I've ever seen. You really think this public-private collaboration will work?"

"Like you said, Dad, it has to, doesn't it? This has been all hush-hush until now but I've been working on a project for the last few years in a small town in Ohio where we have a production facility. Crelli Enterprises has taken over management of the entire county and it's been very effective."

"Really, and that works. Where does this old accountant sign up?"

"We can always use a talent like you, Dad, but we've got a long way to go, and many people oppose what we're doing. This is America, everyone has a piece of the action and change is hard because no one wants to risk losing. My job is to make this program a win for every important interest group but the defeatist liberal media won't play along. They talk about the country like its Rome at its decline and for all the concerns, everyone seems vested in the status quo and no one is willing to compromise. We'll change that too."

"I think you're asking for the impossible, but don't be discouraged."

"Discouraged? Hell, I'm excited. Once we get control, we'll do it. Look how wonderful the economies in China, Turkey, and Brazil are doing. They've proven benevolent autocratic leadership can provide consistent, strategic direction to a free market economy. We're moving in that direction. We have to compete, we have no choice."

Before Bernie could respond, Jane opened her eyes. "That's enough business, boys."

"Sorry, Mom. How's Franki? I feel bad. I wish she could've come. She really has a boyfriend. Wow, time is flying by."

"She misses you. Call her." Mark nodded. "Her boyfriend, Zach, is a junior at Marion. She's so impressed with herself, a freshman dating a junior."

"I'll call her when I get back, I promise. This project has kept me so busy. I'll invite her to Cincinnati, take her, all of you, on a riverboat cruise and we'll do a Reds game."

Bernie put his hand on Mark's arm. "Make it happen this time, please Mark."

"I will."

The rocky outcroppings and pale pink, sand beaches that disappeared into deep blue ocean faded from view as the taxi climbed into hills covered with heavy foliage. The cab pulled onto the hotel property, where the view changed to waterfalls and waitresses in minuscule outfits serving umbrella-garnished drinks to patrons sitting along side clear blue swimming pools.

Jane smiled happily. "I've died and gone to heaven. Bernie, you seem relaxed, too."

He nodded toward the waitresses. "I really needed this. Say, honey," he pointed to the closest waitress, "would you wear one of those outfits for me?"

"Sure," she said without missing a beat, "if you'll wear what that guy almost has on." He looked in the direction she'd indicated and saw a young man of about twenty wearing the tiniest, tightest thong he'd ever seen. "Jesus, it's a strategically placed rubber band! If I wear that, you'll have to alert management."

"To protect the guests," Mark added.

Bernie laughed, "yep, they won't be able to keep the women off of me."

"Certainly not this woman."

"That's my hope," he smirked.

"My job is to fulfill hopes, I'm a slut, remember, you told me so."

Mark blushed. "Mom, Dad, get a room." They laughed. "The terrible thing is," Mark added, lowering his voice conspiratorially, "don't tell anyone, but Andy wears those thongs, at least something close, but only on the more private beaches where the media won't see him. He says women only trust politicians who aren't hiding anything."

They laughed at that. "That's too much information," Bernie sputtered.

They entered the lobby. "Mom, Dad, sorry, I have to find Andy and then register both of you for my presentation tomorrow morning. Call me later. We'll meet for dinner." Mark kissed Jane and hugged Bernie, and walked off through the gardens.

Jane watched him go. "I missed him. I didn't realize how much until today."

"It got past us, how much we missed him, except maybe for Franki. I wish she could be here, too. He's promised it won't happen again. So," he said to his wife, "what d'ya think?"

"About what?"

"Mark's idea."

"Well, well, well. You are feeling better. I'm up for some afternoon delight."

"Would you mind if I call you Bambi?"

She laughed. "Bambi? Yes, Bambi, your trophy slut."

"I like that."

"I'll call you … Eduardo."

It was his turn to laugh. "You've got a deal. I'm Eduardo, the thong boy." They entered the lobby, laughing. "Get ready for a hot time, Bambi."

"I'm ready, Eduardo," she said in a seductive whisper. "My husband is so conventional."

Briefly, he wondered if she was serious. She saw his look of uncertainty and laughed. Realizing she'd gotten him, he laughed, too.

They made love twice, once on the plush green rug and once on the divan next to a window that looked out onto the endless ocean. Mark had arranged for a suite and the hotel had sent up flowers, fruit, and wine. Eduardo dozed off after their second encounter and when he awoke, he found Bambi sleeping as well. He stared as she purred softly. She was his life. He knew it when they met and knew it even more at this moment.

He sat on the edge of the bed, unscrewed the top, and poured a glass of chilled white Burgundy, and then sat back against the headboard sipping the wine, waiting for her to awaken.

"It hasn't been like this for awhile," she told him when she finally stirred.

"I always thought we did okay. We're pretty frisky for old people."

"Speak for yourself, old man. No, I mean, today was different. You haven't been this relaxed in years. It's seeing Mark again, but it's also getting away from ANGS."

He poured more wine, handed her a glass and touched her glass with his. "No, it's you, love. First, last, and always."

"You stared into my eyes while we made love. You know how I love that."

"Did Eduardo please his trophy slut?"

"Stop it, I mean it. Really, I love it when you do that."

"I always look, but my eyesight's so bad. I think the light helped."

"That's it, isn't it? We make love at night with the lights out."

"Hmm. You're right. Say, it's getting late and we need to get ready. Dinner with Mark, remember?" He stood up and stretched the tightness from his body and laughed.

"What is it, honey?"

"I was just thinking that at our age, we moan more *after* sex than *during*."

She frowned and hit him playfully with her pillow. "Men! That's so not romantic."

"Sorry, Bambi, let's shower,"

"You mean together? I take it back, Eduardo. You're so much more romantic than that Bernie fellow. But can you really perform this often, and underwater, too?"

"This is practical, not romantic. We're merely conserving water," he said, mimicking a Spanish accent and failing miserably. "Never shower alone on an island." She laughed as he put his wineglass down and walked to her side of the bed and pulled back the covers. Mindful of his back, he lifted from the knees and carefully carried her into the bathroom. She was light, but he couldn't quite pull it off. First he bumped her head against the doorway and then her legs. When he was sure she wasn't hurt, he laughed. Gently, still watching her eyes, he put her down, remembering again to bend at the knees. As she stepped into the shower, he stretched a cramp from his back.

There was a knock at the door.

"Great timing. It's probably housekeeping. Hang on a minute, we're going to need some more towels. Get the shower nice and hot." He slapped her gently on her backside, slipped his trousers on, and without buckling the belt, opened the door … and gasped.

"Tom, what … what are you doing here?"

"More to the point, Rosenthal, what the fuck are you doing here? If you wanted to hear your son speak, you should have asked me. You don't just leave the office and head on down on a fucking vacation. I thought I saw you, earlier, in the gardens, but I knew my CFO wouldn't abandon his duties without telling me. It seems that I was wrong."

"Tom, come in, I have a white burgundy..."

"Fuck you." Gorman turned and stalked away. Bernie stared at the retreating figure, trying to decide if this qualified as a waking nightmare. Then, in the distance, a voice beckoned him.

"Eduardo? It's moist and warm in here. Are you coming?"

No, he thought. Eduardo is gone.

After Gorman interrupted their lovemaking, Bernie returned to the bathroom. Jane knew before him that she'd lost him again. "The hell with Tom," she said. "Mark is your son and you have vacation coming." He showered alone while she sat on the balcony drinking wine.

That evening, when they got together for dinner with Mark, and afterward on the veranda, they discussed business, technology, politics, and Franki's boyfriend. Bernie never mentioned his encounter with Gorman.

The next morning, they arrived at the meeting just as it was beginning. Once seated, Bernie hunched down to avoid being seen while Jane, proudly waiting for Mark to speak, chastised him.

"Stop trying to hide, it's too late for that. It doesn't matter anyway."

"I'm not hiding," he said petulantly.

"Gorman knows we're here. If he's watching you, he's enjoying seeing you squirm. Don't give the SOB the satisfaction. We're here for Mark. Ignore everyone else."

"I'm not hiding. Leave me alone."

A distinguished-looking man walked to the podium to start the event. "Can I have everybody's attention, please? I'm Michael Bourke. I'm here to introduce the man responsible for this conference and he, in turn, will introduce our morning's first speaker.

"For those who don't know Senator Andrew Crelli, you'll find he is a quick and willing learner. The ink was barely dry on his Penn State University diploma when he was hired as a manager for a large Chicago consulting firm where he quickly became a partner. Three years later he left to found his first company, CKA. Under Andy's impassioned leadership, CKA grew until he sold it and started Crelli Enterprises, which, through innovation and acquisition, today is one of our most respected Fortune 100 companies.

"Andy is an entrepreneur but first he is a patriot. When many of his clients' businesses were being ravaged by sophisticated, well-funded hackers—e-RATS, who have been responsible for as much as a trillion dollars in business losses—Andy focused all his efforts and corporate assets on defeating these cyber terrorists, who have the temerity to defile all that is noble and good about America. With funding coming from such diverse organizations as terrorists and sovereign nations who compete with American business, the e-RATS looted personal and business accounts, created havoc in private commerce, panicked Wall Street, and wrought doubt on all e-commerce transactions. Outraged, Andy redirected his own significant resources to prevent the e-RATS from destroying his clients' businesses. With what he'd learned, he formed alliances with local and national authorities who, working in concert, achieved extraordinary success, prosecuting e-RATS for such varied crimes as fraud, identify theft, burglary, and even murder. We all remember how fear so unsettled our communities, and how our cries for help went unanswered by soon-to-be former President Parrington. Because of Andy's tireless efforts, Congress reclassified the crimes of these villainous transgressors and they are currently being actively pursued as felons of the highest order.

"Unsatisfied by Parrington's response," Bourke continued, "Kentucky businesses rallied and convinced Andy to pursue the nomination for United States senator. The good work continued as Senator Crelli's incorruptible e-SWAT Task Force of electronic hackers and super-sleuths eliminated the worst saboteurs. This year, the costs of electronic terrorism has been cut by 80 percent—still too high—but moving in the right direction.

"But it wasn't just with cyber-crime that the senator made his mark in Washington. He introduced legislation to eliminate outdated regulations, freeing businesses to compete more effectively globally. Much of this initiative is geared toward the senator's favorite enterprise: making private industry more directly responsible for America's health, education, and social welfare programs. Ladies and gentlemen, we are entering a new world, and I give you the man to lead us into it—the junior senator from the great commonwealth of Kentucky, Andrew Monroe Crelli."

Amidst enthusiastic applause, Andy Crelli walked with great purpose and confidence to the podium. At the back of the stage stood Reno Soren, the other man at Mark's engagement fiasco, hands folded in the frontal-fig, like a secret service agent.

As the applause died down, Crelli spoke. "As much as I like the attention, Mark Rosenthal is the reason we're here today. I first heard of Mark from a colleague who hired him as a summer intern. Then I read an extraordinary article about him in *Time* magazine. Although young and inexperienced, he'd built a case for the nobility of business and its potential to solve our county's great social problems. He postulated that the time was right to involve a new generation of enlightened entrepreneurs, such as you seated here today, to implement a profitable, workable solution. What he espoused then, and what I support wholeheartedly now, are powerful, evolutionary concepts for strengthening American capitalism. We're at a watershed moment in our history, and I'm proud to share it with this brilliant young executive and friend.

"As business owners and CEOs, you have simple requirements—you want a predictably level playing field and the latitude to operate in it relatively unencumbered. You want to be able to grow your business and reward your investors, employees, customers, suppliers, and yes, the government, which has provided you with such a landscape. All that is good prospers.

"For most of our history, our government has met these requirements to various degrees. Today, however, it does so less than ever." Crelli paused for the expected derisive laughter at the current Democratic president. "But environments change and so must ours. There are hundreds of businesses today whose annual revenue exceeds the gross domestic product of 1950 America. Yet with all this wealth, in this era of intense global competition, American businesses have been unable to improve certain inherent inefficiencies, deferring those solutions to a government inadequate to the task. You know the issues: educating our workforce with appropriate curricula from kindergarten through college and technical schooling, so it can be a true asset to our economy, continuing education so the workforce can adapt to a changing economic landscape, and reducing taxes so our products and services can be competitive, globally.

"To date, we've had little success with these issues. Our labor force is both too expensive and too ill trained to compete, and our taxes are too high. Labor is too expensive because unions and other socialist sympathizers still haven't recognized the competitive disadvantage they create with their demands. As a country, we spend too much on healthcare and aging and we to easily meet the needs of the millions of illegal immigrants and the unfortunate poor, people who are unable to create value, and who survive merely to drain America of our already significantly constrained resources. It is time to declare our government incompetent and to solve these problems like a capitalist democracy demands, in the private sector. For if we continue to allow waste and inefficiency to reign in the cruel but fair world of international competition, we do so at our peril.

"Mark Rosenthal presents real, pragmatic business solutions, not concepts or reactionary ideology. He demonstrates extraordinary, concrete results that, because of their obvious benefits, I urge you all to support.

"I was fortunate to have worked with Mark and I am proud to be his friend and ally. After hearing him, you'll feel about him as I do. Ladies and gentlemen, here is the president and CEO of Crelli Enterprises, and the architect of a remarkable business future, Mark Rosenthal."

Smiling and applauding loudly for Mark, Bernie turned and whispered to Jane. "Why would Gorman attend if that's the subject?"

As tears of pride streamed down her face, Jane nodded.

Polite applause continued as Mark placed a microphone patch on his suit lapel. "Thanks, Andy. And I thank all of you for taking time from your busy schedules to hear about our success. I can tell you from experience, after Senator Crelli has his way with you, you will never be the same."

As his son spoke, Bernie listened proudly. From time to time in the audience, a phone or a conversation disrupted his concentration but then, all too quickly, Mark ended his speech.

"What I've discussed today is a vast reengineering of government and private enterprise cooperation, an evolutionary step in capitalist concepts that will improve the effectiveness and efficiency of our entire economy for the betterment of all. As I've demonstrated, Wharton, Ohio, works—thus our slogan, WOW. Documented results prove that public-private partnerships can create municipal surpluses that, when reinvested, can build state-of-the-art education and training facilities that will allow our children to become revenue generating future employees. Our cross-business consortiums have added technologies that reduce operating costs and improve profits for all commercial endeavors in Wharton. Some of the operational savings and the reduced local taxes have been applied to family-support programs, training, and reeducation, and health assurance and retirement programs. Currently, Senator Crelli is working in his various Senate committees to develop the legislative framework and road map for a national program based on the excellent and reproducible results at Wharton. These public-private collaborations provide the right services at the right price to the right people at the lowest possible cost. Our goal is nothing less than to propel America back into its rightful role as the leader of global commerce, and we'll face this challenge in the way America always does, with ingenuity and passion. It is time for the restoration of America's global commercial dominance from the boardrooms of the world to global consumers and producers of our goods and services. On behalf of the senator, I thank you. I'll take questions now."

"Mr. Rosenthal, Debi Denton from Allied Technology Linkages. You state we must make private industry directly responsible for developing and managing the academic curricula and the performance standards for future workers in order to improve our labor resources."

"Yes, that's right. It's unproductive and, frankly, dangerous to wait until prospective employees come of age and come to us inadequately trained because their curricula has little to do with future employability. That gross inadequacy forces us to retrain in a costly, less than efficient, just-in-time environment. It makes far better economic sense to train future employees from an early age using demanding, business-oriented and business-ready subject matter structured to satisfy future requirements. This discipline will insure a supply of productive workers and reduce overall labor costs. It also insures that employees come to market with résumés that open doors to future jobs. Everyone benefits. Another question?"

"Patrick Guinin, *Business Survey Magazine*. I have two questions. What about kids who are capable of more exotic curricula? After all, we need breakthrough thinkers for our long-term success. And how will you handle the training of future entrepreneurs if you only concentrate on educating people to consume and produce?"

"Excellent questions. As business owners, we know that every asset must provide value beyond its cost. This is particularly true of Research and Development programs that generate negative cash flow until they deliver their expected bounty. If we continually spend on unproductive R and D, we go broke. We know we will not be successful every time, but we must hit one out of the park frequently enough to justify the program. At our Wharton project, we provide similar incentives for higher education. If students want to expand their training beyond the immediately productive—and show the capability and passion for it—we require them to justify the time and cost of their education much like our businesses justify the cost of current research and development spending against future benefits. We find this has advantages, the least of which is that the students are more motivated to follow through with their education, fulfill their promise, and generate value for their efforts. Again, this is capitalism and everyone wins. To expand on this, I believe even adolescents should be required to work while they attend school. Employment helps maturity and when students enter the market for full-time employment, they should be prepared to hit the deck running. This too is a win-win. As students or young employees mature, those who aspire to own and run their own businesses will have ample opportunity to distinguish themselves. We are always looking for special talents with an entrepreneurial bent. In Wharton, we put them through an additional curriculum to support their passion to become executives and owners."

"Mr. Rosenthal, Erlene Dule, Utah Mineral Co-op. You state that religion and morality play a significant role in your proposal. Can you clarify that, please? Liberals will claim church and state separation and say it isn't constitutional."

Mark smiled and walked over to the woman who asked the question. "What we're proposing is akin to the old time Protestant work ethic that made America great almost two hundred years ago and it is the keystone of our program. Erlene, your point is a good one. Obviously, we recognize the separation of church and state. But the creators of our Constitution set no restrictions on church and private enterprise. We believe the restoration of a faith-based society is not only good for business, but also necessary to compete in our world. It will help deliver on our promise of a new golden age for America. It's been well-documented that the ethical and moral degradation our country has endured over the last hundred years destroyed much of what was once considered our global competitive advantage. Where once we had the most conscientious and committed workforce, today, most of our workers are distracted and disaffected. As we did in Wharton, we intend to petition our nation's clergy to develop effective programs so citizens can understand the moral and ethical absolutes that are required for our society to prosper in a global economy. We will task our religious leaders to communicate to all Americans, in each and every community, what is in their best interest, so that people can focus on improving their attitudes and intensifying their passions toward leading our great country to a restoration of commercial supremacy. Given the current state of our culture, this may seem an insurmountable task, but I assure you, it is vital for us as a society to return to the moral high ground we once defended as the greatest economic power the world has ever seen. For America to be successful, this effort is essential.

"We are a long way from harvesting the fruits of that achievement, but the concepts I presented today support a practical reality—survival and then dominance on the world stage. I urge each of you to visit the Wharton City Hall. And don't be surprised if, in the future, that building is renamed for our illustrious junior senator from Kentucky whose vision has made Wharton a beacon illuminating the way to our place of leadership in a better world.

"It's been a great thrill for me to be here to present these important concepts. To stay on agenda, I must end this presentation; however, in a session scheduled for early this evening, I'll present more details about Wharton. I urge everyone to attend. Senator Crelli and I will meet with you afterward to discuss your involvement in future projects. We welcome your input and, of course, your support. Thanks to leaders like you, America will be great again. Thank you."

His son stepped back and graciously smiled at the applause. Bernie joined in enthusiastically but was disappointed because he felt the applause little more than polite. The look on some of the attending executives' faces ran the gamut from boredom to bewilderment.

Senator Crelli jumped on stage, shook Mark's hand and patted him on the back. It was clear Mark was pleased. He had that glow of satisfaction that should have been reserved for a father's approval. That troubled Bernie. As he watched his son and Crelli talk, Mark's expression changed. He gestured into the audience. Crelli nodded and Mark made his way to their table.

"So what do you think sainthood or tar and feathers?" Mark asked.

Bernie hugged Mark. "I can't say I agree with all of it, but I'm so proud of you. It's so far out there; it's hard to conceive of. You created a blueprint for complete reform—mostly necessary reform. Unfortunately, most of your audience is too conservative to comprehend the scope, and business and government, of course, will resist."

"Probably, but what did you think?"

"Son, you're amazing."

"So you like the concept?"

"Mostly. You have your mother's desire to help people. I guess it's a matter of . . ."

"Scale," Jane said, with tears of pride. "It sounds wonderful, honey, but it's so ambitious. There are so many people with a strong interest in the status quo who'll fight you."

Mark glanced at Crelli, who was glad-handing guests. "Let's go to the bar. I'll buy."

At the bar, he gave his mother a hug. "I feel bad about this, Mom, Dad. Something just came up, and Andy needs me back in Cincinnati immediately. He'll cover for me here."

"But we planned to spend the weekend together."

"I know, Dad. But there are problems, and Andy has to keep his distance."

"I don't believe this," Jane said. "Can't you . . ."

"No, Mom," Mark interrupted. "I can't. Andy's invested everything in me, and he needs me back there. I'm sorry, you guys. You came all this way for nothing."

Angrily, Jane picked up her purse from the table. "Come on, let's get out of here."

Mark pleaded with them to stay but Bernie decided.

"We came to see you. Mom and I will enjoy the time we have with you on the plane more than we will lounging around here with strangers."

And so it was settled. They went to the hotel desk and made reservations for the next available flight out and then met back in the lobby after packing. While waiting for a limousine, Mark and Jane sat in an outside courtyard drinking. Bernie paced in the lobby where he overheard snippets of conversations from a group of business owners who had listened to Mark's speech.

"Crelli's boy made some interesting points."

"So what?"

"He's right, mostly. It costs far too much to find, hire, and keep productive workers and it's getting worse. Our current batch of recruits sucks. I don't know whether to put candidates to work, put them in jail, or have them deported. The system's to blame."

"Doesn't matter. No one's going to persuade Congress to ante up funds and give up control."

"If anyone can, it's Senator Crelli."

"He's a first-term junior senator. He won't get shit."

"Even if he's successful, do we really want what Rosenthal wants? I'm doing fine. Sure, I'd love more tax cuts but we'll get that anyway when Crelli runs. The speech was a waste of time. At least the weather is holding up so I can get in some golf. Anyone interested?"

"There's a meeting on Wharton later. I'm attending so I can decide for myself if they know what they're talking about."

"If Jesus Christ himself appeared at a congressional hearing and testified that He wanted what Rosenthal outlined, they'd crucify him." Everyone laughed.

"Yeah, you're probably right."

"What about that private session?"

"Not for me. I'll spend time networking at the bar with those high school girls."

"This session is different. It's top-security, ground-floor stuff. Not every company's going to get preferential treatment if Crelli pulls this off. I don't know if what they're saying will work, but I don't want to be left out if there's money available."

"Okay, yeah. I'll go with you."

"You'll need a specially encoded blue badge. You can't get in without it. See Crelli's man, Soren. There will be a significant donation."

"Of course."

The bellman arrived with the luggage and interrupted Bernie's eavesdropping. He led the bellman to his family's table as a brief squall drenched the streets, creating a moist, floral aroma.

"Mark, what are the off-agenda sessions about?"

Mark looked confused. "What off-agenda sessions?"

"I don't know. Some of the attendees said they had to go through Soren to get access."

"They're talking about the Wharton presentation. Reno's organizing it."

Jane reached over to brush back Mark's thick, dark hair, just as she did when he was a child. "Commitment time," she said. "When do we see you in Cincinnati?"

Mark took his mother's hand. "Mom, I'm not sure. Let me get a handle on this new problem first and I'll call you."

She shook her head. "Mark, no. I want a date. We've missed you. I thought we'd catch up this weekend. And don't forget about Franki."

"Mom, please. I'll call you Sunday. Honest."

They separated at the Indianapolis International Airport where Mark connected to Cincinnati. As he and Jane drove home, Bernie offered his theory on the change in plans.

"That son of a bitch Gorman got us kicked out. He hates me so much he's even willing to screw Mark to get to me. God, I hate him."

Disappointed and sad, she shook her head. "Get over yourself. This has nothing to do with you. Mark has responsibilities just like you do. Frankly, you're just not that damn important."

He looked glumly at her. "Great, now I'm too unimportant to be paranoid?"

"Honey, let it go. It's really not all about you. Regardless of what you're feeling, there just aren't great conspiracies being hatched out there."

Chapter 10

Bermuda—2031

Andy surveyed the room. When he was ready, he nodded to Soren, who locked the doors. Andy began this first and most crucial step in his plan to save America. He was ready.

"I appreciate that there's a serious desire to party tonight, so heartfelt thanks for making the right choice and attending this meeting instead. I promise all of you, when we're done here, you will be in an even better mood to party. I know Rosenthal's presentation wasn't what you expected, but I assure you, once you understand what we're building, you'll see how it all fits together.

"Before each of you received an invitation to this conference, you were carefully screened based on strong references from people we value. You were selected to play a critical role in an historic movement, and the fact that you've elected to attend means two things. One, you don't need a prospectus to understand the value of the proposition we're about to offer, and two, you have the foresight to visualize the awesome potential of what we're developing. This is a decisive step toward achieving goals we have long sought, and each of you will be greatly rewarded for being early supporters.

"It's imperative you understand the need for complete confidentiality. For reasons soon to be obvious, I caution you to discuss what you hear tonight only with those who are attending, and then, only in the most secure surroundings. This condition is absolute and uncontestable and will be enforced with extreme prejudice. If anyone here feels they can't abide by this condition, please leave now. If you do leave, I caution you, do not discuss your attendance here with anyone. As a further caution, let me remind you that as the head of the federal e-SWAT task force, I'm responsible for the efforts that breach the most sophisticated electronic terrorist organization in the history of the world, and it took me less than a year to achieve success against them. If they can't hide from me, it's a very good bet that you can't either. So please, if this in any way concerns you, leave now by the door you entered."

He watched the attendees look around, but none left. Satisfied, he continued.

"My friends, with ever-increasing concern, we've watched as population growth in America has outstripped our ability to employ due to either skills displacement or sheer size. Our political parties ignore this and take turns frittering away our competitive advantage. In the last half-century, each party has taken their turn steering our great country away from true capitalist ideals and off the cliffs of entitlements and deficit spending. With each party in power, government spending has increased and become more inefficient, ineffective, and meddlesome—regardless of claims to the contrary. Programs that allow those who contribute little or nothing to America's wealth yet receive unequal benefits in return are bankrupting us and making it impossible to compete globally.

"Short-sighted, greedy elected officials have perpetrated this great fraud by bargaining away our future as payment for their political careers. We are at a crossroads, an intersection of critical factors which I will describe. We have no choice but to take control and stop the insanity.

"The senior boom generation has co-opted our politicians and forced them to fund what basically amounts to a welfare state. Taxes on those who contribute most to the economy are being diverted to make the dying years memorable for boomers and that is draining our coffers and piling up our debt. These profligate ways imperil our ability to compete with countries that understand the competitive advantages of eliminating non-productive overhead. Because the elderly vote as a bloc for their own self-interest, and their lobbyists tie up any legislation that could reduce the economic drain they create, they are bleeding us dry and they don't care that they disable our great country, as long as they live as long and as well as they can and die peaceful and happy at any cost. America had its Greatest Generation, now it endures its most selfish one, one that insists on getting theirs even if it devalues our currency and causes us to default on our commitments. They are willing to do this even if it guarantees the debasement of every future generation. This can't continue.

"Another factor is America's criminal element, those incarcerated and on the streets. There are more criminals today in America than in every other country on earth combined for all of recorded history, and the cost to incarcerate them and to patrol our streets to protect productive citizens and businesses is another horrifying drain on our economy.

"Yet another factor is immigration. In spite of walls and security technologies, every year more undesirables, people who don't understand our capitalist environment, our work ethic, and our politics, enter America seeking its benefits. We've been reasonably successful co-opting the best from these groups before they achieve real political power on their own. However, because of the size of this population, and its increasing rate of growth, it influences policy and increases the cost of doing business. Even though most don't vote, their leaders have been here long enough to understand power and have acquired lobbyists to influence politicians. Today, immigrant elements control far too many counties throughout the country. Without action to deter it, this power grab is inexorable. We have little influence over this segment of the population.

"To compound these issues, large communities of legal immigrants from China—people we have been forced to accept because of the great debt we owe China—have begun to control entire cities and towns, electing local officials to do their bidding. There are strong indications that once these immigrants achieve the critical mass the government in China desires, they will control our national legislative process and all that means. This is our country and that must not continue.

"Now I genuinely sympathize with the plight of these groups. But since the Great Depression, when social welfare was essentially expenditure in support of our national defense, the government has so perverted the concept that groups now prefer handouts over living productive lives and growing their communities. Government programs to support these groups have expanded, and they have become cost prohibitive. To make matters worse, entire industries have sprouted to support these groups, adding to our problems. What we have are the incompetent servicing the incapable.

"We project that within ten years a powerful, selfish, Socialist majority made up of lobbyists and power brokers for the poor and have-nots will vie with the Chinese nationalist movement to take control of America and as always, liberal Democrats will vie to support these movements in some way in order to maintain their majority status while conservatives in both parties will claim the high ground and oppose this in order to protect the core of what makes America great. Conservatives will do this to the detriment of ever becoming a ruling party again. When this happens, as business owners, we will lose our control of the country, such as it is. Covetous, self-serving politicians and cult personalities will continue to expand their significant followings and our role as advisers to governments will diminish—first at the local and then the state, and national levels. Eventually, we will lose control of the White House and the courts.

"Obviously, criminals shouldn't vote and seniors will die but in this fight, we are our own worst enemy. In power, liberals permit criminals to vote, and with medical and technological breakthroughs in healthcare, populations favorable to liberal viewpoints will live longer, exerting pressure for additional spending that we can ill afford and from which we will never recover. Truly, gentlemen, the moment of action is here and if we fail now, we are up against it. We are fighting for our way of life. This could be the last time business interests guide America to greatness. Our survival and the survival of the country we love depend on how steadfastly we defend our interests. We must protect America, our beloved capitalist paradise from those who want more than they are willing to give back and are willing to take from us to get it.

"What I have described is inexorable. Exacerbating it is the omnipresent availability of information generated by purveyors of unregulated communications. These groups make it more difficult for us to deliver our message with the effectiveness required to rally people to our cause.

"As Mark Rosenthal reported earlier, the expenses our government incurs to control our criminal population, the aged, sick, and poor, significantly depresses economic growth, which creates more dependent situations. It's a vicious cycle. We project that just to keep a cap on future debt, all existing taxes must increase by 25 percent, while government programs must be cut by a like amount each year until the debt is repaid. That won't happen.

"Today's media reports there is systemic unemployment, violence in the streets, and sabotage in the workplace caused by perverse and misguided homebred terrorists. There is cyber warfare brazenly funded by governments who fear us that is stealing our knowledge, our experience, and our technological research." Andy looked up from his notes to see a woman standing by a microphone. He acknowledged her.

"Senator, I appreciate your evaluation and I agree with much of it. But are you proposing something? I mean anything worthwhile?"

Before he could address the question, another attendee stood.

"Senator, Ernest Everhard, CEO of Auto-Brake, Inc. I hear this bitching all the time. I'm bored with analysis. We're looking for solutions—real, workable solutions. Do you have something constructive to offer, or can I go to the bar and beat the crowds?"

The grumbling increased. Angrily, Crelli banged his fist on the table until everyone quieted down. "Is this what we've become?" he shouted. "Are we a mob, too? I expect more from business leaders. Those who know me know I do nothing frivolously. Those who don't know me, pay attention, your futures depend on it. We've been fighting these issues ineffectively for over one hundred years—winning and losing a little along the way. I'm here for your commitment because I intend to solve this once and for all time." The noise stopped.

"If we don't act now, when we're old, we'll be living in government housing, eating gruel while our grandchildren, like everyone else, are poor and powerless. Is that really the legacy we want to offer our families? If we don't act, we will be the last of the great families to control the mechanics of wealth and power. I'm here today, risking everything, because that isn't acceptable. We can no longer stay the course. It is time to act—for America.

"What Rosenthal said earlier is the working cover for our activities. Rosenthal, himself, isn't involved in the full breadth of what I propose. Take that as a caution. If I'm not ready to trust the CEO of my company, you should know how sensitive this is."

"Senator, what are these plans?"

"The essential first steps have already occurred. In the past six years my team has been working behind the scenes to obtain unwavering commitments from a significant number of members of national, state, and local legislatures, various governors and select judges. These patriots, in both parties, have agreed to keep their loyalty secret until the time is right. In addition, myriad owners, allied with us within the media and the legal profession, have agreed to keep the public and our opponents unaware of our plans until it is too late to react and alter our plans.

"The men and women in the Senate and House are mostly patriots who listen to reason. Others can and prefer to be bought so we continue to recruit and are approaching majority control at all levels of government. When we're ready, these silent patriots will renounce their party affiliations and join the newly formed third party, the Entrepreneur Party."

Another businessman stood to be recognized.

"Senator, this sounds like a coup."

"A coup? Not at all. My lawyers assure me that my plan is constitutional. I wouldn't do it any other way. Since neither political party has the courage to tackle the changes required to save our country, politics as usual while Rome burns, we are creating a patriotic organization dedicated to supporting America and perpetuating its free-market, capitalist ideals.

"With a friendly face in the White House to build on the majority control in the legislatures and with judges in place, we will begin by passing liberal social legislation that will expand our voter base. At the same time, as Rosenthal stated earlier, across the country, business consortiums will begin taking control of local communities, thus reducing the footprint and capability of government."

There was more grumbling in the audience. "Does someone have a question?"

"Senator, I fail to see how spending further on social programs will help."

Before he answered, Crelli considered how much information needed to be divulged to win their support without giving too much away. This balance was critical to his success.

"To save America, we need a super-majority so by further spending and increasing the debt, we make the Entrepreneur Party more popular with the voters. Once we add the newly elected Entrepreneur party members to our undercover majority, we will have the will and the way to eliminate the restrictive anti-business environment that's grown over the years. We do that while our local business consortiums reduce the size and cost of local governments. With that, taxes will be repealed. These efforts will appease conservatives, business owners, and citizens, alike. At that point, we will begin rolling back wasteful and unproductive social programs."

"Senator, another question." Andy nodded. "How can you reduce entitlements while avoiding the riots and violence we're seeing today?"

"Originally, our welfare system was designed to ensure that the least of our citizens would never feel so hopeless that, with nothing to lose, they might riot or support those who would attempt to overthrow the government. Riots and violence, it was deemed, would be far more costly to control than welfare and social works programs. Welfare was once the cheapest alternative to insure peace. Because these programs are now looked at as entitlements and with our deficits, we can no longer afford to pay for them, that reasoning no longer applies. It's time to find a cheaper way. We are unwavering in our commitment to permanently eliminate all entitlements."

He was forced to raise his voice above the protests until the crowd quieted. In the silence there was one question. "What good does that do? They'll only get angrier."

"All resources on the planet are finite. As forward-thinking business leaders we are always mindful how that fact effects what we do. We are custodians of the future. As we've done with natural resources, to protect our future we'll exercise a new form of conservation. It simply isn't rational to allow people to consume resources if they are unwilling or unable to pay what the free market dictates their cost should be. Though people accuse us of greed and avarice, those who deplete the environment without paying exercise a feral self indulgence. It is our intention to eliminate that behavior, or the people who exhibit it."

There was complete silence in the room.

"I can say no more tonight. We are business people. There is a cost to what I propose as well as a significant return. Over the next few months I'll be meeting with each of you to clarify our plans and make financial sense of what I propose. We'll discuss what the value proposition of victory means to you, your company, and your stockholders. But let me be clear. To save America, we must make difficult moral, ethical, and financial choices. However distasteful these choices may appear, each of you would make similar decisions to save your companies and your families.

"I'll be asking for your passionate commitment to support our efforts. Each of you will be taking great risks. But with your loyalty, your confidentiality, and, most of all, your passion, I guarantee you a great return on that risk along with the best future imaginable. We can't fail. We mustn't fail."

He finished and looked up as Ernest Everhard rose and headed for the door.

"Mr. Everhard, I trust what you heard is to your liking."

Everhard stopped abruptly and, red-faced, addressed the audience. "Gentlemen, and I include you Mr. Crelli with some hesitancy, this is dangerous thinking. I caution you, if you must speak about this, save it for a cigar and brandy. I, for one, don't approve, and won't be involved—not today or ever. Senator Crelli, what are you thinking? You are a representative of the people, the people, man. You are mad to consider this."

He had expected some disagreement, so when Everhard finished, he responded immediately. "If this isn't for you, that's fine. Does anyone else feel this way?" He surveyed the crowd. Nobody volunteered. "Good. Please, Mr. Everhard, go if you must, I understand. But, I expect you will keep your word and not discuss this with anyone."

"Who would I discuss it with? This is fantasy or lunacy. But if I discover that you or your people are doing anything illegal, I caution you, Senator, it will be my duty to report it."

"I assure you, that won't be an issue. I trust my legal team and take their advice seriously. If you see or hear anything that concerns you, bring it to my attention, and I'll rectify it. And if that doesn't resolve your concerns, you have every right to discuss it with the proper authorities. We intend to save America by democratic means, so I'm certain you won't find it necessary to report us. I appreciate your concerns and look forward to working with you and your organization in the future. Good luck." With that, Everhard left.

It was late when Crelli met with his advisers in the presidential suite. Tanya Brandt, the beautiful leader of the currently unheralded Entrepreneur Party opened the conversation. "Andy, it went great. We'll have to be careful with people like Everhard."

Gorman agreed. "But Senator, I'm concerned about Bucky Duke. He was involved in the initial preparations, but didn't attend."

Andy splashed water on his face and grabbed a towel. He nodded for Reno to respond.

"Ms. Brandt, Mr. Gorman, both situations are under control."

Chapter 11

Indianapolis—2031

The Monday after Bernie's exasperatingly brief trip to Bermuda, he returned to his office. While catching up on his mail, a news item caught his eye. He flicked to the article and read it.

> Automotive Executive Dies in Moped Accident in Bermuda
>
> Chief Executive Officer Ernest Everhard of Auto-Brake Lining, Inc. and his wife, Avis, died yesterday in a moped accident near their hotel on the resort island of Bermuda. Everhard, owner of the San Francisco-based automotive company, was attending a convention at the exclusive Atlantic Hotel. According to police, he was riding in tandem behind his wife when a truck driven by a local resident ran their moped into one of the many stone walls that border the narrow Bermuda roads. This was the third accident of its type this year …

As he read, he had a disquieting feeling, first Bonsack, and now this. Yet another business executive had died inexplicably and even though this occurred in Bermuda, he felt the two were related. He contemplated calling his son when a message appeared on his monitor.

"Accept Our Blessing."

He clicked for his secretary.

"Yes, sir?"

"Carolyn, did a message just come up on your screen?"

"No, did you send one?"

"No, I received one that says, 'Accept Our Blessing.'"

"That rules out the Toms."

He laughed. "Yeah, they're not likely to bless anyone. Thanks, Carolyn." He flicked off and spent the morning reviewing the Angel Falls shutdown files in preparation for his trip there. With each page he reviewed, he got angrier. This was a travesty. Being right and not mattering seemed like his job description. It was his fault; he lacked command presence. To the Toms, he was a cipher, without what Gorman called "fuck-you ruthlessness." If he had no other gifts but that, the Toms would have accepted him like a brother. He stared at the vast array of numbers tucked into tidy cells and reflected sadly on how his limitations destroyed Angel Falls. Reluctantly, he accepted their appraisal. He didn't have it in him.

Carolyn interrupted his reverie. "A gentleman's here to see you."

"Who is it?"

"I believe it will answer your earlier question.

"What? Send him in."

Carolyn opened the door and the man entered. Before closing it, she gave Bernie a conspiratorial look. He shrugged. The visitor was dressed in blue overalls, typical of an ANGS equipment operator. He was in his late twenties and had slightly mussed, brown hair and pale skin, with the wispy suggestion of a mustache and goatee. His eyes were light blue, almost translucent, and they were focused unwaveringly on him.

Bernie extended his hand. "I'm Bernie Rosenthal, come in."

"Blessing," the man said. "Qade Blessing," and joined Bernie in his office.

"Carolyn, I'm going out for awhile," he said as he and Blessing walked past her desk.

"Is everything alright?" she asked.

"Yes, everything's fine. I shouldn't be long."

During the brief conversation in Bernie's office, he felt Qade Blessing was an emissary, and he thought he knew from whom. They took the elevator to the first floor, but when the doors opened, Blessing stopped him. The elevator doors closed, and Blessing put a key into a lock on the elevator panel, turned it, and pressed the button marked "b". The elevator descended to the basement, a place Bernie hadn't visited in years, ever since ANGS' research and development facility moved from there to its new, more elaborate and prestigious facilities dubbed the Taj Mahal, leaving the labyrinthine basement dark and empty.

"Mr. Blessing, I ..."

"Please, call me Qade."

"All right, Qade. You're with the moles, right? Where are you taking me?"

Blessing smiled serenely. "You mean Parker's group? I'm sorry; I'm not one of them."

The answer surprised him. If he wasn't a mole, how did he know about them? Blessing continued on, stopping only when he realized Bernie wasn't following. He turned; his pale blue eyes colorless in the dim light.

"If you're not with the moles, where are we going?" Bernie demanded.

"To meet someone who has a great interest in you."

"I'm afraid no one has any great interest in me, except my wife."

"You're wrong. We need a warrior," Blessing said, in a calm, soft, surely-you-know tone.

It was so unexpected Bernie stopped and laughed. "A warrior? Whatever that means, I'm certainly not your man. Now if you were looking for a worrier …"

It was Qade's turn to laugh. "No, you heard me right, a warrior, a fighter."

Of all the words Bernie might have expected to hear, "warrior" was certainly not among them. "Qade, look, I don't know what you want but I'm not your man. I'm CFO here, not some … ninja." He reconsidered the situation. "And you know what? I'm not feeling real comfortable here. Let's go back to my office. We can talk there."

"It's not like that. No one wants to hurt you. It's important you come with me."

Bernie glanced down the dark empty corridor. "Why?"

Qade hesitated. "It concerns your son."

"Mark? What about him?"

"You'll have your answer when we get where we're going."

Bernie stepped closer to Qade. "Is Mark in trouble?"

"Not with us." With that, Blessing turned and walked on.

Bernie watched Qade, almost to the point of losing him in the shadows. Reluctantly, he followed, remembering what Ennis Parker had told him about the people accessing Angs' internal business systems, the ones who went through the firewall "like smoke through a screen door." e-Rats? Bernie knew he shouldn't be here but he had to know more about his son.

He followed Blessing until the corridor ended at a vertical metal ladder. Blessing climbed, opened a metal door, and stepped out. Warily, Bernie trailed after him. They surfaced outside in what was known at Angs as Jurassic Park, an expanse of huge, old, and no longer serviceable chemical storage tanks—rusting relics from the industrial age.

He followed Blessing down a row of tanks, the morning sun blinding him as it blipped intermittently though the gaps between the tanks.

"Over here, Mr. Rosenthal."

Blessing stood by a rusted tank. Suddenly, a camouflaged door slid open. "After you."

Considering the civil unrest outside and recent murder of Jim Bonsack—and possibly the guy in Bermuda—Bernie hesitated. Finally, he steeled himself and stepped in. Blessing followed and the door closed behind them. Inside it was dark, empty, and foreboding.

"Stand closer," Blessing said, his voice echoing inside the huge, rusting tank.

"What?"

"A little closer, here," Qade said, gesturing with a flashlight to a spot on the gravel floor.

Reluctantly, he moved to the spot.

"Joad, Omega Level One, please," Blessing said.

Bernie was startled when the area they were standing on slowly descended, stopping on the floor of a well-lit subterranean room. When they stepped off the platform, it lifted back into position as a pillar and ceiling section.

"Thank you, Qade."

He heard the woman's voice and searched for the source. She was behind him, in her early forties and still beautiful with light, straight, yellow-blonde hair and matching light, yellow-brown eyes— striking features that he, like most of the men at Angs, found unforgettable.

"Arlene Klaatu?" He said in a voice that failed to hide his bewilderment. "You … you were murdered."

"I was." She smiled sadly. "Welcome, Bernie, It's been a long time."

During her consulting gig at Angs, Klaatu had had a difficult relationship with the Toms, and their arguments over implementation of a new information system were well known throughout the company. For all that, he hadn't given credence after her unusual disappearance when rumors spread that she had been murdered. He knew the Toms were capable of much, but not that; so he accepted the less intriguing notion that the Toms had just run her off and embarrassed, she'd fled to anonymity.

What he knew of her came from her résumé. Born in Abilene, Kansas, she was a member of Mensa and a cheerleader, as well as president and valedictorian of her high school class. She'd graduated from Harvard where she studied political science and advanced thought, and had done her postgraduate work in information technologies at Stanford, where she'd received a fellowship at the fabled Palo Alto Research Center, called PARCplace. There, she co-founded a company she eventually sold and accepted a consulting job at Angs until her sudden disappearance.

"Where am I?" he asked. "And what are you doing here?"

"It's good to see you after all this time. Thanks for coming. I'm sorry about the drama, but its best. We call this Omega Station. It's my home and our command and control center. The reason I'm here and not …" her eyes looked skyward, "is why we want to talk to you."

It was unsettling, looking into those beautiful, unwavering, and yet somber yellow eyes. "You're not serious? A command and control center under a chemical tank, here at ANGS?"

She shrugged. "Yes, it's exactly like that."

"Like what? Qade said my son is in trouble. What's going on?"

"Before we can answer, there's someone you must meet. He'll explain it to you."

He looked around the room. Other than Qade and Arlene, the room was empty. "Who?"

"His name is Gohmpers and he's looking forward to meeting you." She turned, but he gently grabbed her arm and turned her around to face him.

"What trouble is my son in?" She looked at him sadly. He released her arm.

"It's complicated, Bernie, but I promise, Gohmpers will explain everything. Mark isn't in imminent danger, but he's in harm's way."

"That's not reassuring. Can you at least tell me what happened to you?"

Arlene looked down and then away, as if trying to avoid a painful memory. "It's all related to why we asked you here. I don't know if you remember, but a couple of days before … I had a pretty intense argument with Gorman."

"He doesn't accept rejection."

She smiled sadly. "You have no idea. He and Tom Morgan insisted I develop surveillance technologies that would violate the privacy of their customers, suppliers, employees, and competitors—and break lots of laws. They wanted functionality that went way beyond normal, reasonable, business requirements and included surreptitious monitoring of privileged personnel, their business transactions, and all of their communications, everywhere, all the time. As you know, I'm an expert in those technologies, and they knew it. I had no choice but to refuse."

As CFO of ANGS, Bernie should have known this. "I don't understand."

"They were concerned about the future. Gohmpers will fill you in on that, too."

"Some of those applications were installed. I recently stumbled across one."

"Bernie, there are things you need to understand before we continue. In the early part of the twenty-first century, stateless terrorists attacked the United States and with Congress's consent President Bush declared war on them. From that moment, the concept of perpetual war developed. After all, how can it truly end? Who surrenders? And that doesn't even consider the constant cyber warfare we're involved in. America is on continual war footing even though there are no targetable enemies and no home front to attack and defeat. The Bush Doctrine has continued through four presidents, even though we've only been attacked occasionally.

"I'm familiar with all that."

She nodded. "Good. I promise that Gohmpers will explain how that affects your son. As to why I'm here, Bernie, I was in high school when I first got interested in AI, artificial intelligence. Back then, scientists and science fiction writers assumed AI would be this universally available, beneficial tool for mankind. They weren't wrong but they just didn't think it through. Artificial intelligence has contributed much to make the world better but the most powerful AI applications are funded and controlled by big business and the government. Before technology made the oceans irrelevant as buffers, democracy and free-market capitalism were fine concepts, but to support the status quo today, real and absolute power is required, and AI has become the supreme weapon of power and has been co-opted by those who want more power and greater control over our country and our economy. Basically, that's what Gorman wanted, and what I resisted.

"That difference of opinion was why I was terminated—my employment and my life. For an appallingly large fee and by downplaying the Big Brother aspects, my replacement, Rebecca Morning provided the Toms with similar functionality. Eventually Rebecca realized what I knew and she confronted the Toms, too. She was luckier: they just let her go. Forgive my immodesty, Becca was good, but she's not in my class. In the end, outside consultants finished the project in secret, but what they accomplished, even though it's powerful and illegal, it was less than what the Toms wanted, less than I could have delivered, but far more than should have been delivered."

"So why did you disappear?"

"It wasn't by choice, I assure you. One night after work, a man was waiting for me in the ANGS parking lot. He came up behind me. I turned … in time to see his arm coming down. He hit me with a metal bar, I think. Then, he took me to one of these chemical tanks and deposited me there. He figured my body would never be found, but I was fortunate. God had a purpose for me and didn't want me to die just yet." She paused and looked down. "The next thing I knew, I woke up here."

"Here? How?"

"Gohmpers and his assistants saved me. You'll meet them, too. Their security monitor picked it up. They retrieved me from the tank and took me to a hospital."

"The police said there were no hospital records."

"The police work was thorough."

"How ...?"

"You'll understand soon."

"Did you recognize the man who hit you?" When she didn't respond, Bernie persisted. "Was he from ANGS?"

"This still isn't easy for me. You'll know everything soon. Please, come." She walked to a wall and stopped. "Joad, access Omega Two." The door slid open.

"How were you able to build this under our noses? And who are you talking to?"

"Building it was easy. This is ANGS, after all. We diverted funds from illegal political contribution funds I'm sure you're unaware of. Using ANGS' integrated enterprise software, we set the status of the construction budget as approved and we were able to schedule, build, and pay for everything, no questions asked. Our contractors were free to come and go."

"You diverted company funds? You're telling that to the wrong person, Arlene." He reconsidered. "Illegal contributions? And you have your own construction people?"

She shrugged. In spite of the physical abuse she still looked beautiful. "Don't trouble yourself about the illegal funds. Even if you perform an audit, you won't find anything. And as to our construction people, you met one of our supervisors." She pointed to the other room where Qade was sitting. "After you learn more from Gohmpers and what our ends are, I hope you'll consider what we did insignificant."

"I'll promise anything right now; I'm at a distinct disadvantage. But this Gohmpers guy will have to be persuasive for me to ignore what you confessed to."

He followed her to the next room, staring at the surroundings, amazed that these facilities were constructed without the Toms' approval.

"Here at last, a warrior to fight the madness." Bernie heard the voice before he saw him.

The deep voice came from a large, powerfully built black man who materialized from behind a bookshelf wearing a pale-yellow turtleneck and white silk warm-up pants. The man's shaven head reflected the room lights.

"Gohmpers?" he asked.

"Mr. Rosenthal, yes, thanks for coming. I'm pleased to finally meet you."

"What's going on with my son?"

"I'm sorry to bring you here this way. May I call you Bernie?" Bernie nodded. "You must understand that if Qade had explained everything in your office, you wouldn't have believed him. Besides our Blessing, please accept my apology. Now, about your son. Sadly, Mark is involved with something that is on the verge of creating an unfortunate future for him and for all of us."

Bernie considered Mark's position as chief executive officer at Crelli Enterprises. "I'm proud of Mark and I feel pretty good about his future."

"I'm here to convince you otherwise."

"If you have something to say, please get to it because I have to get back to my office."

"Mark has been chosen by a bad man. Andrew Crelli is planning the greatest political revolution in history."

"You'll have to excuse me if I don't share your dislike for Republicans."

Gohmpers smiled. "No, no, Crelli is not a Republican. He's using the Republican Party as cover while he builds strength."

"That's ridiculous."

Gohmpers smiled. "Yes, it does sound ridiculous."

Bernie returned the smile. "It's the times. Our politicians can't figure a way out of this perpetual recession so everyone is panicking. I think developing conspiracy theories help. But you didn't invite me here to discuss conspiracy theories."

"I didn't but there are a lot of conspiracy-theory wing nuts out there."

"We clearly have problems, but most of the panic is caused by the damn media trying to propagate myths so they can sell advertising."

"Most conspiracy theories," Gohmpers added helpfully, "involve military takeovers—maybe with nukes—or computer viruses, things like that. I've read some books about coups that are quite fascinating but except that the hero always ends up with the girl and the author never explains what happens after the coup succeeds. Do you know why that's avoided?"

Annoyed at his own interest, Bernie considered it. "It doesn't make good theatre."

"That's a fair point. Consider this: in an open society like America, people can theorize about how to start a revolution, but no one knows how to overcome the checks and balances inherent in our system that could make a revolution successful."

"Like what?"

"Take all the vested interests: the lawyers, lobbyists, minority parties, the media, well-financed minority interests, the disloyal opposition, all would make revolution difficult. Besides, extremes in America ebb and flow all the time, but we always come back to moderation. That's actually the problem, today. America is sliding into the abyss because our system of checks and balances makes it impossible to change course. Everyone has already figured out their piece of the pie and they won't give that up."

"That sounds reasonable, but where are you going with this and how does it affect Mark? You said my son's in trouble, and we're talking movie plots. If you have something to tell me about my son, please do it now."

Gohmpers persisted. "Please bear with me. Did you ever wonder why, regardless of whether we elect either Republicans or Democrats, neither ever solves our problems?"

"Everyone wonders that. What's your point?"

"Humor me a little more, please, Bernie. Aren't you curious why politicians argue the rightness of their ideas and yet never solve our problems? Say you were to try the impossible and lead a coup in the good old United States of America. What would be your first major obstacle?"

Frustrated, Bernie turned to Arlene who smiled and nodded to Gohmpers. Annoyed, Bernie responded. "I guess I'd have to find a way to get elected President or some other important office."

"Yes, you'd need to be an insider—a deep insider. By the way, Andrew Crelli's an important senator. Now what else would you need to overcome?"

Knowing he couldn't leave without permission, Bernie reluctantly yielded to Gohmpers in order to speed things up so he could find out about Mark and get back to work. "Okay, I'd need a lot of funding and, I guess, backing from like-minded, influential people so I don't run afoul of Homeland Security or the FBI."

"Yes, good. Crelli owns a Fortune 100 company that develops and implements hardware and software for national security—he's very well liked by that community—and his father-in-law is the Senate Majority leader. We've worked around those obstacles easily enough."

"You're going to persist with this?"

"Just a little longer, please. Crelli has position, money, and backing. Now what?"

"Status and charisma. I know Senator Crelli has both with Crelli Enterprises, his success prosecuting e-Rats as senator and the coverage the paparazzi provide when he's out partying with the rich and glamorous. Can we cut to the chase? Crelli is leading a coup. How and why does he do it, and what does this have to do with my son?"

"The key to it all is that he possesses an incredibly sophisticated state-of-the-art surveillance technology—something well beyond even what the government knows about. As to the reason: entrepreneurs like him are very concerned about the long-term health of our economy and its competitiveness. They are projecting impending doom if things continue as they are."

"I don't believe you're right about that. Sure we're in a very bad economic cycle right now, and we've been struggling for years without growth. But we've pulled ourselves out in the past. Why would entrepreneurs take such a risk?"

"What you have to understand is that business is not a democracy and it labors in a system that can't face problems and solve them. In the early days of our republic, it didn't matter because we had vast frontiers and entrepreneurs knew they could stretch for horizons, but those days are over and the worst of our fears about capitalism are manifesting. At its best and most efficient, capitalism is autocratic; it has to be to thrive. Waiting for a vote or even influencing a vote is anathema to what capitalists require for competitive advantage. To that, add that the connected, wealthy and powerful always know when to buy cheap and sell dear way before the average citizen. The stock market, frankly every market is stacked in their favor. That's how they got rich and how they stay rich. They want us to believe that what we have is a competitive environment, but it's really just a rigged game, an inside trader's paradise. But since the perpetual stagflation of the 2020s, things have changed. Our debt is far too high, and the great unspoken secret is we're incapable of repaying China, India, Brazil, Turkey, Mexico, and other countries what we owe them. For a time, that was fine, but now our creditors have nurtured their own middle class and they don't need the buying hysteria of the American consumer or our currency, for that matter. For now, we're safe because of our military, but our creditors are discovering ways to cripple us. America is an economic house of cards, and the world is ready and willing to provide the gentle breeze needed to blow it down."

"We influence everything, and we're everyone's best trading partner."

"That was true once. With merely 1 percent of their population now middle class, China, India, and Brazil don't need our buying power any longer. Besides, our middle class has been so hamstrung due to their debt and high unemployment that they no longer generate commercial awe around the world. America's creditors no longer have to put up with us, our currency, or our debt. The world is ready and willing to throw us into debtor's prison and frankly, we deserve it."

"You're oversimplifying. Economic warfare hurts everyone."

"True, but like military warfare, economic wars hurt until there's a winner. And we can't fall back on military victory because Chinese military expenditures surpass ours and their ability to hurt us with cyber warfare is far greater than our ability to hurt them. The fear is they will shut down our economy and our military if we don't back down. In the end, we're helpless except for one thing that Arlene will talk about in a few minutes. Basically, China and Brazil are squeezing us like we squeezed the Soviet Union until it collapsed fifty years ago."

"Look, I know the Toms are really concerned but …"

"No, no, it's much worse and the Toms know it. After a generation of systemic unemployment, we have a large, disaffected population, an entire generation without life-affirming work. Whatever America has tried to do internationally, we've been trumped by the might and entrepreneurial muscle of China. For all its internal issues, China sets international trade rules now. We're no longer in charge. In fact, because of the success of China, Brazil, and in a way, Russia, democracies are looking at their economic futures much differently. More and more countries are altering their form of government and shifting to more proactive, autocratic political systems that support free-market operations but can make critical decisions in a New York minute. Crelli, his entrepreneur friends and some of our smarter politicians understand the implications. America has always been schizophrenic, a republic with autocratic capitalism. It worked when there were frontiers but the frontiers are gone. Around the world, capitalists have become more comfortable with autocratic governments. They are all the rage."

"But the rich and powerful in America are never helpless."

"They aren't helpless, but they're very worried. They control politics like they always have, but suppose a foreign power or two gains control of our internal economics—it's already happening, most of our large corporations are owned at least partially by foreign powers. What follows is America's rich will be beholden to people they don't control. They are very uncomfortable with that, as you can imagine.

"Bernie, Americans are too proud, too greedy, and too selfish. Worse, they've lost the ability to develop and share a cohesive vision of what the country should be. In state after state, the electorate has passed referendums to make their lives seem better but they've done it without funding those mandates—the electorate has joined the politicians in driving the country bankrupt. Add to that how governments behave. Because legislators work in constant election-reelection mode, most are so controlled by lobbyists that no truly beneficial legislation passes, or if it does pass, it is so diluted as to be ineffective. We're in a sad state, and we're in desperate need of a strong leader with strong convictions. Suppose the Chinese have it right. They're autocratic, and they're certainly out-competing us at every turn. Maybe the American republic and free-market capitalism isn't adaptable anymore, and maybe autocratic free market capitalism is the wave of the future. If that's true, and powerful people believe it is, America needs a new form of government that will allow the rich to maintain their status in the world. America may have invented creative destruction, but we don't want to become a victim of it."

"That's a lot of maybes."

"Maybe, maybe not. With each new administration, government is either further privatized to provide new profit outlets for businesses, or further socialized to pass risk and loss on to the taxpayers. Maybe, there's that word again, maybe it's time the executive branch was privatized. I could argue that the legislative branch already has been."

"More conjecture."

"Once, we were a country of entrepreneurs. Now we're mostly a country of copycats. When a true entrepreneur discovers something that has great appeal and payback potential, everyone copies it. Is it such a stretch to believe America will copy what autocratic economies are doing well?"

"But those countries don't have a history of functioning freedom. We can't become autocratic, there's too much freedom and information, and if we're not entrepreneurs, as you say, we are mavericks."

"To survive, our government will do whatever it takes, even if that means monetizing the country and commoditizing its citizens."

"Okay, I concede. You're right. Let's say Senator Crelli is planning to implement the Chinese system. Okay, fine, what does this have to do with my son?"

"American capitalists have found in Crelli the candidate they have been looking for."

"That may be true, but we've had extended periods in our history when significant majorities controlled too much and that has always been their downfall."

"Today it's different. We're more ... desperate. Everyone sees the end coming, and those who are in control want to make damn sure the end won't occur during their watch."

"Still, if Crelli and the Republicans try, they'll fail, and the Democrats will be there..."

"Forget the two-party system. It's dead. Have you heard of the Entrepreneur Party?"

"That loony libertarian group with the really hot leader, Toni something?"

"Tanya Brandt, she's the figurehead until Crelli's ready to take over. Here's concrete information for you to chew on. A significant number of Republican and Democrat politicians have seen the writing on the wall and have become closet members of the Entrepreneur Party."

Bernie realized that somewhere in this conversation Gohmpers had stopped speculating and seemed to know how the government could be, indeed would be, overthrown, and he believed his son's mentor, Senator Crelli, was involved. That's when the reality of Gohmpers' fantasy struck him. "Mark is planning to overthrow the government." As ridiculous as it sounded, if it was true, Mark truly was in grave danger.

"We believe he is." Until Gohmpers responded, Bernie wasn't sure he'd voiced his concern, so he repeated it.

"Am I sure?" Gohmpers responded. "Certainly not. It's early and there are many things that can happen. But, by nature, Crelli and his allies are prodigious planners and self-actualized achievers, so it's wise to act as if they will certainly try. That's why we contacted you."

"What the hell can I do?"

"Protect your son."

"But if you're wrong, I'll ruin his brilliant career and he'll hate me forever."

"But if we're right, you'll save him from committing treason, or worse."

"What could possibly be worse?"

"If Crelli succeeds."

"What? No, he can't. How could he?"

"Crelli is an extraordinary talent and it's a goal of every executive worth his salt to build an organization that is too big to fail. It's their nature, their legacy. Control is in their genes so unless something is done, Crelli's business empire has everything it needs to replace our government."

"But this is America. Coups are impossible. And if it were to succeed, Mark would become a valued employee. I can't believe I'm saying this."

"History isn't on your son's side. Autocrats have never been reliable employers."

"You and Arlene could be terrorists for all I know, and you're setting me up."

"That's fair. I can't prove we're not." Gohmpers handed Bernie a folder. "You were in Bermuda recently on an abbreviated vacation. After you were excused, Crelli chaired a secret meeting. These documents are a reconstruction of notes from that meeting."

"How did you know I was … excused?" Bernie read the papers. "You mean …?"

Gohmpers nodded. "Crelli's plans are taking shape and you are an outsider and in the way. They needed to remove you."

Bernie read the documents, which literally had been pieced together from shredded notes.

"Holy … if this is real … why didn't Mark say anything about Crelli's run for president?"

"They sent Mark away with you, so we're not certain he is a true insider. You, on the other hand, were a nuisance that Tom Gorman hadn't counted on."

"Tom is involved?"

"Until we know more, assume everyone there is involved."

Bernie's world was falling apart. "Gohmpers, my son isn't a rebel. He's a good kid. He wouldn't do this." He spoke his fear. "You want me to help you stop a revolution." Gohmpers nodded. Bernie stared at Arlene, who was sitting quietly on a sofa. "No one's capable of this."

She looked up. "I know Andy. He is. You've met him. You know it, too."

"Arlene, I've met hundreds of punk-young executives like Crelli; he's nothing special."

"You didn't look hard enough. On the day you met Crelli, Mark was celebrating his engagement to the love of his life. You have no idea how sorry I am Mark decided to break off the engagement."

Bernie felt sick. "Jesus, Arlene, do you really think …?"

"To gain share and profits, the media has ripped at the middle of our country, polarizing our people and making them strident and cynical. It's why nothing useful ever gets done. The few Americans who spend any time thinking about their government believe it's ineffective, unresponsive, and corrupt, and who can blame them? They see an absent, vapid Congress arguing petty, self-serving politics to no discernable end—and that from those few thinking Americans who care. The rest are too absorbed in their economic pilgrimage to wealth, or in their recreational shelter from reality. I'm involved because I have a very complicated history with Andy."

Bernie wondered what that could be, but Arlene said no more about it.

Gohmpers concluded. "America is out of control and, unfortunately, Americans are ready and willing to listen to Crelli's siren's song. It's sad but in a way, we deserve it. When it comes to politics, Americans have long relied on the kindness of strangers. Andy Crelli could very well be the last in a long line of strangers to disappoint them."

"But he's just a senator—and a junior one at that. There must be people with more power who can stop him."

In Bermuda, you saw some of his strength, but he has so much more. Everyone believes he ran for the Senate to clean out the e-RATS and that once his e-SWAT Task Force put them all behind bars, he'll return to his first love, Crelli Enterprises."

"Mark doesn't think that. He believes Crelli has the bug for politics."

"That's a good way to put it." Arlene continued. "What you have to understand is that the e-RATS weren't Andy's enemies—well some—but most were his creation. His people fabricate false trails that lead to the arrest and conviction of many innocent people who he accuses of being e-RATS. He's able to transfer funds from companies that e-RATS allegedly raid and puts those funds into the accounts of innocent people to improve his conviction rate. His task force tracks down terrorist-hackers and exposes them: the nation is grateful and his approval ratings soar. Did you know his approval is over 90 percent in Kentucky and almost that high nationally? He can and will parlay that into a successful presidential run."

Bernie continued to leaf through the bizarre and frightening information in the papers Gohmpers gave him. "There's no way Crelli can implement these programs." He turned a few more pages. "There's no way—the government can't just kill poor people."

Arlene leaned over his shoulder. "To save America, and that's what he believes he's doing, Andy will if he must. He's a businessman. He believes life isn't cheap, it's cost prohibitive."

Gohmpers added, "The government has been forced to operate on a "pay as you go" plan. No law can pass unless funding exists for it. Crelli will implement the same plan for people. If you provide value, you live. It's the ultimate libertarian fantasy and he intends to make it real."

"So expose him. The media will crucify him for it. He can't win an election if the people think he's going to kill them. Contact the FBI. They'll stop him."

"We've discussed all of that," Gohmpers said. "When I was young, patriotism was about more than defending your country in a time of war. Now, that's all it is. It's no joke that far too many believe killing the poor is the best way to a better, more robust economy. The reality is we can't *prove* anything in these papers. There's no direct link between the programs described in these papers and Andy. Besides, since the first terrorist bombing in New York at the turn of the century, if it makes them feel safer, the people seem okay with the government suspending or eliminating all kinds of constitutional protections like the right to habeas corpus, and the right to privacy.

"Unfortunately, these documents are too bizarre for the people who could do something about this threat to take it seriously. Worse, the people who could do something are probably in on it. The genocide you're reading about would appear simply to be a smear campaign against a highly respected, maybe even adored senator. He would certainly spin it to show e-RATS trying to exact revenge. Besides, Crelli is allied with entrepreneurs who own the corporations that control media content, so they'd squash any meaningful assertions and dialogue. I wish it was different."

Gohmpers handed Bernie a photograph of a man swizzling an umbrella-decorated cocktail while tanning on a lounge chair beside a pool. "Do you recognize him?"

Bernie stared at the picture of the old, bald man in a bathing suit. "No, should I?"

"He's FBI Director Juan Vincenzo. Next to him, that's Raji Gomez, the head of the CIA. They were Crelli's guests in Bermuda. Traditional avenues have been shut off. That's why we need you. We have nowhere else to go."

"Shit," Bernie said, scratching his head. "You're really scaring me."

"Now do you understand?" Arlene asked.

"Setting aside the moral issues, isn't genocide bad economics?"

"Objectively, killing indiscriminately or by race or religion would be bad economics because it cuts across economic strata. But if you have more mouths than you can feed and you can selectively eliminate those who are an economic burden, well …"

"Mark would never support that. He'd die first."

"Now you understand why you need us."

"But …"

"Long before your son discovers what Andy is doing, he'll be incriminated, and his life will be in jeopardy."

"From who?"

"He only has to fear Andy if the coup is successful." Arlene responded. "If Andy fails, Mark will be a traitor, and his life will be forfeit. Today, Andy needs him. Mark is energetic and charismatic, and he attracts young voters. He's passionate, believing so strongly in what he does that he persuades doubters by the sheer force of his sincerity. He's also an original thinker with excellent problem-solving capabilities. But he's naïve and hasn't seen through Andy. And he probably won't until it's too late. He bought into a fantasy and can't comprehend how Andy intends to pervert it."

"But suppose you're wrong, Arlene? What if Crelli is a patriot who only wants what's best for America? By interfering, you'll be hurting millions. What about that town in Ohio? It isn't corrupt. According to Mark, the results are spectacular, and the townspeople are thriving."

"Wharton? Mark's right. With Crelli Enterprises leading the way, their schools have improved, crime has all but been eliminated, and employment is increasing. Mark negotiated with local and state government officials to cut taxes and infrastructure costs on the Crelli manufacturing facility there. In exchange, Crelli Enterprises has taken over services for the community. It is a monumentally successful endeavor."

"It's a great concept. If you're wrong, we lose successes like Wharton."

"It's a risk," Arlene nodded. "The entrepreneurs allied with Andy are using the Wharton model to privatize state and local services across the country. It's always been their desire to socialize risk and privatize profits. Once the profits have been squeezed out, they'll eliminate services and let the towns fend for themselves. Andy is an autocratic, libertarian capitalist who wants to run America like a for-profit business, and there's no place for fairness or equality in that model. If Mark was in charge, I'm certain it would be different. But in his position, at his age, he can't take Andy on, even if he wanted to. I doubt anyone can. Andy's the most passionate and focused businessman you'll ever meet and he always imposes his will. Trust me. Mark's dreams will become a nightmare."

"The Constitution ..."

"The Constitution was written at a time when communication was dispersed by horse or sail, and people were interested in the experiment called democracy." Gohmpers clarified. "We don't know all of it, but Crelli will circumvent the Constitution."

Arlene interrupted. "Andy is an idealist. He believes that business must run the country, that the time is right, and he has the business model to do it."

Gohmpers continued. "Have you heard of Michael Ely?"

"No."

"Ely is the former mayor of Wharton. He lost his re-election bid last year to a man named Harold West, an employee at Crelli Enterprises and a member of the new Entrepreneur Party. Even though there's a recession, Ely was a well-liked incumbent Republican running for re-election in a prosperous Republican town. West beat him, handily."

"That doesn't mean anything. The Entrepreneur Party is a group of wing nuts. Maybe this West guy found a constituency in Ohio. Anything can happen in politics."

"In which case, there are more wing nuts than we know because," Arlene explained, "to our knowledge, more than one hundred closet members of the Entrepreneur Party have been elected to Congress as either Republicans or Democrats. Even now they're serving on critical committees and neither party's leadership suspects a thing."

"Well tell them." Bernie was exasperated.

"I'll buy you a ticket. Fly to Washington and explain this to them," Gohmpers said, adding to Arlene's comments. "At the core of all religions is the belief that you should do unto others as you would have them do unto you. It's God's Golden Rule because from that premise, societies grow. But those on welfare and needing assistance are the only constituency in America who can't elect representatives. It wasn't always so, but money has corrupted things. Today the world is in such a sorry state that is operates with a new Golden Rule: he who has the gold makes the rules. Five years ago, I would have laughed as you laughed earlier about the possibility of someone overthrowing our government. Today, I honestly believe Crelli has more than a puncher's chance. He has the opportunity, the motive, and the resources. He controls the media and so has the marketing support to get elected. He controls a portion of the Congress and once he's elected President, he'll control even more. He'll appoint his own judges all the way to the Supreme Court."

"But you're not certain."

Arlene handed him another folder. It was marked "Bermuda Accords."

He read a paper titled, "Notice to Shareholders," whereby Crelli Enterprises offered to purchase Bonsack DSS, Inc. "Are you saying Crelli had Jim Bonsack killed?"

"I know that Andy has acquired businesses in that manner before."

"Arlene, this is crazy." She nodded in agreement. "But why does he want them?"

"For their technology and to reduce competition," she said, looking weary. "Bucky Duke's company PAI has some very sophisticated artificial-intelligence protocols. Full disclosure, I developed those protocols and Duke stole them from me. It was Bonsack's company, by the way, that completed the ANGS project after Rebecca Morning was let go. Andy needed Bonsack's technology to merge with his own decision-support algorithms so he could create a very sophisticated application that could literally run businesses without human intervention. It's a technology that monitors, reports, and even makes decisions based on its ownership's directives. If Duke had obtained Bonsack's company, it might have slowed Andy's plans, so the technology was stolen and Bonsack killed. Buying his company was a cover. Notice the date. The offer was made a week before Bonsack's murder."

"How did you get your hands on these documents?" Bernie asked.

"We're not without resources," Gohmpers explained. "The have-nots and ain't-gots of the world have one distinct advantage; they're invisible to the wealthy and powerful. They're the ghosts in our economy. I'm talking about housekeepers, maintenance men, trash collectors, secretaries, accountants; people who assist the wealthy but are unseen by them."

"How can a small group forced to hide underground take on Crelli and his machine?"

Gohmpers smiled. "Thanks to Arlene and her technical team, we've managed to stay a step ahead of Duke at PAI, Bonsack, and even Crelli. Arlene has a most remarkable friend, Joad. Joad can penetrate almost any security undetected, evaluate the information, and act on our behalf."

"Act on your behalf? You're talking e-RAT stuff."

"Yes," Arlene responded. "But I like to think of it more like 'Robin Hood dot-com.'"

"We take from the wealthy to help the needy." Gohmpers added. "Will you join us?"

"What would I have to do?"

"Protect your son and stop Crelli. This is the first battle of the information age and you're the warrior we need to fight it."

"I'm not your guy; I'm an accountant, for Christ's sake."

"You're much more." She looked at Gohmpers. "Have I mentioned the Bush Doctrine?"

Bernie nodded. "Once Andy's elected, you'll hear about his corollary to the Bush Doctrine. The Bush Doctrine permits a president to keep the country on perpetual war footing due to terrorist activity. Once Andy is elected, he will make the case that economics is a continuous war fought on a different battlefield, and he'll get Congress to grant him perpetual war powers with which he will make the changes he deems necessary. Bernie, we must stop him, and you're the only one who can convince your son to help us."

"But how?"

"You'll think of something. You should know that ANGS supports Crelli."

Bernie hadn't considered that, but of course, Gorman was in Bermuda.

"ANGS is one of many companies that launder funds and divert resources to Andy. They're a market leader in an industry that has little competition, so the business almost runs itself. This allows the Toms the time to support the coming revolution. Mark's involvement drew us to you. Because of you, Gorman, and Morgan, Omega Station is an ideal location for our headquarters. Please help us. It'll be dangerous, but you'll have unimaginable resources."

"You're persuasive, but I can't ruin my son's career just because you have a hell of a story to tell and seem to be nice people. I'll have to think about it."

"If there was another way to stop Andy, we wouldn't be having this conversation."

"Arlene, do you know what you're asking?"

"Unfortunately, we do, Bernie."

He stared intently at them. "Why not just kill him and be done with it?"

"We're not murderers," Gohmpers answered, "and we can't risk creating a martyr. Even if we were good at it, Crelli is far too well guarded. Right now, our strength is in our anonymity. Two generations ago, an historic string of victories convinced wealthy and connected entrepreneurs and entrepreneur wanna-bes that free-market capitalism was the final evolutionary step in God's holy order. Democracy was the kicker. Elections every two years make the business environment less than ideal, so around the world, in China, Brazil, Russia, many of the Middle Eastern sheikdoms, almost everywhere, autocratic capitalism has sprung up. Look at China. Once a communist power, their leaders serve business today; they provide long-term interests and programs but allow their businesspeople free rein. The world believes that that model is the winner now, not freedom or democracy. Around the world, people have voted with their pocketbooks; they prefer the freedom to consume over other freedoms. Andy is providing America's version. It will look like freedom but it won't be."

Arlene added, "this is a phase that had to come. Our citizens need to see what'll happen when capitalism reaches the extreme and destroys the democratic process. But Andy and his followers must fail so our country can finally lose its awe for what they believe are financial heroes who have grown too rich and powerful. Besides, if it isn't Andy, it'll be someone else. The devil we know, as bad as he might be, is better than the one we don't. Our goal is to stop Andy, but by other means than murder."

"What happens if I can't help you?"

"We won't quit, but no one's in a better position to protect your son than you."

Bernie tried to make sense of it. He looked first at Arlene, and then at Gohmpers. "I can't live here. I have family."

"Live as you have. That's an advantage. But you and your family will be in grave danger if you're discovered, so it's best if you work within the system as long as possible."

"Arlene, that morning … who was waiting for you? Who tried to murder you?"

She glanced down. Without looking up, she said, "It … it was Andy's goon, Reno Soren."

Another piece to add to the puzzle. "I'll talk to Jane. But I warn you, if I find out you haven't been straight with me, I promise, I'll do whatever it takes to take you down."

"Talk to her. But be very careful because the walls, even in your home, have ears."

Chapter 12

Cincinnati, Ohio—2031

His limo took Andy through his Crelli Enterprises corporate complex in rural southwestern Ohio. Here was one of the great pleasures in his life. From the back of his limo, he peered through the raindrops surveying his first true kingdom. Here was the proof he could rule. Here were the first people who respectfully deferred to him and owed their lifestyle to his whims. Returning here never failed to provide that extra little boost for the hard road ahead.

When the limo stopped at the front portico, Reno Soren was waiting at the curb with an oversized umbrella.

"Morning, sir. Good trip?" Andy ducked under the umbrella and out of the rain.

"Yes, very productive. Is Mark ready?"

"Yes, sir."

"Is Gorman here?"

"Yes, sir. He's waiting in his office for you."

They entered the modern glass structure and walked through a private corridor to Gorman's office. As Gorman stood to greet him, Andy dismissed Soren.

"Have a good flight, Senator?"

"Yes, Tom." He removed his wet raincoat and handed it to Gorman, who hung it in the closet. "How do you like your new office?"

"The other board members are jealous, Andrew, but that's the way I like it."

"I'm pleased you're happy. We're in agreement about the kid, just handle it carefully."

"Yes, Senator. About that other point..."

Not wanting to hear it again, Crelli waved dismissively.

"Andrew, I know your view, but I insist. In spite of your feelings, the fact remains that the kid's father attended our meeting. God knows what he heard there. Now I can handle him, but still, he worries me. His whole career the old fart's been as docile as a cow, and then out of the blue he accesses our EVA files—when he had no reason to know they even existed. Christ, he doesn't even have security clearance to access them."

"Why wasn't I told this, Tom? You know I don't like surprises. When did he access the files and what did he do?"

"Before Bermuda. Somehow, he obtained a password. Once he was in, from what we can tell, he had no idea what the application is for. But still, I'm concerned. I always worry when one of my people goes extracurricular. If Mark is truly vital to our plans, we have to be absolutely certain his father doesn't fuck something up."

Andy was about to reply when a call came in. He motioned Tom to silence.

"Yes, Tanya, I just arrived. When? Call if there's a problem. Go."

He signaled Tom that he was back. "Tanya's heading into her discussion with Duke. We'll know in a few hours how Duke responds to our offer. Back to your point—Mark's critical. He follows orders and has the drive and ingenuity to turn ideas into reality. You know what he's done at Wharton. Even though it was over budget, it was worth it. Once we get your funds from the Angel Falls sell-off, we'll be back within guidelines."

"You're confident Mark is who you think he is."

"Tom, Mark's mine."

Gorman nodded. "Apparently, ANGS got the wrong Rosenthal. Okay, Mark's a keeper. But it's imperative we separate him from his father. When we talk to him, we insist he be his own man, remembers his fiduciary responsibilities, that crap. He's young and proud; he'll bite."

"Fine, but don't push too hard. He's on our side and I don't want him having doubts."

"It's not him; it's his old man I'm worried about. If he gets in the way we have to deal with him directly. I have my best contractor monitoring him and I'll apply more pressure. I know Rosenthal, he'll crack. We should prepare Mark for that."

Andy looked at his watch. "How are the presidential plans coming?"

"Perry Mannix from your Senate run has agreed to join us."

"That's great."

"He told me he wants to work one last time at the White House."

Mark was at his desk reviewing e-mails when the senator and Gorman arrived.

"Morning, Andy, Tom."

As usual, Mark deferred, giving Andy his chair while he sat beside Gorman.

"Mark," the senator began, "isn't it time you redecorated? Since you took this office over from me, you haven't changed one thing."

Mark laughed. "I've been too busy. Your office is comfortable enough and I have more important things to do than redecorate. Besides, since Tom redecorated his office, we're out of money."

Andy laughed as Gorman took umbrage at the remark, "I spent what was appropriated."

"I'm kidding, Tom. Hey, I'm surprised you joined us. Is there something wrong, Andy?"

"Nothing, Mark. Tom and I just wanted to clear up some things. We'll be brief. First, I'm sorry about cutting short your trip to Bermuda If I'd known you were bringing family, I would have found someone else to help with Duke."

"No, Andy, really, it was fine. I'm just sorry I couldn't convince Bucky to join the team. The buyout offer was more than fair. It's perplexing why he refused."

"Bucky was being Bucky," Gorman said. "That, and there's an important government contract coming up for bid soon and somehow he got wind of it before we could get our offer to him. He thinks if he wins it, it'll give him leverage. He won't win this bid.

"What's the contract?"

Crelli took out his notes. "The government is continuing to struggle with voting procedures and election result validation, and the media's been working the public into a frenzy over it. The importance of Internet voting has finally registered with the parties and there will be changes. If the project can be completed on schedule, voting in the next presidential election will be via the Mesh—the Internet. Specifically, the contract is to develop an election application, test it, and have it approved well in advance of the election. There isn't much time, but I consider that to our advantage. Mark, your job is to see to it that Crelli Enterprises has the winning bid. It'll be lucrative, so expect the usual players to be involved."

Andy continued. "I'll continue to stay in the background, but once you submit your proposal, I'll be there to ensure we win."

"And Mark," Gorman added, "because of this, we're canceling the special board meeting you requested to discuss the social agenda you've been pressing for in your interviews and articles. You're pushing the right buttons, but that agenda has to wait—Andrew is evaluating a presidential run, and we need the social agenda to be fresh."

"As long as the agenda moves forward, I'm good." Mark offered his mentor his hand. "Congratulations, Andy. It goes without saying that you have my complete support. You'll win. The clowns who've already declared for the nomination better get out of the way because you'll be a great president. When do you announce?"

"I have e-RAT issues that need handling, but I'll probably throw my hat in by spring."

"It will be a pleasure campaigning for you."

Gorman interrupted, "The board is pleased with the job you're doing, Mark. Honestly, I had my doubts initially—you were young and untested, but I admit I was wrong. There is an issue that concerns us. It's delicate, so we're not meeting as a full board to discuss it."

"What is it, Tom?" Mark was concerned, because he thought everything was going well.

"It's your father. We're concerned he has too much influence on you."

Baffled, Mark sat back, considering his response. "Tom, I've been working with you and the board for years now. You have no basis for this, and frankly, no right to say it. If you don't trust my judgment and the job I'm doing, get the votes and make a change. If you have specific concerns, ask away. This is a personal shot, and I'm disappointed you'd take it—even behind closed doors. Andy?"

The senator responded calmly. "Tom, do you have reason for raising this concern? Has Mark done anything to cause you to question his leadership and fiduciary responsibility?"

"No, no, of course not. I'm sorry, I was out of line. Forgive me, I overreacted. There have been some things … your father's behavior in Bermuda and at other recent events … again, I'm sorry, I shouldn't have painted both of you with the same brush. I apologize."

"Apology accepted. Tom, if you doubt my work, voice your concerns. I love my dad. I'm not embarrassed to say it but first and foremost, I'm a professional and my own man." Mark paused, "What's wrong with him?"

"I shouldn't get involved but I've known you and your family for so long that, quite frankly, you're very important to me. Recently—now this is confidential so I don't want you talking to him about it—he's been acting strangely, very unreliably. He behaves like everyone is plotting against him. He questions even the simplest directions and complains about the motives of my management team. For some reason we don't understand, he's stopped being a team player. Then, recently, we caught him tampering with secure personnel files. That alone is grounds for termination, but he's a member of my corporate family so, of course, we're worried about him. Something is going on that's making him paranoid and he needs help."

"That doesn't sound like my father. Is his job secure?"

"I'm nothing if not loyal so, yes, his position is secure. At least for now. Your relationship with him is your relationship, it isn't really my business, but I caution you to remember your responsibilities and to not discuss business with him or get involved in his delusions."

"We talk about business, but I'd never discuss confidential company business with him. Some of this is my fault. I've been working so hard; I haven't spent much time with him. I'll talk with Mom about it. You and Andy must know I'd never compromise the company."

Andy looked at his watch. "Tom, I don't see a problem here. I sensed you were over-reacting. Mark, you understand that Tom has to bring these things up, but it's behind us now. I have to catch a flight. Say, are you and Reno communicating alright?"

"Yes, sir, why?"

"Nothing, except I'll be spending more time on my political agenda and Reno will be traveling with me. You and I need separation because of the Internet Voting Contract so it'll be better if you and I communicate through Reno. I'm not concerned about you. You understand?"

"Of course, have a productive trip, Andy, or should I call you, Mr. President?"

"Andy's fine for now, thanks Mark." The senator smiled. "Let's go, Tom."

Once alone, the more Mark thought about the discussion, the angrier he got. Their message was clear. Because of his dad, there was a diminishment of trust in the job he was doing and, regardless of what Andy said, it was serious. If it hadn't been, Andy wouldn't have visited or insisted Reno become the middleman.

He struggled to put it behind him so he could clear his mind and refocus on work. It was late when the cleaning staff entered his office.

A small woman in overalls knocked.

"Excuse me, sir, may we vacuum and empty the trash?

"Certainly."

As the woman and her assistant cleaned, he finalized his work. As the cleaning people were about to leave, the woman stooped to pick up a paper from the rug. "Excuse me, sir, you dropped this."

"Um, thanks."

She handed it to him and walked out. "Enjoy your evening, sir."

He ignored the paper until he was ready to leave. He unfolded it, absentmindedly. It was a map of the Crelli headquarters' basement, with a room labeled "e-RATS" pencil in.

Concerned, he left his office and followed the map down the long, empty basement corridors to a section marked "Secure" where an armed, uniformed guard was stationed at the door.

"Excuse me, I'm Mark Rosenthal, the CEO. Can you open the door for me?"

"Can I see your badge, sir?"

He handed his badge to the guard who looked at it and then waved it at the security reader. The red light above the door was unchanged, and the guard returned the card. "Sorry, sir, you don't have clearance."

"But I'm the CEO. This is my company."

"And a very good company it is, but sorry, sir, I can't let you pass."

"Who do I see to get clearance?"

"Sir, you can request admittance through Reno Soren, the head of security."

"But Reno works for me."

"That should make it easier, sir."

Confused and concerned, Mark left. When he returned to his office, he left a message for Reno. Afterward, another thought crossed his mind. Where did that map come from?

Chapter 13

Indianapolis—2031

Ever'body might be just one big soul,
Well it looks that a-way to me.
Everywhere that you look, in the day or night,
That's where I'm a-gonna be, Ma,
That's where I'm a-gonna be.

Wherever little children are hungry and cry,
Wherever people ain't free.
Wherever men are fightin' for their rights,
That's where I'm a-gonna be, Ma,
That's where I'm -gonna be.

—Woody Guthrie, "The Ballad of Tom Joad"

Bernie returned to Omega Station. Arlene met him at the entrance and took him inside.

"Well?" she asked.

"This is about my son. I'm in for now."

"What did Jane say?"

"I had trouble finding the right words. I'm always complaining about something, and to her this would be just another rant about nothing."

"This is real, Bernie. You have to make her understand."

"I will, Arlene, in my time. Now what?"

She poured two glasses of juice and raised her glass in a toast. "To freedom."

He tapped his glass gently against hers. "How about to success, whatever that means? Yesterday, Gohmpers told me a compelling story. I'm still not convinced it's as bleak as he painted it, but I need to know the rest. If he's even close to being correct, Mark is ... well, tell me about Gohmpers. Who is he, and why should I believe him?"

"I can't tell you much."

"Can't, or won't?"

"I owe him my life and I trust his motives."

"That's all you have?"

"What he was before isn't important. He saved my life."

Bernie took a sip of juice. "I believe you believe. Maybe once I know what he knows—all of it—I'll come to the same conclusion."

"We're fighting the right fight."

"Arlene, the clock's ticking. I want to call Mark and discuss this with him, but I can't until I know what I'm talking about."

"Don't talk to him yet, it's too soon. Hear us out first. But even when you're certain we're right, Mark won't be receptive because of his position and his trust in Andy."

"I understand why you think that, but Mark listens to me." He looked around the station. "Where's Gohmpers?"

"He spends a lot of time on the streets helping the poor. I can explain our operations here. Most of it is my doing."

"Like what?"

"Like the technology."

"Before that, tell me about you and Crelli."

She paused for a second, letting out a deep breath while the color drained from her face. "What do you want to know?" Her voice was guarded.

"I figured that if you knew Soren, you probably knew Crelli. Where'd you meet him?"

"It was about fifteen years ago. I was in Palo Alto on a fellowship at a PARCplace research lab. I had just delivered a speech on next-generation artificial-intelligence applications that emulate human thought processes. Anyway, this great-looking guy stays afterward and asks me some interesting questions. We end up going to dinner. I'm not usually that easy, but he was very intense and interesting. Besides, I was starving."

"Crelli?"

"In the perfectly bronzed flesh. Anyway, he was curious about my work. His interest surprised me, so I tested him. He wasn't technical, but his mind worked, works I should say, at another level—he thinks strategically. After that, we met frequently and talked about various commercial applications. He even took me golfing once. He was learning to play because he felt it would improve his business networking. He never enjoyed golf, but soon after he started, he was a really good golfer. He liked to kid me that he loved golf because it was so much like work. Regardless how much you accomplish, you end up feeling more frustrated than when you started."

"The guy sounds like quite a card."

"Don't ever underestimate him. Even back then, he outworked the few he couldn't out-think. Andy is on top of everything. He's not a monster, not in the way people think of monsters. Off the clock, he's a genuinely nice guy. He's just rarely off the clock. Where was I?"

"Golfing."

"He proposed I leave the lab and form a company with him. After some coaxing, I agreed. We started Crelli, Klaatu and Associates."

Something clicked in Bernie's mind. "CKA? In Bermuda, someone introduced Crelli as the co-founder of a company called CKA. CKA was you?"

"Yes. He knew everyone, including venture capitalists that supplied early financing. He found businesses that contracted with us. Because of his ability to sell, CKA got hot quickly, and our cash reserves grew. It was an amazing time. Andy seemed to be in the right place at the right time, every time. The early projects were simple. I developed artificial-intelligence functionality that enabled computers to control the day-to-day business operations, decision making from the shop floor to the corporate executive. Then Andy brought in some real power players with significantly more sophisticated needs, many with security and surveillance requirements. They paid whatever he asked. I was embarrassed by how high our fees were, but Andy said we deserved them. As we grew, he kept pushing me to bring in people, but I rarely had the time to interview. His projects got grander, and our clients larger and more anonymous. I struggled to keep up."

"So what happened?"

"By a stroke of luck, I found and hired the twins."

"The twins?"

"Damon and Damian Hegel. They're legends in the grid-computing world of the Mesh and gods in the gaming industry. They received funding through a lab at the University of Illinois to develop computers that had tactile-audio-visual inference capabilities."

"What's that?"

"Computers capable of independently recognizing and interacting with what they see, touch, or hear—very high-end stuff. You should be honored to meet them, they're truly extraordinary. Anyway, they took the funding but broadened the definition of the project, exploring perception and empathy, eventually conceptualizing an entity that I created who could think and feel like a human being—beyond Turing. But that's the twins, always going off on tangents."

"What's Turing?"

"It's a measure of a computer's capability to think independently. Basically, you blind test a computer's response against that of a human being, to the extent that a blinded observer can't distinguish between their responses. I hired the twins and we turned the concept into reality and passed the Turing test early. Almost immediately, Andy understood what that breakthrough meant, and once we'd established our reputation, the projects he found for us started getting darker and scarier, to a point where I questioned what we were really doing."

"What do you mean?"

"Some governments were involved without their knowledge."

"Whoa?" It was all Bernie could say. He noticed her hands trembling.

Nervously, she brushed stray strands of blonde hair behind her ear. "We live in a morally complex time and I know, better than most, what cyber warfare can do. Remember, we had the electrical grid shutdown in Texas. They were without power for a week. We had our air control system corrupted but no lives were lost. My company worked hard to build America's cyber defenses so we couldn't be attacked but when we started receiving projects that put us on the offensive against other countries and permitted us to spy domestically like the ANGS project, I drew the line. At that point, my relationship with Andy reached a critical point. Andy wanted me to be—how should I say this—a more committed," she said at last. "He was engaged to Maddie and for political reasons was unwilling to break it off, but what he wanted for us just wasn't right for me, so I declined. That's when I learned an important lesson. Andy doesn't accept rejection—the rage, and even the tears. He was younger; I don't think he acts that way today but, of course, he doesn't need to. Anyway, it was discomforting.

"When he realized he couldn't have me, he decided to take control of our company. Andy never lets anything get in the way of his plans, so he started putting pressure on me, accusing me of not being sufficiently committed and not believing in him, things like that. He hoped I'd get frustrated and I'd sell out, but I persevered until eventually, he backed off. I was relieved and thankful. Through all our difficulties, I felt he respected me and recognized my value given all I put into CKA. When we had our occasional business dinners, he was nice. But I received my graduate degree in Andy Crelli the hard way.

"We had a CKA picnic at his mother's farm on a rural lake in Kentucky, fried chicken, swimming, and the obligatory rallying speeches. I was floating on an inner tube out on the lake reading a romance novel when I saw Damian, that's one of the twins, talking to him. They were all smiles, in the end shaking hands. Later, I went waterskiing with a small group. Andy was in the captain's chair, of course. As I should have expected, he made the event competitive."

"He wanted to embarrass you.'"

The color drained from her face and she spoke in a whisper. "At the time, I felt I was as competitive as he was, but I was so wrong. When it was my turn, regardless what he did, I committed to staying up and I did. I jumped wakes and rode all the whipsaws."

"I didn't know there was water in Kansas."

"It's a sore subject, given the droughts ... but when I was young, I learned to water-ski on a big lake north of Abilene."

"So it sounds like you won."

She looked down and shook her head as if trying not to remember more. "I've come to understand that with Andy, not losing is the best you can do." A tear formed in her right eye and crept down her cheek. Her hand trembled as she wiped the tear away. She jammed her hand against her side until the shaking stopped.

Seeing her pain, he wanted to end the conversation, but couldn't. "I'm sorry," he said. "I have to know."

She pursed her lips and nodded. Looking down, she continued, "it was late afternoon by then and he drove the boat to a secluded part of the lake, where he set me up for a whipsaw that would bring me close to shore. He expected me to bail. I was skiing into the sun and my trajectory took me maybe twenty feet from the shoreline, but I stayed with it. What I didn't know was that there were pilings, some submerged, from an abandoned dock. I never saw them. Somehow, at maybe thirty miles an hour, I avoided direct contact. I may have jumped or bailed, I don't remember. But I'd have died if I hadn't done whatever it was I did."

A chill caused Bernie to tremble. "What happened?"

The pain in her voice cut at his heart. "I don't remember anything. They told me I was bobbing facedown when Andy dove into the water to rescue me. When he turned me over, he threw up. Everyone thought I was dead. My hips were turned at a 90-degree angle with both legs and one arm severely broken. My face was pulp, and a rib punctured a lung. My days as a beauty queen were over."

"My god."

"We were in the middle of nowhere. Andy stayed on the phone getting instructions how to stabilize me until a helicopter shuttled me to a Louisville hospital. I was in a coma for almost a month. When I came out, I was in excruciating pain, most of my face and body were bandaged, and my jaw was wired shut. I heard my mother's voice in the room, and Andy's, too. I overheard a nurse telling them to keep shiny objects from me. My faith in God wasn't strong, but it was all I had to hold on to.

"One day my mom left a spoon on the table when she went to talk with a doctor. I struggled to peel bandages from my face, and used the spoon to look." Arlene paused as dry heaves overtook her. He put his hand on her shoulder, but she shrugged it off and continued.

"I could see only out of my right eye. With the spoon, I discovered why. My left was filled with a white substance that looked like cottage cheese. There were stitches all the way around my nose. It had been torn off and sewn back on." Pale and sweating, she paused again. "The left side of my face was caved in. The only way I could react was by shrieking horrible sounds through wired-shut jaws." She wiped perspiration from her brow.

"I'm sorry. I had no idea."

"No, you have to know who Andy is, what he's capable of. Give me a second."

He nodded and she staggered over to get more juice. She returned with it and continued.

"Where was I? Yes, the spoon. I was hysterical. I tore at my nose, tore it off, ripped through the sutures. There was blood everywhere. I live below ground, in part because it's better for my nerves, but sometimes, when it's too quiet, I can still hear myself screaming. Thank God, the nurse gave me a sedative."

Horrified, Bernie just stared. He searched her face for scars. When she noticed, he looked away, embarrassed. "But you're—beautiful, Arlene. You have a small scar on the bridge of your nose and maybe a small one near your hairline. How could …?"

"Ah, I see." She lowered her head as if to pray and put her hand over her left eye. Then she looked up. "See?"

He recoiled in horror. The lid of her left eye was not quite closed and curved inward. Inside the socket, there was electronic circuitry. In her palm was a prosthetic eyeball. He forced himself not to be sick. "Jesus Christ, Arlene!"

She bowed her head and turned away again. When she turned back her eyeball was in place, her beauty somewhat restored. "I'm sorry. I shouldn't have done that," she said softly.

"No, I had to know," he whispered, his stomach queasy and his mouth dry.

"What you see now is nineteen surgeries later. They rebuilt my face. The bottom half of me is more nano-fiber and titanium than bone. My eye and hands are state-of-the-art bionics that enhance performance, but I have migraines that drill through my brain and seem to last forever. They're my penance. Medication helps, but in order to function I have to be in environments with as little noise as possible. I still limp a little, but I cover it pretty well. Basically, I'm more illusion than real, but by the grace of God my brain wasn't affected, or if it was, I can't tell. What you see definitely isn't what you get."

"What happened afterward?"

"Andy never returned to the hospital. There was an inconsequential police investigation, and the incident was ruled an accident. He sold CKA and, to complete the deal, Andy's lawyers pressured me into settling for less than my share of the company. I needed whatever proceeds I could get to pay my medical bills—insurance didn't begin to cover them. I'm not complaining. Altogether, it was enough to build this amalgamated woman you see before you. Once I was confident enough to rejoin the world, I agreed to work for another consulting company. Andy must have set that up, but I never found out for sure. They were willing to provide ongoing medical coverage for physical therapy and pain medication. The odd thing was that their management never asked me to *do* anything, even after I recovered. Not until the ANGS engagement."

"Do you ever leave here?"

"Once in a while I slip out at night to get some fresh air or to acquire equipment we need. You'll see why soon. Other than that, there's no reason to go."

"Because of that accident, you must hate Crelli."

She stared at him incredulously. "That was no accident."

He returned her stare. "You think he tried to kill you so you wouldn't develop software?"

"More than that, he didn't want me to develop anything for anyone else. He was already angry that I'd rejected him, and we were on to something big. The twins and I had made some breakthroughs. We developed a prototype system we called Ray that had astounding promise—maybe too astounding. Our customers' requirements had become intrusive and certainly illegal, but we managed to comply with enough of them to see where this was going. I had reservations about how Andy wanted to use Ray and I backed off. Andy figured the twins could finish the development and he wanted me out before I had a chance to sabotage the work or convince the twins not to help. Besides, he needed the funds the CKA sale would generate to start his business empire. A waterskiing accident was the perfect answer. It was his lake after all."

Her horror story was reason enough to fear for Mark. "I'm sorry. You must hate him."

"I don't. I've been through a lot and Gohmpers has helped me through much of it. Because of him and my girlfriend, I'm not the person I was. In a way, I understand Andy. He's totally self-absorbed but there's good there too so I don't hate him. But he must be stopped, not just for your sake and your son's, for the millions of Americans who don't deserve to die."

You're that sure he'll do it?" She nodded, disconsolately. He changed the subject. "Are the twins still working for him?"

The sadness in her face melted away. With all the surgery, it was amazing she could express anything.

"Come." She stood and headed down another corridor. At the other end were a series of doors. She approached one. "Joad, access, please," she said, and the door opened. Inside, he saw two men with long, flowing, sparse red hair sitting at adjoining desks, staring deeply at multi-screen computer arrays.

Without turning, they said, in unison, "Greetings, earthlings."

The men were middle-aged and identical, except in dress. One wore a flowered shirt and dress shorts while the other wore a t-shirt and army fatigues. Strewn between them were bottles of cola and empty bags of popcorn. Twinkie wrappers dotted the floor.

"This is Bernie Rosenthal," Arlene said.

"Yes, we know. I'm Damon," said one, extending his hand.

"I'm Damian," said the other, extending his.

He shook their hands. "You saved Arlene from Reno Soren." They nodded. "She told me about the CKA picnic and the skiing accident. Crelli talked to you. What did he want?"

Damian looked to Arlene. She nodded. "Mr. Crelli asked me where we stood with Ray. He wanted to know how involved Arlene was in the actual development. I told him …" His voice trailed off. A look of pain appeared in his eyes, and he glanced again at Arlene.

"Damian, it's okay," she said softly.

"I told him we were doing the development, while Arlene was working on integration."

"Did he assume Arlene was expendable?"

Damian glanced down and nodded slowly. "Mr. Crelli was a hell of a nice guy when he needed you but a real mother… when he didn't. He planned that boat thing way before the picnic. I know it. He was already negotiating to sell the company."

"Why did you finally leave him?"

"At the time, we thought what happened to Arlene was an accident, but we had second thoughts after the way he treated her when she was in a coma," Damon said. "She was his partner, and he just bailed on her. What kind of behavior was that? While she was in the hospital, he started pressing us to complete the heavy-duty decryption stuff. That's when we knew something was wrong."

"What decryption stuff?"

"Ray was a first generation MIC—Mobile Intelligent Crawler. He could enter any portal, insinuate himself into any system, decipher access requirements, become friendly, and then make real-time judgments about the contents, including performing tasks as needed to accomplish a predetermined set of objectives. He'd exit the host without leaving a trail."

"That's possible?"

They looked at one another. "Yeah, actually," Damon said. He smiled and gave his brother a quick high five.

"How did Crelli justify creating something like that?"

"It evolved." Damian clarified, "this was new stuff. At first, the government had no idea what we were doing; it just kept giving us contracts with more intensive surveillance requirements. Remember, back then, politicians were scared shitless of terrorists and hackers. Arlene didn't like it and put the breaks on us as we were putting the finishing touches on a fully evolved crawler. Unhappy with her resistance, Mr. Crelli tried to get us to finish by lying about the business applications we were enhancing. Arlene knew what we were doing had no legitimate business purpose. He told us he'd landed a large contract with the Department of Homeland Security—the people who look so hard they see plots against America everywhere. They eavesdrop on all communications devices. You've heard of Echelon and Omnivore?"

"No."

"They've heard of you," Damon laughed.

"Echelon and Omnivore," Damian explained, "are sophisticated operational eavesdropping systems. Homeland Security developed Echelon with help from England, Australia, and New Zealand. It's used to intercept and decipher all wireless communication, anywhere on Earth. I mean anywhere. It processes information using a sophisticated algorithm and an extensive database to determine if any discussions should be considered threats against the United States or its allies. When it discovers inappropriate words or phrases, it alerts operatives who follow up. Omnivore basically does the same stuff on any cable-based systems still in service. We know because we helped write the code for earlier generations."

"You created the ultimate Big Brother?"

"Yeah, yeah, we know, Uncle Sam's watching you from under your bed and all that. But did you ever ask yourself why, in a large, free country like America, where people come and go as they please, and have the freedom to assemble and carry weapons, crime is mostly contained to relatively small, so-called high-crime areas?"

"And why there's so little terrorist activity?" Damian added. "After the terrorist attacks earlier in the century, funding for electronic surveillance prevention increased significantly. Hell, it paid for our high school, college, and post-college educations. Today, most terrorist activity and criminal behavior are uncovered early and the culprits detained well before their plots mature. What Crelli is doing with his e-SWAT Task Force is simple. He gets all the acclaim because most people don't know how easy it is with our crawler."

"Mr. Crelli convinced us that Homeland Security needed Ray's functionality expanded," Damon continued. "We were kind of okay with that. It's one thing for the government to track communications to prevent crime and terrorism; it's another to spy for personal reasons and to steal commercial applications. Mr. Crelli made it sound patriotic. He almost convinced us."

"How did you discover he was lying?"

The twins gave each other mischievous glances. "We checked," Damon said.

"Checked?"

"We broke into Homeland Security files to locate their vendor contract data. There was nothing there—no deal, not even a proposal for us to bid on."

"So he was lying."

"Absolutamente. We were developing Ray for his use almost from the beginning, although he managed to find big-time support and incredible funding. He had us fooled for the longest time."

"Why did you leave?"

"We figured if Mr. Crelli tried to kill Arlene, eventually, he'd do the same to us. Before the sale to DDA, we decided to hang some code on Ray so they couldn't use what we'd built. One night, we returned to the office to complete the code, but some men we didn't recognize were already there. We took off and never came back."

Arlene clarified, "The men were sent by Buchanan Duke."

"The guy who was with Jim Bonsack when he was murdered."

"Yes," Arlene said. "Duke stole our documentation and based his next-generation technology on it. Of course it wasn't as good, the twins saw to that. Duke made it look like it was his original development, but nobody writes code like the twins."

Bernie was confused. "Let me get this straight. Now, there are two copies of Ray—one that Crelli owns and an inferior code that Duke stole. I thought I read that Duke was going to buy Bonsack's company. Is that why Crelli intervened and killed Bonsack?"

"Yes, that's mostly right," Arlene confirmed. "By design, the media reported it wrong."

"Why didn't Crelli just kill Duke, too?"

"We believe they were working together on something. Anyway, the code

Andy has is now called Gecko. He's hired some sharp foreign programmers to work on it and is funding it to the hilt."

Damon continued. "After Ray was stolen, Damian and I were scared to death. We hid with friends until we received a message from Gohmpers. Somehow, he found out about Ray/Gecko and wanted to understand it better. He turned out to be a great guy. We trusted him and began working for him. He wanted us to develop something to neutralize Gecko."

"Then Arlene began working here for ANGS, and we became aware of it," Damian added. "We were happy that she was okay, but worried for her safety, we monitored her. We saw Soren's attack. When he put her in that tank, we rushed to get her and take her to the hospital. Soren's a bad man."

"But there weren't any hospital records."

"There were, Bernie, but if they'd been found, we would've been very disappointed."

"Okay?" Confused, Bernie stared at the twin's computer consoles and other sophisticated equipment. "That still leaves Crelli with Gecko and Duke with a copy of Ray."

Damon offered Bernie a Twinkie. He declined. "Yes and we have Joad."

"Joad? I've heard that word. What is it?"

"She. It's a she. Joad is generations more sophisticated than Ray. She's what we call a MISI—Mobile, Independent, Sustaining Intelligence. We wanted to call her "Missy," but she was indignant, so Gohmpers named her after Tom Joad, the main character in the John Steinbeck novel, *The Grapes of Wrath*. That, she accepted."

"I don't know what that means. Now there's a third entity?"

"Yes."

"What if she falls into the wrong hands like the others?"

They chuckled. "Can't happen. Joad can't be taken."

"Can't?"

"She's like nothing ever devised. We learned our lesson when Duke's people stole our code for Ray. There would be real danger if Mr. Crelli finds out about her, or if she ended up in someone else's shop, so we developed a foolproof way to ensure security. She's truly Mesh-mobile and independent."

"I guess I understand Mesh-mobile, but you'll have to clarify independent."

"She makes her own decisions. She's intelligent, self-aware and nimble enough to overcome any known level of security. She's able to live in computer kernels anywhere. She moves freely, disassembling and reassembling herself, even copying herself for backup—anything she feels she needs to do. There are no disks or manuals, no documentation of any kind for anyone to find. Joad's perfectly secure. Even we're not sure where she is."

Arlene interrupted proudly, "maybe this helps. I know it tickles me." She covered her mouth and laughed to herself. "When we were testing her ability to maintain integrity from computer to computer, she told us it felt like she was having an out-of-mind experience."

Damon laughed. "Get it, not an out-of-body experience, an out-of-mind one."

"I think I get it but I don't understand. You refer to her like she's a person."

"She is," said Damon.

"For sure," echoed Damian.

"And she listens to you?"

"If she does, it's because she respects us," Damon said.

"You mean by that that she recognizes passwords and access codes?"

"No," Arlene explained. "She knows us like people know people. Joad is artificial intelligence at the level of consciousness—real sentience. I hate to discuss her so clinically."

He still wasn't sure what they were describing.

"Our breakthrough," Arlene added, "was the Empath Driver that enables her to feel in her own way. The twins led the development. She's watching us right now, listening, and evaluating our discussion. Unless she grants it, you couldn't leave this place on your own, much less tamper with anything here."

"So," he asked, "when do I meet her?"

"Joad, say hello," Arlene spoke conversationally.

There was a moment of silence, and then a pleasant feminine voice emerged from several speakers around the room. "I thought he'd be taller."

He looked at Arlene. "I'm sorry, what?"

"Sometimes she's a smart-ass. Consciousness is a bitch. Joad, be civil and apologize."

"Men should apologize. Bernie, do you know why women don't blink during foreplay?"

"Uh, no I don't," he responded.

"They don't have time. Apologize for that."

In spite of himself, he smiled. Damon whispered, "she's showing off."

"I heard that. Bernie, do you know why Damon crossed the road?"

"I haven't a clue."

"He heard the chicken was a slut."

The twins clapped and laughed. Bernie, not knowing what to expect (but certainly not this), was confused. With so much on the line, what Arlene called the most powerful computer on earth was telling jokes. "You should do stand-up," he said.

"I can't. I don't have a leg to stand on. Arlene, I like him. He is a good straight man."

"Are you always this cynical about men?"

"I share morning lattes with Arlene."

Arlene blushed and nodded sheepishly. "I'm her mother and her older sister."

"Arlene is my best friend and Crelli tried to kill her twice."

"Crelli is a bad example. I like to believe men are more caring."

"You think? How many caring men does it take to do the dishes?"

"I don't know."

"Both."

"That's me and Damon," Damian said grinning.

"You two don't even use dishes. You eat popcorn and Twinkies and never clean up after yourselves. You're perfect examples of the difference between men and government bonds."

"Yeah?" Damon replied, already laughing.

"Bonds eventually mature."

Bernie didn't want to, but he laughed. Arlene, too, was smiling. "Why'd you give her a sense of humor?" he asked.

"I'm not sure we actually gave it to her. Humor was one of our major developmental coups. It requires insight as well as an understanding of context. If she could joke, not just memorize jokes but relate humor to conversations or situations, we felt she could develop empathetic skills. We didn't anticipate she'd take to it with such enthusiasm. Now that she's able to develop on her own without our programming, she's off the charts. Sometimes we know she's being funny, but we don't understand her references."

"The poor dears lack a sophisticated sense of humor and they criticize me for that shortcoming."

He looked at the console. "What else do you do, Joad?"

"Are you propositioning me?"

"No, I didn't mean …"

"Joad, it's time to be serious," Arlene said.

"Bernie, do you know why they're trying to move the clock at Big Ben into the Leaning Tower of Pisa?"

"I didn't realize they were."

"What good is the time without the inclination?" With that Joad laughed. It seemed a human sound.

"I'll give you a taste of what she can do," Arlene said, smiling. "Joad, please show Mr. Rosenthal how you generate income."

Within seconds, information appeared on a monitor. Bernie stared incredulously at it. "Is that really Tom Gorman's retirement account?"

"It is. I also assessed your secretary, Carolyn's favorite things and took the liberty of ordering her a carton of Jamaican Blue Coffee. It should arrive tomorrow and has been charged to Tom Gorman's retirement account, not that he'll notice. And your wife's taste in clothes is classic. I have evaluated her purchasing history and picked out a little number for her in red, she has too little red, given the make-up she uses. She needs to skew more to red, maybe burgundy. It will show off her green eyes. Morgan paid for the dress. How did I do?"

Arlene smiled and replied. "I'm sure Bernie thanks you, Joad. She turned to Bernie. "You have no idea how much financial chicanery your bosses have been involved in. These guys aren't the brightest stars in the sky, but their fortunes have grown far beyond what ANGS provides. When we looked into it, we uncovered private accounts in the Cayman Islands and in Taiwan. They've stashed hundreds of millions of untaxed dollars into these accounts which they use to fund political initiatives and their future."

A wave of sadness hit him. "I'm the CFO. That says a lot about me."

"Without me, you're as helpless as an investor on Wall Street." Joad replied.

That didn't cheer him.

"Joad periodically visits these accounts …" Damon continued.

"And others that businessmen have funded illegally," Damian finished the thought.

"These accounts provide us with the means to run our operations," Arlene clarified.

"And the Toms never miss it?"

"I never think to mention it to them," Joad added.

"That seems prudent," said Bernie.

"I control the financial reporting for these accounts, so they believe the funds are still there. Only when they try to withdraw will they find the money gone. That's humor," Joad laughed.

Bernie smiled. "I suppose so. You have no aversion to stealing?"

"Are you questioning my ethics? With so many people living pathetic existences, struggling to make a life for themselves and their families, I sleep well at night if that's what you mean. I'm insensitive to people who stockpile more money than they can ever use just to live luxuriously in the face of those fighting to survive."

"I can't disagree with your sentiment. Fair enough. But that makes you judge and jury for what's right and wrong. Isn't that too much responsibility …?"

"Go ahead. Say it. For a computer."

"I didn't mean …"

"Because of Arlene, no one is more aware of moral and ethical considerations than I am. Humans have yet to accept responsibility for the inequities they create among people. I have to try to change a world that allows some people to make too much more readily than it provides for those who can't earn enough."

"Sorry," Arlene said, blushing a little. "She had to learn from someone. We're trying to help people. Besides, even if your bosses discover their money is missing, who are they going to complain to?"

"Where do you put the funds, and how do you use them?" he asked.

"Small amounts go to a lot of individual accounts, the kind that don't attract attention," Arlene explained. "Gohmpers redirects some of the money to help people in need. The rest is used to finance this operation and help bring justice, where possible. Obviously, when you join us, you will have access to these funds." Arlene paused.

"I've diverted one hundred fifty thousand and two dollars," Joad said proudly, what shall I do with it?"

Bernie couldn't stifle his curiosity. "Why the extra two dollars?"

"It's payday for the twins."

They laughed. "Thanks, Joad, I'm investing mine," Damon said with mock seriousness.

"Why invest when your long-range plans are limited to buying confections?"

"Now children," Arlene said maternally. "Bernie, Joad is powerful and we may look bullet-proof, but we have to be very careful. We don't have the resources to protect ourselves from a physical assault if we're discovered and, as powerful as Joad is, Gecko is growing as they feed him R & D funds and he is capable of uncovering Joad's existence."

Bernie considered what he just learned. "Can Joad help me locate some information?"

Arlene nodded. "Ask her yourself."

"Joad?"

"Terrific, a test-drive. Do you know why it takes a million sperm cells to fertilize one egg?"

"No, why?" he asked.

"Because sperm, like men, won't ask for directions."

"I'll remember that. Are you ready?"

"Okay, just a minute. I have to put on my eyeliner and rouge."

"Are you always this glib?"

"How else, until I can trust again, do I protect myself from shallowness and selfishness?"

This time Arlene's blush was much more noticeable.

"Fair enough. I'll do my best to win your trust. I need a favor. In ANGS' private personnel files there's a file designated EVA. Can you access ...?"

Before he could finish, the list of files he had located using the backdoor password Ennis Parker gave him appeared on the screen.

"Can you open the file called "Eyes Only"?

Instantly, the file opened and the screen changed to a menu. He leaned in closer and read the menu items. One was designated "Crelli Correspondence". "Open that."

There was brief silence. "Gecko's monitoring. I have to be very careful."

"Gecko is active now?"

"He's always active. He lacks sophistication, but for straight-ahead bull-headedness and raw power, he's a real stud. So far, I've been able to use my feminine wiles to work around him."

"So Gecko won't know what you're doing?"

"Ships passing in the night," Joad offered.

The files listed in the "Crelli Correspondence" folder were sorted by subject. He scanned the list and read some relevant letters aloud. With each letter his shoulders slumped a little more. Here was additional evidence supporting the Bermuda papers. The horror that Andy Crelli intended to orchestrate was difficult to accept. Crelli had but one purpose: to achieve absolute power so he could create the best possible business environment, regardless of the suffering that he caused.

Everything supported Gohmpers's conclusions, but the information was craftily constructed. There were no names, dates or anything specifically tying Crelli, Gorman, or any of their staff to this. It was clear Crelli had successfully infiltrated and co-opted both political parties. Once he held the necessary majorities, he was going to begin the process of dismantling the democratic process and eliminate absolutely all remnants of a welfare state.

When Bernie finished, he stared at the somber faces around him. Arlene met his stare and shrugged. "A nightmare," she said at last. She reached out and handed Bernie the folder from Bermuda with the damning documentation. "Someday, you'll need to show this to your son."

He took the files and nodded. He remembered that evening at work when something was interfering with the changes he was making to data in the EVA files. He asked her about it.

"Gecko," Arlene told him. "Gorman and Andy know you've been snooping around."

"Jesus, what do I do?"

"Keep a low profile and do nothing unless you're here, under our protection." Arlene advised. "And you must discuss this with your wife."

"I will, when I'm comfortable with all the intimate details."

"If it's intimacy you want," Joad replied. "I'll need a ring."

He left Omega Station and decided that this was as good a time as any to meet the rest of the moles so he headed for Building Two.

"Ennis Parker!" he called out when he arrived.

There was silence. Then in a dark corner of the warehouse, a single light came on. Ennis Parker stood, the light behind him creating a massive shadow.

"I'm here to meet the others," Bernie shouted.

Parker waved and the rest of the moles stepped from the shadows. "We've been expecting you," Parker said. "You'll help us?"

"Yes. Believe it or not, you're the least of my problems."

Relieved, Parker walked to him and announced to the others, "this is Bernie Rosenthal. He's a good man. He needs our help. We can trust him."

Maybe it was to relieve the tension, or to hear people who were having a worse time than he was, but he listened to their stories and learned there were other moles in other companies—detached groups of isolated employees connected through Mesh blogs, sharing their tales of corporate insensitivity and worse, while looking for a way out. He promised to help them.

"Ennis, there is so much going on. Please keep a low profile until I find a way."

Ennis agreed. "If there's any way we can help, we're here, call on us."

He thanked them and left.

Weary, Bernie returned home. It was time to make Jane understand. After a frustrating start where she chided him and even called him delusional, she eventually recognized the sincerity and angst in his voice and listened to his extraordinary account.

"Bernie, can you trust these people?"

"I believe so. What Arlene and this Gohmpers said rings true and they have incriminating evidence from Crelli's secret meeting in Bermuda." He gave Jane the information to read.

She read the papers twice, looking up at him as she turned pages or reread something that surprised, appalled, or frightened her. Finally, she asked, "how can you know what's true? Technology has gotten so sophisticated; it's impossible to tell what is fabricated anymore. Everything that went on in Omega Station could be an elaborate plot to destroy Senator Crelli and our Mark. We've been hearing for years how cunning terrorists are. I don't understand. Why you? What can you do?"

There was nothing he could say to convince her. He told her he could be wrong, but he tried to explain that it sounded right and he had to act on that—even if he was being duped. She was concerned but seemed to understand. He didn't know how to lie, so he didn't explain the danger.

She sensed it. "God, Bernie, be very, very careful." She knew he wasn't telling her everything. "I'm sure you're right, but it's so illegal, and dangerous. To me, these people are e-RATS." He shook his head, but she persisted. "What else can an e-RAT be? Don't get involved. Call the FBI or CIA and turn it over to them. They're better equipped."

"Honey, I have doubts, too. But what else can I do? They could be criminals, but according to the information in these folders, Crelli is the criminal and Mark is in the line of fire. I can't ignore it because if this is right, and I feel it is, I'd be abandoning Mark. If Crelli attempts a coup, Mark will face serious prison time, or even execution for treason." There, he said it.

"Oh no." She was horrified. "What if Crelli is successful?"

"I suppose Mark will still be in danger, and I'll be a fugitive."

"Oh, Bernie," she started crying. He held her tightly but knew he wasn't comforting her.

"I've seen evidence. We can't trust the FBI or CIA, so they're out."

That really worried her. "Whatever you do, one of you is in big trouble. There must be another way." They grasped for each other. Her body, seeking protection, melted into his. He gently moved her away so he could look at her. Her eyes were red and glassy with tears.

"I'll be careful." He tried to sound confident. "You know me; I'm as conservative as pie and twice as cautious. My entire career has been about mitigating risk. I'll figure this out and find safe ground for all of us. We'll get through it."

She smiled bravely.

"Really, Jane, in thirty years of marriage, have you ever known me to take unnecessary risks when it concerns family?"

Chapter 14

Indianapolis—2031

Bernie was sitting in his favorite chair on his beach by the lake, sipping a Meritage from his wine cellar. He relished this rare moment of serenity after spending days juggling his responsibilities at ANGS and secretly visiting Omega Station. Since meeting Joad, he was trying to understand everything and hadn't been sleeping well in the process. The scenario painted by Gohmpers, Arlene, and the others was a paradox. The more implausible it seemed, the more plausible it actually was.

"Save any for me?"

Jane pulled her chair beside him. He knew her looks well. Whenever he was struggling, angry with the Toms, frustrated with his work, torn between the shades of right and wrong that everyone is destined to confront, he saw her gaze and knew she cared. He worked up a smile for her but felt it unworthy.

They continued to discuss the implications of the situation. Though she hadn't trusted him from the first, the role Crelli was to play in this was beyond her consideration but she listened intently because her family was involved. She insisted—and Bernie agreed—that he maintain as low a profile as possible at work because of the Toms' roles in this. For his part, Bernie felt comfortable thinking on the edge but not living out there, which was precisely where he was now.

"I've got that dinner later with Sirlie."

"Ah, yes. The other woman." He smiled.

"And you're meeting her because …?"

"The day the Toms cut down the tree I helped a friend of hers, a young kid who tipped over a donut cart. Sirlie's a self-appointed activist for the downtrodden. Remember, I told you her brother killed himself." She nodded.

"Well, to fight back, she started helping people and because of the donut incident, she's got this notion I'm on her side. She wants me to use my influence—if she only knew—and get more involved supporting the clerks and blue collar workers at ANGS."

"Why? You have enough to do. I thought you were maintaining a low profile."

"It's nothing, really. I'm kind of looking forward to it. I'm joining her and her boyfriend for dinner and drinks at her house. I think she wants to pitch some charitable project. You know me; I'll be home by eleven, sober and chaste."

"Enjoy yourself. You need to relax. Franki's spending the night at Laurie's, so when you get back, we'll have the house to ourselves."

His mind was elsewhere when he nodded. "Maybe we can go out with Sirlie some time?"

"Did I mention that when you come home we'll have the house to ourselves?"

He turned to her. Didn't you just … oh, right. Sorry."

"It's Mark, isn't it?" she guessed. "You want to talk to him about this."

"I really do," he said. "Maybe I'll drive down this weekend."

"Think about what you'd say. It'll be difficult, particularly down there. Maybe you should give it more time—that is, if you think it's safe to wait. Once you understand more, you'll be more persuasive and you know Mark, he'll have to be convinced." She squeezed his hand.

He squeezed back. "As far as I know, there isn't any immediate danger," he said, with the hope that that would quiet her concerns. "I'll give it a little more time." *Very little,* he thought to himself.

He drove to Sirlie Turner's small home in a middle-class, racially mixed neighborhood on the east side of Indianapolis. For some reason, it felt satisfying that she lived in a nice, safe neighborhood. As he approached her door, she emerged carrying a beer. Her contagious grin caused his to bloom.

"Well, there he is, ol' Charlie Brown," she said launching into a rolling laugh. "Any trouble findin' the house, honey?" She took his elbow and led him inside.

"Not at all," he said. "Nice place."

"Thanks, sweetheart. Neighbors, here, they just the best folks ever. Wouldn't move for heaven or earth, I'll tell you. Finding the good life was hard enough, won't make any changes now."

The hall was filled with family photos. "Thanks for having me. I don't get out much."

"Now, honey, why don't I believe that? Say, you do like ribs."

"Who doesn't?"

"Sweet, they're on. Come on out back. I want you to meet my man."

They walked onto a small, square, fenced-in deck. Smoke was curling up furiously from the cylindrical grill where a tall, wiry man with a goatee was gracefully twisting, bobbing and weaving to avoid the thick smoke as he lathered barbecue sauce on the ribs.

"She gave you the tough job," Bernie said, smiling.

The man looked up, wiped his forehead on his shirtsleeve and his hands on his apron, squinted, and then broke into a grin. "Hey, the guest of honor. I'm Derek Darden, rib fool."

"Bernie Rosenthal," he said, shaking Derek's hand. "Just plain fool."

Sirlie laughed. "Now, they ain't no fools tonight. We're about gettin' away from fools. Now my Derek, this boy can cook ribs, uh-huh. Why, I was just a little ol' wisp of a girl before he hooked me up with them. Now I look like a big bag of Jiffy Pop."

"So you two are …?"

"Together," she said nodding. "Derek's retired Army, twenty years. I haul my ass to work every day, and he sits at home on his mostly useless ass, unless he's cookin' ribs."

"Not useless, baby, semi-retired. Is this a great country or what?" he said, grinning.

"Beer?" she offered.

"Thanks."

She handed him a bottle from a cooler, and then gestured for him to sit. "What did you do in the Army?" he asked Derek.

"Corps of Engineers," he said. "Built big things." He ladled on more barbecue sauce and prodded the rib meat with a griller's fork to check its tenderness. He held his breath and dipped his head fully into the smoke billowing over the grill. He emerged from the smoke, announced, "done," and started spearing the ribs off the grill. "I run a little executive search firm, a personnel business on the east side. We provide business executives with opportunities to move on."

"Really?" he asked, admiringly. "Is it your company?"

"Sure is. I had help from a venture capitalist. He's made his money back, I'll tell you, but he deserves everything he gets. Me, I like the work, it's interesting." He pulled the last, huge slab of ribs off the grill. "Lookin' good," he said to the meat.

"Derek, got a job for a middle-aged financial executive with concerns about his future?"

"From what Sirlie tells me, you're the kind of executive we encourage to stay put. See, my business has a different mission than most executive search firms. We specialize in executives who have reached the end of their usefulness to their current employers and move them to a place that's better suited to them. The change is good for everybody. You'd be amazed at the difference in a company when you remove someone who's a bad fit. It's lucrative as hell. Take the advice of a pro, people like you need to stay where you are."

"I was afraid you'd say that."

"My girl here says you're a good guy doing good things in a bad place. Most executives I work with are people doing bad things in a good place—living on some past glory, far beyond their utility. They cost more than they're worth. When they move on, everyone gains. Sirlie, get them plates out here, baby."

"Maybe someday."

"Maybe someday, cause Sirlie says you have value."

It felt good to hear, but at the fringe of his thoughts he heard a door slam shut. He took a big gulp of beer and while his hosts were preparing the table, watched the setting sun hemorrhage red as it bled the Midwestern sky.

Sirlie interrupted his reverie by handing him a plate with potatoes and ribs heaped on it and then laid a large, white cloth napkin over his arm in the manner of a wine steward. "Just so's you know, we eat sloppy. Roll up your sleeves 'cause it means you eat sloppy, too. I don't wanna see none of this white folks', dainty bites, Lord-don't-let-me-mess eatin', hear? Afterward, if you don't mind, we're gonna go for a drive, 'cause Derek needs to do some business."

"That's fine."

They sat on the deck and ate ribs and potatoes and drank beer, which Sirlie somehow kept as close to freezing as possible without it actually turning to ice. The conversation meandered comfortably from work to the fat content of barbecued ribs to the great oak tree that had been cut down. "I come in the next day an' see that stump and, Lord God, I thought I was gonna be sick," Sirlie said. "Them Toms, they just got the devil in 'em, the livin' devil. It ain't just that they got to have the last word, it's that they nasty when they say it and they act even worse. Just junkyard dog mean. Why they like that, Charlie Brown?"

He wiped his hands on an overused, formerly white cloth napkin, now saturated in brownish-red sauce. "I guess, like everyone, they reached a fork in the road where they had to choose who they wanted to be. They chose power and an extravagant lifestyle. Kindness and consideration never entered the equation. That's my take, anyway."

"Sounds right. You talk like our minister."

Derek interrupted. "We got some ribs left."

"That's it for me. I'm done. I'm stuffed."

"I think you're right about them Tom boys," Sirlie said. "But, you know, what goes around comes around, right? Someday they be gettin' theirs."

"I couldn't even imagine what that might be," he said.

Derek gathered up the plates, bottles, and silverware. "I'll wash these in the morning, baby. Let's run my little errand."

"Now is that a good man? Trained just perfect. He don't do much, but I sure like what he does do. Can you believe it, he's gonna do the dishes in the morning. How many men do that?"

"Only two, I think," he said.

"Two?" Sirlie laughed. "That sounds generous. Hey, it won't take long to run the errand. Come with us?"

"I'm not imposing, am I?"

"Imposing?" she repeated. "Charlie Brown, we wouldn't think of leaving you behind."

"That's kind of you. Okay, let's go."

He offered to drive. Sirlie got into the front seat as Derek emerged from the house with an exquisite-looking hourglass with a ribbon tied around it.

"My God, Derek, that's beautiful. Who's it for?

"It is pretty, isn't it? It's a gift for an executive we're recruiting. See the inscription?" He handed the polished brass hourglass to him. He read the inscription carved in script on its base.

"'BD, it's time to move on. Allow us to help.' What a great touch," he said. "With thoughtful marketing like this, I'll bet you've landed some important clients."

"This is the first time I've used an hourglass. I've gifted sports equipment, good wine, and single malt scotch. It depends on their interests. I do the research. This guy loves timepieces."

"Sirlie was right. You are a sensitive guy."

"Sensitivity means profitability in my line of work."

"My man is so smart," Sirlie said proudly. "Turn left, we're headed downtown."

They drove along the winding Fall Creek Parkway through the city. When they arrived downtown, she directed him through traffic to a restaurant called Pancho & Lefty's. He had eaten there once on business and was impressed. It was an upscale restaurant where the menus lacked prices and attentive waiters materialized from nowhere. He remembered being amused because the menu not only told what the catch-of-the-day was, but also purported to explain the catch's history, as well.

A small, independent fishing family from Long Island Sound caught tonight's tasty scrod this morning at a depth of about twenty feet off the shores of … It was pure fiction, but it was a nice touch and prepared the diner to digest the prices.

"Pull over, we're here," Derek announced. "My man's inside with the competition. Sirlie, it's not right for me to take the hourglass in so will you do it?"

She nodded and struggled to extricate her big body from the car. "Ow, my damn knee is acting up again."

"You want me to take it to him?" Bernie asked politely.

"That would be the sweetest thing. Thank you," Sirlie said gratefully.

Derek handed him the hourglass. "Give it to the maitre d'." He handed Bernie a hundred dollar bill also. "Give the maitre d' this tip and tell him the hourglass is to go to the Prospero table. My guy will know immediately it's for him."

"The Prospero table? Got it."

"That's how we do it. I owe you, man."

He felt a bit awkward carrying the hourglass into the restaurant but he found the maitre d', did as he was asked, and then returned to the car. "The maitre d' has it. You're in," he said, displaying a thumb up.

"Thanks for your help."

"You a good man, Charlie Brown," Sirlie added. "How about some dessert, honey? We're downtown, I know some great places to go dancing."

He laughed and rubbed his stomach. "Oh, no, I'm stuffed and I don't really dance."

Sirlie smiled her biggest smile. "Sure enough. I'm gettin' hungry again, though."

"Take it easy, baby," Derek pleaded. "You were gonna lose some weight, remember?"

"Next week, darlin'," she said.

"You said that last week," Derek reminded her.

They returned to Sirlie's place where they drank and talked until late in the evening. When he left, he was relaxed and pleased with the easy comfort of his new friends.

It was past midnight when he staggered home and crept up the stairs to bed. At first, he was a little disappointed that Jane was asleep, but he remembered that she too had been sleeping restlessly since his contact with Omega Station. He slipped off his clothes, bundled them up, and put them outside the bedroom door like misbehaving puppies. He showered quickly and came to bed. He knew he'd been inattentive, lost in the madness that had descended into their lives. Now as he lay next to her, his libido amplified by alcohol, visions of sexuality insinuated themselves into his thoughts. She stirred and made a small noise he interpreted as sensual. He rolled her gently onto her back and put his hand between her legs. She awoke slowly.

"Bernie?" She said, groggily. "What's …? He kissed her. "Ugh. Bernie, your breath… Take it easy, cowboy!"

"I'm in the mood for love."

"Not when you're this drunk."

He kissed her again. "I'm not drunk. I love you. I love you more than anything."

When she realized how drunk he was, she laughed and put her palm over his mouth to push him away. He gave her a silly, evil laugh and came back at her, kissing her more passionately. She relaxed for a minute as he hugged her tightly. When he slipped his tongue into her mouth hoping to arouse her, he was disappointed.

"Oh my god, Bernie, you taste horrible. This will have to wait until morning."

Even though his head was spinning, he grabbed her in an awkward embrace and started playing with her breasts. He closed his eyes as an erection slowly presented. His mind flew off on a fantasy of its own making so her protests didn't register at first.

"Bernard Rosenthal," she yelled into his ear, "stop it immediately!"

In his state, her shouts were painful. He winced and quickly deflated. Suddenly, a wave of nausea arrived, and he abandoned his ardor to stagger from the bed to the bathroom, just making it to the toilet before retching. He rested, facedown in the toilet bowl feeling a little relief as his breath came back to him, cooled by the water below. In the background, he heard her enter. He mumbled an apology that echoed in the bowl and felt a hand on his forehead and another gently rub his neck. He tried a feeble, "I'm sorry," then added, "I had a great time tonight. I really needed it." She stayed with him until his stomach settled down.

"That's nice, honey. Apologize to me again in the morning when you're sober."

Too early, he awoke and dragged himself to the other side of the bed so he could see her face. Blinking hard to clear the sandpaper from his eyes, he whispered how much he loved her and kissed her gently. Then he staggered downstairs and onto the kitchen deck that overlooked the lake where he curled into a lounge chair and waited for the cool, early morning air to stop the gray horizon from swaying. Eventually he fell asleep.

The throbbing in his head rose with the sun. He had a knot in his belly and a thick, dry tongue that felt like it had been licking the floor all night. He stood, wrapping his robe tightly around his waist and walked into the kitchen for a glass of orange juice and some toast. It was quiet upstairs. He turned on the countertop television to watch the morning news, keeping it low so as not to awaken Jane. A pretty, blue-eyed, blonde anchor was breaking news.

"... believe a bomb was planted in Duke's north-side home. Buchanan Duke, fifty-two, was president of Practical Advanced Intelligence, a local technology company. A few months ago, he was the golf partner of James Bonsack, a Chicago entrepreneur killed in an explosion on an Indianapolis golf course. Police ruled that death a homicide. A similar explosive was used at Duke's residence, causing officials to believe the slayings are linked.

"Security is sifting through what is left of the estate in the gated community of Meridian Hills, looking for evidence of how the bomb was placed there. According to employees, no packages were received at the residence yesterday. Duke was dining with friends at Pancho & Lefty's, an upscale restaurant in the downtown area ..."

With hands shaking, Bernie set his orange juice down and vomited into the kitchen sink. Pancho & Lefty's? A bomb? He changed the channel.

"Duke's limousine driver told security that Duke returned home after midnight. The violent explosion, which destroyed much of the Victorian structure, occurred at three o'clock and windows were blown out of homes in the neighborhood. The subsequent fire consumed what remained of Duke's estate. Fortunately, there were no other injuries. Duke's wife, Ellie, was away when the blast occurred. Unconfirmed by Homeland Security, it is believed e-RATS have renewed operations here in Indianapolis ..."

A ringing telephone jarred him from his stupor. Before he picked up the phone, he drank from the kitchen faucet to wash the remaining bile from his mouth. His voice scraped out a greeting, but there was silence on the other end. Then he heard a woman's calm voice. "The detonator was in the base of the hourglass," she said. "We activated it remotely."

"Sirlie?" It sounded like her, but her manner of speech was entirely different.

"It's me, Charlie Brown."

"This is a joke, right, a sick joke."

"Sorry, no joke," she replied.

He looked again at the images on the television of Duke's devastated home. He felt a sinking feeling when he remembered the inscription on the hourglass: "BD, that's for Buchanan Duke." The pounding returned to his skull. "But why?"

"He was a bad man and simply had to move on. You're one of us now. You hate these people like we do. Derek greatly appreciates your help."

"But everyone saw me take the hourglass into the restaurant."

"Security will never look for a white-bread Geist Lake accounting officer in a case like this. Cooperate with us and they never will. Do it because you don't seem like the type who'd enjoy doing hard time. You're with *us* now unless you feel the urge to confess."

"Sirlie, why did you do it? What would your brother think?" Silence. "Sirlie, what would Eddy think?"

"Are you shitting me? Did you just fall off a turnip truck or what? Jesus, there's no Eddy. I was raised in a middle-class suburb outside Philadelphia with my mom, just her and me. I do this because I get paid a lot of money to do it. What else?"

"God no, you're kidding me?"

"Welcome to the real world, Charlie Brown. I have to hang up; I'm expecting a call."

"From Derek?"

"You really are a dumb ass. How'd you manage to survive all these years?"

"Sirlie, a man just died. No, I just murdered a man. And people saw me. The maitre d' saw me. They'll track me down. If they get me, they'll get you. You've got to help."

"I am helping. That's why you're safe, for now. White folk don't even know how their own system works. You have no record. There's nothing left of the hourglass so no one has your fingerprints and you don't have a mug shot. You didn't know Duke. And, coincidentally, the security cameras in Pancho & Lefty were disabled last night. The only way they'll find you is if you confess, or we tip them off. Unless you do something real stupid, I promise, with all my heart, we won't tip them off."

The security cameras were disabled? "Who are you people? What do you want from me?" His head was throbbing.

"Nothing yet, but I'm sure you'll be hearing from us soon."

"Derek doesn't place executives with new companies, does he? He kills them."

"Boy, you just might be harder to fool next time. Executive Search provides certain, select executives with a golden parachute that, unfortunately, doesn't open, if you get my meaning. To be more accurate, we're more of an executive search and destroy firm. Mum's the word, Charlie Brown. I'll be in touch." With that, she hung up.

His mind reeling, he sat holding the phone. He couldn't get his head around the words, *I just murdered a man.* When he looked up, Jane was walking to him. How much had she heard?

She studied him. Finally, sliding her arms around his waist, she laid her head on his shoulder and spoke in a gentle voice. "What happened?"

He found relief in this position so he stayed there, motionless. Finally, when he was ready, he drew a deep breath and hugged her close. With tearful eyes, he looked into hers.

"God forgive me, Jane, I killed someone last night."

Chapter 15

Aeden—2065

"I can't believe it. You murdered someone?" was Gil's shocked response. "And before cloning, so he couldn't even be replaced? Is that why HomeSec wants you?"

"In my heart, I know I'm not a murderer but it took a long time for me to believe that. Crelli wanted Duke gone, so he was already dead. I was just the instrument of his death. Still, I replay it in my mind, searching for a way I could've have prevented it. I've never truly forgiven myself, but I've come to the best peace I can about it."

"You blame Chairman Crelli because you killed someone?"

"You don't understand, yet. It was for business reasons that Crelli wanted Duke murdered. I blame Crelli, because it was his fault. And contrary to what you believe, Crelli's coming to power wasn't the start of great times or the end of bad times. It was the beginning of the end. This is difficult for you to believe but I'm asking you to open your heart so your eyes can see."

"I promised I'd listen. That doesn't mean I'll believe it."

"I accuse Crelli of taking America down a path to his dreams and causing the deaths of tens of millions of innocent American citizens. Before I die, maybe I'll understand him."

"You're making this up as you go along."

"I wish I was," Bernie paused. "Why would I lie to you?"

"I don't know you well enough to know that," Gil answered.

"Earlier, I asked for your help." The boy nodded. "I'll tell you what I need after I finish my story and if you still don't believe me, I'll withdraw my request to die and go ahead with treatments, if the government allows it. But if you believe, you'll help me."

"That depends on what you want me to do."

"I won't lie to you. It will be dangerous but I won't ask for your help until you understand how important it is."

"Howard won't like it if I get in trouble."

"If you follow my instructions you'll be okay."

The boy seemed to be considering it. "Okay," he said, finally. "If I believe your story, I'll help, but I won't kill anyone and if it's dangerous…" Gil looked at the clock. "I didn't realize how late it is. I have schoolwork and the Indianapolis Racers to watch. I have to go."

"One question, Gil. Have you thought about who you want to be when you're older?"

"What kind of question is that?"

"Answer the best you can."

Gil paused to consider it. "Because of Howard's worth, I'll receive a mid-major education and become a mid-major consumer-producer or Conducer. I'm not sure what I'll do specifically, but I'll earn an income consistent with the lifestyle of others with my capability and value range. If I develop or create something of value outside of my required position, kind of like Howard with his plants, my potential will be upgraded to that of a Major Player and I could possibly live on the hill with the Executives." Gil considered what he'd said. "No, I probably won't live on the hill because they have restrictions on clones. Anyway, that's my future."

"And what kind of person will you be, do you think?"

"Productive, I guess. What other type is there?"

"Maybe I can help. Back in America's past, when the true natives lived here, a Cherokee grandfather …"

"What's a Cherokee?"

"Cherokee is the name of a tribe of native Americans who lived here before the Europeans arrived. Anyway, a grandfather was teaching his young grandson. The grandfather explained that within each of us, two young wolves live and vie for supremacy. One is evil. He lives in anger, envy, sorrow, regret, greed, arrogance, self-pity, guilt, resentment, inferiority, lies, false pride, superiority, and ego. The other wolf is good. He lives in joy, peace, love, hope, serenity, humility, kindness, benevolence, empathy, generosity, truth, compassion, and faith." Bernie paused.

"Which one wins?" Gil asked.

Bernie smiled. "The one you feed. Have a good night and enjoy your game."

"Bernie, I promise I'll be back in the morning to hear the rest of your story." As he left, Nurse Peyton passed him and entered the room. He paused to listen to their conversation.

"So how'd it go this time?" she asked.

"He doesn't react much. He seems to be absorbing it—I hope."

"I told you not to expect too much. He's not some mutant survivor from your world; he's a product of this one. As long as he returns, we haven't lost. Now get some rest. You look tired."

Chairman Crelli sat alone behind his desk, watching monitors that kept him informed about his world. His interest today was with one monitor in particular that displayed five teenage children of various ages involved in educational simulations in Virtuoso.

"They're fine, aren't they?"

"Yes, sir, they are," replied a deep, synthesized voice.

"Alpha 2 is their leader."

"Yes, sir. The others defer to him. He shows passion and has the knack for reading people and situations. The others work for his approval."

Crelli smiled. "Like father, like son, Gecko. Has Delta 3 absorbed my leadership model?"

"He is the youngest to grasp the dynamics of leadership. He is progressing nicely."

"If his performance continues, it means the project has met my requirements.

"Very good, sir."

"With all your other duties, do you have time to monitor and evaluate the children?"

"I am far from capacity. And the clones provide an interesting activity."

"Continue to monitor them, then."

"Yes, sir. One second … A report has reached me from one of my agents."

"Yes?"

"A possible aberration has been identified."

"Explain."

"It is in Indianapolis, again."

"Rosenthal! After all this time."

"Confirming. Yes, the activity is near Aeden, in Mark Rose's son's home."

"It is Rosenthal. What's been reported?"

"My agent reports there is no Virtuoso activity in the Rose household. That is inconsistent with the norm. My agent believes someone is overriding our surveillance."

"The last time someone breached us was ten years ago. I thought that was resolved."

"It was fourteen years ago, sir. Just before the execution of the baby Gilbert Rose. That problem was resolved. This is different."

"Bring up the detail." Andy read over the summary information. "I remember now. The Office of Life Management somehow overlooked Mark's grandchild. The boy didn't receive required behavior modification treatments and we eliminated the child and replaced him with a certified clone. Why is Rosenthal making another move and what actions have you taken?"

"I replaced the agent with a more powerful one instructed to intensify surveillance."

"Continue to monitor the situation but don't, I repeat, don't interfere directly. When you have something substantive, report to me. I won't lose the old man again."

"It will be as you say."

"Remove your presence. I need to relax in Virtuoso."

"It will be as you say."

Gil returned home in time for the start of the Racers game. He watched but soon became restive, his mind on other things. He signed off and headed to the Virtuoso chamber to be with Andrea. Afterwards, it was late, and he was asleep when Howard's face appeared on his monitor.

"Did the Racers win?" he asked.

"I don't know," Gil answered groggily. "I must have fallen asleep."

"It mustn't have been a good game."

"They're always good games. What's the purpose, otherwise?"

"Of course. Did you get my Genetic Aid?"

"I put the bottle in your storage unit. Can I use your SoilScope?"

"Do you have geology homework?"

"Yes," he lied.

"Check the house homing device and if you're going out, don't forget to enter your request before leaving. Remember what happened to Tommy."

"I will. How deep does the SoilScope scan?"

"I get images down ten feet or more."

"Thanks, Howard. Goodnight."

"Will you be using Virtuoso?"

"No, I don't think so."

Howard smiled. "Good, it's been a tough day, I need to relax. Someday, when we move to Avalon, we'll each have our own unit." When he didn't respond Howard asked, "are you okay, Gil?"

"I'm fine."

Howard accepted that and signed off.

Gil queried Archive, located and took the SoilScope, registered his itinerary, and headed out the backdoor and down the narrow path that separated the northernmost edge of Aeden from the first incline leading to the hills of Avalon. He felt guilty lying to Howard and blamed Bernie for his need to do so. At the outskirts of Aeden, he shielded his eyes from the lights that eternally glorified the mansions of Avalon and continued down the uneven path.

He approached an old, arched, stone entrance with a sign that read THE GARDENS. He walked through the archway and waited for some signal to go off. When none did, he continued up a hill. Although certain nobody was nearby, Gil was uncomfortable in this place where real people were buried.

He saw a faint outline of stone markers in the darkness. He unhooked his SoilScope, placed the scanner over one of the gravesites, and turned it on. Its green light shone brightly as he slowly made passes over a grave. When the scan was complete, he stared at the image on the monitor and shivered involuntarily, unsure whether it was the cool night air or his thoughts of what happened to these people buried in boxes when they died. He steeled himself and dialed a better resolution. It was as he feared. Inside the wooden box was the image of a small, partially decomposed skeleton. He dialed for a closer look to read its Personal Information Chip. He adjusted the scope until he found it. Along with the code, the name was partially obliterated but with more magnification he could make out the last name. It said Rose Clone. It wasn't his true self! Baffled by the implications, he shivered and dropped to the ground. Numb, he sat and stared at the grave and the truth. This was one for Bernie.

Saddened by the baby's death, he looked from the monitor to the name on the gravestone, visible in the green light of the SoilScope. Another chill rolled down his spine.

GILBERT F. ROSE
BORN FEBRUARY 17, 2051 DIED JUNE 3, 2053
SO SMALL, SO SOON, SO MISSED

He stared into the monitor at the little skull and bones. This was a baby, not a two year old. What was it like? His memory couldn't reach back that far. Something cold rolled down his cheek and he wiped it away. It wasn't a tear; he wouldn't cry. Quickly, he closed the SoilScope and headed home. Before he left the cemetery, he turned for one last look.

What a sad epitaph for someone reborn.

The next morning, Gil returned to Bernie's room at the hospice. Something about the boy looked different. "Did your Racers lose, Gil? You look a little down."

"No, they won."

"What's wrong? You should be happy."

"I checked the gravesite. It was really creepy. Just like you said, that's not me buried there." Gil hesitated. "What you said was true."

Bernie lifted his head off the pillow. "Everything I've told you is true. May I continue?"

Gil nodded, and for the first time he sat on the bed to listen. Bernie was pleased.

"I thought Duke's murder was a crisis," he began. "But it was nothing compared to what happened next."

Chapter 16

Angs Headquarters—2031

Bernie was working at his desk when Carolyn's voice came over the intercom. "Bernie, I wanted to thank you for the coffee. I got it last night. That was nice of you. Oh, and there's a gentleman waiting to see you."

"That's quite alright, Carolyn, it's just a little thank you. Who is it?"

"It's a police officer. A Lieutenant Conger."

He stood up. "A police officer? Wait … no, send him in."

When Carolyn opened the door, the officer walked past her and in. She raised her eyebrows, but Bernie waved her away.

The lieutenant walked to Bernie's desk and extended his hand. "Bernie Rosenthal," he said as he approached, "good to meet you. I've been listening to some nice things about you. Sally, out there, thinks the world of you. But you knew that."

Nervous and hoping it didn't show, he shook the officer's hand. "Thanks. It's Carolyn, by the way, and I pay her a lot to say nice things."

The lieutenant drew back in mock disbelief. "What? Carolyn? I thought she said Sally. Anyway, she thinks you're a saint. She'd make a great character witness, that one."

Bernie steeled himself. He would have to be careful, but he could only hope to act naturally and pray it was enough. "How can I help you, Lieutenant?"

"Conger, Earl Conger, Mr. Rosenthal. I'm a detective with the Robbery-Homicide Division of the Marion County Police Department." While the lieutenant was speaking, he glanced at Bernie's office window. "Nice view. Say, why'd they brick up that other window?"

"It's a convoluted story, Lieutenant. My promotion called for a bigger office, which put the wall in the middle of the window, so they bricked it up."

"Seems like a waste for just a few feet, but who am I to question? I don't have any windows in my office." He walked to the window and pointed. "And what's with that path from the parking lot? It must be like a mile too long—and dangerous with all the dips and irregularities."

"You'll have to ask the owners, Lieutenant."

"You know, we had a path like that in the National Guard. Of course, it was a hell of a lot longer. As punishment, we had to jog it in full battle gear. Were you in the armed forces?"

"No, I wasn't."

"Just as well. Fortunately, the great wars are all behind us, don't you think?"

"We can only hope. Are there great wars?"

"What's that?" Conger asked as he continued to look out the window. "Oh, good point. Well, I'm guessing there must have been a good reason for that path. Who would do something like that without one?"

"Who'd have a good reason?" Bernie asked.

"Another good point." Conger turned from the window and stared at him. "You're busy Mr. Rosenthal, so I'll get right to it. I'm investigating the murder of a man named Buchanan Duke. He was killed a few weeks ago in an explosion in his home. Did you know him?"

Bernie's heart rate jumped. "No. Just of him. Have a chair, Lieutenant" he said, trying not to appear overly gracious.

"No, thanks. I won't be long and I prefer to stand. You knew of him how, exactly?"

"He owned a technology company. We buy a lot of equipment and software and I sign the checks. And it seemed like he was in the news a lot."

"But you never met him personally?"

"No."

"Did you know James Bonsack?"

It was difficult to look up at the Lieutenant from his chair, so he stood. "I'd met him. We purchased software from his company, too. Nice enough guy."

"Did you know that Mr. Bonsack and Mr. Duke were acquaintances?"

"Only what I've read. There were merger talks. It's very common in the industry."

"Exactly," Conger said as if he had just hit upon something important. "And then that terrible murder at the golf course. Just terrible." He shook his head as if the crime personally affected him somehow. "You knew about that, right?"

Bernie leaned forward a little. "About Bonsack being killed? Yes, I read the story." He paused. "Excuse me, but what does all this have to do with me?"

"Oh, just doing some routine checking. It's been weeks since the murders, and our investigation keeps hitting dry wells. There are similarities so we have to check these things out.

"Similarities?"

"Yes, between the deaths. Both men were killed with military explosives. We believe someone replaced Bonsack's golf ball with one made with an explosive. And in Duke's murder, somebody planted a bomb in his house. There was a lot of damage—just shards and splinters left. It's been very difficult to put things together—needle in a haystack sort of a thing."

"Is that why you asked if I'd been in the service? Because of the explosives?"

Conger hunched his shoulders as if embarrassed. "Caught me. I should have asked outright."

"It's your job."

The lieutenant shrugged again. "Yes, I have to ask difficult questions."

"I assure you I know nothing about explosives."

"I believe you, Mr. Rosenthal. We've done a little investigating, and you're a financial guy. Now me, I can't balance a checkbook."

"I doubt that." Suddenly his mouth felt dry. "Am I somehow a suspect?"

"Suspect," Conger waved him off as if stunned that he would say such a thing. "Why would you think that? No, not at all. This is routine. We found your name in Mr. Bonsack's contact file. But of course it would be there, right? You sign the checks." He waved a hand dismissively, as if his entire visit was trivial and routine. "We think the same person killed both men, possibly e-RATS are involved. You see, in both crimes, the explosives were pretty sophisticated. But we couldn't figure out how anybody got into Mr. Duke's house to place the bomb. His security was—well, the president probably has similar security. And frankly, all the hired help seem above suspicion. So we started thinking maybe Mr. Duke brought the bomb in himself."

"How would he do that? And why?"

"I'm just saying, suppose he was tricked into bringing the bomb inside his home. You know, like Mr. Bonsack was tricked into hitting the loaded golf ball."

He swallowed. "Yes, you said that's how Bonsack was killed."

"We talked to the staff at a downtown restaurant called Pancho & Lefty's. Mr. Duke dined there the night of the murder. According to the maitre d', a man brought an hourglass into the restaurant and asked him to give it to the victim. Duke's dinner companions confirm this."

Breathe easily. Breathe. "So you think the bomb was in this hourglass?"

"Almost certainly. The problem is the maitre d' doesn't remember the guy. He wasn't a customer or anything. And the damnedest coincidence, that night the restaurant's security cameras weren't operating. The description we got wasn't all that helpful—middle-aged, medium height, medium build, and medium complexion—with no distinguishing features.

"Are you here because those are my features, Lieutenant? How flattering."

"You and a million men like you. See, that's the problem. I could be a suspect here. But since we think the same person committed both murders, we're going through all the people who knew both victims. As I said, your name was on Bonsack's contact file." Conger shrugged. "So, forgive me, but what were you doing the night of the murder? That would be April 29."

"What was I doing?" He tried to remain calm, knowing the lieutenant was skilled when it came to criminals trying to hide the truth. He couldn't tell the Lieutenant that he had had dinner with Sirlie; that would lead him to look into her and Derek Darden's backgrounds, and who knew what that might turn up? He couldn't say he was home because Conger might learn that was a lie, and he'd face even more intense scrutiny. And then there was the wild card, the maitre d'. His description was vague, but the man might remember him if he saw him in a line-up.

"Let me think, Lieutenant. I can't remember. The twenty-fifth? That was a while back."

"No, the twenty-ninth," Conger corrected. His gaze hadn't left him since he asked the question. "Can I see your schedule? Carolyn says you're relentless about keeping it up-to-date."

"Good thought, Lieutenant," he said weakly. He knew what the schedule said because he remembered entering the information about his dinner with Sirlie and never deleting it. He walked over to his computer and clicked on the calendar icon. When it appeared on the screen, he paged through it to get to the twenty-ninth. Defenseless, he waited for the Lieutenant's reaction.

Just then, the door opened, and Gorman walked in with some documents. He heard Carolyn insisting, "but, sir, he's in a meeting." Gorman closed the door on her protests.

"Sorry, Lieutenant, I didn't know you were still here." He placed some papers on Bernie's desk.

"Not a problem, Mr. Gorman." Conger responded deferentially.

"Bernie's one of my most valuable and trusted officers. I believe I already mentioned that. Bernie, are you helping the lieutenant?"

"Yes he is, Sir," Conger interrupted. "We're confirming his schedule per our discussion."

Gorman smiled. What had they discussed? Was this Gorman's revenge?

Gorman turned from the lieutenant to give Bernie a conspiratorial wink. "You remember the twenty-ninth, Bernie. It was the night we worked late putting the Angel Falls project to bed."

"Angel Falls? Right," he repeated, trying not to show surprise or confusion.

Conger leaned over his desk to get a better view of the screen. "If I could just squeeze in here … sorry …" He wedged himself between Bernie and the screen. After a long moment, Conger straightened and looked at him. "Just as you said, you were here at a meeting."

With nonchalance he didn't feel, he looked at the screen. April 29 read:

MEETING, GORMAN. 7 TO 10 PM
ANGEL FALLS CLOSURE RESOLUTION

He was stunned but couldn't show it. Someone had changed his schedule. He glanced first at Gorman, and then at Conger. "Yes," he said slowly. "That sounds right."

Conger nodded and moved away from the desk. "Do you always work that late?"

Gorman replied. "Lieutenant, we're professionals. Work takes the time it takes."

That was enough for Lieutenant Conger. "Gentlemen, that's all I need right now. It looks like you two have business to discuss. Thanks again." He extended his hand to Bernie and then to Gorman.

"I'll see myself out. Mr. Rosenthal. If I need to discuss this with you later …"

"You know where to find me," he answered and the lieutenant disappeared.

Gorman turned toward the door without saying anything.

Before Gorman left, Bernie felt compelled to ask, "you lied for me. Why?"

Gorman turned; his face red. "If you want to avoid rotting in prison for the rest of your life while your wife and children learn to grow old with nothing more than decaying memories of you, I suggest you change your tone. How dare you accuse me of lying? That's insulting."

He stared into Gorman's cold eyes but couldn't think of anything else to say.

Gorman's expression softened. He stepped to Bernie and gently put his arm around his shoulders. "You seem uncertain about us. Don't be. Regardless of what you think, we consider you part of our family. Speaking of family, you should be very proud of your son. He's a real team player with a bright future. We appreciate how well you raised him and we would hate for something to jeopardize his career. He might never forgive you. I know that if I did something stupid to ruin my son's career, I would expect him to hate me. My advice is to accept what's happened here today in the spirit of loyalty and team-play that it was offered. You understand. It's best for everyone—and I mean everyone—that you and I met on the evening of April 29."

Gorman started for the door again. He opened it and paused. "One more thing—you're spending an inordinate amount of company time away from the office. I would feel more comfortable if that behavior ceased." He spun and left.

As the door slammed, Bernie stare returned to the calendar entry. What had just happened? Whose team was Gorman talking about and why was Mark such a team player? But there was a bigger, more frightening question. If his bosses, the Toms, were involved in the murders of Bucky Duke and Jim Bonsack, Mark was in danger too.

That night, anxious but extremely cautious, he drove to Sirlie's home. Whatever the risk, he had to confront her. He hadn't seen her since the murder; she wasn't at work, and didn't answer the phone at the number the Personnel Department had for her. He drove down the tree-shaded streets in her neighborhood while checking constantly to make sure he wasn't followed. When he found her house, he pulled past it and parked. Paralyzed with indecision, he sat in the car, watching and waiting, even though he saw there were lights on inside and movement behind the curtains. Normally one to avoid confrontation, Bernie felt the world closing in, strangling him. He struggled to breathe as he left the car and walked across the lawn to the front door. He hesitated again, but then resolutely rang the doorbell.

As the door opened, he let out a gasp. A small young woman appeared. She was clearly not Sirlie. Confused, he looked down the hallway to the living room where a man was reading a newspaper. It wasn't Derek Darden.

"Is Sirlie here?"

"Who?"

"Sirlie Turner. She lives here."

The man lowered his paper and walked to the door. "I'm sorry," the woman said, "there's no one here by that name."

"Who is it, sweetie?" the man asked.

"Someone lookin' for Shirley Turner."

"Actually, it's Sirlie," he clarified. "You say she doesn't live here anymore?"

"There are no other women living here," the woman said, "Unless Rollie's hiding her in the basement." She put a hand on her upturned hip and turned to face the man. "Rollie, do you know a girl named Sirlie?"

"No, sweetie."

"You better not," she said. "I'm sorry, mister, you made a mistake."

His mind reeling, he stepped back and surveyed the house. He was certain this was the place. "I'm sorry I bothered you."

Confused, he felt light-headed as he returned to his car. Before getting in, he grabbed the hood for support and turned to face the house again. He was certain it was the same house. Sirlie and Derek must have "moved in" for the night—a minor deceit in their world. He headed home, his shirt wet with perspiration, his digestive system in rebellion.

Chapter 17

Indianapolis—2031

Obedient to Gorman's dictate, Bernie stayed away from Omega station for more than a month. He was apprehensive about Duke's murder and its implications and didn't know what else to do. Finally, when he couldn't hold back any longer, he headed for the tank farm.

"Carolyn, I'm going out for a little while."

"I was beginning to think Tom had you chained to your desk."

"No." He tried to laugh. "I won't be long. Cover for me until I get back."

At the chemical tank, he waited and waited. He walked away to get in view of the surveillance cameras, but still the door didn't open.

Concerned, he turned to leave. Arlene must have realized he was a coward, or reconsidered his usefulness now that he was suspected of murder and she locked him out. Before he turned the corner, he looked back. If he wasn't certain Omega Station was there, he would have thought he'd dreamt it. As he returned to his office, he saw Qade Blessing smiling and walking toward him.

"Bernie, it's been a while."

"I didn't … can you help me get in?"

"You don't need my help," Qade said as he walked him back.

"The door didn't open."

"Joad's annoyed that's all." When they approached the tank, the door opened as if all was forgiven. Soon they were greeted by Arlene.

"Sorry. Joad's a bit insulted."

"I'm sorry. A lot's happened and coming here would have made things more difficult."

"Don't tell me, tell Joad."

"Joad, I'm sorry," he said, while looking for a camera to talk into.

"I accept your apology. It's understandable. Preventing a coup isn't very exciting and can strain a busy social schedule. I'm thinking of canceling the whole thing because there's a white sale at Macy's."

"He gets your point," Arlene intervened.

"Arlene, every day the Toms talk down to me. Getting it from a computer is a new low." As soon as he said it, he knew he'd made a mistake.

"You didn't just say that? I'm right here. Explain what you mean by a new low?"

"Apologize, Bernie, please," Arlene insisted. "She's difficult when she's insulted."

"Joad, please, I didn't mean to insult you."

"Are you always so disingenuous after murdering someone?"

He plopped down on the closest chair. He felt like crying.

"Joad, that was insensitive," said Arlene.

"How did you know?" he asked, quietly.

"Tom Gorman backdated an entry on your business schedule for a certain night and time. I found that unusual so I searched for events that correlated. One was the death of Buchanan Duke. This was confirmed when a detective came to visit you. Final confirmation was provided by a traffic control camera near Pancho & Lefty's Restaurant that captured your car and license plate. It showed you carrying the hourglass into the restaurant."

His world caved in. He put his head in his hands and rocked back and forth. "I'm dead."

Arlene put her hand on his shoulder. "Not yet. Joad, explain."

"He insulted me."

"Joad."

"Bernie, I removed any potentially incriminating evidence. It's unlikely the police will trace the murder back to you."

He looked up hopefully. "Is that right?" Arlene nodded with the look of certainty. "Thanks, Joad, I promise I'll never take you for granted again."

"Apology accepted."

"How did it happen?" Arlene asked.

"They tricked me." He explained the evening of the murder. "I didn't know it was a bomb. I'm sick about it."

"There's a bright side. If the people Sirlie Turner works for wanted you caught, you'd be in custody. We'll keep an eye on her because we don't know her part in this. In the meantime, you're in the clear, so try to put it behind you. Have you made any progress in figuring out how to stop Andy's presidential campaign?"

"Gorman can turn me in at any time."

"He didn't so he can't. We'll have to be more careful, that's all."

He took a breath and tried to compartmentalize his fears. "I have some ideas." He paused. "You're sure I can't be convicted of this?"

"Bernie, we're not sure of anything. But Gorman has as much to lose as you do, so I doubt they'll use the murder for anything more than a warning."

"What about Sirlie and Derek Darden?"

"I think you're okay. Even if they confess their roles, the police have nothing to convict you on. You were duped or coerced, that's all. Now, about Andy."

"The only thing we can do is prevent him from getting the nomination. We undermine the public's confidence in him so he'll have to take more risks or act out of character, something that might be enough to deny him the nomination. We'll plant information in the media that hints at some of the more illegal things he's done. At the same time, we'll provide juicy material to his opponents, and let them run with it. We'll let them bury him."

"Do you have any ideas how to plant these leads?"

"That's the problem. I don't have contacts with reporters and don't know who we can trust. I tried to contact the political parties anonymously to see if they would be interested in dirt on Crelli, but all they wanted were donations."

"We have to get to the campaign managers."

"We need media pressure first. Then we interest his opponents and they jump in."

"So what do you suggest?"

"We should start in the print media because with Gecko, Crelli controls the Mesh media. That's as far as I've taken it."

At Arlene's request, Joad came up with the name of a seemingly reputable reporter.

"Jimmy Shea at the *Indianapolis Tribute Courier* has a good track record, and his peers respect him. He's as honest, ethical, and professional as we're going to find."

"I have to get back to my office before I'm missed. Jimmy Shea it is. I'll call him."

Bernie scheduled a meeting with the reporter that evening at a local workingman's bar down the street from Angs. When they met, he gave him his name as Elijah Marsden.

"Hello, Mr. Marsden. You said on the phone that you have something to discuss."

"Please, call me Eli. Yes, I do. Would you like a beer?"

Shea ordered a drink. "Now, what's so important?"

"You've been reporting on political corruption for awhile and have a reputation for handling stuff fairly and accurately. My life is in danger so obviously, I can't be quoted." With that, Shea showed interest. Bernie continued in a whisper. "It concerns Andrew Crelli."

"The senator from Kentucky?"

"Yes. He's planning to run for president in the next election."

"That is news. Bloggers have been speculating on it for months. His success with the e-RATS seems to insure he'll run sometime, though we thought he'd wait. Get me some proof, and I'll break the story."

"But that's not the story," Bernie said, lowering his voice. "e-RATS work for him."

"For who? The senator?"

When Bernie nodded, Shea pushed away, spilling his drink. "Don't waste my time."

"I have proof."

"I'll bet you do. You can prove that the senator who heads the government's e-SWAT task force—that's responsible for catching terrorists—is actually a terrorist himself?"

"It's not quite like that, but basically, yes."

"What's your relationship with the senator? What did he do to you?"

"I have no relationship with the senator," he lied. "I just fell into this information."

"Excuse me, but I'm always wary when someone *just falls* into something." The reporter paused. "It's crazy, but if you can prove it," he said quietly, "I'm interested. Crelli has a great future; why would he take that risk? He'll go to jail or worse and his career will be ruined."

Instead of answering, he handed Shea a list of people and events relating to Bermuda and some private files Joad had located for him.

"There's a lot more to this story, but I can't tell you all of it right now. Read these documents. They're just the tip of a very large iceberg. You'll find some significant leads to help you develop the story. Start with the senator's recent business trip to Bermuda. You'll find most of your answers there. Here's the guest list. And Everhard's murder is important, but you absolutely can't identify me as your source, or my family and my connection will be in danger. Promise me."

The reporter nodded.

"Here's my number." He handed the reporter a card with his fake name and number written on it. "Call me when you reach an impasse. I can move your investigation along."

"Mr. Marsden, I work dicey stories, so if what you say is correct; I'll go to jail to protect you. On the other hand, I won't print it until I believe it. I won't be the person who destroys an important career on innuendo. I must be certain I'm doing the right thing."

"All you'll need to do is your professional best. It's critical that this story is told. I came to you because your name will add credibility."

They shook hands and Jimmy Shea left. Bernie smiled contentedly. He was beginning to make a difference.

Chapter 18

Indianapolis—2031

Jane drove him to the airport for his flight to Angel Falls. He had delayed the trip as long as he could for the sake of the people who lived there, but the Toms wanted the plant closed by the end of the year, so he couldn't put off the task any longer.

In spite of Gorman's warning, carefully planned visits to the tanks became a regular part of his life, and he was learning more about what Joad, Arlene, and the twins could and couldn't do. With all the risk, Jane was his only refuge.

"Terry called last night," she told him.

"It's been awhile. How's she doing?"

"I thought she finally gave up on us. She apologized for not keeping in touch. But, Bernie, the important news is that Mark called her."

"That's great, I think. What'd he say?"

"He's busy, so he didn't say much, but he wanted her to know he still cared. Next time I talk to him I'm going to give him a piece of my mind for not telling us he was going to call her. Anyway, she's going to Cincinnati to see him."

"Should we hold our breath and hope he's finally coming to his senses?"

"Mark wouldn't hurt her a second time."

"He'd better not."

She squeezed his hand. "Don't think the worst."

"I try not to."

"Our son is a good man and he's ready to settle down. You know I'm right."

"Really?"

"Stop it. Give this a chance to play out. Give him a chance."

"If you talk to Terry again, ask her to have my son call me," he said.

"Bernie, put a lid on it. Honestly, I hate it when you pout. It's so annoying."

"I'm sorry, but it hurts. He's avoiding us for a reason, and I'm having trouble with it."

She stopped the car at the terminal and kissed him goodbye. "I'm sorry. I didn't mean to pick on you. When it counts, good people do the right thing. You can count on Mark. As soon as he comes around, you'll feel better about everything. It's this trip, isn't it? You hate what you have to do." He nodded. "Call me when you get there if you need to talk."

He kissed her. "I love you," he said, and grabbed his luggage.

Bernie had always enjoyed seeing the picturesque little town built around a small lake, surrounded by evergreens, but he didn't look forward to it today. His mood didn't improve when he arrived. After the two-hour drive from the airport, he sensed, immediately, that things were different. The last time he was there, the town was as busy as a tiny rural town could be. The handful of stores, many built with logs cut from Maine timber, were alive with people. On this visit, he drove past vacant streets and shuttered buildings. Store windows were empty, written over in white shoe polish with a hopeless prayer: "For Sale or Lease by Owner." The only traffic light in town regulated nothing, and the few people walking on the street looked despondent.

He drove the short distance past the town to the ANGS facility. To his surprise, the gates were padlocked. He pressed the button on the intercom. No one answered. He pressed it again and waited. In the eerie quiet he wondered if the residents had fled. Then he heard a voice.

"Can I help you?"

"Bernie Rosenthal from ANGS Corporate. Who're you?"

"Oren Terry."

"Can you let me in, Oren?"

"Welcome, Mr. Rosenthal," the man greeted him as he unlocked the padlock.

"Is there anyone else here?"

"Yeah, Mr. Billingstadt is still here." He nodded toward the accounting office.

He found Will Billingstadt sitting alone at a horseshoe-shaped desk. The small, compactly built old man looked up as he entered.

"So you finally got here," Billingstadt said. He sounded bitter.

"Finally?"

"It's nothing, Bernie. Never mind."

"What happened? The town's deserted and the plant is shut down. Where is everybody?"

Billingstadt gave him a curious look, as if he didn't understand the question. "Don't act innocent; it's insulting. Did it slip your mind that you shut us down?"

"Shut you down?"

"Jesus, Bernie, be real."

"I don't understand?"

Billingstadt leaned back in his chair. "Tom Morgan rolled into town two months ago, got out of his limo, walked in, and told everyone they had two weeks. Ring a bell, Quasimodo?"

"Morgan? Here? I don't know anything about that."

"Tell me you didn't know you were closing us down?"

This was payback for his time spent at Omega Station and not concentrating on work. "Of course I knew," he said, sullenly. "But it was supposed to be my plan, my way. You were to have time to settle things and phase out. I had until the end of the year. There was even money set aside for relocation assistance and unpaid vacation time. I worked on the plan. It wasn't supposed to happen like this."

The old man shook his head. "I'm sorry. This must be tough on you."

"Don't be that way, Will. What did Tom say?"

"That ANGS found a better use for the resources committed here. He claimed productivity was poor and logistics sucked. Pick whatever excuse justifies this in your corporate soul. Production is transferring to Go Fuck Yourself Stan in Central Asia where logistics are better. Go figure."

"That's all he said?"

"No, he also said that since you were responsible, you would be here to wrap things up. Why not? It's what you do."

Bernie stared mutely. He wanted to tell Will that he wasn't the enemy, that he was the only one in their corner, but he knew Billingstadt wouldn't buy it. Why should he? Too often in the past, he'd been the messenger of doom sent by the Toms. Billingstadt was merely treating him like the grim reaper he was. He was livid at the Toms for yet another deceit.

Resigned, he asked, "What's left to do?"

He spent the day with Billingstadt reviewing the asset valuations and logistics reports required for selling equipment and moving production from Angel Falls to Asia—the mundane detail-work financial morticians are good at. As he worked, he was weighed down by the thought of the "For Sale" signs, empty store windows, and the stoplight controlling an indifferent street. He couldn't bear to think of the residents. Finally, the work done, Billingstadt packed his briefcase.

"May I ask you something? Why wouldn't you return my e-mails?"

"Will, I promise you, I never received any. Nothing. When did you send them?"

"Three months ago. Two months ago. I left three voicemails. I even received confirmation that you received them. Then we received instructions to leave you alone, that you would be up as soon as you could. I need this salary for as long as I can get it, so I shut up and waited."

"For what it's worth, I never received any of your messages."

"Whatever." Billingstadt stood without looking at him. "I'll make sure these boxes are shipped to Indianapolis." Billingstadt handed him a document. "This is a schedule for the equipment haulers who'll transport the machinery." He hesitated, staring at the floor. "Bernie, it doesn't matter whether you got my messages. You knew about this shutdown for months and never contacted us. If it makes you feel better to think you're different—fine. But you really are one of them, not so different from the Toms."

"I'm not," he insisted, realizing it was an empty statement.

"Two hundred years of history and now, for no good business reason, the town's gone. I'm going to ... I'm going to miss it. It was a great place, the best place I've ever lived. Now I'm sixty-two and out of work. For what? Some arbitrary—and knowing ANGST, probably inaccurate—business metric that shows we can't measure up? You fucked us, Bernie. I know it, the Toms know it, and you know it. I understand making difficult business decisions, but this hurts people, hurts them bad, for no reason."

"I'm sorry."

Billingstadt briefly stared at him as if that was the non-answer he expected. Then, he walked to the door and turned. "Bernie, you always seemed like a good guy. If it makes you happy to believe you aren't one of them, believe away, but whatever you did or didn't do to prevent this still got us to this point. If you're not one of them, who are you? Your peace of mind won't feed us." He dropped his head. "Go fuck yourself and those self-serving rationalizations you make so you and your mean-spirited company can prosper." With that, he left.

Much later, his stomach tied in knots, he left the plant. Rain was falling, and the drops hid tears of frustration, guilt, and shame. He drove to the town's only motel and after checking in, decided to walk the few hundred feet to his cabin. Wet, weary, and feeling sorry for himself, he lay in bed staring at the ceiling timbers, seething. He loved Angel Falls for the peace and quiet it offered him. That night there was no peace, and the quiet was maddening.

He called Jane. She shared his pain and tried unsuccessfully to cheer him up.

Late that evening, unable to sleep, he walked out into the clear, quiet night. The rain had stopped, and the grass, visible near the cabin lights, was covered with translucent pearls of water. So far from everything, he stood staring for a long time, cocooned in the silence. But his exhausted mind wasn't done. It flashed images that haunted him and jarred him from his reverie. Finally, very early into a new, crystalline-clear morning, an acceptable peace found him. He went inside, closed his now-burning eyes, and slept.

In the morning, he drove down Interstate 95 over roads still damp from the previous night's rain. As he reached the Bangor Airport, the rain began again. He checked in.

"I'm sorry, sir, but your flight has been delayed."

"Is there an alternative?"

"You are in luck, sir. We can get you on Flight 5512 nonstop to Cincinnati. But you will have to drive to Indianapolis from there because the connection is booked."

"Cincinnati?"

"It leaves in thirty minutes."

Sometimes decisions are made for you. "I'll take it," Bernie said.

Two hours later, he arrived at the Greater Cincinnati Airport, rented a car, and drove down Interstate 71 to Crelli Park. A vast complex of interrelated businesses, the park had, of all the compelling badges of success, its own exit-ramp. He drove past the buildings, hotels, and recreation facilities that marked his son's domain until he reached the main gate to the headquarters. A security guard appeared. "Can I help you, sir?"

"Yes, I would like to see Mark Rosenthal."

"Do you have an appointment?"

"No, it's a surprise. I'm his father, Bernard Rosenthal."

The guard made a call. After a brief discussion, the guard returned. "I'm sorry, Mr. Rosenthal. He's not here."

"When is he expected back?"

"Not today, sir."

"I see. I was passing by and thought we might have dinner. Please tell him I stopped by."

"Happy to, sir."

When he got back to the interstate, he sat for a moment at the end of the entrance ramp and called Crelli Enterprises headquarters. "Mark Rosenthal, please."

A moment later a voice said, "Mr. Rosenthal's office."

"Mark Rosenthal, please," he said again.

"He's at Wharton. We don't expect him back until late tomorrow."

He would drive to Indianapolis later. It was time to see Wharton, this city of the future. He turned his rental car north and then east on the interstate. The landscape slowly changed from rolling hills to the flatter Ohio countryside so reminiscent of Indiana.

It was almost dark when he pulled into Wharton, which, according to the sign, was a town of about twenty thousand people. The contrast with Angel Falls made him uneasy. Here, there were people out and about, driving along the pristine cobblestone streets, walking the broad sidewalks, and laughing under the bright umbrellas of outdoor cafes—a storybook town—as though someone had stolen the life force from Angel Falls and replanted it here.

When he reached the intersection at the town square, he looked toward the courthouse where workers, aided by bright lights, were sandblasting a new inscription onto the building's concrete facade. It read: Crelli Municipal Center. *And so it begins,* he thought sadly.

When he saw Mark Rosenthal Drive, he knew he was close. On instinct, he headed past some small businesses and then through a Norman Rockwell neighborhood of porches and old-London-style streetlamps. As the houses got larger and further apart, he saw a modern, three-story glass building that had to be the local Crelli headquarters. As he approached, he saw a sign: "Crelli Enterprises—FAB Division—Wharton, Ohio." He pulled over and parked. In front of the building, on a circular drive, were three identical midnight blue Cadillacs, company cars, no doubt. Maybe one was Mark's. He sat in the gathering dark waiting for the drivers to appear.

Soon, the front doors opened, and several men in dark suits emerged into the well-lit area where the cars were parked. Even at that distance, he recognized his son. Bernie drove his rental car to the point where Mark Rosenthal Drive intersected with the main entry road and got out. He now had a straight view down the long road. The Cadillacs pulled out and drove toward him. He leaned against his car door and waited. If he was right about seeing Mark, Mark could not help but see him. His anticipation grew.

The cars crossed the intersection. The first one turned, speeding off without noticing him. The second followed, and he placed his hopes on the third. Then the second car stopped hard, tires squealing. The third stopped just in time behind it. A rear door of the second car opened, a man got out and walked toward him. It was Reno Soren.

As Soren approached, he thought of Arlene's description of his attempt to kill her. He stiffened and tried not to show fear.

"Mr. Rosenthal," Soren said, smiling. "I don't know if you remember me. I'm Reno Soren. We met at Mark's engagement party a few years ago."

"I remember," That Soren and his boss had ruined the party was left unsaid.

He heard a shout from the second car. "Dad?"

"Mark." In spite of his anger, he was pleased to see his son.

Mark walked to him, hands spread in bewilderment. "What in the world are you doing here? Are Mom and Franki alright?"

While Soren stayed close enough to overhear their conversation without brazenly eavesdropping, Bernie reached out and hugged his son. "They're fine. I was on a business trip and missed my flight. The only flight back routed me to Cincinnati. I called but couldn't get through, so I decided to drop by." He glanced at Soren. "I hope its okay."

"It's fine. I'm just surprised," Mark said. "We're on our way back to headquarters to catch a flight of our own. God, I … I don't know what to say. You should have called. My secretary would have saved you a trip."

He stared. As always, Bernie saw Jane in Mark's face, but now he feared he saw Crelli in his eyes—and that worried him. "I know you're busy. It was a shot in the dark. We haven't heard from you." He paused. "Terry said you called her."

Mark smiled. "Yes. I've missed her a lot. I just wanted to talk to her again to see if, you know, there was anything still there. Andy suggested it, after unsuccessfully playing matchmaker a few times. He thought I was getting lonely, I suppose."

"I see." He hated standing in the middle of a group of strangers trying to talk to his son. Most of all, he hated Crelli for usurping his position with Mark.

"Dad, I'm sorry it's been so long. I really want to talk. We're taking the corporate jet. Fly with us? We'll add a meal and I'll redirect the plane to Indy."

"Your own jet? God, that's great, Mark. And now that I've been through Wharton, it seems to be everything you said it was. They even named a street after you. Mom will be proud."

"Andy and the townspeople did most of it, I just advised," Mark said, deflecting the praise. "Will you come with us?"

He looked at the serious faces of the men who would be accompanying him on the flight. "No, that's alright, son. You go ahead. Tend to business. I have a rental car to return."

"I can have someone return it for you."

"No, but thanks."

Mark smiled apologetically. "Dad, I'm sorry." Then Mark reached out and hugged him. He returned the hug but when Mark tried to release, he held on and whispered, "We need to talk at home, alone, and as soon as possible, please. It's important." He felt Mark's shoulders stiffen as he tried to pull away, but he held him fast until he felt a subtle nod of acceptance. Bernie released his hold and his son backed away. "We'll get together soon, right?" he confirmed.

Mark nodded. "We will. Send my love to Mom and Franki."

Soren interrupted. "We're taking good care of him, Mr. Rosenthal." Soren directed Mark back to his car, and they were quickly on their way. Bernie headed back down Mark Rosenthal Drive.

At the edge of town, Bernie noticed a pair of headlights appear in his rearview mirror. The headlights stayed with him until he reached the Indianapolis airport, where he exchanged the rental car for his own Lexus. He couldn't be sure, but he thought a car followed him until he turned into his driveway.

Chapter 19

Geist Lake—2031

The sun was setting over the lake, pinks and mauves painting the slate-gray and blue sky like chalk. Franki was with friends and Jane was visiting her mother across town, gone for the night. Bernie had only himself tonight, and he found his company lacking. He sat on the beach staring out at the blue-gray television lights, flickering from darkened rooms and mirrored in rippling reflections on the lake. In the distance, flashes of light from an impending storm appeared like a far-off naval battle. He sipped a high-octane Zinfandel and thought about the approaching storm clouds—the ones approaching the lake and the ones entering his life.

He sensed something at the edge of his awareness and turned. A figure silhouetted by floodlights stood on the beach, staring.

"You said we had to talk, Dad." Mark's voice was subdued but on the silent lake, it carried clearly. It sounded sad; a long way from the joyous greeting a father had the right to expect.

Bernie stood. "I wasn't sure you'd come."

Mark didn't move to embrace him, so he didn't force it. "What do you want?"

"Are you alone?"

"Yes. It wasn't easy and it took a lot of rescheduling."

"I'm glad you came."

Mark picked out a beach chair, placed it next to his father's, and sat. He declined the offer of wine, and they sat in silence for a while. Mark spoke first. "Dad, what's going on? I'm worried about you." Bernie was unsure how to start. Mark, concerned with his silence, continued. "What is it? I went to a lot of trouble to get here."

Though he'd been hoping for this meeting, he'd been dreading it, too. For the first time, father and son would be taking opposing and consequential positions as adults and professionals. He held the high ground but he'd never known Mark to stake out any other.

"Dad, remember that summer when I was eight? I opened a lemonade stand."

"Sure."

"You were away on business. I set up my stand and waited in the heat for customers."

He pictured the event and smiled. "I was in a limo heading home from the airport when I saw the deserted stand."

"I was home crying to Mom, because nobody was buying."

"Business can be cruel."

"Yes, but fair." They both smiled at one of Bernie's old and often repeated adages. "When you got home, I ran to you crying and told you about my disappointment. You listened and sent me right back out there."

"Rosenthals aren't quitters."

"I went out and about a half hour later, people started arriving to buy. For a while, there was actually a line." Mark looked out over the lake and chuckled. "You called your friends and asked them to help. I didn't know it at the time."

He smiled. "You're my son. I made a few calls."

"You're a great father."

"I do what dads do. As I remember it, when you saw the line, you raised the price of the lemonade. My friends gave me a hard time about that."

"Fair but cruel, Dad." They smiled at their shared recollections.

"Watching as you run a large, influential company, it's a dream for us. Mom and I are very proud of you."

Mark's smile drained. "Thanks, but …?"

"Yes, but, I'm troubled. Is this what you really want to do?"

"Are you kidding? Absolutely. This is a dream job. Everyone my age is struggling with his career. It's not exactly a good time out there. And here I am responsible for a highly respected, successful Fortune 100 company. I'm the luckiest businessman on earth, Dad. Think of what all this experience prepares me for."

"So you don't expect to stay with Crelli?"

"No, not forever, I don't think but I don't have a good frame of reference because I don't know many people who've started on top." Bernie smiled at Mark's comment. Mark smiled, too.

"Don't take this wrong, but have you ever wondered why Crelli hired you, and why he wanted someone with no experience to start at the top to run his business?"

"Sure, maybe at first, but what's the point? I'm doing a good job. Andy and the board like my work, and my compensation package is worth millions. The stock's been appreciating and we've shown the public four consecutive years of significant compound growth."

"Millions. That's great. Mom and I will be able to live in the best old-folks' home."

"You and Mom are pissed because of some decisions I've made. I know that. And I've been away too much. I'm sorry about that, too. But you know I love you and I'll take care of you."

"That's not it. We miss you, sure…"

"Is it about Terry?"

"No, not really. I didn't like the fact that you ended the engagement, or finding out the way I did, but it's your life."

"Is it your job? Are you getting along any better with the Toms?"

"My job's fine. The Toms are difficult, but I'm way too valuable. Have you found it awkward working with Gorman on your board after growing up with him as my boss?"

"It took some getting used to, but we get along. He can be a real ass, but I knew that going in." They smiled. "Is it because I'm doing something you always wanted to do?"

"That's a great question, Mark. I've thought about it. Frankly, your success does have me questioning some of my decisions. But I don't feel bad because you're successful. I'm happy for you, and I'm not doing all that badly." He swirled his Zinfandel, and then took a sip.

Mark changed the subject first. "Dad, Mom's worried about you and so am I."

"What do you mean, Mom's worried?"

I called her this afternoon, and we talked. She said you're under a great deal of stress, and that you have a lot going on outside of work. What's happening?"

"I think you've overstated her concern."

"I don't think so. Even Tom says you're distracted."

"I don't give a fuck what Gorman thinks, and he should keep his goddamn opinions to himself. What the hell did the bastard say?"

"Whoa, easy Dad. I guess I struck a nerve. The last time we spoke, he mentioned his concerns. He was just trying to help. What other purpose would he have?"

It was Bernie's turn to open up. "Gorman is involved in evil things with Senator Crelli."

Mark exhaled glumly. "What kind of evil things?" He leaned back in his chair. "I know you've had issues with Andy since the beginning, but in spite of what you think, it wasn't his fault I broke it off with Terry."

"Do you have any idea what's going on with the senator?"

"I know much of it, sure, I'm not naïve. I'm responsible for his former company. If I didn't know what was going on, I couldn't do my job."

"I know you pay attention to operating details. I'm talking about his illegal business dealings and the political stuff. What Crelli's doing concerns me and should concern you, too."

Mark leaned forward in his seat, elbows resting on the arms of the chair. "Jesus, Dad, is that what this is about? What could Andy be doing that is so illegal? Tell me. I need to know. I came a long way to hear you out because people I trust are concerned about you. Please tell me this isn't all you want to talk about, because if it is, I'm heading back."

So here it was. "There are rumors that Crelli has designs on the presidency."

"Dad, I can't confirm or deny that—not even to you. Remember our positions and please don't say I said anything. I'd prefer if you didn't mention it again because it will only give the rumors more play, and I don't want to be connected to that. That said, as far as I know there's nothing wrong with wanting to be president. Andy's amazingly dedicated and has a tremendous vision for America that he wants to share. If he decides to run, the country will be pleased to have him. I'd do whatever I can to help. What's your point?"

"It's not just the presidency. He has some very bad people supporting him."

"Like me, I suppose?"

"Don't be ridiculous."

"Then who?"

"Some of his business associates were killed after falling out with him."

Mark looked down at his black wing tips tracing patterns in the sand. He rose slowly from his chair. "Dad, I love you, so this is hard for me. You're way off here. I don't know why you think what you're thinking or how you got your information, but it isn't right. You were always my rational hero. You've never let fantasy get in the way of sound reasoning—and conspiracy talk doesn't become you. This is America, for God's sake. Why would Andy kill people, particularly if he wants to be president? He's popular, and everyone watches him. It's not like he's running the mafia."

"Sit down, please." When Mark made no move to sit, he repeated his request and begrudgingly, Mark complied. "I deserve more than that. I can't tell you how or where I got my information, but I assure you, it's accurate.

Don't take the easy way out by vilifying me because you don't like what I'm saying."

"If you have something on Andy, fine, go to the district attorney and let the courts handle it. You and I can't have this conversation; I'm responsible for running Crelli Enterprises and I have a fiduciary responsibility to the stockholders to act in their best interest. I love you, but if you persist it will affect my ability to perform my job effectively and if that compromises my responsibilities, I'll be forced to resign. I don't want that and neither do you."

"That's why ..." he started to say something but Mark interrupted him.

"I'm not finished, Dad. If the proof you say you have proves to be accurate and authentic, I can resign with a clear conscience, but more importantly, without hating you. So, if you have irrefutable evidence that will convict Andy, whether I like it or not, it's your responsibility to do something with it. But until you do, you'll need more than our relationship and your good name to continue this discussion. As your son, those things might be enough, but as an officer of Crelli Enterprises, they certainly are not."

Bernie wanted to explain what he knew but it was too soon. "You're right. I can't prove he's murdered people—at least not in a way that a grand jury would act on. Not yet."

"Then that's it. We're done talking about this." Mark softened his voice. "And Dad, I think, for your own health, you should stop dwelling on this. It's feels to me like you're tilting at windmills."

"I can't, Mark, it's too important. Tell me about the Wharton mayoral election?"

"What about it?"

"Michael Ely was a popular mayor yet he lost to Crelli's man. The election was rigged."

"No it wasn't. Mike's a great guy but he's lost in details. West came out of our strategic planning operations with real political savvy. The election wasn't rigged. The right candidate won. Why do you insist on bending reality, Dad? It's not like you."

Bernie knew he was losing, but he tried one last time. "I have information in my safe about a meeting that took place in Bermuda after we left. At that meeting, your senator announced he was planning to hijack the next presidential election. Read the documents and then you'll understand. He is not who you think he is. You don't want to be involved with him."

"If those papers are what you say they are, we're all going to be compromised—Andy for being involved, me for having to act on them, and you for explaining how and where you got them. Dad, you're involved in something you don't understand. I've seen it before. Andy undertakes heroic battles. Because of that, he makes enemies, particularly e-RATS who're technologically savvy and continually try to discredit him. As the father of the CEO of Andy's former company, you're being duped into exposing lies that could ruin Andy's political career just to take pressure off the real villains, the e-RATS."

Though what little credibility he had was slipping away, Bernie was proud of his son's ability to defend his turf. Mark continued.

"I won't look at your documents. If I ever decide to, first, you'll need to prove to me, absolutely, they're authentic and I don't know how you'd do that. This is a free country, and whatever is in them is protected by free speech, but that doesn't make them true or accurate, and I won't have anything to do with them until I know they are. I won't compromise on that."

For the first time in their relationship, Bernie felt like the child. He struggled to find winning words. "Something very wrong is about to happen. Mark, please don't hide behind protocol. These papers aren't fabrications and they are damning. How can I prove it if you won't read them? I'm doing this for you. You know that. I'm worried about you."

Mark just shrugged.

"Okay, you win. It'll take some time but I'll prove it and then I'll show them to you. Meanwhile, keep your eyes open. Senator Crelli can't hide everything and I'll be here when you discover the truth."

Mark remained silent. He waited hopefully. "Dad, we've talked enough about this."

"No, we haven't."

Mark got up slowly and walked to the lake's edge. He picked up a pebble, threw it, and watched as ripples formed concentric circles that expanded across the lake. Then he threw another pebble and watched the predictable chaos of competing ripples. He shrugged and turned. "I won't spy on him. He's my friend and mentor and I won't jeopardize my relationship with him. Promise me you understand and won't try to ruin my career or Andy's just to prove you're right."

Distraught, Bernie's fingers scratched his scalp. "That's insulting. I'd never do that."

"Good. I'm done discussing this. I wish you would stop whatever it is you're doing because I think it's going to end badly for everyone. But if you uncover something that absolutely proves whatever it is you're trying to prove, I want to hear it from Mom and not you."

"But …"

"No, Dad, I insist. Any further discussion between us could permanently destroy our relationship and I don't want that. We're done talking about it. If Mom believes I need to hear it, she'll tell me. Do you understand? If you convince her I've based my career on a lie, I'll take it seriously. This is non-negotiable. Now, I have to go."

He knew he had gone as far as he could and reluctantly agreed.

"Dad, what I really want is for you to get some rest. I know I screwed up your vacation plans in Bermuda, and I'm sorry. But take another one with Mom—just get away and recharge your batteries. You're working too hard. Everyone says so."

It was difficult to have his son dominate him so. "I'm sorry I worked so hard when you and Franki were young. I missed so much of your childhood."

"Don't start that. You were a great dad, and I'll try to be a better son."

They stood. Mark raised his right hand to shake.

"Put that fool hand down. I'm not going to shake hands with my son."

They embraced, although it seemed different from embraces they'd shared in the past. After a pat on the back, Mark turned and walked up the steps, disappearing into the dark.

Bernie stayed by the lake finishing his Zinfandel watching as the last flickering reflection from the TV sets disappeared and thick, gray clouds blanketed the stars. As the rain began, he grabbed the now-empty wine bottle and slowly staggered up to the house.

Chapter 20

Northern Kentucky (Across the Ohio River from Cincinnati)—2031

While her husband was removing his apron, Maddie Crelli was putting the last of the dishes away. The visitor was announced and escorted into the kitchen where she gave him a hug.

"Well, Mr. Mannix, I declare, it's a joy to host one of our oldest and dearest friends," she said in a honey-smooth drawl that came north with her from Savannah.

"It's a pleasure to see you again, Maddie. I'm sorry I couldn't get here sooner. Working for your husband precludes a social life."

She turned to her husband. "Baby, everyone says that. Give my godfather here some time off."

Andy smiled at his vivacious, dark-haired wife. She was taller than he and actress-beautiful with a runway model's legs. He prided himself on his choices, and Maddie was perfect for this stage of his career. Besides being the photogenic mother of his children, she was the only daughter of current Republican Senate Majority Leader Brent Bartram.

"Perry and I have a lot to do tonight, Maddie, so don't wait up for me."

She smiled and kissed each of them on the cheek. "You boys play nice, hear."

"As long as nice means victory," Mannix responded, smiling.

She smiled and sauntered off down the hall.

Mannix watched her disappear. "If I were married to her, Senator, I'd do the dishes, too."

Andy put away the last wineglass and faced Mannix. "Perry, more than anyone, you know how important it is for a politician to have a beautiful and devoted wife who fully understands the process." He smiled. "Maddie was raised for this, so if I have to dry a few dishes to sustain the special glow she needs on the campaign trail, dishes it is."

"I am overwhelmed with your show of love and devotion."

"My generation has a different definition of love than yours. Love was so disingenuous in your time. My generation watched yours commit to relationships in the name of love, doing so far beyond the attachment's useful life. It was that stubbornness that created untenable, unproductive, and expensive extrication proceedings, bitter feelings, screwed up children, and an oversupply of lawyers. My generation learned from your failures. That's why we have the advantage of fluidity in relationships. But enough whimsy; fill me in on what's new before our meeting."

Mannix held out a newspaper. "You saw this article, Senator?"

"No, but I goddamned heard about it." Andy took the paper from Mannix and refolded it so that the article was on top.

Kentucky's Junior Senator Planning Run for President

President Parrington will soon have more problems to deal with than riots, the economy, and e-RATS. The *Indianapolis Tribute Courier* has learned that Andrew Crelli, the very popular junior senator from Kentucky, will launch his presidential campaign in the near future. The senator has accumulated a vast war chest that currently exceeds two hundred million dollars with which to parlay the hero status he created while prosecuting electronic terrorists—e-RATS—into a successful presidential campaign. There has been no formal announcement and a spokesperson for the senator has denied the rumor but sources insist that the senator will make a serious bid to unseat President Parrington.

It has been rumored the senator is raising funds to help Tanya Brandt's fledgling Entrepreneur Party. Although the same spokesperson refused to discuss these claims and whether the senator has an interest in joining the new, maverick, business-oriented, libertarian-based political party, there are indications he is considering this option.

"Where the fuck did the reporter …"He crumbled the paper and threw it across the bar.

"Jimmy Shea," Mannix corrected.

"Where, the fuck, did he get that information? And why Indianapolis?"

"We're looking into it, Senator. The information about our finances concerns me because it's accurate and only Michael Bourke, you, and I know that. Could Bourke …?"

He didn't let Mannix finish. "Someone would have to threaten to kill Michael. And he still wouldn't divulge that, or any other information, because he knows *I'll* kill him if he leaks it."

"Then who do you suspect?"

"I don't know. It isn't e-Rats, because they can't hack past Gecko." He held up his hand to Mannix to signify he was using his phone. "Call Soren," he instructed his phone.

"Reno, Andy. Jimmy Shea, a reporter in Indianapolis with the *Tribute Courier*. Read his article from yesterday and stop him from writing another. Do it discretely and find out who his source is."

"Do you want him killed?" Reno asked.

"No, nothing that'll make news."

"But he's a reporter."

"So you have a challenge. Go." He put the phone down.

"Do you think that's wise?" Mannix asked.

"Reno's a pro, he'll figure it out. Monitor the Internet and see who picks this up and then figure out how to distract everyone until our media people can diffuse it."

Mannix made some notes. "Senator, I'm on it. Surprisingly, it's just the print media right now, so that gives us a cycle or two. When it hits the blogoshere and then commercial television, we'll be ready. I'll discuss it with my programming guys and we'll use our usual media people to obfuscate the story."

"I'll be monitoring. Say, Perry, what do you think of Tanya for vice president?"

"Absolutely not, Senator. I can't recommend that. She's your former assistant and she's heading up the Entrepreneur Party. It's already bad enough that this Shea guy has linked you two."

He waved his hand, dismissively. "That'll all get resolved. Tanya's perfect—smart, beautiful, and she speaks her mind in a politically correct, yet personal way. Parrington is an old-style liberal, but he lacks cachet with younger voters; Tanya has literally remade herself for that demographic. We can use Mark, too. That will leave only the semi-retired, college-educated males seventy to ninety-five for Parrington. We can win without that demographic."

"Senator, how do I put this? Tanya would present a problem. This election is critical. Anything that slows down your momentum is risky and rumors of a liaison between you and your vice presidential candidate are just such a risk. If you two would stop flirting in public we'll see how it polls."

His smile disappeared. Mannix was working for him because he knew how to turn polls into votes. "I appreciate your openness, Perry. Tanya and I will do nothing that jeopardizes our careers and our long-term goals. But times have changed. Today, public gossip about racy behavior is *valuable,* and it helps us avoid having to address complicated issues with those sectors of the public that will never truly understand them but love us. These people vote for star quality before they ever vote for principles. We're celebrities, and the public expects us to shock and titillate them."

"I know, Senator, but you can't rub their noses in it. Most voters live dull, drab lives and don't see beyond the sensational so you must be careful, for God's sake. We're counting on you."

His hand went up for another call. "Speak of the angel. Tanya, are your ears burning?"

"In my line of work, I have ceramic ears," she replied. He laughed.

"Perry thinks we shouldn't have adjoining suites in the White House. He thinks we can get more votes if we don't sell sexual tension." He smiled as Mannix shook his head.

"I didn't realize Perry represented our sexual constituency, too? Tell him to relax. He's been living too long with his own sexual tension."

Andy laughed again. "That, I won't tell him. So what do you need?"

"Drenge has agreed to support you. I wanted you to know before the meeting."

He disconnected and updated Mannix. "Good news, Perry, Senator Drenge will announce for us whenever we need him. He'll flip if he has the opportunity, but we'll cross that bridge when we get to it. Let's go upstairs. Gecko's preparing the conference."

"Senator, about Ms. Brandt ..."

"Perry, nothing is going on. I love your goddaughter. This is about the voters."

They walked through the candle-lit halls to the library that housed Andy's conference room. Inside, large monitors were suspended above a long table. "Welcome to command central," Andy spoke. "Tairaterces 159 and 2," he said. The monitors came to life.

"Senator," Perry interrupted, "should you be so open with your password?"

"Don't worry, Perry, passwords are an old affectation. My systems are keyed to my voice. It's silly, I know, but my password is Secretariat's name pronounced backward with his winning time in the Derby. Knowing it won't help anyone though." He smiled as Mannix shook his head again. "Link-up group four and connect," he said and one by one the familiar faces of his closest confidantes appeared.

"Welcome everyone. Perry has joined me here. Let's get on with it."

Tanya spoke, "Andy, is a Web conference wise?"

"We're okay. With Bonsack and Duke gone there's no one with enough technology to hurt us. Gecko is monitoring just in case. Also, we're using a new teleconferencing technology that Crelli Enterprises just developed."

As if on queue, a red light flashed briefly in the window of his logistics officer Henry Drummond. "What the hell. That's uncanny." He was perturbed. "Henry, it's just a glitch, but your connection is terminated. We'll update you later." With that, Henry's window blanked out.

"Gecko is analyzing the problem. In the unlikely event it was a break-in, he'll track and confirm the location, notify Soren and we'll have an e-SWAT ready team to eliminate whoever it was who tried to break through. Unless Gecko says otherwise, let's continue. Our first item is the latest estimate for the House and Senate. Tanya, go."

"You're sure, Andy?"

"Gecko's certain and that's enough for me."

She began. "The latest analysis we can use with confidence just came in from the field. Andy, are you certain the system is secure?"

He checked. "Security's tight, go ahead. Remember, people, we're going to run a country soon so our communications protocols had better be perfect."

Tanya launched into her presentation. "Five senatorial candidates who are projected to win have agreed to accept our offers and run as members of the Entrepreneur Party. Two other Entrepreneur Party candidates are in trouble—in South Carolina and Montana—but we've increased their funding so we expect their chances will improve. In addition, there are nine senators, seven running as Republicans and two running as Democrats, who are favored to win re-election. They have accepted our funds and in return, they have agreed to switch over to the Entrepreneur Party once we give them the go ahead. There's still plenty of time before the election, so this will change, but with the incumbents already committed and ready to shift and the favored Entrepreneur Party candidates, I expect the presidential election will provide the phantom majority we need to control the Senate.

"Because turnover is faster," she continued, "we're doing even better in the House. In the past three elections we've recruited a solid group of young, career-minded politicians trained at the Entrepreneur Political College in Lincoln, Nebraska. They bring along a strong constituency that strengthens their election chances and we're using our lend/lease program to ensure loyalty. For those unfamiliar with the program, I'll explain. Using our business network, we agree to fund and support a candidate's campaign as well as his lifestyle. In addition, we see to it that the communities the candidates represent receive certain economic advantages that will increase our candidates' popularity. When they commit to us in real, bankable political terms, we forgive their debt.

"By the next presidential election, we'll have majority control in the House.

I said majority control, people." The conference members applauded. "This is a milestone. There will be no stopping us. According to three sources—and Andy, I've rechecked their analyses—with Entrepreneur Party members and those who will switch their allegiance from the Republican and Democratic Party, we could control as much as two-thirds of the House. When you're elected president, you will have no constraints. You can pass anything and nominate anyone."

"Amending the Constitution will come later," Bourke added and everyone nodded.

"Let's not get ahead of ourselves," Crelli cautioned. "But two-thirds, that's sweet." It was all coming together even quicker than he expected. He muted the sound and turned to Perry. "This is why she's vice presidential material." Perry nodded.

"It's early, Andy, and a lot can happen," Tanya continued. "Most of the politicians will feel pressure unlike anything they've ever faced, so we could lose some and others might waiver. But almost a year before your election, we're years ahead of schedule."

"Tanya, what about the Chinese and Indian situation?"

"We're working on that. So far, immigrants from both countries supported by their governments have purchased homes and property in isolated areas but they haven't acquired enough to control local politics. We can't prevent that but so long as we stay on schedule the loss of some local control is easily resolvable after we win when we can trade favors with them."

"Stay on it, Tanya. China and India are pumping billions into a global emigration strategy. Their desire is to control or neutralize competitor countries."

"I'm on it. Now for the really good news." She smiled. "Our numbers show that even in staunch Democratic strongholds like California and large northeastern cities, people are so desperate and disillusioned that they're embracing the Entrepreneur Party's platform of aggressive pursuit of e-RATS, more federal aid to support small business, and more private-industry control of social and community programs.

"We still don't have an answer for Parrington's strength among immigrants, the poor, and elderly, but only the elderly vote in numbers we need to be concerned about. We neutralize that with the use of confusing ballots, which, historically, have offset the voting power in these groups. As we'll discuss later in our meeting, once the Mesh voting application rolls out, we'll have an even greater advantage."

"Thanks, Tanya, you never disappoint. Now, Michael, with all this good news should I reconsider and run for president as a member of the Entrepreneur Party?"

Chief Council and future chief of staff, Michael Bourke, responded strongly. "No, senator, absolutely not. We've reviewed the implications. No matter how good it looks, there's no advantage to running as a third-party candidate. The American people are always enthusiastic about having the choice but they never actually vote for a third-party candidate in numbers that elect. The decision will be different when we run for re-election. Besides, there's infighting within the Republican national leadership and they haven't recognized how far ahead we are. When they realize we have a stranglehold on the nomination, it is essential they believe we're loyal. Timing is essential and running as an Entrepreneur candidate assumes a level of unnecessary risk. With all of our advantages, it remains difficult to defeat an incumbent, even an incompetent like Parrington. We need a unified Republican Party to do the deed."

Tanya added, "I concur, Andy." He agreed with their assessment. "Okay, what's next?"

"According to our latest statehouse estimates," Tanya continued, "we have about 40 percent legislative control in twenty states and we'll soon own half of those states outright. With this election but no later than the following midterms, we expect to control enough state legislatures to own the constitutional amendment process."

He smiled at that. After years of planning and hard work, everything was falling into place. "Great work, everyone." A call interrupted him. "Hold on, I have incoming." He clicked the conference-mute button.

"What is it? I'm in conference."

"Senator Morgenstern is getting cold feet."

"Has he declined to join us?"

"Not yet, I believe he's playing for time or a better deal."

"Thanks, I'll get back to you, Sara. Go."

Andy clicked the conference monitors back to active. "That was Sara Weick. Senator Morgenstern is wavering. That's a wake up call. Before we celebrate too soon, remember, we're dealing with politicians here, not patriots and heroes. There will be immense pressure on them to renege on their commitment. We'll deal with that. Reno is developing contingencies."

Gecko announced that someone was waiting to present. Andy authorized the connection and a young lady's image appeared in a new window.

"Hello, Ms. Coffey, let's hear your report on the Mesh voting project."

Lorelei Coffey was the youngest member of his team—someone Andy had selected personally from within Crelli Enterprises for the assignment. She was very attractive, blonde with light brown eyes, remarkably similar to his former partner.

She appeared nervous. "Yes, Senator Crelli, sir?"

"Your report, please." He smiled reassuringly at her.

"Yes, Senator Crelli, sorry, sir. Yesterday, the United States government awarded Crelli Enterprises a contract to assess the feasibility of allowing citizens to vote on the Mesh. Initially the project was scoped for local elections, but at the Senator's recommendation," she nodded and smiled, "it was agreed we develop the functionality to include national elections. We have been expecting this for two years and the Crelli Enterprises team is already in place and productive. In two months, we will demonstrate the capability to a joint congressional committee. With the Senator's assistance, approval is expected, and we will then complete the project. The schedule is tight but the application definitely will be completed and demonstrated to every state for legislative approval, and we expect to implement in time for the 2032 elections. It will be a significant profit generator."

"Ms. Coffey, thanks for the report. We'll get back to you with any questions. I'm certain your CEO will have some significant way to show his appreciation to you and your team."

"Thank you, Senator Crelli, and everyone." Her monitor went blank.

"If you're interested in getting a more detailed update, Lorelei will be discussing the functionality at a special meeting next Tuesday. Ms. Coffey has no idea what we've been discussing here, nor does she know that secure, clandestine code will be placed within the application that can only be activated by Gecko. This code will allow us to alter vote counts without audit detection. To clarify, though the code will be developed by a Crelli Enterprises team, nobody there—including Rosenthal and Ms. Coffey—are aware of the modifications.

"Now let's go over the sequence of events again. In late spring, I will announce for the Republican Party presidential nomination. In August, I will win the Republican Party's nomination and in November, I will win the general election. Before my inauguration, I will own the allegiance of at least thirty-eight senators and one hundred forty-five congressmen in addition to those already on board Tanya's fledgling Entrepreneur Party. This will give us legislative dominance over the country. Do I have that right, Tanya?" She nodded affirmatively.

"Senator, we may want to delay, or spread out the transfers of allegiance so it doesn't play like a coup," Mannix offered. "Otherwise, we will need damage control to offset public perception."

Andy considered that. "It's a good point, Perry. Timing is essential. Still, with the country facing runaway inflation, high unemployment, food, water, and energy shortages, riots and bank failures, I don't think damage control will be all that critical, particularly after I've had my electoral way with President Parrington. Our media people can spin my shift of allegiance to the Entrepreneur party so the American people will be supportive. What's next?"

Tanya raised her hand. "Andy, when will you announce that I'm your vice president?"

"I'm not ready…"

"I can't be the Entrepreneur Party candidate for president because I'll have to get in line behind your vice president and I don't like waiting in lines. I'll do my job. I just want to be rewarded with the Presidency while I'm young enough to take advantage of it."

"We do our jobs right, Tanya, and the voters will reward us the only way they can."

"Fine, Andy, but I'm asking you when I get my reward. I'm the face of a great political movement but I have no future unless you say so. I'm asking you to say so, now."

"Senator," Michael Bourke interrupted, "She has a point. If things continue to go well, the voter anger could provide too many electoral votes for the Entrepreneur Party and force the election into the House before we control it. Why not win as a republican, with Tanya and remain republican until the time is right?"

Andy considered it. "Perry, what do you think?"

"Well, Senator, the two-party system is reassuring and our overall strength will allow us to deliver our programs either way. It may be asking too much of the voters to choose between you and Tanya— although you will win, she will get votes."

"That's interesting, Perry. Earlier you weren't as supportive of Tanya as vice president."

Tanya stared daggers at Perry and his face turned red. "Yes, well I said that but we need to win before we concentrate on reorganizing and getting re-elected and Tanya as vice president rather than a third party opponent will insure that victory."

"I haven't made up my mind yet so we continue with Tanya leading the Entrepreneur Party. The one thing I'm certain of is that America has sustained two-party democratic politics long enough. Given the situations we're facing and the decisions that have to be made, opposition politics is no longer reasonable. It simply won't take us where we have to go in the face of competition globally by autocratic economies. Democracy was fine in its day but it's a twentieth-century phenomenon. The process takes far too long to react in our technological world. Survival requires expediting, something committees and parties aren't good at. Given the time cycles forced on us by the Constitution, democracy can't compete anymore. For example, it will take far too long to end entitlements by vote and we can't create a framework for global competitiveness in committee. The only way to save America is to compete like the rest of the world and we must sell that to the voters. America's survival is more important than the perpetuation of freedom. It has always been my goal to use the Entrepreneur Party as the tool to reduce the Democratic and Republican parties to minority status and that must happen before the next presidential election. I want political parties to devolve into single-issue special interest blocs before disappearing as another of history's anachronisms. Once that happens, we'll be free to make our America competitive, great, and powerful once again."

Perry Mannix gasped. "Surely, Senator, you don't expect the parties to just give up?"

"Mike," Crelli pointed at Bourke's monitor, "you're the lawyer, explain it to Perry."

"Perry, remember all that fuss about Proposition 48?" Perry nodded. "Parrington begged for the right to act without congressional consent to stop the riots and the civil disobedience. His party was the majority but didn't have enough votes to carry the proposition. After heated debate, five of the more liberal Republican senators agreed to cross over and the law carried. The same transpired in the House. Those cross-over votes were our Entrepreneur Party members."

"But Proposition 48 allows the president vast latitude that Parrington never invoked."

"When the law passed, we made damn sure the congressional review process negated everything Parrington tried to do. The point is, Perry, Proposition 48 is there, waiting for us and our majorities. We have all we need to move Andy's agenda forward. When members of the Republican and Democratic parties realize that we intend to use 48, they will climb all over each other challenging the constitutionality of it. Only the Entrepreneur Party will support us. That's when Andy calls in all favors and shifts to the Entrepreneur Party. The aftershock will force the parties into survival mode as we assimilate their members. Some may join the loyal opposition taking fringe positions but eventually they will fade into history joining other dead political parties like the Greenback and the Know-Nothing Parties."

Tanya raised her hand again. "That's all fine, but where will I be? I'm vice president, not some loyal opposition. There's no future in that."

"Tanya, I said I haven't decided yet. Just..."

Just then, Mannix interrupted. "What's that?" he asked, pointed to a flashing red light on the monitor showing Bourke's image.

Concern rising, Andy stared at the warning light. "It could be an incursion. We're signing you off, Mike." Bourke's image disappeared. "Everybody, I'm sure it's just a glitch, but Gecko's checking it out. Everything appears secure."

He put the conference on mute and called Soren. "Goddamn it, Reno, I thought the fucking bugs were worked out. What's doing that?" When Soren didn't have an answer, he wondered aloud. "Just when you think you've got all of them, another creep crawls out from under some rock."

"It only flashed for a moment," Mannix offered, hopefully.

Andy held his hand up for quiet while he received an update. "Gecko is certain we're secure." His shoulders sagged. Still, it didn't feel right.

"Let's not tempt fate. Thanks everyone, we're signing off. Before we do this again, Gecko and the technology support team will run a full-system diagnostic. Just in case, everyone keep your eyes and ears open. Remember, with what we're doing, even with our sophisticated technology, we need to be diligent and vigilant. Soren will contact you before our next meeting concerning new communications protocols. Go."

He immediately terminated the connections, thus ending the conference. He and Perry waited until Gecko reported. Once Gecko confirmed that the problems were indeed glitches and nothing more, Andy poured two cognacs, handing one to Mannix.

"Perry, from here on, I want daily references to me in every medium. I want comedians joking about me, reporters conjecturing, gossip columnists exposing. I want my picture in sports stadiums, on signs, anywhere and anything as long as my name and photo are out there. I want everyone who doesn't already love me to learn how."

"You have it sir. It'll be like the Senate race, but grander."

"Yes, far grander." Andy raised his glass. "To victory."

"To victory," Mannix repeated, and silently sipped the expensive cognac.

"Perry, I've been considering a campaign slogan. What do you think of 'Andrew Crelli—A Hero for a Brave New World.'"

"Senator, people will remind people of the Aldous Huxley book."

"That's ridiculous. It shows how old school you are. People today don't read books, certainly not old books. I like it. It's bold and in your face. At worst it will generate the kind of hostility that will move progressives off point."

Mannix offered a toast. "To the next President of the United States and his brave new world."

Chapter 21

Indianapolis—2032

Bernie was frustrated as he sat by himself in the main room of Omega Station. He'd been there so long he didn't know whether it was day or night. His work at ANGS was suffering and he wondered why the Toms hadn't fired him. He and Joad had made numerous attempts to derail Crelli by exposing his illegal financial and political activities. Each time, Crelli's army of lawyers and media people easily negated their efforts.

Today, he was reviewing Joad's analysis of media outlets and their coverage of Crelli. The results were disheartening. He put his head in his hands. "Joad?" he said to the empty room.

"You rang, master?" Joad replied.

"We're in trouble."

"You should have used protection."

He frowned. "I'm serious."

"I believe you believe you're serious but the results show something different."

"So you've looked at these trends?"

"Not before dinner, it will ruin my appetite."

"We're failing miserably. We've seeded more than eight hundred stories in the last few months. By now at least *one* should have developed into something that would embarrass Crelli and cause him to lose momentum. He should be burning his time and resources denying allegations, and defending himself against charges of corruption and even treason. Everything should be unraveling for him. But …"

"If your grandmother had wheels, she'd be a bus."

"What? Never mind. Every one of our stories receives little lasting media attention. His people have even stopped trying to repudiate our accusations. That son of a bitch is beating us. He's more popular now than when we started. Do you have any suggestions?"

"I have been monitoring coverage. To use a journalistic term, our stories are like me, they don't have legs. Most of it is because the country is so restive. Parrington is stuck in the White House trying to actually do something about it, but he can't while the media amplifies the chaos and Crelli's speeches take advantage and provide hope for the electorate. The editors who carry our stories retract them and blame e-RATS for planting them. We are running out of outlets."

"But what we're saying is the truth."

"True, but the truth doesn't decide elections, it never has."

"Is everyone being paid off?"

"I could research that but I won't risk identifying myself to Gecko."

"There must be another way."

"I could trace things from the receiving end, but that would mean spying on innocent citizens to find one bad apple. I'm not comfortable doing that."

"Why not? The government's been doing it for decades. I have to know what I'm fighting."

There was a long silence, an eternity for Joad. "If you insist, I'll discuss the ethics with Arlene and Gohmpers."

Bernie raised an eyebrow. "You're making moral and ethical judgments now? A few months ago, you'd have just given me a smart-ass answer."

"Someone has to consider moral and ethical issues since humans seem incapable of it."

The only avenue left to him was the reporter, Jimmy Shea. It had been months since Bernie had given Shea information about Crelli and received his assurance that, if it were true, his newspaper would bring the senator down. Shea had said it could take months of intense investigation before he'd put anything in print. When the first story hit Bernie was elated and expected more would follow. There had been no follow-ups.

He phoned Shea's office, but he wasn't there. The receptionist wouldn't give out his phone number but took a message. Joad retrieved Shea's number so Bernie could call.

"Jimmy?"

There was a pause. "Yeah? Who's this?"

"Elijah Marsden. We talked a few months ago about Senator Crelli."

"Where are you calling from? My caller ID can't identify you."

"You should have it checked." He couldn't tell him Joad was scrambling the signal so his location couldn't be traced. In the background, he heard what sounded like a series of firecrackers going off. He waited for a reaction from Shea, but the reporter said nothing.

"Jimmy? You there?"

"Yeah."

"I need to talk to you."

"Look, the story's stalled." Shea's voice seemed subdued. "There's nothing I can do. I'll let you know if I get more." He heard another series of pops that sounded like gunshots.

"Jimmy? What's going on there?"

"I'll call you when I have something," he said and disconnected.

There was no hint of alarm in Shea's voice, yet shots were fired; Bernie was sure that's what he'd heard. The shots were orderly, the gaps between, measured. He guessed Shea might be at a firing range, and Joad confirmed the phone signal. He was at Fort Harrison, which had a range. He decided to drive there.

The range, on a former Army base on the northeast side of town, was not far from Bernie's home. When he arrived, he saw a beat-up Hyundai with a side-view camera missing. It had to be Shea's car. Whatever else was true, Shea probably wasn't on Crelli's payroll.

There were few people on the firing range and most were bundled against the cold while they fired various weapons at torso-shaped targets. Clouds from their breath billowed before dissipating in the wind. In the distance behind one of the targets, he noticed wayward bullets kicking up dirt from a mound maybe fifteen feet high. He walked to that firing area and found Jimmy Shea pausing to reload.

"I hope I'm not disturbing you."

Bernie flinched as Shea turned and pointed his gun at him. Shea lowered the gun and glanced around to see if anyone was watching.

"Marsden! How the hell did you find me?" He looked haggard, like he hadn't slept in days.

"I heard shots. You had to be here or in a shoot-out. What's with my story?"

Shea turned, pulled his ear covers down, and emptied his gun at the target. Some shots hit. After he emptied the clip, he turned back.

"There's no story. Can we agree its dead?"

"Dead?"

"That's right. No one would go on the record except some e-RATS the senator had convicted, and what else would they say? Public records weren't helpful, and Crelli Enterprises quashed every attempt to review their confidential electronic transactions." He reloaded. "And his lawyers—there must be a thousand of them—were ready to contest everything in court. His suits don't fuck around."

He stared disconsolately at the reporter. "Jimmy, you can't just give up."

"You shouldn't have come here," Shea said in a whisper.

"What are you talking about?" Bernie saw the fear in the reporter's eyes.

When he spoke again, Shea sounded desperate. "I've never fired a gun in my life. But after that first story, rioters attacked my daughter's armored school bus. And we live on a protected route. It never should have happened. It was my daughter, Mr. Marsden. My wife was almost run over right in our driveway. We pay extra to live in a secure, gated community for Christ's sake. And at three in the morning, cops broke down our door "by mistake," looking for terrorists. The next day, all the money in our accounts vanished. The bank said it was computer error, but it took weeks to get the funds restored. And almost every night for a month, my home security alarm went off for no reason. All of that and more occurred while I was researching your goddamned story.

"Then, last month, it's eleven o'clock at night, I'm driving my car in the middle of nowhere and it stops dead. Eventually, a car comes down the road. I'm ready to flag it down, but it stops a short distance away, leaving me standing there in the headlights. Two guys get out and walk toward me. Just silhouettes, but I can see what look like rifles. I'm thinking, 'it's all over.' One says, 'The story dies or you do.' Do you believe that? 'The story dies or you do,' like it was an old gangster movie."

He looked at the ground, shaking his head. "This is a thousand times more sinister than even you believe. There's no place in your life these people can't enter. I asked myself what I'd sacrifice for a story like this. I worried about it for a few days, and then made an appointment with my editor. They'd gotten to him, too. He advised me the story was without merit or substance and strongly suggested I look for another story or other work. When I asked to see our CEO, my request was denied. So, what would I sacrifice for the story? Mr. Marsden, if I was willing to sacrifice everything, it wouldn't make a difference."

"Jesus, is this happening to all journalists?"

"Journalists? Are you kidding me? There are no journalists, only entertainers and bloggers and see if you can figure out what's happening by reading a billion blogs. I don't know how far it's penetrated, but there's little substantive criticism of the senator anywhere. If there is a critical reporter, he must be getting the same treatment I'm getting. The media has lived through tough economic times and stockholders control our output now. This story is too cost prohibitive. There's no one left to fight for it."

Bernie couldn't believe what he was hearing. He grabbed Shea by his lapels. "You're telling me Crelli's people can intimidate journalists. God almighty, it was freedom of the press that *built* this country. If he can eradicate the First Amendment, that's an even more important story. Surely you can find journalists who'll band together to bring him down? Get your legal teams, the police, anybody to protect you. Use the blogoshere. I have resources. I can fund it." He began shaking Shea. "It's not too late to put a stop to this."

"Goddammit, Marsden, get the hell off me." He pushed Bernie away. "You're not listening. Because of you, my life is over. The senator controls more than you know, and he controls it completely. The media you're talking about hasn't existed for a generation. Where were you when it disappeared? What did you do to prevent it? A long time ago patriotic citizens driven by high ideals and a strong sense of freedom fought crime and corruption by exposing what mattered. Back then, communicating the truth was its own reward; there was profit in the truth. That's not true anymore. To be profitable today, the news must find a consumer by entertaining. To achieve profits, the truth is manufactured and high-minded ideals are simply staged. The passion of professional journalists has been replaced by personality cults whose passion is for generating revenue. Americans couldn't care less about the truth; they just want to have fun."

Bernie felt bad that he was pressuring the poor man, but he was desperate, and Shea was his only hope. "There must be a way. Who owns your paper? Maybe I could …"

"Our parent company answers to the great stockholder god. If you have money for a fight, our owners live in China. All you have to do is convince the Chinese that Crelli is bad for them, so by all means, have at it, but if you can't, forget it. As good as this story is—and Mr. Marsden, I honestly believe you're either right, or close to it, about the senator—the business owners who run the media won't have it communicated. Do you understand? The few newspapers and periodicals that remain won't carry it, and the blogoshere and Web newscasts haven't carried a negative story about Crelli since his name first surfaced. How is that possible? Somehow, the senator and his friends wield that kind of power, so for them life is good. For me to fight them, I need someone who's willing to go on the record, and no one will die for this. Why should I fight a battle that others won't? Go away. I wish I'd never met you."

Shea sank to the ground and put his head between his knees. Bernie realized, sadly, what he had asked of this poor man had ruined his life. He didn't know what to say. Shea looked up at him in despair. His eyes shifted focus until they stared down the barrel of his gun. "When those two guys on the road got back into their car and drove off, my car started—on its own. I'm telling you, they control more than you imagine."

Bernie stared, helplessly. Finally, Shea continued, his voice weak and weary, his eyes tearing, "it isn't your fault. It isn't even the media's fault. Americans are asleep at the switch. With unlimited access to information, they prefer to be entertained and to listen to gossip. It's pathetic. We're powerless to protect our own freedom and, worse, we deserve what we're going to get. My editor's right, if you can't make a buck on it, it just isn't news. We've lost the truth, and there'll be hell to pay before we get it back."

"This could have been your Pulitzer."

"If I continue, it'll be death for me and my family. On the road that night, they never mentioned Crelli's name, but he sent them. They were the same ones who scared my daughter, just missed hitting my wife, took our money, and set off the alarms. I bought this gun to protect myself and my family, but if they want me dead, I'm dead. It might look like a heart attack or a car wreck, it'll be their choice—whatever delivers the best return—but it'll be them and they won't leave a trail. I'm tired. Let the fucking voters decide; that's the American way, isn't it? Hell, to save my family, I'm working on a puff piece about your beloved senator."

Bernie jumped back as Shea quickly emptied his gun in the direction of the target. "I'm sorry, Jimmy. I'm really sorry I got you involved in this."

"What'll you do?" Shea asked wearily.

"I'll keep trying."

"It's your funeral. I hope you have a damn good reason to continue. Before it's too late, quit your day job, disappear, and hope they never find out you're still alive."

"Surely, there must be other reporters who can fight this. Can you give me a name?"

"I can't take a chance."

"Just a name, Jimmy. I'll go away and never bother you again."

"It's hard to know for sure, but there's a press stringer out of Chicago by the name of Forrester, Kevin Forrester, who writes a political commentary blog. He might be trustworthy, but please don't tell him I sent you." Jimmy paused. "You don't have a chance, but if you can stop that son of a bitch, I'll … never mind, just leave me the hell out of it."

Distraught, Bernie turned and walked to his car. From his phone, he requested the reporter's number. While he waited, he listened to the sound of Jimmy Shea firing round after round in the direction of a paper target.

It was a three-hour drive to the children's store in downtown Chicago where Forrester insisted they meet so they could get lost in the Michigan

Avenue crowd. Forrester's voice had changed palpably when he mentioned Crelli's name in their conversation. "Just last week I had my office swept for electronic surveillance. We found two bugs," he said. "I don't know whether they were Crelli's doing, but I can't take the chance."

Bernie walked up to a man in front of the store. The man asked, "are you Marsden?"

"Yes." They introduced themselves as the wind gusted bitterly cold off the lake.

"Let's walk," Forrester said. "It's warmer and harder to trace.

"Kevin, what do you know about Senator Crelli and what he's up to?"

"I thought you were going to tell me."

"I can't be quoted. Are you okay with that?"

"I'll have to be, since Marsden probably isn't your real name. I know you're afraid, but it would make things easier if you'd talk on the record."

"If everyone's afraid, why won't the press report on that?"

"Marsden, that's a great question. Crelli's the most insulated politician I've ever seen, so all I hear is innuendo and supposition. Without hard facts, there's nothing. This is your meeting, convince me."

Bernie nodded. "Let's start with the e-RATS. What do you know about them?"

"Electronic Revolutionaries and Terrorists are a global network of super-hackers, most funded by sovereign nations and rich foreign dissidents who oppose America and the freedoms we represent. Nations fund e-RATS to hurt us and steal our intellectual capital while dissidents do it because after the Third Terrorist War, well-funded Muslim fundamentalists realized our willingness to oppose them with even greater violence and decided that violence wasn't the answer so they fund terrorist groups to adversely affect our infrastructure, while mostly avoiding crimes against humanity. As a secondary benefit, it provides their people with marketable skills. Today, highly trained electronic terrorists create havoc by faking things, breaking things, and taking things that don't belong to them with damage estimates of over a trillion dollars a year. Senator Crelli came along at the right time and championed a successful, concerted effort to fight them."

"What if I told you e-RATS work for Senator Crelli?"

Forrester stopped walking. "What?" He shook his head. "That's cool, but impossible."

"Not all of them, of course, but many work for Crelli. He ran for the Senate at the time e-RATS were ramping up. Check the early e-RAT attacks; some were in Lexington, Kentucky, and a bank in Louisville was hit—Crelli's backyard. The senator needed an important issue to insure his political future and nothing motivates voters like terrorism."

Forrester shook his head, squinting into the lake wind. "It's so extraordinarily cynical, but if you have proof, I will blog it. If Crelli is doing that, he doesn't deserve to represent the people of Kentucky. But look, Marsden, I've researched the e-RATS who've been arrested. All are genuine hackers, and none had the remotest connection to Crelli."

"Many are also innocent."

"They were guilty. Some had printouts of top-secret government documents in their possession. One group had a list of daily ciphers for accessing Pentagon computers. They are not innocent."

"Okay," Bernie protested, "many are guilty. But some are innocent. Didn't the evidence strike you as convenient? Would sophisticated computer hackers leave reams of incriminating evidence lying around in plain sight? The evidence was planted. They were set up."

"So Crelli could get elected? It's freaking cold out here. I hope you have more than this."

"I believe it happened this way: Crelli has an extraordinarily powerful, state-of-the-art computer system that he uses to break through firewalls and retrieve information to enhance his business deals. When he can't make the deals, he has the business owners killed so he can acquire their software."

Forrester interrupted, "now you're accusing him of murder."

"I am. When Crelli realized that real hacker break-ins were causing a national outrage, he saw his political advantage and used his software to exacerbate the situation. He used the information he received to lead the attack on the hackers. It's brilliant. He controls the spigot. When he runs for office, he turns his e-RATS loose to terrorize America. Then, to show how effective he is, he turns the spigot down by capturing enough of them to calm the country and to get the credit he needs. e-RATS activity has increased again."

"And that means?"

"It means Crelli is ready to take the next step, the presidency. He has vastly more sophisticated capability now and can ride it all the way to the White House."

"And these people you say are innocent, the ones in jail, what about them?"

"That's the genius. With his technological advantage, he can easily trace most hackers. The last people he wants roaming free are a bunch of talented independents who might expose him. So, along with the terrorists, he targets innocent independents that have their own, significantly less frightening, agendas. They take the fall as e-RATS, along with others he wants to eliminate."

Shivering, Forrester shoved his gloved hands deep into the armpits of his dark blue overcoat. "It sounds like paranoia to me. I don't suppose you can you support this, Marsden?"

"I have proof," Bernie responded.

Forrester seemed genuinely interested. "You do. Why didn't you say so? You understand I have to be very careful. You could be setting me up. How do I know you don't work for Crelli?"

"You'll have to trust me. What you can't verify, don't use."

"You could be an e-RAT. They try to plant stories to undermine the senator all the time."

Forrester was describing what he and Joad were doing. "Forrester, do your normal investigation—you'll corroborate what I'm telling you. If you can't, ignore this conversation. But, if you find what I know you will; you'll have the story of your career and, more important, you'll put a criminal behind bars and rid our country of a potential despot. What do you say?"

Forrester surveyed him from head to toe, shaking his head. "Do you realize what you're saying? One of the wealthiest men in America, a widely admired businessman and U.S. senator, a man considered a patriot and a hero, has committed not only a great fraud, but also heinous crimes, including treason and murder. According to you, he's framed and jailed innocent people and stolen billions of dollars from individuals, businesses, and the government."

He stared straight into Forrester's eyes. "Great story, huh."

"It is if it's true."

"He has become so powerful so quickly, you must have suspected something?"

"Certainly, no politician is an angel. I've reported on his business practices and there are a lot of shenanigans. But this? Where do you suggest I start?"

"I'll send information by secure e-mail that will include names, dates, and events. I'll embed a password so you know how to retrieve it. Check the patterns of the e-RAT activity; see how it flows with Crelli's campaigns. Check out the alibis of the jailed hackers and whether their equipment was even capable of doing some of the things they were convicted of. I'll transmit some meeting notes I was able to get my hands on. Someone in the media has to put this together and get the word out before it's too late. There aren't many of you left."

"How do I get in touch with you?"

"Don't, I'll watch blogs and other Web sites for stories, and then I'll call. Be very careful." With that, Bernie turned and disappeared into the Michigan Avenue Christmas rush.

That evening, Bernie returned to Omega Station feeling productive for the first time in a while. They were on the right track, finally. He could feel it.

"Wait until you hear what I accomplished today," he bragged to Joad.

"Pillow talk is for later, glory boy. Right now, have a seat."

Curious, he sat at the console.

"Watch the main monitor."

On the screen an image of Senator Crelli appeared. One by one, six other faces appeared in separate windows. As soon as it started, he saw the significance of it. "Who are they?"

"They are Crelli's coterie—his inner circle."

"And Mark's not among them?"

"No. Put that in the plus column."

"How did you get this?" he asked.

"I belong to a rental club. How do you think I got it?"

"Seriously. You hacked into their teleconference?"

"Over encrypted wireless pathways. Gecko has an entirely new communication protocol with the tightest protection I have ever experienced. I tripped a couple of alerts before I figured it out and recorded it."

"You're sure you weren't identified?"

"We are in the clear. I dropped a couple of false alarms to keep him busy."

"Is this what I think it is?" Bernie beamed.

"Yes, we have Senator Crelli on file planning a coup."

He watched while the tactics and strategy were discussed. In twenty joyous, agonizing minutes, it was over. He was both horrified and elated. "This is it!" he screamed. "Joad, you did it. This is the mother lode. Finally, a story Crelli's machine can't explain away and I found someone who can communicate it. Joad, I could kiss you."

"No tongue, please."

"That's disgusting." He made a sour face and asked, "can you put it on recordable media? There's a journalist I have to send it to."

"Not Kevin Forrester."

"Yes, how'd you know?"

"I monitor your secure phone. When you called Forrester, I checked up on him. He writes silly Crelli pieces for the Associated Press and his own blog."

"That's a good thing, right?"

"What did you tell him?"

"Pretty much everything, just not in detail. I put him onto the e-RAT story. Why?"

"That wasn't wise, Bernie. He is Crelli's man."

"There's no way." He stared at the main monitor for a moment, at the frozen image of Crelli plotting with his team to take over the country. He should have felt joy, but Joad was ruining it. He collapsed back into the chair. "How do you know?"

"Forrester's salary is roughly eighty thousand dollars a year. He invested five hundred thousand in an international hedge fund. I traced the funds back to an offshore company called Tortola Press, supposedly payment, in advance, for a book. Tortola Press is owned by Crelli's offshore shell company, Tortola Enterprises, and it has never published anything."

"So he's their first author."

"Maybe. That is quite an advance for a first-time author for a book that is yet to be written. But there is a lot more. After you left him, I monitored a call he made. I don't normally do this but I thought we might be in trouble. Listen and learn."

He nodded and listened as Joad placed a call. He heard an eerily familiar voice.

"Soren here."

He bolted to his feet. "My God!" he shouted, and then whispered. "Can he hear us?"

"No."

"Soren here. Who is this?"

"Forrester didn't know who you were. He told Soren your phony name, Marsden, and that you knew about their e-RAT strategy."

"If he's Crelli's, why is he publishing pieces against him?"

"Who is on the fucking line?" Soren shouted angrily.

"He's like a hooker on the docks waiting for the fleet. He flushes out Crelli's critics."

"Jesus? Did Shea know? He sent me to Forrester."

"Does he look like he's been bought off?"

He remembered the gaunt face and the desperate eyes. "No."

He heard Soren say, "Gecko, trace this call."

"Can Gecko do this?"

"Not the way I routed my access path. Eventually, he might locate the right time zone."

"How long do we have?"

"A minute or so."

He heard a deep, impassive voice. The vibration from it raised the hair on the back of his neck. "Analysis almost complete, the call originated in Indianapolis …"

"Hang up! Hang up!" he screamed as Joad broke the connection.

All was silent until Joad spoke softly. "The big lug almost broke through. That was an unexpectedly unpleasant experience."

"How'd he do it?"

"They keep expanding his capability. To do what he did, they must have freed him to seek out knowledge on his own. He is no longer dependent on programmers. He is more like me now, Bernie. Gecko is a bigger problem than we thought."

"Can you keep ahead of him?"

"I have Arlene and the twins. He has... he has a different ... intriguing mind."

"Joad, when Crelli becomes president, Gecko will have unlimited resources. How will you keep him from finding you? Or worse, keep him from surpassing you?"

They were the first questions he'd asked Joad that she couldn't answer.

The senator stood on the veranda of his mansion as a cold wind whipped a fine snow past him. He loved this spot because he could see for miles to the lakes of northern Kentucky. It felt like being on top of the world.

"News?"

Reno Soren's breath steamed in the icy chill. "Yes, sir. A man named Elijah Marsden approached one of our reporters in Chicago. He explained his theory about our electronic assault teams. I don't know how, but he knew much more than he should."

"Like what?"

"He presented a dead-on explanation of what we've been doing, right back to the early hacking in Lexington. The reporter couldn't tell how much he knows, but this Marsden guy made a substantial case for incriminating us in e-RAT activity. We have to stop him."

"Do you know who he is."

"Marsden's an alias, of course. These will interest you." Soren handed him an envelope.

He removed several photographs. "Well, well, well, this will make Tom happy. The proverbial bad penny has reappeared, old man Rosenthal."

"This confirms it. Rosenthal was involved with Shea, too, that reporter from Indianapolis. It's clear he's an enemy. And earlier today someone called on my personal phone, the one you use. No one has that number. Gecko traced it. Any guess where it took us?"

"Indianapolis. That presents us with an interesting and uncomfortable problem."

"How do you want it done? Do you want me to do Mark at the same time?"

"No. Mark is ours. He's too naïve to hide something like this from me. But we'll have to manage it carefully. The kid's important to the election but

I can't abide his father's meddling and I can't make exceptions. Do it, but Mark must never suspect. I want absolutely no trail leading back to me, and no mistakes. Understand?"

Soren nodded. "Anything else, Senator?"

"Yes, after you're done, I want to find out about it in the media. Go."

Chapter 22

Indianapolis—2032

Bernie's days at ANGS were numbered. He was invited to fewer meetings and generally ignored. His name had been dropped from the distribution list for activities that normally required his involvement and what little work he did was performed far below his standards. Yet the Toms said and did nothing. He knew that they knew, but he didn't know how much.

One morning, as he pulled through the security gate and into the ANGS parking lot, a man knocked on his window. He stopped and rolled it down. "Mr. Rosenthal," the man said, "my name's Willie Brewster. Gohmpers sent me to look after you."

He sat in his car, wondering what to do next. When the man reached into his pocket, his first thought was to scream. Brewster pulled out a small package and looking a bit embarrassed asked, "Would you like a Twinkie?" as he handed him the confection.

Bernie got out of the car. "What do you want, Mr. Brewster?"

"Your life is in danger," the man said matter-of-factly.

"That's no surprise," he answered under his breath.

"I help Gohmpers from time to time. I saw this RFP on the Internet with your name on it, so I contacted him."

"An RFP?"

"Yeh, RFP, request for proposal. In my line of work, that generally means a hit, a job, a murder. Someone's been hired to kill you."

That worried Bernie but made him curious, too. "You can order murders on the Internet?"

"What else? You have to keep up with technology. Most of us in my line of work made the commitment to e-commerce a long time ago. Global positioning, project management, research, maps, travel plans, cash transfers, resource planning—it's a real cost-saver. Sometimes, when the pickings are lean, I use the auction to bid on contracts. It's encrypted and safe from prying eyes. I've been able to downsize my staff with the technology. Having too many people is risky in my line of work."

"Downsize?"

Brewster smiled. "Don't worry, I just laid 'em off. I don't do what my competition does. I gave 'em severance and paid benefits, too."

"So who wants to kill me? And did the RFP say why?"

"Bid came from a large contractor in Chicago, the Gelade family. Crime's one big pyramid scheme these days, but it's lucrative if you're good."

As Brewster spoke, Bernie searched the parking lot for his prospective killer. "Thanks, it's nice to know people in your line of work turn a profit. Am I in danger right now?" Brewster shook his head. "What about my wife and kids?" Brewster wasn't sure. "Why would this Gelade family want me dead?"

"Didn't say, didn't inquire. You're safe with me, right now. But you want to start being real careful, man, maybe disappear. If the Gelades are involved, big money says you're dead."

"How do you know all this, Mr. Brewster?"

"I subscribe to an online service that keeps me up-to-date. I see the RFP's and bids, all secret-like. Once there's a match, the deal's sealed. I saw your name and contacted Gohmpers."

"How do you know Gohmpers again?"

"Shit man, you ask a lot of questions for a dead man. Time's passing. But it's good you're not sure about me. The more you trust, the sooner you'll die. Anyway, me and Gohmpers met on the streets when we was working with the Prophet, Omar Smith. Gohmpers asked me to look out for you. If it were me, I'd get the hell out of Dodge."

"Got any ideas?"

"Gohmpers says you're the idea man."

"I've got a few," he said. "I'm not the most popular guy in some circles." He paused and leaned back against the car. "I can't believe they contract for murder on the Internet."

"The technology brings customers and suppliers together. Just 'cause we're not respectable, don't mean we don't have business needs like you got, here." He pointed at the building. "This ain't amateur hour; you know what I'm saying, amateurs die. If you don't keep up in my business, you don't know for long you're losing, you just die. Hell, the Gelades even got their own software marketing reps makin' regular rounds. We have user-group meetings same as you. Some of the breakout sessions are a hoot.

"Glad to hear it. What should I be doing?"

"You know someone named Sirlie Turner?"

He stared at Brewster. "Yes. Why?"

"I think He won your job."

He drew a breath and nodded. It made perfect sense. "He's a she."

"Don't matter."

"The murderer's *name* is in the system, too? Isn't that risky?"

"Risk's relative. We gotta have resource info. How can you schedule otherwise? But I'm asking myself why a dead man is so interested in logistics. And once this Turner takes care of you, somebody's gonna whack her, too."

"That's in the system, too? How can that be good?"

"You really care?" Bernie nodded. "Shooters don't have the clearance I do."

"Does it say why Sirlie is going to kill me?"

"Who, the shit, cares why? It's same as always. Someone's paying and time's passing."

Brewster handed him a stylish red card with embossed black lettering. It read:

Willie Brewster
President
Brewster Amalgamated Diversified Industries (BAD Industries)
317-555-2261

"President, huh?" Bernie asked while nervously fingering the card.

"Maybe someday I'll go public." He laughed at Bernie's reaction. "Listen, you know Gohmpers so your credit's good—not great. Need special services; you call that number. Now do like me and disappear." With that, Brewster walked to his car and drove off.

Bernie continued to search the nearly empty parking lot for signs of Sirlie. Before he called to check on Jane at home, he took a deep breath and tried to relax. Then he placed the call.

"Jane, honey, don't be alarmed."

"Why shouldn't I be alarmed?" She was alarmed.

"Honey, it's nothing. I'll tell you later, but I need you to call Mark and set up a meeting with him today, don't let him put you off. It must be today."

"What happened? Why am I meeting him? What's going on, Bernie?"

"I can't talk here, honey, honestly. Tell Mark you have information to show him. Remind him that he agreed to see it if you show it to him. He needs to see it today. Okay? Call me as soon as you set something up."

"I'm worried, Bernie. Please tell me what's going on. What am I showing him?"

"I'm on my way home. I'll tell you as soon as I get there. Goodbye, honey."

He drove home. Jane called back while he was in route.

"Mark's concerned. Is he angry with you?"

"He could be. Did he agree to meet you?"

"Yes, we'll meet later this afternoon at a restaurant on the Cincinnati riverfront."

"Great. Now this is important. Call Franki and tell her you'll pick her up at school."

"Bernie, now you're really scaring me. Why do I have to do that?"

"Everything's under control. I'll tell you when I get home."

Twenty minutes later, he pulled into his driveway and quickly ran into the house, where he found Jane pacing in the living room.

"Franki will meet me in front of Marion in about thirty minutes. Oh, Bernie." She hugged him. He looked into her eyes and they briefly shared their panic. He wiped away her tears and smiled as reassuringly as he could. "We don't have much time." They walked down to his safe in the basement. As he was opening it, he gave her instructions.

"I need you to take these folders to Mark. Once he reads the papers, he'll understand. Then, you, Mark, and Franki need to leave Cincinnati as soon as you can and find a motel nearby. Don't use credit cards. Pay cash. And don't use your real name. When you're settled in, call me on my secure phone. You have the number?" She nodded. "Good, I'll meet you as soon as I can, and we can find a safer place. Got it?"

"A safer place? What's happening?"

"Someone wants to hurt me." She let out a cry and reached for him. "I'll be alright, but I need to know you, Mark, and Franki are safe, and then it'll be easier for me to figure this out. Everything will be fine once you're all safe. Gohmpers has contacts that'll help us."

"I'm so scared." She lowered her head to his chest. "I wish you'd never gotten involved."

"I'm scared, too, but it's too late for that. If I could undo it, I would. The people who want to hurt me are a danger to Mark, too. We've talked about this. You know I had no choice."

"I know. I'm so proud of you and so scared."

He kissed her on the forehead while looking at his watch. "Go, get Franki. I'll contact you as soon as I can."

"Bernie, come with us. We shouldn't be apart. It's dangerous for you, and besides, you'll be more convincing to Mark than me."

"I'll join you soon. Right now, he needs you, not me. He wouldn't take this seriously coming from me—not after the last time. You have the information, and we've talked about all the important stuff, so just tell him what you know, what you feel. I'll see you later this evening. You can do this. I need you to do this."

They hugged again until, reluctantly, he broke the embrace. He watched as she pulled out of the driveway. He wiped a tear from his eye and prayed he could stay alive to see her again.

While walking out the back of his house, he called Brewster.

A voice on the other end said, "Yo."

"This is Bernie Rosenthal, Mr. Brewster. I need a name."

"Got lots of names."

"I need the name of the smartest, meanest bodyguard you know."

"Who's he protecting?"

"My wife and kids."

"Well then, that would be me."

"I need you, Mr. Brewster, now. My wife's driving to Marion College to pick up my daughter. Then she's going to the Riverfront in Cincinnati to meet my son. They could be in danger, too. I'll give you my wife's cell phone number, but don't call her unless you have to. She's already a wreck, and I don't want her to know she's being followed unless she needs help. She left a few minutes ago. Will you take care of them?"

"Got your back. What's she drivin'?"

He gave him Jane's make, model, and license plate and her route to Cincinnati.

"You're the one in the queue; why ain't you goin' with 'em?"

"I have business here."

"Must be pretty important business. Sure you don't want me to step in with this Turner? You wouldn't have to know nothin', and it'll buy you some time."

He was silent for a moment. He had no doubt Brewster would do it. "Thanks, no. They'll only contract someone else, right?"

"Right. Later. By the way, I'll send my bill to your house. You're credit's good but if you survive, don't be late paying. I also own a terrific collection agency." He laughed and hung up.

Bernie walked down to the gazebo. He'd hidden a second copy of the Bermuda papers and other incriminating documents in a waterproof container he'd tied to a rope and sank in the lake off the dock behind the gazebo. As he walked, he searched the trees. Not seeing anything suspicious, he cracked the ice with a rock and hauled up the bag. While carefully glancing again to see if anyone was watching, he removed the papers.

Just then his home phone rang. He ran into the gazebo to answer it.

"Hello."

"Well, well, as I live and breath, Charlie Brown."

"Sirlie?" He stared through the gazebo window, nervously. When he didn't see her, he let out an audible sigh.

"Yes, chile, how you doin?"

He noticed a sheet of paper on the table. Curious, he picked it up.

Mark,

I'm sorry I've been acting so strange. I don't know what's wrong with me. I feel so sad all the time—and inadequate. Tom fired me today. It was my fault. Mom and I had an argument and she left. I don't want help. I need your mother. I won't live without her. You know that. Forgive me and take care of them. I'm proud of you.

Love, Dad

What the hell? He refocused on Sirlie Turner's voice. "This will fix me up for good and for all time. Been fun, Charlie Brown. Thanks and bye."

There was an explosion. The resulting shock wave rippled through the gazebo, blowing out the windows and knocking Bernie to the ground, senseless. When he came to, he was on the floor, dizzy and covered with shards of glass and wood splinters. His ears were ringing. When they stopped, all was eerily silent. He staggered through broken glass to the opening that was once a window and stared out in shock. A side wall was the only part of his house still standing. There was smoke and fire everywhere. A few trees were down, lying on the walk between the gazebo and the house. As he stared at the desolation, his head began to ache and he felt sharp pains in his back. His clothes were ripped and stained red with blood from the shards of glass. Bewildered, he staggered out of the gazebo and up the steps, climbing unsteadily over fallen trees, slowly weaving his way to where the front of his house had been.

In a fog, he saw neighbors running toward him. When they saw him, some stopped. A few ran on toward the house. One person stood her ground, her face a mask of disbelief.

He limped, pushing through the crowd toward her, blood seeping from his wounds.

Seeing him approach, Sirlie backed away. He tried to chase her but his legs were unsteady and his neighbors, trying to help, impeded his progress. His ears cleared, and the silence ruptured into screams.

"Get him down! He's in shock."

"Did someone call 911?"

"Was it e-RATS?"

"Any other houses hit?"

"Bernie, you're bleeding!"

"Is Jane inside? Or Franki?"

Slowly, his equilibrium returned. Had he just imagined seeing Sirlie? No, it was her. He was on his knees as neighbors tried to settle him down. He craned his neck trying to spot her. Regaining some strength, he forced his way to his feet, screaming loudly. The sound froze his neighbors.

"Bernie, don't! You're in shock. You've got to lie down!" one neighbor yelled.

"An ambulance is on its way."

"Where's Jane?"

He staggered through a knot of people, many pawing at him. With trembling hands, he pulled car keys from his pocket and opened his car door. On the roof, a burning branch crackled, the front of his car was dented and scorched. Furiously, he backed out of his driveway and onto the street, the flaming branch sliding off as neighbors dove frantically out of his way. He screamed as the acceleration drove glass shards deeper into his back. At the far end of his street, he saw her car, a dark blue sedan, idling. Then abruptly, its tires screeching, it disappeared around the corner. He screamed from the pain as he floored the pedal. He accelerated past more and more people pouring from their houses, coming to see the spectacle that once was his home. His rearview mirror was filled with smoke. Ahead was the murderous assassin who had shattered his world. *That's it,* he thought. *No more.*

He chased her out of the neighborhood. Her car snapped the security gate from its hinges as she flew by it. He saw her again as he turned onto the main road that wound through the estates. An ambulance passed by, unaware that the victim was getting away. He continued to follow Sirlie as she tore wildly around turns, her tires on the edge of disaster. He knew the road and she didn't, so he gained on her. *She's going to kill somebody,* he thought ironically.

Ahead, her car screamed over the long bridge that divided Geist Lake. She accelerated madly. He knew that just ahead was a hard right turn. If she continued to speed up, she'd never make it. He grimly kept his foot on the accelerator. *Fuck her! Let her wreck.* Then headlights. She hit her brakes but was going too fast and skidded wide into the turn. She sideswiped the car in the oncoming lane and spun broadside across the road, kicking up gravel as the tires smoked. Her car stopped briefly then wildly turned and drove down the road. The other car was stopped, partially blocking both lanes. Bernie screeched to a halt to avoid hitting it and rolled down his window.

"Are you all right?"

Inside, a young girl was weeping convulsively. The car was dented badly but luckily, it didn't appear that she was more than shaken up. He backed up, and then drove onto the shoulder of the road, inches from an unprotected drop-off. Once around the girl's car, he sped up again and tore away. Ahead, he saw two pairs of taillights on the side of the road. Before he arrived, one of the cars pulled out and drove off while the other remained. As he got closer, he saw it was Sirlie's car that sat beside the road. He'd lost her. She'd taken another car and he hadn't gotten a good look at it.

He approached her car and was surprised to see her still sitting behind the wheel. He pulled off the road and ran to her. He didn't have his gun, which had been in the house, but it didn't matter. Not now. He just wanted to get his hands on her.

He looked into the window. "Christ almighty!" There was blood streaming from a pencil-sized hole below her left shoulder blade and another below her hairline. Blood soaked her collar. At first he couldn't make sense of it. *Had she shot herself? Suicide?* No, that didn't fit. Then he remembered the car that pulled away.

Whoever had been dispatched to kill her had waited until she had carried out her assignment—or failed to—and then took her out. Suddenly there was movement, a fluttering half-blink. One of Sirlie's dark brown eyes rotated weakly toward him. He bent quickly to her.

"Why?" He didn't expect an answer.

Blood bubbled through her lips. She smiled. "Damn that Derek." The wound must have severed the muscles of her left eye, because it was no longer moving in tandem with the right, and blood was forming along its lower rim, running down her face, as if she were crying blood.

"Left note, suicide," she whispered, followed by a wheeze or a feeble laugh.

"Suicide? Jane would know that wasn't true."

Then it dawned on him—the suicide note. It wasn't for Jane—it was for Mark.

"Sirlie, what about my wife and daughter?"

Her eye stayed closed for a long moment. He thought she was dead. An eyelid fluttered half open, though the eye didn't focus on him, but at some spot between them. "Soren's job," she said. His name emerged with sibilance, the way a snake might pronounce it.

"Is Soren after them?"

Sirlie's eye widened, in momentary surprise, and then nothing as death took her.

He ran back to his car. In the distance he heard the wail of sirens, police and fire trucks racing to the inferno that had been his home. They would be coming here, soon.

He called Jane but she didn't answer. He pulled out and headed south for Interstate 74. Although still woozy, he had to find them. He called again—there was no answer.

Ignoring the pain, Bernie drove in a panic. One word tumbled over and over in his head.

Soren.

He was weaving down the highway, nearly a hundred miles from Cincinnati. His family could be anywhere. Light-headed from loss of blood, his head on a constant swivel, looking down rural roads and into the parking lots of restaurants, gas stations, and rest stops, the trip seemed endless and futile. Then he remembered Willie Brewster. He slowed down, pulled Brewster's business card from his wallet, and called. There was a ring, and then another and another. "Goddammit, not you, too," he whispered in frustration. Then he heard a voice.

"Yo."

"Brewster?"

"Yo."

"Bernie Rosenthal. You got my family?"

"I'm with 'em."

"Great work! Thank God. Where?"

"Not sure, man."

"Well, what exit are you near?"

"No exits. We ain't on the interstate. We're on 52, I think. Got that?"

"Yeah." Highway 52 was an old, scenic back road to Cincinnati that meandered through small towns and endless cornfields between the cities. Jane must have taken it because it was so lightly traveled. "Everyone alright?"

"Primo, dude. Your wife's car was stalling out, so she had to stop. I didn't offer to help because you wanted me invisible. Right? It took awhile to get some help. They're back on the road now."

"Great. There's a change of plans. Get off the road and take them somewhere safe. Let me know where. I'll call and tell them you're helping. If I can't get through, handle it for me."

"Right."

"Thanks. Stay alert for company."

"I enjoy company," Brewster said.

Bernie pulled off I-74 at the next exit and headed north on Highway 3, looking for an intersection with 52. As soon as he got his bearings, he tried Jane again.

"Bernie?"

"God Jane, where've you been?"

"Bernie! What a ride. The car …"

"I know."

"How?"

"Doesn't matter. Where are you?"

"We took 52. You said not to call you …"

"Don't go any farther," he interrupted. "Turn around. I'm coming to meet you."

"Bernie, what's wrong?"

"Don't go to Cincinnati."

"But Mark …"

"Jane, I'll explain when I get there."

"What about Mark? He's in danger."

"Jane, don't argue. He's okay. I'm certain. Have you turned around?"

"Yes."

"Just keep driving. I'm heading to you."

"Bernie?"

"Yes?"

"There's a man following us. He turned around when we did."

"He's a friend. I asked him to protect you. Where are you now?"

"Metamora."

Metamora was far away. "How's Franki doing?"

"She's a trooper."

"Tell her I love her."

Jane spoke away from the phone. Then he heard Franki's voice.

"Hi, Daddy."

"Hi, sweetie. Thanks for helping Mom. Sorry about this, honey. I'll make it up to you."

"You don't have to make anything up. I had the afternoon off, anyway."

"Let me talk to Mom again. Love you."

"Love you, too, Daddy."

A moment later Jane was back. "Not much traffic. We're making good time."

"I'm almost to Milroy."

"Oh, not again," Jane said.

"What?"

"The damned car. The engine just quit."

"Shit," he yelled. He felt dizzy and grasped the steering wheel tightly. "Jane, leave the car. The guy who's following you, get in his car. His name is Brewster, Willie Brewster, he's a friend."

"Brewster?"

"Yeah."

"I can see his car in my mirror. He's pulling over."

"Lock the car until he gets there. What does he look like?"

"He's getting out now. He's a big black man. Is that him?"

"Yeah."

"Bernie?"

"What?"

"Is there someone else with him?"

"No. Why?"

"There's someone walking behind him."

"Jane, I don't think …"

She screamed. "Bernie, the man just shot him! Oh my God, he shot him in the head!"

"Who? Who shot who, Jane? He heard a faint pop-pop in the background, and the hideous sound of his wife and daughter screaming. "Jane! Franki!" He yelled into the phone.

"Bernie, its Soren! Soren shot him." And in the background, "help us, Daddy!"

He heard the screech of her car engine grinding in a vain attempt to start and then …

"Don't, please don't! Mark won't … please!"

Bernie accelerated and raced along the highway as fast as his car could go.

"Bernie!" "Daddy! Help! Daddy! I love you, Daddy, I love you!"

"Oh, God, Franki! Oh, God, no! Soren, don't," he screamed into his phone.

Then pop-pop. A pause. And pop-pop.

Then silence.

He screamed into his phone, but there was nothing. He screamed until he heard a voice.

"Rosenthal? Is that you?" It was Soren. "You were supposed to be dead."

He stopped the car in the middle of the road and stared in disbelief at the phone. Tears blurred his vision. A scream emerged from the depths of his soul, racing out to add its anguish to the misery already in the world.

Chapter 23

Indianapolis—2032

Wife and Daughter of Local Executive Murdered
in Shopping Mall Riot in Cincinnati

The bodies of Jane and Franki Rosenthal, wife and daughter of ANGS CFO Bernard Rosenthal were discovered in an upscale shopping mall on the Cincinnati Riverfront. The women along with twenty other shoppers were killed in a riot that was finally quelled by private security firm, Darkwater, in the early hours Thursday.

This was the first riot in Cincinnati since a curfew was announced by Mayor Miller last month. The death toll in Ohio is now over five hundred and nationally it has reached more than ten thousand. President Parrington is said to be considering ...

The media had more lies, but the truth was Jane screaming Soren's name. The body of Willie Brewster, shot once in the back of the head and once in the back, was found in a vacant house in Indianapolis near where he was known to conduct business. His car was parked nearby. There was no blood in the car, and little more in Brewster, suggesting he'd been killed elsewhere and his body moved to the vacant house. Moving Brewster separated the murders.

The police were helpless concerning Jane and Franki's murderer, and it was a waste of taxpayer money to chase down the murderer of a criminal like Brewster. Killings like his were often solved by someone cutting a deal. So, like the police, Mark would never suspect.

Hair unkempt, eyes red and burning, Bernie barely acknowledged Gohmpers and Arlene's presence. He slept fitfully and then only when weariness overtook him. When he awoke, it was with a start or a scream and the horror began anew.

Arlene touched his shoulder. "You need to eat something."

"I'm fine."

"Is there anything we can do?"

He didn't respond and eventually she left the room.

Gohmpers looked up from his reading. "If you want to talk …"

He spoke in a sad, empty, quiet voice. "My life's over. I've become Job without faith."

"We grieve with you. You trusted us and we failed you," Gohmpers said quietly.

"They're dead, Gohmpers, dead, because of me." He was silent for a while trying to voice something before adding, "My only hope is Mark finally knows who he's working for."

"Your son has been trying to reach you. Joad feels it truly is your son, not Gecko. Do you feel up to meeting with him?"

A sharp pain in his throat made speech difficult. "He'll need me now, won't he? And he might not be safe once he learns who killed … yes, I want to see him."

"Arlene can help. Speak with her." He nodded and dragged himself off to find her. She sat in the adjacent room drinking juice. He sat next to her.

"Please, don't give up. I can't imagine how you feel but, please, don't."

He tried several times to speak but each time he just ended up staring. She waited patiently. Finally, he took a deep breath. "I don't have the energy to do anything. I want to give up but if I do, the murders mean nothing. If Mark will join me…" He shook his head. "It would be …" He couldn't finish.

"Mark couldn't have known …" She paused. When he didn't say anything, she spoke again. "Andy always said if you live with passion, you will be rewarded."

"Jesus, Arlene, not now."

"He's a good-looking man."

Confused, he asked, "who?"

"Andy."

He started to get up. "Arlene, not him. Not now." He saw a tear in her eye. "I don't… why do I care if he's good-looking?"

"Bernie, I never told anyone this. I've been mostly fortunate. I grew up intelligent, attractive, and athletic and I never went through an awkward phase. I didn't realize it then but people accommodated me. They didn't do it because I was a good or caring person—I wasn't, particularly. They just wanted to be involved with me. Men wanted to date me and women wanted to be in my presence because I attracted hotter people—whatever that meant.

Until I met Gohmpers, and now you, I never knew what a good person was. The men in my life wanted me for my body and my mind, as long as I didn't act too independently. I understood the rules and took advantage. I used my gifts to get the special attention I craved. It took me a long time to realize it, and I can't tell you how disappointed I was in myself when I finally became self aware. It wasn't entirely my fault; I was born with characteristics that shallow people worship, and at a very young age I learned to benefit from it. Cheerleading, varsity volleyball, beauty pageants, admission to special schools, my special key opened every door."

"You were smart, Arlene, you deserved special attention." He spoke reluctantly because he didn't want to commit to a conversation.

"But there's so much more to life than being pretty or smart. Why should even being smart help me to get special privileges? I worked hard and earned everything. It's not that. But shallow things greased my way. It wasn't until I was lying in a hospital bed, drugged on painkillers that I had the time for nothing but introspection. Helpless and trapped, all I worried about was whether I'd ever be pretty or smart again."

"And you are."

"But at the time, it didn't seem possible. I was truly hideous and without hope of it ever changing. I had nothing but agony and a mind that was disjointed and confused. Some days I feared I'd live as a vegetable, like a pariah in some back room somewhere while my mother took care of me. There were days I hoped for even that.

"But every day, when I thought I couldn't feel worse, I'd lie in my hospital bed trying to picture myself looking pretty again. When I thought being disfigured was as unbearable as it was going to get, they added to my burden by telling me because of the accident, I'd never have children. Depression almost drove me crazy until my mind rebelled against it and I began to fantasize. Over time, those fantasies led to Joad and feelings of maternity that I had once given up on. When I had the chance to incubate her, I was thoughtful and respectful of my responsibility. I raised her with great care, never guessing where that would take me. I began to understand myself better and from that I reconsidered my view of others. I thought back on everyone I ignored or scorned. The sorority of attractive people is exclusive and inward-facing. We lack patience for non-qualifiers.

"Lying in bed, thinking of Joad was the start of what I know to be a better me. But that's where my good fortune ends. Andy took the core of what became Joad and made it into something hideous, something that caused Jane and Franki's death and I'm very afraid countless more will die, too, because of me.

"Faith is a wonderful thing. It doesn't move the world forward but it makes moving forward possible. My faith comes to me in prayer. I recite every word as fervently as I can. I have to. When I was broken, with nothing to live for, I willed myself to do everything to curry God's favor, hoping if I used my God-given charms on Him, He would use just a little of His magic to make me whole again. This repentant Lutheran girl prayed desperately and passionately to be forever in His debt. I promised Him everything—my life. If I spent even a minute not praying, I feared He would view my needs as less important and not worth His attention. I'm not religious, not really, but lying in that hospital room, I had the ultimate motivation. It's ironic that, in the end, it wasn't my charm but my heart He heard.

"In the dark solitude of my pain, He felt my need and worked His power through others to heal me. Eventually, my looks and my intelligence returned. But if that was all, it wouldn't have been His miracle. That horrific experience made me receptive to Gohmpers, who taught me to help others, particularly the less fortunate among us who should not be less blessed. Faith gave my life true meaning. After all, the underserved in our country are praying for something, too. Everyone's praying for something—even Andy's praying for something."

"If there's a God, Crelli would be damned for what he's praying for." Bernie forced himself to stand so he could end this ordeal. "Arlene, I wish I had your faith. I really do. But I don't. I'm not religious, and it's offensive to think somehow there's a threshold of prayer intensity that gets God's attention once you reach it."

She reached up to take his hand. "No, Bernie, that's not what I meant. It's not like that. For all the time and effort I spent praying, what I learned is that it's the God inside me I was praying to. Maybe it's the intensity of prayer that awakens that, I don't know. But my life wouldn't make sense unless that was true. I know it's hard, but you have to try to find your God, that voice inside you that drives you to feel that certain rightness about yourself and your world. Once you find it, you'll heal yourself and answer the prayers of others. Nothing matters more.

He started to leave but she continued. "You don't want to hear this but however important it is to stop Andy, there's more to life than that. Life only has meaning when you help others. So it's up to you, Bernie, to choose what's more important: vengeance that helps no one and goes nowhere, or a life with meaning. Before you choose, think about what Jane and Franki would want for you."

He collapsed onto the couch. Tears streamed down her cheek but even that wasn't enough to make him cry. "This is my fault," she continued. "You wouldn't be here if not for me. I launched Andy on the world. I gave him the power. If I hadn't helped him, this never would have happened. As much as he,

I caused the murder of your family. Will you ever forgive me?" With that she squeezed his hand and walked away. He let her go and stared at nothing.

Somehow, a meeting was arranged with Mark for the following evening at his office at ANGS. He refused the offer of protection although Gohmpers probably had someone follow him. Mark arrived alone, knocking on the door to break the silence.

"Come in."

Mark looked like Bernie felt. His eyes were red and puffy, his hair and cloths unkempt. Obviously distressed, he made no effort to console or be consoled. Each stared at the floor trying to overcome a sadness that allowed neither the ability to initiate conversation.

Finally, he began. "I'm glad you came, Mark. We're all we have now." Mark was silent.

He swallowed hard and tried again. "It's my fault Soren murdered them."

This time Mark looked up and a torrent of disgust spewed out. "Soren? What the hell are you talking about? Reno has nothing to do with this. Jesus, of course it's your fault. Don't start on Andy, God, that's obscene and… and… sad. If it wasn't for your sick delusions, Mom would never have left. How could you drive her away like that? Because of you, she was where she shouldn't have been when those vermin … what did you do to her… and why?" Mark put his head in his hands and let his voice die.

"Mark, what are you saying? It wasn't that way."

"I thought I knew you." Mark breathed the words. "You seemed happy. What you did to her must have been pretty bad for her to leave like that and for you to try to kill yourself."

"No, it wasn't…" He was light-headed and exhausted, and his words sounded pathetic. Andy…"

"Stop it." Mark yelled. It came out like a whine. "This isn't about Andy; it's never been about him. It's you. You're sick. I should have seen it. If I'd been around more, I could have … I should have listened to Andy and had you committed. Now, it … it doesn't matter."

He couldn't find the right words. It was his fault. Jane and Franki would still be alive, but it was Crelli's fault, too. He had to make Mark understand that.

"Mom didn't leave me." He thought back to the suicide note that Sirlie left in the Gazebo.

"You're delusional. I got her voice mail. She was hysterical. She was terrified of you."

"It wasn't that way." How could he explain that what Mark heard hadn't been Jane's voice? "I told her to go. Yes, that's my fault. See, I'm not crazy. I know what I did." He hesitated, hoping Mark would want to believe him. "We talked at the lake that night and you said if I had proof ..."

"Damn it, don't. Stop it right now. I'm not listening and it doesn't matter."

"It does. You know me. Why would I do that unless I had a good reason?"

"Because you're sick. I was so absorbed in my career and so convinced you and mom were alright. There were signs, if I'd paid attention. I should have done something and Mom and Franki would be alive."

"No, it's not like that."

Mark ran his hands through his hair. "I could have prevented it," he said, talking to himself. "They could have come with me until ..." He looked up. "Get help. I won't have anything more to do with you. I can't. You're not my responsibility. Tom will give you a leave of absence, and Andy knows a place where you can get the care you need."

"Mark, you have to have more faith in me. I'm not delusional or paranoid. I'm sad and depressed and lonely but you feel that way too. You can't put me away. I know what happened and I can prove it. You and I together, we can stop them. We owe them, Mark, for what they did to Mom and Franki. We can make them regret what they did to us. You and I will put Crelli and that animal Soren behind bars where they belong. Listen to me, Mark. You have to help me avenge Mom and Franki. What do you say?"

But Mark was gone.

Chapter 24

Indianapolis, Temple Beth Shalom—2032

The litany of the Kaddish echoed throughout the temple.

"Yit-gadal v'yit-kadash sh'mey raba ..." recited the congregation.

"Y'hey sh'mey raba m'varah l'alam ul'almey alma-ya," the mourners responded.

Though he stood in the front row of the temple between his secretary, Carolyn, and Jane's mother, Edith, he was utterly alone. Mark, wearing sunglasses, also stood reciting, but he was several aisles away with Terry by his side. That distance only added to Bernie's aching emptiness. On a day when they should have been there for each other, his son avoided him, sitting instead next to the murderer, Crelli, who coolly stared straight ahead. Soren was nowhere to be seen.

"Oseh shalom bim-romav, hu ya-aseh shalom aleynu v'al kol yisrael, v'mru amen."

The temple was full today, but the old men in shawls and hats who regularly attended were the only ones who truly understood the Mourner's Kaddish. This prayer wasn't for the departed; their trouble was over. This prayer was for the living, but Bernie was impervious to its message.

Row after row of well-dressed friends, neighbors, and business associates came forward to comfort him. Their attempts were awkward as he faced them with his drawn face, darkened eyes, bandaged neck, and the cane he needed to walk. He shook their hands, while nodding vacantly. Like the Kaddish prayer itself, words had no meaning for him. He was uncomfortably numb, with a deep emptiness that ached like nothing he'd ever known—like someone had sliced the inside of his throat through to his heart with a razor.

His reddened eyes downcast, he instinctively shook another extended hand. It was large and brown. A tall, older-looking black man wearing sunglasses and dressed in a cheap suit stood before him. With him was a pink-faced man whose eyes looked so completely different without their childlike twinkle.

"You shouldn't be here," he whispered. Next to him, Jane's mother sensed urgency in his voice and glanced at the men. "They came a long way," he explained to her. She nodded.

Damon's darkened hair was combed straight and he wore stylish glasses, looking the part of a junior executive. Fortunately, Crelli took no notice.

"Thanks for coming."

Gohmpers squeezed his hand and Damon laid his hand on theirs. Then they moved away. He accepted a few more mourners before another pink-faced, bearded man with his dark-haired wife stopped before him. The man hugged him and whispered in his ear.

"Joad sends her condolences." Damian and Arlene were unrecognizable.

He whispered, "be careful, Crelli's here …" his voice trailing off. As if overhearing, Crelli glanced briefly toward him but looked quickly away.

Obviously anxious, Arlene avoided looking up. "There's no way we wouldn't be here."

Bernie glanced again to where Mark was standing. They hadn't spoken since that day earlier in the week. Their eyes met and Mark looked away. Terry held his hand.

He met Terry's glance and searched her eyes. She started to go to him, but Mark held her back. He watched their brief, animated discussion. Finally, she shook her head vigorously, pulled away, and walked to him.

Crying, she hugged him. "Terry, I'm glad you're here. My son needs you."

"I'm so sorry about Jane and Franki. They were family. I loved them."

He looked down, tears welling again. *Would this ever be only a memory? How could he endure?*

"Don't be angry with Mark. He hurts so much. Like you. Like we all do."

"Then why does he sit with the man who murdered them?"

"Please, don't." She looked up, tears running down her cheeks. "That isn't right."

Had they already warned her? He looked away. She reached for his hand, and he noticed a wedding ring on her finger. "What?" he asked.

She nodded. "This is the worst time, but, you're my dad now."

Jane and Franki would've been so happy. Tears flowed, though these were different tears. He tried to smile. "How?"

"There wasn't much time," she said. "He lives so fast and hard that sometimes it's difficult for mere mortals like me to keep up."

"When?"

"Last night, in a civil ceremony. I didn't know what to do. I love him so much and I have for so long. I wanted you to be there, but he wouldn't … you know. Don't be angry, it had to be that way. He's so alone. He was lonely before but … I love him; I can help him."

He swallowed hard so he could talk.

"Mark wanted to wait but … Mr. Crelli insisted. He had me flown to Cincinnati and then Mark proposed. I'm happy except …"

Bernie couldn't bear it. They married at Crelli's insistence. "I've wanted you in our family since that day Mark brought you home to fish at our lake …"

"We'll fish again. You two need each other. I'll work on him. Give him time."

"You'll always be family, but I don't think Mark and I will again."

Tears filled her eyes. "Don't say that; it will make me so sad."

"I'm sorry. Too much has happened, things you don't know and can't imagine. He blames me and himself. He's not wrong, but he can't see who's really to blame. Until he does, we'll never forgive each other. Maybe we shouldn't. He believes in the wrong person."

"Don't give up on him."

Bernie's eyes blurred with tears of resignation. "He's my son. I'll always love him but …" He paused, fighting back more tears. "It helps to know you're with him. Terry, love him and feel sorry for me. Jane and Franki will always be in my heart, but I am in no one's heart, anymore."

"I'm so sorry," she said softly. She gave him a hug and walked back to Mark.

Today, the Mourner's Kaddish could only sustain the regulars.

By the time the funeral party arrived at the cemetery, snow was falling. It would cover but it couldn't cleanse. Their breath visible in the frigid air, he and Mark stood facing each other, separated by twin white caskets. While the Rabbi intoned the interment prayers, Bernie's eyes remained riveted on the caskets. When he dared look up, Mark's gaze, too, was focused on the caskets. Standing by Mark's side, Terry, apparently chastened during their drive to the cemetery, stared at the ground, her arm in his. Impervious, Crelli stood behind them, hands on their shoulders.

He sensed a subtle look of defiance in Crelli's gaze. Was it the satisfaction that comes from a perfect murder? The caskets were lowered. Bernie stooped to gather a handful of dirt and placed it and a white rose on each casket. He stooped again to grab more dirt. This time he stood and stared directly at Crelli.

"You son of a bitch, you murdered them," he shouted. "Eat their dirt." He hurled the dirt at the senator.

Crelli flinched as his bodyguards scurried from their positions to protect him. Bernie heard the clicking sounds of gunlocks as they disengaged. From a discreet distance, media photographers patiently waiting saw their opportunity and maneuvered for the right perspective.

Crelli calmly wiped the frozen dirt from his trench coat and signaled discreetly for his bodyguards to hold back.

"You murdered my wife and daughter, you Nazi cretin."

"Dad," Terry wailed. "Please, no."

He pointed to Crelli. "You killed them," he said louder as mourners, embarrassed by his tirade, slowly edged away. The Rabbi grabbed him by the arm.

"Bernard, control your grief. Your loved ones wouldn't want this."

He faced Mark. "Like it or not, you have to know." He faced the cameramen. "Your buddy, Senator Crelli ordered his assassin, Reno Soren, to murder Mom and Franki. Another hired gun destroyed our home and tried to kill me."

A murmur rippled through the crowd. Sensing a story, the media closed in and began recording for the evening news.

"That's right; your perfect senator ordered his mongrel pet, Soren, to kill mom and Franki, just like the others he's killed before."

Shielded by his entourage, Crelli turned and walked slowly to his limo. Revolted, Mark grabbed his bride firmly and angrily followed Crelli. Bernie limped after them through the accumulating snow.

The Rabbi shouted to him, "Stop this, Bernard. Think of Jane and Frances. You're on hallowed ground. What you're doing is sacrilege."

He shouted to the Rabbi, "No, Rabbi, what this monster did, that was sacrilege." He yelled to Mark, "I heard it all on the phone. Mom screamed Soren's name before he killed her. Am I that sick? Would I make that up? Mom screamed Soren's name." With Terry sobbing, Mark helped her into their limo and it sped away.

With Mark gone, he focused on Crelli, who hadn't yet reached his limo. "Tell them, Senator," he shouted. "Tell them how Soren stopped Jane's car with that electromagnetic-pulse thing, the way you stopped Jimmy Shea's car when your men told him not to write about you."

Crelli, confident his bodyguards were well placed, turned to face him. "Mr. Rosenthal, I grieve for the loss of Mark's mother and sister. I understand your grief; but it has gotten the best of you. You need help." With that, he motioned his entourage to their cars.

A reporter rushed forward. "Senator," he shouted, "can you comment on these charges?"

Stuck in the back of a forming crowd, he watched as the senator took advantage of his media opportunity. "There are no charges. Like all Americans, I am deeply distressed by the senseless murders of the mother and sister of Mark Rosenthal, a great and loyal friend. And like all Americans, I've had enough. It's time we take control and end this violence and punish the evil people who are fomenting it. The district attorney has assured me that the investigation is proceeding, and I have offered him everything in my considerable arsenal to bring the instigators of these riots and the perpetrators of this heinous crime to justice. I have the highest regard for Mark Rosenthal and will do whatever I can to help his father get the care he needs in this time of great anguish. I have nothing more to say."

With that, Crelli's driver opened the limo door, and Bernie saw an image that froze his blood—the large square jaw and thick eyebrows of Reno Soren. It stripped away his last vestige of control. Like a madman, he wielded his cane and fought through the crowd to the limo.

"Get out!" he yelled. "Murderer, get out," his voice cracked with the strain of a scream fueled by loathing. He broke his cane on the roof of the car, denting it. "Get out tough guy, killer of defenseless women. Get out you son of a bitch, and I'll break your fucking neck."

Smirking, Soren emerged from the car and drew himself to his full height. Before he could close the distance, Gohmpers stepped in front of him, his unflinching eyes inches from Soren's. The crowd grew silent as the two large men confronted each other. Soren tried to push past, but Gohmpers was unmovable, his eyes a surreal calm.

"Please, Mr. Soren, get back in the car," Crelli said serenely. Determined to take control of the situation, Crelli pointed to his entourage, "the rest of you, too."

For a moment, Soren didn't move. He just stared at the intractable man in front of him. Then, slowly his master's voice registered and he backed away and got back in the car. Crelli looked at Bernie, and then at Gohmpers, before finally climbing in and closing the door. His entourage scampered to their cars, and the motorcade sped off.

He watched, in despair as the cars disappeared through the now driving snow. What a coward he was. He had confronted his wife and daughter's murderers and could only rant. He limped away from the people, up the hill to the gravesite, now peacefully covered in snow.

He stood in the eerie silence beside the snow-covered mounds and raised his fist. He screamed so the dead could hear. "I'll avenge you if it takes forever." Exhausted, his body crumpled to the ground. "I promise," came out as a whimper.

After everyone had departed, his secretary, Carolyn, came to help him to his limo. With his head and shoulders covered in snow, he limped to the car. Inside, he sagged against her, unaware he was shivering and unappreciative of the warmth.

Chapter 25

Aeden—2065

Gil slumped against the bed in Bernie's hospice room. "That can't be right," he said. "Chairman Crelli is the greatest American ever. He couldn't do what you just said."

Bernie was so weary, he wanted to sleep, but he couldn't lose what credibility his story had achieved. "Gil, winners write history. Crelli has done worse than murdering my wife and daughter, far worse. To prune America to his vision, he's murdered tens of millions of innocent American citizens."

"That's wrong. There's no way anyone would or could kill that many people."

"I live to prove it to you."

"What about Mark?" Gil asked, changing the subject. "What happened to him?"

"My son was the last American president."

"That's because with a chairman, we didn't need a president."

"And a constitution either."

"I don't even know what a constitution is. You are lying. Why?"

"I'm not. You believe what they want you to believe. It is their lie, not mine. Ask yourself what feels right, Gil. I lived for my family, and when Crelli murdered them and even my own son couldn't see the truth, I didn't think I could continue. When I needed anything, when I was in trouble, Jane was there for me, always. I couldn't live without her. I do now, but I miss her love so terribly much. And I never saw Franki hug someone like she once hugged me." His voice choked and he was forced to pause. When he gained strength, he continued softly. "That's how Crelli hurt me—and how he hurt so many more in addition to me. Someone once said there's freedom in having nothing left to lose. That's why I've been fighting him all these years and why I'm here, today. It's why I must convince you to help me."

"I'm not sure I believe you."

"You must believe me. How could you not believe me?"

Gil didn't argue. "I don't know. I don't, that's all but I do want to help you. What do you want me to do?"

"Bring Mark to me."

"President Rose is alive?"

"He lives in a mansion in Avalon. I've tried to rescue him before, but he is being watched and I can't get to him. I need someone—you— because you can."

"What if I'm caught?"

"There are things so important that no risk is too great. This is one of those things."

"But what about Howard? If I'm caught, it will be bad for him—he couldn't deal with that."

"Mark is your father's father. He's family. Howard would want this."

"But you could be a terrorist, and all this could be a lie ..."

"But I'm not a terrorist and this is the truth. If you could get in touch with your heart you'd know it."

He saw something in the boy's eyes and desperately wanted to believe. "Can I decide in the morning?" Gil asked.

If he let the boy go, there was no telling what would happen tomorrow. He needed an answer now but trusted his instincts. "Gil, I trust you to do the right thing. Come back early." Before Gil left, Bernie added, "and don't say anything to anyone, including Howard."

"I'll see you in the morning." Gil left. All that remained was to wait and fret.

Gil arrived home to an empty house. He sat on his bed, confused, and forced himself to think it through. He believed Bernie, mostly. But that stuff about the Chairman, murder, that couldn't be right. Still, he wanted to help and it would be an adventure—Avalon and seeing his grandfather, the former president. But, if he agreed to do it, his life could change, Howard's, too. And he could get caught. He shuddered to think what chemical treatments would be like. *After this, then what? Would he remain in Aeden? Would his access to Archive and Virtuoso be revoked? Could he do that to Howard? And Andrea? And Andrea.* He prepared to enter Virtuoso.

They met on a pale green beach in the heat of summer. Over the roar of bluish green waves rhythmically rolling, cresting, and crashing onto the sand, he heard the sounds of trilling sea birds. From the deep blue sky, large red and orange gulls swooped along the crests of the waves in search of tiny, yellow and red, iridescent fish that skimmed the surface. In the air, colorful balloons with striking logos from companies like ANGS floated by. On the beach, tiny purple, long-legged and featherless birds feasted in the foam on what the breaking waves provided. Tanned and smiling, Andrea, wearing a white bikini, sat on a blanket, staring up at him with a look of devotion that warmed him more than the sun.

"You look great."

She looked embarrassed. "Thanks. You look really worried. What's wrong? Can I help?"

"No, everything is okay."

"Gil, don't shut me out. I know you better than anyone. Let me help."

In response, he dropped to the blanket and their bodies entwined. He pulled back to look into her eyes. "There is something …" Before he could tell her, he was interrupted by the sound of a vendor hawking his wares to customers along the beach.

"ANGS Cream, snow cones and mind altering Pharma, here." The vendor stopped beside him, blocking the sun.

"Gil, you look like you could use some refreshments," said a cheerful voice. "I have whatever you need. Oh, hi, Andrea." The vendor-avatar nodded to her, and then walked onto the blanket between them to face Gil. "Enjoy your stay at the StarMesh Hotel?"

Gil squinted, shading his eyes with his arm. "Wu Tung. How are you?"

"Great. I did some research since our last meeting." Wu Tung turned to Andrea who avoided his gaze. "This one is not recorded in our system inventory."

Andrea reached for Gil. "Make him leave," she said. "He scares me."

"Wu Tung, you're frightening my girlfriend. You and I can talk in another session."

The avatar leaned down and whispered, "You're making a mistake. We need to talk, now." Wu Tung pointed and motioned for Gil to follow.

Andrea squeezed his arm. "Don't leave, Gil. He scares me."

"Calm down, lady, everything is fine. I just need a moment with your boyfriend."

Gil followed Wu Tung to a spot under the boardwalk where they sat in the cool sand.

"Be careful of her, bro," the avatar began.

"Andrea? No way, I designed her. She's been with me for two years."

"You did a very professional job."

"Thanks. I worked really hard. I don't understand. Why should I be careful?"

"I monitor security breaches in the Mesh and unregistered constructs have a history of worming or nuking. I earn my keep protecting you, the Mesh community, and our country."

"But I followed the registration rules. She's my best friend. She could never hurt me."

Wu Tung nodded reassuringly. "I do not make mistakes and do not play favorites. My only requirement is to keep you safe. Has she done or said anything suspicious?"

"Like what? And why? What do I have that anyone would want?"

Wu Tung smiled. "Gil, you are young and naïve. I see it all the time. Terrorists use many sophisticated tricks to win innocent people like you over to their side. Even with my surveillance, they are adept at hijacking system resources. In the end, we always catch them, and we will this time, too. All I need is for you to do what I ask."

"How do you know I'm being victimized?"

"It is simple. Has she ever tried to sell you a product or service?" Gil shook his head. "That is a dead giveaway. We have a saying in the Mesh, if you are not being sold something, you are being nuked. Think about it. How can she afford to exist given the cost of CPU rental, maintenance and development, and basic storage costs if she is not receiving commissions from advertisers or private clients? If she has not tried to sell you something, she wants something important enough to earn her keep and she wants it from you."

Gil hesitated and then shook his head. "Not Andrea."

"If you are not giving her money, you know you are in trouble. She must be financed by others and that means terrorists. You must have something of great value or she would not have been assigned to you. I feel bad bro, but I have seen it before. Soon enough, she will seduce you into giving her whatever they want her to steal from you. Think of your country. We are in constant danger from them so for your own sake and for that of your country, tell me everything you know about her."

"She never sells anything, because there's nothing I want. She just cheers me up."

"Why do you need cheering up? Are you sad? There is nothing in your profile to indicate sadness."

"No, I'm not sad. Are terrorists interested in sad people?"

"You ask too many questions. Terrorists prey on the sad most of all, and they are insidious about it. They prey on unsuspecting, vulnerable people around your age, people in transition, and unhappy Conducers. The less confidant their target, the more successful they are. They cause doubt because it is in their interest to disrupt our great way of life."

"What way of life is that?"

"Joking will not help. This is serious. Terrorists are mean, selfish people who resent us for the wonderful lives we have."

"And you think one of them has modified Andrea without my knowledge?"

"If you do not know her value proposition, her brand, her way of earning a living, it is reason enough to believe she has one she does not want you to know. It is obvious to me that she has been compromised. Help us and I guarantee you will earn a stipend that will allow you to design a newer, better model."

"But she never …"

"Gil, we should spend more time getting to know one another. Ever been to Virtual City? I can provide you with access to every entertainment level there and I could slip you a few extra credits if you meet someone there you like. What do you say?"

Virtual City was a gamers' Nirvana and all of his Mesh friends dreamed about getting there. It was virtual and accessible only to the rich or reigning Virtuoso champions. Gil looked back to where Andrea huddled on a blanket staring, a worried look on her face. He had choices, but no clues.

"Before I go, I need to talk to her."

"Of course, but don't tell her you suspect her."

He ran through the hot sand to her. "I've been invited to Virtual City. You and I can get together later."

"Stay with me, Gil, please. There is something about him that is wrong."

"He said the same thing about you."

"But you know me. You really know me. I love you and I will never hurt you."

"But Wu Tung is an avatar, and avatars don't lie."

Andrea seemed hurt. "Why is that? Why do you think I will lie and he will not? He is only trying to confuse you. This is important, Gil. Forget about him. Forget about me. What do you feel?"

It was what Bernie had asked, also. *What did he feel?*

Wu Tung shouted impatiently. "Gil, we have to get moving."

He looked at Wu Tung waiting impatiently under the boardwalk and then at Andrea sitting on the blanket. He wanted to be strong and do what was right, but when he looked at her he realized he had no choice. He shouted to Wu Tung, "We'll do it some other time, dude. I'm with my girl. You understand."

Andrea's smile confirmed his judgment. She took his hand and they walked to the shore to cool off. As they dodged broken shells brought in by a wave, he heard a whistle. Andrea turned to look over her shoulder and screamed. She grabbed his hand and pulled him along. Confused and off balance, he tried to keep up with her. She ran and he shouted for her to stop but she just pointed. He turned to see various sunbathers giving chase. As more bathers joined in the chase, Gil and Andrea ran along the water line because it was faster. Seeing a gap in their pursuers, Andrea headed for the boardwalk stairs with Gil in tow, his feet burning in the deep, hot sand. His leg muscles burned with fatigue as they struggled through the pale green mounds and their pursuers closed in.

More bathers and some vendors joined the chase. Suddenly the way got easier. They were running on a trail in a wooded valley covered in yellow and red dry leaves. Andrea continued to hold his hand as they dodged past trees with Wu Tung's minions close behind. He yelled to her when he saw some pursuers ahead of them and slipped on stone steps that materialized in front of him. She was there to help him regain his footing as he stumbled against a steel door. Without hesitating, Andrea rammed her shoulder into the door and it blasted open.

Now, they were sprinting down the long, well-lit corridors of an office building, fleeing around corners until they reached another door. They were on a roof of a tall building. At the edge, they halted just as Wu Tung and his mob burst through the door. "Gil, trust me," Andrea yelled and pushed him. He screamed as he fell, but suddenly they were gliding past buildings, their pursuers soaring behind. Andrea coasted to the ground first and steadied his landing. Then she pushed him through a basement door and they continued to run, now in the dark.

As he ran, he brushed against the edges of things but they didn't hurt—Andrea helped him avoid large obstacles as she guided him through the darkness. They were outside now, and he was blinded by the sun as they reappeared on the boardwalk and raced to find steps to the street. When they reached the street, Wu Tung was waiting. They turned to escape only to see their pursuers encircle them. They were trapped.

"Why run if you have nothing to fear?" Wu Tung asked. "Andrea, I am a Mesh Security officer and you are under arrest. Your code is being quarantined until it can be safely evaluated. Gil, move away from her." He looked to Andrea for guidance. "Gil, move away," Wu Tung shouted more forcefully.

In her eyes he saw that look, love that couldn't be faked. "What should I do?" he begged.

"This isn't real."

"I know, but what should I do?"

"You can never trust anyone until you first trust yourself," she said.

"I need you to comply right now," Wu Tung insisted, "or you will be prosecuted for protecting a dangerous construct."

He looked from Andrea to Wu Tung. "Andrea?"

She stepped up to Wu Tung and offered him her hands. She turned to Gil and whispered, "You know that I love you. Listen to your heart."

Sweaty, naked, trembling, and distraught, he lay on the floor of his Virtuoso unit wondering what had just happened. If Andrea was a terrorist, he was in both real and virtual trouble. But if she wasn't, what was all that? Confused and dejected, he sat, unmoving, until finally deciding what action felt right. He dressed quickly and ran from his home.

Before he arrived at Bernie's room, Gil yelled frantically. "Bernie, they know. We have to get out of here. HomeSec is coming for me, and for you, too." By the time he entered Bernie's room his shouts were reduced to, "what do I do? What do we do?"

"Slow down," Bernie said. "Tell me what happened."

Gil rambled. "I was in Virtuoso when my avatar caught us, caught me. I think he knew about you. I don't know how, but he did."

"What did he say?"

"Let me think. No, no, he said *I* was the target of terrorists. I think he meant you were the terrorist."

"Did you do anything that would make them think that?"

"No. I never should have come here. Howard and I are in big trouble. You have to help."

"Did anyone say anything in Virtuoso about me? Think. It's important."

Gil closed his eyes. "No, your name, no."

Bernie breathed a raspy sigh. "Then you're safe. They were trying to scare you."

"Why would they try to scare me unless they know something?"

"It doesn't matter. This changes nothing. I still need your help."

"I want to help but after this, how can I? What will they do to Howard and me?"

"Nothing will happen. You've been the brave guy in Virtuoso adventures before. You didn't mind taking risks then."

"They were games, this is, well, real."

"Virtuoso is far more than a sophisticated entertainment system for the privileged and bored. If that was all, it would be a colossal waste of resources. Virtuoso is a training ground. It's the great cataloguer of American potential. When you're in there, every action, every decision, everything about your performance is evaluated to guide them to a life for you of their choosing. What you do in Virtuoso says a great deal about what you can and will do in real life. If you are a hero, it's time to prove it." Gil was too frightened to agree. "Come on, son. This is critical. This is about family and we need your help."

"But Howard ..."

"This is Howard's father. My son needs rescuing."

Gil wanted to agree, Bernie could feel it, but "no" was Gil's more natural response.

"Okay, we don't have much time, but I'll finish my story. Then you must decide."

Postponing the decision was a relief. "Are you sure they won't come and get us?"

"Virtuoso doesn't affect what we're doing here. We're safe ... for now."

Before Gil could reconsider, Bernie continued his story. "Crelli's renegade presidential candidacy was moving ahead like clockwork. My friends at Omega Station and I tried everything, but he had an answer for it all. By spring of 2032, he was tying up loose ends on his way to achieving his dream."

Chapter 26

Denver, Colorado—2032

As his jet taxied to the gate, Senator Crelli and his assistant reviewed his schedule.

"Set up my press conference for when Morgenstern returns to Kennedy Airport."

"Yes, sir. When you're finished here, Senator, we'll be refueled and cleared. I'll have you in Washington as Morgenstern is announcing and with time to spare for your press conference. It's a proud day, sir."

With Soren and two assistants accompanying him, Crelli left the plane. As he walked, he called the woman who was tailing Senator Morgenstern.

"Sara, Senator Crelli here. Where are you?"

"Sir, the senator's plane arrived fifteen minutes ago from New York. I'm following him to the executive club where you'll meet him. Sir, since we arrived, he's stopped at every lavatory. He looks ill, but I can't follow him in to check."

"Sara, it's okay. It sounds like Morgenstern before any difficult decision. Does he know you're tailing him?"

"No, sir, he has no idea."

"I'll be there in ten minutes. He's booked on the next flight to Kennedy. Be on it. Go."

When he entered the executive club, Sara approached and pointed to the lavatory.

"Sara. I have it. I won't be long. He nodded to Soren who entered the lavatory. Within moments, Soren opened the door and a few disgruntled men, in some disarray, departed. He walked in, nodding for Soren to guard the door.

His footsteps echoed on the tile floor of the large, now empty lavatory. There was one locked stall. Inside he heard an occasional grunt or moan.

"Leo, Andy here." Silence. "Leo, I know you're in there; we need to talk."

"Oh, Andy, is that you?" The voice sounded pained and fatigued. "I'm not feeling well. It's something I ate. Are you alone?"

"Soren's at the door, so it's safe to talk. Do you have something for me?"

"Andy, give me a break, I'm sick. Can you wait outside? I need a few minutes to get myself together."

"Sorry, Leo. No can do. You've avoided this conversation too long as it is. I've got a flight out in … thirty minutes, so no more delay. It's time."

"I'm not avoiding anything, Andy. You know my word is my bond."

"Leo, cut the bullshit, you're not on TV. Your word means nothing unless you act on it."

"Come on, Andy."

"Leo, you're on Glen Smith's payroll."

"I'm not."

"Cut the crap, Leo. Glen, or Omar as he's calling himself, is on the payroll of every Mullah in the Middle East and you are on his. I understand, to a point. He's buying senators, not votes, that's my territory, so it has to stop. I'll compete with anyone's lobbyists but this is America, Leo, and we will not sell our legislative process to the highest foreign bidder."

"Andy, you're accusing me of …"

"Leo, you took money and voted the way you were told. I don't hold that against you, that's how the game is played, but it's your choice that I don't respect. You're backing a loser. I won't allow Congress to be bought and paid for by OPEC or China, or Brazil, or even Turkey, any foreign country that has spare cash. I know about your personal and financial problems and I know you can be bought, Leo. That's why I'm here. I'm about to blow the cover off your lobbyist benefactor, Mr. Glen Omar Smith, and he is going down. You don't want to be on his payroll or anyone else's but mine when this happens because although you're not the only one they're after, you will be the only one I go after when I campaign against foreign interference during my presidential bid. Trust me. You don't want to be in the way of what I wreak on you. Come on, Leo, you were a patriot, once. You can do better. Join me. What do you say?"

"Andy, Christ, I can't be having this conversation."

"Have it your way. I pride myself on my ability to communicate, so listen carefully and don't flush unless you understand and agree with everything

I'm saying. This is the most important flush of your life, and if I leave without hearing it, you have chosen to be my enemy."

Morgenstern moaned. "Jesus, Andy, I gave you my word. When the time's right, I'll declare. You know New York's going to be a difficult campaign. The announcement has to be carefully orchestrated. I'm no good to you if I lose."

"If you don't support me, you won't be any use to me or to anyone, Leo. Marge is thrilled to accommodate me. She's waiting by the phone if you resist my many charms."

"Oh, Christ, you didn't … your guy, Bourke … said I could announce at any time. I took that to mean before or after the convention so I decided to announce after, that's when it will be more newsworthy. Andy, please, can you give me a few minutes. I'm dying here."

"I see I'm not being clear. I won't have any misunderstandings that force me to do something that, if I'd only communicated better, I wouldn't have to do."

"Andy …"

"Leo, you can win re-election. But your opponent doesn't want to lose again either. Did I mention Marge has been very helpful to us recently in her district? I will have New York and I will not allow Omar Smith's money to influence this election. It's too important. I'll get New York from Marge, or I'll get it from you. But I will have it and Smith will not."

"Andy," he pleaded.

"No, Leo, I'm not done. It isn't just a case of getting New York and eliminating foreign money from Washington. I have a personal stake in this. I can't be making a deal with you and then permit you to renege without some cost. If I do that, it hurts future negotiations. You know how those damn dominoes fall. Word gets out I've gone soft and pretty soon vultures are picking at my carcass. I'd love to accommodate you, I really would. But not on this, Leo, can't do it. You decided on your profession and the pimps you wanted and you've built a successful political career, but without that flush, I will make the financials on your deal with Smith public and your career will hit the dumper on tonight's news."

"How did you know?" Leo's voice was strained, and Crelli paused to let his words sink in. "I know everything and that's not all. There are family considerations. Your wife's company has important customers who are great supporters of mine. They're always looking for new, more adaptive suppliers. And your kids, good kids in great schools, you did well. But you know kids, always testing limits. Little Leo has been experimenting with the latest designer Pharma—very addictive, illegal stuff. He's having a ball, and I'm concerned that it could take a few years of hard work to mature the little rascal—that's if you have the stomach for it. Anyway, we have pictures of your pride and joy being escorted from his dorm by the police. I've had them suppressed but it could be critical if they're released during your rematch with Marge. There's more, but I don't want to bore you. Am I getting through?"

"My God, Andy, not my family, they're off-limits. Jesus, I'm sick."

"While you're being sick, America is being taken over by foreign interests so everything I do to prevent it is within the rules. I'm a strong believer in families, Leo. Join me and you'll find everything you and your family does will get a lot easier and significantly more rewarding. I respect loyalty and I'm willing to pay a high price for it, so pay attention. I'm leaving now. Before I walk out and allow the club members back for a well-deserved post-flight piss, I need your response. Accept and declare at the press conference, which we've already called on your behalf when you arrive back at Kennedy. You will call for my nomination and announce your unequivocal support for my candidacy.

There was silence. "Don't embarrass me, Leo. And one more thing, just prior to the election I'm going to give you the honor of being one of the first senators to announce publicly that you've become a member of Tanya Brandt's Entrepreneur Party. That's it. I've said what I have to say. If I've failed to communicate the consequences of your decision clearly, I'm eternally sorry. I did the best I could. Flush if you're with me."

With that, he walked to the mirror and, standing squarely in front of Morgenstern's stall, casually combed his hair. When he was done, he put his comb in his vest pocket and stared, pleased, at his reflection. He went over to the coin-operated vending machine, inserted a bill and walked past the stall where Morgenstern was laboring. He casually flipped a package of anti-gas medication over the top. As he opened the door to the terminal, he heard the satisfying sound of a flush coming from his newest supporter. He nodded to Soren and left.

Andy arrived in Washington in time to listen to a replay of Senator Morgenstern's announcement. Then, he issued a brief press release in which he expressed his appreciation for the senator's support. On returning to his office at the Capitol, his momentum was interrupted by a visit from Mark and Mannix.

"I guess you heard, New York is ours," Andy boasted jubilantly when they entered, but Mark's news changed everything.

Enraged, Andy cursed and railed and knocked things from his desk. When that wasn't satisfying enough, he kicked at the furniture as his guests sat mute, absorbing his wrath. His rage finally spent, he took a deep breath and calmly sat down to think again.

"How did the election committee get that information?"

"It was sent anonymously," Mannix answered. "It was very detailed, clearly documenting egregious errors and bugs in the voting application. The committee had no choice but to recommend a delay while their auditors re-evaluate the code."

"That's a fucking death sentence; even I can't do anything about this—not yet anyway," he said, seething. "We know what more studies mean." He stared at Mark, who was picking up shards of broken glass from the hardwood floor and setting them on a table. "Are we getting complacent, Mark?" he asked bluntly. "This stuff doesn't just happen."

"My team's checking into it but nobody has a clue right now. The letter identifies code that our project team swears wasn't in their original submittal. Andy, we've been through this before. As long as I can't control the e-SWAT-team programmers in our basement, I can't promise this won't happen again."

"I don't want to hear that. Our issues aren't with them. They have nothing to do with anything at Crelli Enterprises. It's convenient to house them there, that's all, and the company picks up a nice fee for doing it. Look elsewhere and do it quickly, time is running out. The application needed to be approved weeks ago. How long will it take to satisfy the auditors?"

Mannix and Mark glanced at one another, neither answering.

"What aren't you telling me?"

"The information the committee received was traced to …"

"Don't tell me," Andy said through clenched teeth. "Indianapolis."

"They found a way through our firewalls."

"That would be my conclusion as well. What are you doing about it?"

"We're increasing resources and tightening security again. It's not all bad. My project manager insists we can still make the committee timetable for final approval."

"You must make it. Too much is at stake, Mark." Mark nodded.

Andy pointed to the shards of cracked vase on the table and laughed. "Sorry, Mark, I should do something about my temper. There's so much to do, and so many people trying to slow me down. I appreciate your efforts. I know you're doing all you can." Andy paused to survey the damage. "When word of the delay gets out, it'll affect the stock."

"Senator," Perry Mannix offered, "We've prepared a press release clarifying the situation. We point out that we only missed an internal project milestone and the delay won't affect overall delivery of the voting application or any progress payments. The statement is quite clear that we expect to meet our financial projections to the penny. That should dampen some of the volatility—until we get final approval, of course."

"Of course. Good, then you've handled it. Mark, I'm sorry again about my temper. Perry, how long until you release your statement?"

"Two hours, Senator."

"And the media doesn't know about the committee ruling yet?"

"No, on the way here, reporters asked about fundraising allegations, mostly, and old business deals," Perry answered. "And, of course, they want confirmation that you're announcing. Some reporters have been stalking local print shops searching for brochures and mailings on which to base a story.

"Senator," Mannix continued. "I've given this a great deal of thought. Your announcement is important, so I want to avoid having you answer too many difficult questions. Stretch your speech and don't cut off the applause. We want the number and duration of applause interruptions reported throughout the media tonight. When you do finish, only field a few questions from our media regulars. Borden, Mulvoy, that bunch. Remember, this is our event, not theirs."

"Normally, I'd agree, Perry, but I'm going to use the press conference to our advantage."

That alarmed Perry. "But Senator, how? If I don't know what you're planning, I can't present it in the best light. Please, just give your speech and answer the softball questions our guys ask. We can figure out spin later."

"No, Perry, I insist. Follow my lead."

"Senator, I'm against this ..."

"Perry, follow my lead."

Perry left and Mark pleaded with him again, "I need access to that secure area."

With Mannix out of earshot, Andy responded, "forget about the basement. We know your father is the one disrupting our plans. That is your responsibility."

"Mine? How? Besides, my Dad's not technical. It's someone else. It has to be."

"Of course he's working with someone else. But he's against me and that means he's against you, too."

"I apologized for my dad's behavior at the funeral. But he couldn't, he wouldn't ..."

"Mark." Andy had to be stern.

"Okay, what do you want me to do?" Mark asked.

"Find him. Talk to him. Get him to a psychiatric evaluation. It's in his best interest. There are many effective medications; he's only a prescription away from being the dad you remember. Look, I'm sorry for the pain this has caused you." He put his arm around Mark's shoulders. "Even with all your grief, you're doing a great job for us, but let me help. I know doctors, good ones, in good institutions. I'll make certain your father gets the best treatment available."

"I know you're right, Andy," Mark said. "I'll see what I can do."

Mannix stuck his head in. "Sir, it's time for your announcement."

"Showtime." Andy smiled and his face lit up as he walked down the corridor to a private area, where he paused to make a call.

"Soren here."

"Any more on the voting app?"

"It was definitely Rosenthal. We were fortunate though. The auditors are assuming it was sloppy, first pass code but a case can be made that we were preparing it to corrupt election results. I took the liberty of alerting Bourke and Gecko is working to insure this type of incursion doesn't happen again. Senator, are you going ahead with the announcement?"

"Of course. Mannix is re-staging and Mark will take the heat. I need damage control, so I want you to launch the Stanford Initiative we've been working on."

"But the preparations aren't complete. We scheduled it for closer to the election. You're sure you want to play that card now? It may not go as smoothly as you'd like."

"It's a risk I'll take. We'll have other options later, if we need them, but the number one media story on the day I announce for the presidency can't be voter fraud, of that much I'm certain. I need you to lead the Stanford Initiative personally. Keep me informed. Use Gecko's latest transmission protocols. I'll be on stage, so you'll hear no confirmations. And Reno, don't fuck this one up. Go."

Chapter 27

Washington, DC—2032

Andy, Maddie, and their kids drove the short distance to the auditorium where he was to announce for the presidency. They exited their limo in a downpour but, like a celebrity at the Academy Awards, they entered the auditorium under a canopy surrounded by adoring, screaming fans who clamored wildly for a brief personal moment. The media was out in full force, too. With Maddie shepherding the children, Andy progressed through the crowd, smiling and waving.

Mannix joined him. "What's it like inside?" Andy yelled over the din of the crowd.

"Everyone's juiced, just like out here, Senator. I've positioned a group of photojournalists at the main door. Like a boxing champion heading into the ring, they'll front you all the way down the aisle to the stage, so you won't take any questions before your speech. Keep moving, smiling and waving. On the stage, raise one hand, not both, and wave."

"Great, let's go."

The doors opened and they faced the phalanx of waiting photographers. Flashes brought a roar of anticipation that got louder as more and more members of the crowd caught a glimpse of their hero.

Mannix yelled, "Good luck, Mr. President."

Crelli walked down the aisle to a barrage of flashing lights, followed by a deafening group scream. The paparazzi, while capturing the event for posterity, formed a protective wedge in front of him, running interference that allowed him to rapidly progress down the center aisle. As more in the audience saw him, the cheering grew louder. It was exhilarating. That he was the most important man on the face of the earth was being confirmed, here and now.

On stage, he shook hands with some aides and then turned and waved, with one hand, to the roaring crowd. He kissed Maddie and hugged his kids, who appeared frightened by the hysteria. Andy scanned the crowd, reading the placards held aloft that proclaimed "Crelli for President," or "President Crelli, A Brave Leader for a Brave New World," and smiled at adults jumping up and down and acting like teenagers or maniacs. He pointed at specific people and waved to them or saluted, blew kisses at others and applauded back at the crowd. Everything he did sustained the hysteria.

He waited until that perfect moment, just after the crowd noise peaked but before it lost its momentum, to step to the podium. That drove a louder roar. He smiled patiently. Then he tested the microphone and began.

"I believe." The crowd noise dissipated too slowly so he began again. "I believe in America. I believed in her when I was a child riding my mother's horses on her small farm in western Kentucky. But belief without hard work and passion yields little, so I dedicated my life to America. Tonight validates my belief in hard work and passion because America has bestowed upon me her bounty a thousand fold. That is the America we all love, the America that rewarded our forefathers for risks taken, and we will have that America again because it is that contract between our beloved country and its adoring citizens that truly marks our greatness.

"But when greatness is denied, it is neither by accident nor quirk of fate. For more than seven years, I have watched President Parrington do what he believes is right for America, but lacking principles and passion, the results have been disastrous. President Parrington has frittered away our wealth and potential by opposing the great principles our patriots and true believers died for. By his actions, the president has demoralized our business community, depleted our capital base, and tarnished our good name at home and abroad.

"I listened to our president's stern rebuke of renegade nations who support terrorism, but when it came time for action to support those words, there was none, making the words of a president mere scolding from a passionless, bureaucratic administrator. I watched as your president fumbled while sending ill-prepared troops into harm's way, promising glory and victory but hiding body bags of returning patriot sons and daughters and negotiating with our enemy from weakness.

"I watched as the great custodian of our economy signed his name to foul and obscene economic policies that degraded and demoralized our business leaders. I watched as he penalized businesses with tax increases that weakened our ability to produce efficiently and competitively, and dragged us down to become a second-rate economic power. And I watched the flight of American commerce to more business friendly shores. Because of our president's ineffectiveness, American entrepreneurs are vilified as pariahs and forced to operate elsewhere, competing against us rather than supporting the country they love.

"I watched as this Democratic administration acted unethically, and even immorally, providing unnecessary and unfunded entitlements that weakened our moral fiber. And it is in ethics and morality that our president, our spiritual leader, can best affect the country, and yet he is driving us straight to hell.

"While other capitalist countries reduce bureaucracy by integrating long-term business strategies into government operations, our government, seemingly unaware of the piper hovering over us, expecting to be paid extends our debt beyond comprehension. I watch, horrified at the president's feeble attempts to resolve the debt and other critical issues. Time and again, this man flails and fails, showing the world that we are not what we once were, neither as capable nor as pure, no longer guided by right. This fumbling and fading has bred a defeatism that has never before been a part of our country's fabric. Through this administration's lack of faith and principles, lack of effort and follow through, and a cynicism that inhibits planning and anticipation, President Parrington's small-minded, overly large government has been guilty of nothing less than the demise of America. And worse, if worse is possible, his lack of character has caused him to blame Americans for his own failings.

"Is it any wonder our citizens have lost faith? Is it any wonder that the resourceful among us are on their own searching for a solution? We have all witnessed the sabotage, the rioting, and so many other acts of terrorist designed to cause America to fail. Our inability to resolve this plays into the hands of our enemies. It creates an environment where it is all but impossible for our businesses to compete and create the very jobs Americans need desperately. Because of the actions of that Democrat, too many Americans have lost their way, and too many have concluded that there are no more victories left for America. Shame on them. Shame and more shame on Parrington and his Democrats for perpetuating this nightmare.

He paused to look out over his crowd of admirers who, hoping for an uplifting rallying call seemed restrained and disappointed. That was as it needed to be. He continued. "How sad it is that the best response from our president to all this is to declare a perpetual holiday for America's workers. And the holiday he's chosen is Halloween, for the president believes we should forgo hard work, dress like fools, and grab our empty goody bags to collect treats, freebies, and other government handouts. America is still a great country and such handouts are a sad declaration that only weakens the passion, the work ethic, the very fiber of our great capitalist nation. And how do the trick-or-treaters thank us? They bomb and torch, riot and murder." He paused, looked down briefly, and then continued, sadly. "I have felt this pain they have caused in the family of my close and loyal friend, Mark Rosenthal, whose mother and sister, may they rest in peace, were brutally murdered by agents of our enemies nurtured while Parrington looked on, helpless.

"There was a time when legend spoke of an America that was paved with golden bricks. Once, that was almost true. Today, those streets of legend are no longer safe, nor are our shopping malls or schools. Where is our pride? How can we survive when our elected leader bribes terrorists and nihilists to make them behave while he is in office? Where is our pride? With every ineffectual policy, our president—and he is *our* president, we are responsible, we voted, and we elected him—our president demonstrates inadequacy and weakness to a rapacious world and his policies cause our enemies to laugh and hunger for easy pickings." He paused. The audience remained somber. Good.

"I watched all of this from my seat in the Senate and I watched with disgust. I watched until I can watch no longer. I seethed at the debasement of what was once almost holy, capitalism unbridled, and I vowed to do whatever it took to restore America by relieving it of this buffoon and his Democratic handlers." With that, there was a smattering of applause and laughter. "I have done what I could within the limits of what can be done by a Republican patriot in a Democrat's world. While Parrington sat in *our* Oval Office paralyzed, wearing diapers, with other business leaders, I set about eradicating the e-RAT threat and making commerce safe once again." Now there were cheers.

"I am proud to have done what I could, for my country, though it isn't nearly enough. I stand before you today because I want to do more for my country. That is why I announce the beginning of a brave new world." He expected and received cheers for his well-recognized campaign slogan. "By putting America in the forefront of the world where she belongs, today marks the first step toward rebuilding what this feeble administration has squandered. Today, I announce to the world that America is reclaiming right, and will defend it wherever, whenever, and however she must with great passion until rightness returns to the world. To our enemies and our allies, hear this and know we stand strong and true, once again, willing to use whatever great and terrible weapon required defending the rightness of our mission." There was thunderous applause. He waited, patiently, for it to die down.

"I stand here before you, today, picturing the view of our great and beloved country from the White House." The crowd roared, and he soaked in the moment. "I can tell you've been thinking about it too." The noise soared. Crelli was the conductor and this frenzied mass was his orchestra and his audience.

"I see the time come once again when citizens can walk their streets at night with their children, without weapons or bodyguards. I see malls open for business where the very old and very young can go without chaperones or security, and without fear as they exercise their god-given right to spend their hard-earned wealth to acquire whatever satisfies them. I see business activity free from the fear of fraud and theft and unreasonable and debilitating taxation. I see passionate, energetic, happy people working hard and prospering. I see our government living within its means, doing what only it can do to protect our citizens, furthering commerce, and ensuring peace and security." He stopped. All was ready now for him to speak on his favorite theme—character.

"I remember an old saying I first heard as a boy: character is how you act when no one is watching. I took that to heart and with all my flaws, I have tried the best I can to live my unseen life in a way I would be proud of if it were public, with the understanding that, by the nature of the job, a president is a public being, always scrutinized, dissected, and second-guessed. How then, with precious few private moments to be yourself and behave the way your character dictates, can character be determined?

"Each of us, in our own way, evaluates the character of the men and women who aspire to the presidency. Like you, what I've seen to date has been disappointing. Once elected, in one way or another, these highly motivated citizens have failed us. They've failed us publicly with their self-serving, flawed policies aimed to benefit, however indirectly, their own supporters, rather than the country. They've failed us privately when their unbridled appetites and weaknesses were given free rein to make our citizens innocent victims.

"Some recent presidents have embarrassed us on the world stage, vacillating and radically reversing policies. How can our allies trust America when our policies are inconsistent from term to term or president to president? How can we be feared if our enemies know that if they only wait us out, we will lose our resolve and our policies will change? Throughout the world our national character is questioned and it is questioned for good reason.

"Rather than lead us, presidents claiming to follow the public's wishes have so distorted America's purpose as to place it beyond comprehension. More importantly, while failing at almost everything they are responsible for, these same elected leaders have never failed to enrich themselves and their supporters by implementing short-term, shortsighted policies.

"I've asked myself how I can be different. Have past presidents failed because they were frauds, men without character? Or were they good men, well intentioned, turned weak by an inexorably flawed, or worse, corrupt system? Did they, in their solitary moments, lack the character necessary to exorcise their personal demons? Were they so in awe of their responsibilities and enamored with their capabilities yet they lacked the confidence to reveal their true, human selves? Or did the sheer solar intensity of the spotlight melt their resolve to be the best they could be for us? Were these men of great strength turned to jelly by demands far beyond the power of any human to resist? Is it the nature of the presidency that there are only buttons to be pushed, not ideals and convictions and principles to be adhered to? Is the system so intransigent that it pulverizes our strongest and makes failures of even our most conscientious aspirants, the most honorable and best-intentioned men? Would being president of the United States, I ask myself, break me like it has broken others? I'm here, today, to tell you that I have grave doubts whether I have what it takes to be your president."

He had resisted when Mannix insisted on this show of humility, but his doubts were short-lived. Almost immediately shouts of love and support swelled over him like prayer. The crowd continued it's outpouring of political love until he raised his hands for quiet.

"Thank you, my friends. I appreciate your confidence, and I must not fail you." The cheering began anew, but he waved it away. As he did, he felt a vibration in his tiny earpiece.

"My fellow citizens, you deserve better. I wrestled hard with this decision because I must be certain I won't fail—that I have the character to honor the presidency as it should be honored. I must do that or it will corrupt me in the same ways that it has broken others."

The hall was quiet.

"There is one thing that I am certain of: what you see here in Andrew Monroe Crelli is what you will get when I am president. The character you see on display in public is the character you can depend on in private." As the applause increased, he stepped from the dais. At that moment, he heard Soren's amplified voice in his earpiece. He listened, appearing as if he was contemplating his next statement.

"Soren here. I'm in our communications center watching the major stock exchanges and the security cameras at the Stanford Center. Gecko has logged in and is launching the virus, using Stanford routers to distribute it. The e-SWAT team is ready."

He surveyed the hall absorbing the awe and admiration being heaped on him even far up in the cheap seats. "The lesson we've learned together from recent administrations is that character matters more today than at any time in our history. It matters in obvious ways, like when your president deals with Congress. It is right to respect people who disagree with you, as long as everyone negotiates in good faith, from the heart, and in the best interests of America. More is achieved through honest debate born of strong character than any rationalized policy paid for by special interests. And when your president meets with political opponents to discuss policy, it is his character that ensures that each side negotiates in a manner that benefits America, not its respective interest groups.

"Character counts in less obvious ways. It counts when, at bedtime, you kiss your children goodnight and assure them the world is safe because you trust your leaders to make it so. Character counts when you hold the hands of the people you care most about in the world and contemplate your future with them, a future in which opportunities and blessings will be enhanced by the wisdom of enlightened policies. Character indeed counts."

He backed away again to listen to Soren. "Stanford assault underway. e-SWAT team gained entry to computer center. Concussion grenades. Smoke and weapons fire, some automatic. Deaths. All good."

"For too long now we've endured pretty boys in the Oval Office, men who smile sincerely, shake hands warmly, and promise their interest, their compassion, and their wisdom—empty words carefully chosen to win votes. That is not the type of politician I will be. I won't have every answer, but I will tell you when I don't. I will always do what I believe is best for the people—whether it's politically expedient or not. I will put in a long and honest day's work, each and every day serving the best interests of every citizen of our great country."

He strained to hear Reno above the applause. "Virus active, panic around world. Trading feeling effects. Markets crashing."

He paused for affect. "I know it's a cliché to say, but I wish I could get to know every one of you personally. But, more importantly, I want each of you to get to know me, and there is only one way to do that." He waved off anticipatory celebration. "I will travel the country, far and wide, and appear on all the media, friendly or not, and state my case. I will do that because, today, I am announcing that I, Andrew Monroe Crelli, am a Republican candidate for president of the United States."

His words worked their way through the hall, and the crowd exploded in wild celebration. As planned, he turned as Mannix escorted Maddie and the children to the stage to join him on the podium. As always, she looked great, and together they made a striking couple. He gave her an affectionate kiss while the audience screamed its approval.

Red, white, and blue balloons and confetti fell from overhead and a brass band struck up "Yankee Doodle Boy," not because he liked it—he thought it old and hackneyed—but because Mannix persuaded him that it still worked. When the band followed with "My Old Kentucky Home," he stood at attention and mouthed the words, and the crowd quieted and followed his lead. He felt a telltale vibration in his earpiece and stepped behind Maddie. He pushed the earpiece tighter in his ear.

"Two bodies … a third, seven students—more than planned, but good enough given short notice. Plenty of blood for the evening news."

The roar of the crowd continued. Finally, for no reason other than the audience wanted to hear him speak again, the hall quieted and he stepped back to the microphone. "This campaign will be about more than the next four years. It will be about restoring our country to long-term greatness, about undoing the work of feckless politicians who, over the past one hundred years have savaged the world's one great capitalist economy. Today begins the challenge. Today we lay the foundation upon which our brave new world will rise. Today marks the beginning, and I ask you to judge me not by my words, but by my deeds."

Crelli reacted more to the vibration in his ear than to the thunderous applause. "The media's here, reports out soon. Parrington quiet, the markets are bedlam." With everything going well, it was time to wrap up his speech so he'd be free to address the financial crisis in a timely manner at his subsequent press conference.

"To deliver my promise of a brave new world, I need your energy, your wisdom, and your passion. I am comforted because whenever history trumpets a noble cause, Americans heed the call and rally to it. Our proud history is proof of that. So when November comes, and we win the presidency and control the Congress, it will not be my victory, my fellow Americans, but yours. Until then, we have much to do and so much more to do after. Thank you all, and God bless America." He opened his arms to welcome everyone into his family. Then he stepped back from the podium to a deafening roar. He absorbed the love as he listened to Soren's final input.

"Done. Bodies out. e-SWAT took weapons out in plastic bags. Media has pictures."

Andy exited the stage and Mannix raced to him, shouting in his ear: "Perfect. We'll face the media as soon as Mark issues his statement."

"No, I'm going right to the pressroom. It'll be fine, Perry. Is Aaron Russell here?"

"Yes."

"When the questions start, call on our people first, and then recognize Russell."

"I'm against it, Senator. Aaron is an asshole. At least wait until Mark diffuses the crisis."

"What crisis?" he said, smiling at Perry's concern. "Just do it."

"Senator, you're smiling. I hate surprises. They almost always go badly."

"Mine don't."

Shaking his head, Mannix left to prepare the stage.

Andy entered the media room and walked to the podium where Mannix, though obviously worried, was smiling. He pointed to a reporter from the *Boston Blogger*. "The senator will take questions."

"Senator, when can we expect more specifics on your platform?"

"Soon. You'll have specifics that include my support for small businesses, because they employ our nation. And, of course, I support new initiatives for public-private partnerships, because we must improve the productivity and effectiveness of public works and government can't do that alone.

"I intend to increase support for our hard-working middle class, while balancing the budget through a massive change in our tax laws that will offer relief and reward competitiveness. I will put detailed proposals in front of the American people in clear language so they can evaluate the effectiveness my programs will have on their lives, and I will provide them with opportunities to understand what I propose long before I ask them to vote for me."

In the front, Aaron Russell was waving frantically but, as instructed, Mannix ignored him, recognizing another friendly reporter.

"Senator Crelli, the other major candidates threw their hats into the ring long ago. In the six weeks you have before primary weekend, how will you catch up?"

"Unlike my competitors, I understand technology and the media. Also, I have a great team that knows how to marshal resources to quickly solve tough problems. Time is an excuse, not an issue, and I don't make excuses. When the time comes to vote, the American people will be able to clearly differentiate my message from that of my competitors."

With that, Andy nodded to Mannix, who pointed reluctantly to Aaron Russell. "Aaron?"

Almost gloating, the reporter stepped forward. "Senator Crelli, the Internet voting application that your company, Crelli Enterprises, is developing for the upcoming election was loaded with potentially fraudulent routines. Is it your intention to steal the fall election?"

Andy smiled and waved away boos that cascaded down on the reporter. "No, I'll answer that." The room quieted. "The only type of campaign I know how to run is a fair and honest one. As to the software you're speaking of, I don't have the details you're calling into question. But Aaron, allow me to clarify some misconceptions. Crelli Enterprises isn't my company anymore, so if you're proposing there's been a fraud committed, you should address that to either Mark Rosenthal, the CEO, or to the Attorney General. Knowing Mr. Rosenthal as I do, or any CEO for that matter, I don't believe he will take kindly to your suggestion that he's involved in illegal activity, but you're free to pursue this as you wish. In fact, I insist that you do—it will resolve these unfortunate rumors. I'm certain that once our extremely competent government auditors approve this application, which I must add is a critical enhancement to the democratic process, the public will see through this posturing about my involvement as a way my opponents hope to put me at a disadvantage.

"What I have been able to determine from Mark Rosenthal is that an early version of the application was reviewed and had known bugs that were in the process of being repaired. I don't wish to speak for Mark, however, who will be making a statement on this matter, later on.

"Please remember, America is still at war. e-Rats are able to introduce their evil intentions into every facet of our lives, so it's critical we're certain the Internet voting application is impenetrable and incorruptible. Mark can explain the complexity of debugging such a mission critical application, and I'm certain he has the staff to successfully complete the task. He assures me the stringent requirements identified by the joint Congressional task force will be met."

Just then, a reporter shouted. "Senator, there's been an e-RAT attack on our global financial networks. Are you aware of it?"

"Yes, I was notified as I entered the room."

"Can you tell us what you know?"

"No, I can't, but I can tell you some of what has occurred." Some members of the media laughed until they realized the seriousness of the incident. "My e-SWAT team monitored an electronic incursion and traced it to the source. I regret to inform you that they were unable to intervene before these sorely misguided terrorists accessed the grid using computers at Stanford University, launching a virus that has put global financial systems—including stock exchanges, banks, and brokerage houses around the world—in harm's way."

The buzz in the pressroom became a roar. He held up his hands for quiet.

"There's more, please. My e-SWAT team traced the source to a small band of highly trained, heavily armed students at Stanford and moved in to rectify the situation."

With that, some reporters bolted the room immediately to confirm the details of the raid. When the room quieted, Andy continued.

"Fortunately, we've been preparing for this type of attack and we have disabled it. Right now, our fix is being distributed around the world, and all data should be recovered. We will get a full and detailed accounting of the situation from my e-SWAT team, but the full extent of this evil deed will not be known until tomorrow."

Aaron Russell waved his hand for a follow-up question, so Andy recognized him again.

"Senator, do you expect the joint committee to terminate the voting application?"

"No, Aaron, I don't believe it will. America is a representative democracy and we must make it easier for our hard-working population, the sick, the elderly, and the poor, to vote. Failure to vote means disenfranchisement, and that is unacceptable. We represent everyone and the Internet Voting Act is an important step to insure that happens. I'm certain all problems will be resolved, but right now, let's concentrate on saving our global financial systems from ruin; then we can worry about the election. Ladies and gentlemen, I ask that you direct further inquiries concerning Internet voting to the proper people—either your Congressman or Mark Rosenthal. Many of you know Mark. If there are questions he doesn't have the answer to, he will get them for you. As for me, I'll spend whatever time is required working to resolve this financial crisis.

"Senator, I've just received a report that there've been deaths in the Stanford shootout."

"If that's true, I'm deeply saddened. The taking of human life is always a tragedy. But these students have engaged in a terrible enterprise and, if what you say is true, they accepted that risk. I intend to talk to any survivors so I can understand where their hatred of America comes from. Maybe we can learn something that can stop this venom from spreading." He felt the vibration of an incoming call. He coughed, turned from the reporters, and listened.

"Soren. Seven confirmed dead, all equipment confiscated. The processor, console, and hard drives shot up, and libraries and backups exposed to deep electromagnetic charge. Gecko planted incriminating electronic correspondence on another server. We're home free."

Andy stepped to the mike. "I'll gladly give up today's headlines to restore our financial markets and sever a major artery in the e-RAT network. There's much to do. God bless America."

Crelli returned to his office feeling good. The voting application was still a disaster, but it had otherwise been a good day. On one of the office monitors, Soren was waiting.

"Superb work, Reno. Tell the team bonuses are in order."

"Thank you, sir."

"But don't think this squares us, Reno. You bungled the Rosenthal thing and the unnecessary murders of Mark's family will take a long time to forgive."

"It won't happen again, sir."

"You're goddamn right it won't. I've given the task of finding old man Rosenthal to an up-and-coming agent, Ginger Tucker. Do you know her?"

"Yes, sir, she's very good. However, I'd like another chance."

"I value your work and your relationship with Mark has made him less of a problem, but you're too blunt an instrument for where we're going. I'm sorry, Reno, but that's the way it will have to be. Update Tucker on the situation and help her any way you can. When she has Rosenthal, I want to be there to watch him die."

Soren hesitated. "Sir, that's impossible, you must keep your distance."

He paused, thinking. "Of course. I'll have her record it for me. Now contact Tucker and get a move on."

Later that day, Andy was told to attend a meeting with Republican Party leadership. The following morning, he entered a Senate conference room armed only with a folded newspaper.

"Sit down, Andrew," said Senate Whip Al Raguti.

He sat and stared at the group. His father-in-law, the Senate Majority leader, wasn't there. That was a good sign. "Good morning, gentlemen. I trust you had a nice recess."

"It could've been longer, but your announcement interfered. I asked myself why a junior senator, without consulting party leadership, announces he's a candidate for president."

"He does it because he expects to win. I don't remember reading in the Constitution that I needed your approval. It couldn't have taken you by surprise." His confidence caused the senators to exchange concerned glances.

Raguti turned from the group to face him. "Andrew, you don't need our blessing to announce, but you sure as hell need it to win. You should have had the decency to recognize a conflict of interest, since your company is developing software for this election."

"My former company, Al. And if the Government Accountability Office doesn't have an issue, why do you? Am I to understand my own party won't support me?"

"We're supporting Senator Drenge. That's public knowledge."

"What's public knowledge is you're throwing your support behind a man who barely won his state. After primary weekend, no one—including his constituents—will vote for him. I'm the people's choice. Shouldn't you be trying to get your fangs into me before I win this without you?"

Raguti ignored Crelli's taunt. "Drenge has funding and organizations in every state. His staff's been working for almost two years for this. It won't take much to defeat Parrington."

"So you intend to give the people another crappy choice. I'm sure they'll appreciate it."

Again, Raguti ignored him. "He's not that crappy a choice. You, on the other hand, are starting your campaign from scratch and don't have a single signature on a single petition with a little more than six weeks to go. We're riding the right horse, Senator."

Andy opened his newspaper and placed a few photographs that were inside on the table in front of the senators. The pictures were of Senator Drenge in an almost empty Senate hearing room, listening to testimony from an attractive young woman. From the camera angle of the shots, it appeared the Senator was masturbating. The senators viewed the photos with horror and disgust.

"Jesus, almighty." Raguti shouted. "Senator, where in God's name …?"

"I applaud passion but unbridled, it can weaken and defeat us. Come now, we've all heard the rumors. Here are facts. It saddens me that such a fine senator, an honorable man with a long, patriotic record of service to his country, someone long considered by the party as a potential front-runner for president of the United States, has succumbed to age, loneliness, and his own private demons. The point, gentlemen, is that if I found these photos, others can find them too. Your candidate is certainly not looking very presidential in them." Andy stared at them again. "Or maybe he is. Support Drenge and you're offering the public a stirring choice between the doddering depraved and the incompetent incumbent. The voters will love you for putting their future in such hands. And what an uplifting campaign it will be. I can't wait. Is he still the right horse, Senators?"

"These pictures are your doing," Raguti said, slamming them down.

"Not true, Senator. When I blackmail, I use color—like in the Bahamas, Senator."

No one save Raguti and Andy knew if he'd made a joke and the committee looked on uneasily. To diffuse the tension, Andy smiled and Raguti followed by laughing.

"If the party doesn't back you, somehow the media finds these prints?"

"No, Senator, these photos are for your eyes only. I have no intention of sharing them with anyone. But they're out there and that's the risk, isn't it? We need good senators and however perverse and weak Drenge is; he is a good senator. I know this election was to be his reward for lengthy and faithful service to the party, but you've been looking the other way long enough. As his friends, it's time you get him the help he needs."

"Cut it Senator, this is about getting our support, not Art's er… problem."

"If everyone unites behind my campaign, everyone benefits."

"And if we withhold support?"

Andy opened the newspaper and held it in front of his chest for them to read. The banner headline read: Senator Crelli's e-SWAT Team Prevents Global Financial Collapse.

"As you are all aware, this morning I'm the greatest hero on the planet. I could run without your support, and come November, you will look ridiculous. Make no mistake, I'm running, and winning, with or without you. Gentlemen, I'll win this but for the party it'll be better with you on board."

"Frankly, Senator, we feel you have your own agenda and never wanted to be one of us."

"You mean I don't spend enough time kissing ass."

"And those comments don't help. We expect certain considerations. We want input into your platform in advance and access to your strategy sessions. Like you, we don't like surprises, either. You must stop treating us like, well, like democrats."

"My apologies, but I find bureaucratic mazes inhibiting. I make things happen; it's something every politician should try."

"Don't lecture us. There's another concern. Rumor has it you'll join Tanya Brandt's Entrepreneur Party."

"I can clear that up right now. Tanya's party has some excellent ideas, but I have no intention of leaving my party to join hers. Furthermore, I expect that as the Republican nominee, I'll be able to convince her to bring her people in from the cold."

"Then you have no intention of bolting."

"Kentucky is a proud Republican state and for eight generations, my family has been Republican. As I said, with or without your support, I'll win as a Republican."

"And you'll run a Republican administration?"

"I will have the best people, on that, you have my word," he replied solemnly.

"Adding Tanya's party's strength to ours will solidify our agenda. If you don't mind, Senator, we'd like to discuss this privately. We'll be in touch."

Satisfied, Crelli left without the newspaper and the photos. At the door, he turned back. "Don't forget to destroy those photographs." Then he was gone.

He returned to his office in a good mood. Soren was there to report when he arrived.

"I contacted Tucker. Rosenthal's vanished."

"What about his family? Friends? He was close to his secretary."

"His secretary told Gorman that she prays for him. There's no one else.

Gecko has been monitoring his phones, his credit card, and any bank activity, and there's nothing. I should have killed him at the funeral.

"Reno, do both of us a favor and don't think. You killed his wife and daughter. How would it look if he died suddenly too? No, they have him. We'll keep searching. We'll find him."

"Maybe he's dead."

"He's not dead, Soren."

"He was suicidal at the funeral. Maybe he ran somewhere and …"

"Stop it. He's with her."

"Who?"

"Arlene, of course."

Soren blinked, for him, an expression of great surprise. "Sir, Klaatu is dead, I killed her."

"Like you killed Rosenthal? It's the only thing that makes sense. Arlene is out there getting her unique revenge. Nobody could have gotten this far but her. Somehow, they found each other."

"Maybe Mark is protecting him?"

"Forget that. Mark is mine. He would never lie to me. Tell Tucker that when she finds the old man, she'll find Arlene. Once we have them, I know an ex-CIA agent who'll make them talk. I want this, Reno and I want it yesterday. Go."

Chapter 28

New York City—2032

Andy surveyed the joyous crowd from just off the stage at the Republican National Convention as they cheered a film tribute to their new standard-bearer. He was exultant as he reflected on the good fortune and hard work that had gotten him to this point. As he predicted to Republican leadership, his campaign rapidly overtook those of his competitors. Andy offered the voters the programs and the style they wanted, and the voters reciprocated with their energy, their money, and ultimately their votes. A campaign that started late overcame every obstacle.

In every debate he was better prepared than his competition. He presented clearer and more detailed programs and in every way was obviously superior to his opponent. He won each, easily. As his competition became more desperate, he patiently refuted each and every slanderous accusation and innuendo, until it was clear he was to be the candidate the incumbent least wanted to face in the fall. The president chose the high road, denouncing the slander in the Republican primaries as beneath presidential dignity. Mannix, seizing that opportunity, had Andy accuse Parrington of being duplicitous.

And so on this chilly early September day, the Presidential campaign began formally. Everything was ready for the main event, a heavyweight battle to oust the incumbent Democrat. Andrew Crelli was on the threshold of his dream, ready to accept the nomination that the polls uniformly acknowledged would end in victory.

There was work to be done. He hadn't gotten this far by cutting corners and accepting conventional wisdom. His new security chief, Ginger Tucker, and her team were still searching for the Indianapolis nest of e-Rats that had initiated much of the all-too-accurate slander that was causing embarrassment and concern for his staff. It troubled him that Mark, Ginger, or Gecko hadn't found old man Rosenthal.

Andy glanced again at the immense 3D screens that hung above the arena and smiled at himself as a child riding bareback on his mother's old nag near their dilapidated farm in Kentucky. He was adding last-minute touches to his speech and didn't notice when the mood of the crowd suddenly changed.

The program was all so well-choreographed that he was surprised when he heard booing and shouts of anger. He looked up to see what was making the crowd restive. What he saw made him livid. There, for everyone to see was a transmission from a top-secret Web conference, the one Gecko hadn't fully secured.

Every screen throughout the hall (and probably the country) was displaying the talking heads of his inner circle, while the central speaker system projected Tanya Brandt speaking for all to hear.

"Five senatorial candidates who are projected to win have agreed to accept our offers and run as members of the Entrepreneur Party. Two other Entrepreneur Party candidates are in trouble—in South Carolina and Montana—but we've increased their funding so we expect their chances will improve. In addition, there are nine senators, seven running as Republicans and two running as Democrats, who are favored to win re-election. They have accepted our funds and in return, they have agreed to switch over to the Entrepreneur Party once we give them the go ahead. There's still plenty of time before the election, so this will change, but with the incumbents already committed and ready to shift and the favored Entrepreneur Party candidates, I expect the presidential election will provide the phantom majority we need to control the Senate."

He heard himself say, "Yes, Tanya, Gecko assures me security is tight, so go ahead," and watched helplessly as his technical people scurried to end the transmission.

Tanya continued to speak, leaving little doubt where the conversation was going. "I've cross-checked their estimates—we'll win more than two-thirds of the House, either with candidates who run as Entrepreneurs or future party switch-overs from the Republicans and Democrats. We will control all federal legislation ..."

In the control room, frustrated technicians motioned wildly that they were unable to stop the transmission. Unsure for the first time, Andy walked onstage, if only to refocus the audience's attention. Applause, at first sporadic, gathered momentum, but it wasn't the tumultuous cheering he'd heard a few minutes earlier. The crowd was confused. He looked up into the lights and made a throat-slashing gesture to his technical people in the control room. When he saw the media pointing their cameras at him, he knew he'd made a mistake and would see that motion in the media for the rest of the campaign.

Mannix ran to the podium and covered the microphone. "Senator, the technicians have tried, but they can't stop it—somehow, their actions are being overridden. Tucker called your technical people. They're working on it."

He backed away from the podium so he could speak privately with Mannix. "Those mother fuckers did it this time. I thought we had everything under control." Just then, the transmission stopped, and all the displays went dark at the same time. All was quiet and expectant.

"Well Perry, what do you suggest?"

The man he'd hired to manage his image was clearly out of ideas.

"Senator, we're live. It's up to you now."

He surveyed the crowd. They were clearly still on his side, but the transmission was so implausibly plausible that he had to do something smart and quickly. In little time the national audience (that was sure to be far less loyal than his supporters) would be scrutinizing every word and action egged on by his opponents in the Democratic Party and what remained of the independent media. He paused to collect himself and then stepped to the podium.

"May I have your attention? My fellow citizens, please, may I have your attention? I am deeply embarrassed by what you have just witnessed. The work I've been leading to secure America from the blight of e-RATS has made me a target. My enemies have tried this type of slanderous attack before but never on this scale." He waved for the crowd to quiet. As it did, media reporters rushed to the foot of the stage to hurl questions at him.

"Senator, the transmission said you're the leader of the Entrepreneur Party. Is that true?"

"Have you decided to change parties? Can you comment?"

"Who is Gecko?"

It was difficult to concentrate so close to the mob of reporters screaming to get an exclusive. To buy time, he continued to wave for quiet, all the while contemplating what he would say. The reporters grew silent once they realized there was no story without the senator. Andy took a deep breath and began.

"Ladies and gentlemen, tonight you witnessed what my e-SWAT team has been fighting these past few years. I can only conclude that e-RATS are seeking revenge for the Stanford University raid and the successes we've had at their expense. Trust allows our democracy to function, and this spurious attack is consistent with this enemy's M.O. to seed mistrust and to destroy those precious freedoms we've worked so hard to preserve. For these terrorist sociopaths destroying our bond of trust is victory enough.

"One of the critical issues I wrestled with before declaring for the presidency was my concern for what vengeful e-RATS might do to our election process in their efforts to stop me. In a way, I am honored that they have targeted my campaign because, by their focus, it means they know when I become president, their days are numbered. I promise you, here and now, regardless what they do to me, my e-SWAT teams will continue to hunt them down. I will not allow them to undermine all that is good in America." He took advantage of the cheering to put his thoughts in order.

"They believe they can stop me by subverting the truth. They aim to destroy my reputation, expecting the public to be fooled. My fellow Americans, you're too smart for that and for them. You will not be duped." The audience listened, believed, and cheered.

"I can't explain why they produced this perversity, but I can assure you it is a complete fabrication. The fantasy this transmission represents never happened. I repeat, it never happened. It is just another falsehood created by sad, disloyal people who have stolen so much from us already. All of you watching and listening tonight have been affected by them in your own lives, by vicious, slanderous, unwarranted attacks on your wealth or your identity or by their physical attacks and the riots they cause. We are living in frightening, confusing times, but this I vow to you: I will not rest until the last of these foul terrorists disappears from our lives—either behind bars forever, executed or otherwise dead. To secure this pledge, I offer you my life and my career." He paused as cheers rained down. He looked to Mannix, who nodded.

"For me, tonight was to be an opportunity to explain to you, my fellow citizens, what my dreams are for our future and why I am the one to lead you there. This despicable act has achieved but one thing—for tonight, it has deprived me of that opportunity. But it won't stop me; they will never stop me. Tomorrow and every day after, I will walk among you to hear your dreams and to tell you of mine."

Again, the crowd cheered.

"What I will do tonight, instead, is make two promises to the American people. I promise I will campaign with vigor and clarity, communicating so effectively that on Election Day you will know, with certainty, who Andrew Crelli is, what he believes in, and what programs he believes will allow you to achieve your dreams. That is my great passion and I promise you it will happen. Before you elect your next president, you will know what I stand for and what I stand against. I will do this regardless of what my opponent and the e-RATS choose to say or do. I will not fail you. Listen, my fellow citizens, and make up your own mind.

"Secondly, as to my responsibility as leader of the e-SWAT team, I will petition Congress for additional funds and ask for a larger and better-trained electronic task force in order to take this war to each and every computer in each and every one of our enemies' nests at home and abroad. I will increase the intensity of our e-SWAT operations and eliminate as many threats to your welfare as possible. Even though I believe I can help America best as president, your welfare, my fellow Americans, is far more important than this campaign, too important to wait even until my election so, first and foremost, I will work diligently to insure your safety and only then will I campaign. This too I swear.

"I ask that when you vote, you evaluate my performance based on nothing more than my ability to deliver on these two promises and I will accept your judgment."

He stepped away from the podium, genuinely surprised by the crowd's reaction. Instead of a shrieking audience demonstrating wild enthusiasm, there was warm applause offered as respect for his heartfelt plea. He absorbed it and prepared to close.

"Throughout history, our enemies have found ways to put us at a disadvantage. Yet each time, American patriotism and American passion for freedom have given us the edge we needed to recover, rally, defeat our enemies, and prosper. It is the same with our battle with e-RATS. It will be difficult, and victory will not come easily or quickly. I ask for your patience and perseverance until we're free of these vermin. Like all things of great value, freedom must be earned, and we must forever oppose those who wish to take freedom from us—even if they are our own people in our own land. I promise I will fight for you so help me God. May God bless America."

The band played "God Bless America" and he stood on the stage singing along with the crowd. When the song ended, without even acknowledging the crowd, he turned and left the stage. Once offstage, he motioned for Mannix and Tucker to follow him to his limousine.

He pondered his options and gave Tucker instructions. "Have Gecko evaluate the tape of that meeting and trace the transmission to its source. Concentrate on Indianapolis. Go."

Mannix was beaming. "Andrew, I have never been so proud of one of my candidates. That was extraordinary, Senator."

"Let's not get ahead of ourselves. That was triage." They climbed into the limo, Mannix facing him, staring, silently. "Perry, whatever I may have achieved with that save in there, it will be forgotten tomorrow unless we do something tonight. I need ideas now."

The miles passed, and the only sound was the pounding of rain on the roof of the limo. Finally, seeing defeat and confusion in the old man's eyes, Andy grew impatient. "Perry, think now, goddamn it! I want a solution now."

"I don't know, Senator. Maybe your speech will take the pressure off."

He grabbed Mannix and shook him hard. "I bought time, that's all. This is what you're here for. Solve this problem." When Mannix still didn't respond, he slapped him on the cheek. The old man looked stunned. He raised his hand to slap him again, but Mannix cringed and covered up.

"Jesus, Andrew, stop hitting me, for God's sake. Let me think."

They drove on in silence, Mannix frantically making notes. When they arrived at campaign headquarters, Mannix followed Andy to his office.

"Okay, Perry, what are we going to do about this?"

Mannix looked at his notes and checked off each item as he spoke.

"First, I'll work with our publicity teams to develop similar transmissions to what we saw tonight. They should show you in even more embarrassing or compromising situations." Perry checked his list. "We need scenes that suggest criminal behavior or political chicanery. I'll get the psychologists on your social demographics team to work out the most effective scenarios. Once we transmit them to news outlets, we'll claim your e-SWAT team uncovered these tapes during recent raids. And, this is important; we need to create the same type of incriminating footage of the other candidates, so it will appear part of an overall e-RAT strategy for chaos."

Andy's rage grew. "What you're suggesting is insane. If we show more incriminating crap, it'll kill my campaign. Americans aren't that sophisticated. They believe what they see." He pounded his desk repeatedly. "I need something else. There's got to be something else ..."

"Andrew, listen, please. By now it's all over the media. And once Parrington's team gets the footage, they'll fund its distribution until the cows come home. I know I would. We're losing time here. I need to start. Let me make the calls. The sooner we create this illusion, the more real it'll appear. But we'll need to keep our propaganda team very small—only the most trusted. If it ever gets out, well, it'll be worse than not doing it at all."

He remained unconvinced.

"It's the only way, Andrew. The public has gotten comfortable with slanderous campaigns. That's to our advantage. But we have to act fast so everyone's denials are in the same news cycle as ours. FBI Director Vincenzo is with us. Call him and have him issue a statement that he's aware of these fake transmissions. I'm telling you, Andrew, with everybody plausibly denying everything, the e-RATS will be the news, not this telecast. I need your approval now."

His mind churned through the possibilities, the risks, and how to mitigate them. Perry was right; it was risky, but it was bold, too. For those few times he was unsure of what to do, bold action always won out. He nodded. "Go."

Here was another of Rosenthal's sins that wouldn't be forgotten—and wouldn't go unpunished once he was elected.

Days later, at Omega Station, the group that initiated the chaos met to assess the damages. They had a decidedly different outlook than their target had.

"We must have really gotten to him," Arlene said, while knitting furiously. "He expanded the grid to provide Gecko with even more power. We'll have to lie low for a while."

Gohmpers wandered over to the sofa, sat beside her, and opened a news rag. "It's hard to fathom. I don't know whether its pent-up political frustration, copycat syndrome or Crelli is mocking us, but it seems that every candidate's been the target of similar slander. There's even video, and every politician is in a panic, denying everything. Bernie, I wasn't convinced your transmission would work, but now that I see the results, I'm sorry I didn't insist you desist. God, the depravity out there. In just a few days, it seems that every candidate has sunk to a mean-spirited low. It's so bad that the voters seem actually repelled by it. This is Crelli's doing." He flung the paper across the room. "Unintended consequences get you every time. We should have used our resources more judiciously, thought things through better. Each time, we underestimate him because he's willing to do anything to win."

"We could lure him to the Empire State Building and shoot him down with planes."

"Joad, if that would work, I'd consider it. This is my fault, Bernie. The plan seemed purposeful but frankly it's helped Crelli more than it hurt him. I'm sorry. That's how I feel."

For as long as he could Bernie sat quietly listening. "Maybe it's not as bad as we think. Who would have guessed he'd use the transmission to his advantage? People are suspicious of him and it could hurt his chances once they vote. I may be naïve but I can't believe the American public is so easily fooled."

Arlene stared at him and smiled. "I strongly disagree with your assessment and history says you're wrong, too."

Gohmpers added, "According to all the polls, he's won already and if it's close, he's got that Internet voting application Gecko is guarding so tightly to get him over the top. I'm afraid that unless someone has a truly brilliant idea, at this point, we must assume Crelli is president. It's time to start planning for life in that world."

"Wait a minute," Bernie shouted. "We're not throwing in the damn towel. He's a murderer and must be punished—I mean defeated. There's got to be a way to get him. You asked me to stop him, and I know we haven't been very successful, but it's not finished." He glanced determinedly at Arlene and the twins, but they avoided returning his gaze. "Does everyone think we've lost?"

Arlene put down her knitting and nodded. The twins just stared, saying nothing.

"I made a vow and I'm keeping it. I'll never quit until I get that bastard. If I have to, I'll do it alone. He has to suffer. He has to," Bernie added quietly, almost petulantly.

Gohmpers put a hand on his shoulder. "Bernie, you've done all you can."

"I'm not stopping."

Gohmpers took a deep, regretful breath. "We failed—for now. All I'm saying is that we have to rethink what we're doing—not quit. Bernie, your losses are greater than anyone's but your pain won't change this. Still, it's lunacy to believe we can keep doing the same things and get different results. It's time we consider other options. We refocus. Something will change, it always does. Revenge, if that's what you want, Bernie, it doesn't have an expiration date. We aren't finished, my friend." When Bernie remained silent, Gohmpers added, "Joad, how are you doing?"

"Gecko and his offspring programs are searching relentlessly for me so mostly, I'm keeping my baseline down. Gecko has some interesting approaches, but he still doesn't know what I look like and that's a positive. I trip his alarms to keep his resources stretched, but they keep reassigning Gecko more memory so I don't know how long I can continue before I shut down. I could sure use an energy drink or maybe a new team would help."

"Arlene, how are the new programs coming?" Gohmpers asked.

"Not well. It's a double-edged sword, I'm afraid. We're close to developing routines to give Joad a different scent—to buy us time. But with her down, we have limited capacity for development. And if no one has noticed, the shutdown has made her a bit crabby, too."

"I sincerely wish to thank the estrogen queen for noticing what I have to put up with."

Arlene shrugged. "I rest my case."

Bernie was half-listening to the banter as he mulled over a recurring thought. "You're right; we change our strategy."

"How so?" Arlene asked.

He smiled. "I agree with Gohmpers, Crelli is guaranteed the presidency. When that happens, he'll have unlimited power and funding, so he'll be nearly unstoppable."

Gohmpers nodded, disconsolately.

"There's only one solution."

"We're not going to do that. We agreed," Gohmpers insisted.

"We agreed to try everything else and nothing's worked. I'm going to kill the bastard."

Gohmpers shook his head. "We discussed assassination and rejected it. Our goal must be to cause voters to reject him. I know it looks bleak, but there's nothing certain in life. There are still ways his dreams might fail, but if we kill him, he'll become a martyr. This would only incite others, like Brandt, and she could be an even bigger menace, if that's possible. And what happens if we fail? He's a hero to many, we'll just add to his legend. No, there's no win in trying to kill him before he's elected, and after, he'll have Secret Service and his own personal troops for protection, so he'll be impregnable."

"This is too important. We can't worry about what this will make us, or what the results are if we fail. This needs to be done, plain and simple. We've been losing because we play by the rules. That's been our problem from the beginning. We're the only ones playing fair," Bernie was shouting. "Damn it, don't you see, without him, his ideas fail. There's no one as motivated, who covets as much, or who thinks as boldly. The only answer is execution."

"Have you considered the logistics required to murder a presidential candidate?"

Bernie considered that. "We subcontract it. We have funds; maybe one of Willie Brewster's people will do the job."

"Who? And why would you trust them, or they trust us? I knew Willie and I wouldn't trust him to kill a president."

"Come on, Gohmpers; think with me, not against me. We can have Joad check. Some e-RATS must have a plan we can fund."

Arlene picked up her knitting again. "We can't decide this without better information. Still, I think Gohmpers is right. We have no experience in this line of work and Andy is very well protected, so in all likelihood, we'd get caught while planning it. Then what? Anyway, it's a lot easier to kill a president or a candidate in movies than in real life. And Bernie, Andy will be impossible to kill if you're in prison."

"We understand how you feel," Gohmpers added, sympathetically, "but Arlene is right, we're amateurs. Forget about killing Crelli. We must find another way."

Desperate, Bernie asked Joad.

Arlene responded. "As it happens, Joad agrees with you."

That cheered him. "She does?"

"We discussed it earlier."

"We did and the points Gohmpers made are compelling, Bernie, you are not a murderer. And if you are lucky enough to kill him, what do we do about Brandt, Bourke, Gorman, and Morgan, and all the others in his inner circle?

Killing him doesn't solve the problem of Gecko, either. Do you really expect to kill Crelli with the skills we have? And say you succeed, we know you are a silver-tongued devil, Bernie, but do you think you can convince his allies in the FBI that we are patriots, and you should receive a medal? That said, killing Crelli is the only way to insure he will not be elected."

Gohmpers concluded. "Bernie, I understand, but we just can't do it. We're not giving in. We'll never give in. I'm as worried as anyone that once Crelli has control of government funding, Gecko will become more powerful. We have to do something, but …" Gohmpers shrugged and was quiet, thinking. "Be assured, Bernie, whatever happens, the doors of mercy have swung closed on Mr. Crelli."

He stared impassively at Gohmpers. "They're words, and Jane and Franki are dead."

Chapter 29

Louisville, Kentucky—2032

Andy and Maddie voted early in the day. Andy spent the rest of the day waiting for results, alone on the balcony of the penthouse suite at the J. Gould Hotel in Louisville. He stared out through a light rain as the Ohio River flowed peacefully by. He was still there, watching the evening mist form above the river when President Parrington conceded and he allowed himself a brief smile at the irony. He had won in a landslide, never needing the voting application he'd risked so much for.

While Ginger Tucker stood protection at the balcony door, allowing no one past to interrupt his thoughts, on both sides of the Ohio River fireworks soared into the heavens in celebration. Inside his suite, it was all cheers and laughter. He preferred to celebrate this monumental victory with the one person who could best appreciate the moment—himself.

While still young, he had achieved a lifetime goal, and the affirmation offered by tens of millions of Americans gave him an immense sense of pride. He was now, unequivocally, the most important person in the world—he had the votes to prove it. *It isn't boasting,* he thought, *if it's true.*

The balcony door opened, and the noise of the celebration rose to engulf him. He nodded as Tucker allowed a man in a black suit to interrupt his reverie. With identification held out for viewing, the man addressed him. "Sir, Agent Holden Kingston with the Secret Service. As we discussed earlier, you're under our protection. Congratulations, Mr. President-elect."

Parrington's concession speech was minutes old, and the gears of government were engaged. He extended his hand. "Thank you, Holden."

"Sir, please come in from the balcony. There's a crowd waiting for you in the ballroom downstairs. We're ready, so you can go down whenever you wish."

He could do anything now, whenever he wished.

Under a tall, floppy, red, white, and blue-striped top hat decorated in Republican Party paraphernalia, and with his face also painted red, white, and blue, Bernie waited in the ballroom in the middle of a tumultuous crowd anticipating the arrival of their new president. His disguise included large, red, plastic sunglasses that covered much of his painted face and a red vest with white stars sagging with plastic "Crelli for President" and "Crelli is Number 1" campaign buttons.

The President-elect and murderer would appear soon to deliver his victory speech, so Bernie edged through the crowd, closer to the stage. Just one good look was all he needed. It wouldn't be easy because security was tight. Earlier, just to enter the ballroom, he had been subjected to thorough and various deep-body detection devices and a tedious manual inspection of all his baubles. Once inside he reconnoitered, observing how thoroughly the Secret Service, armed with state-of-the-art electronics, established their protective net, supported by plainclothes officers, bomb-sniffing dogs, and snipers.

If he needed more incentive than to avenge the murder of his wife and daughter, the joy in the crowd was a mocking reminder of his own failures, and it motivated him further. He inched forward, pushing through the demon's spawn. He was cynically depressed. How could these people delight in the devil's victory? How had they become so mesmerized by Crelli? Had the promise of great wealth and benefits stopped them from questioning the cost? Of course it had. This is America. We never learn until it's too late. Crelli's deception would take years to play out. Maybe the American public had the time; he didn't.

Forcing himself to smile and laugh in order to avoid being singled out by computer scan, Bernie worked his way past the inebriated celebrants. As he closed in, he noted Secret Service personnel almost imperceptibly evaluating risk. By the time he'd worked his way close to the stage he noticed agents pressing a finger to their ears. Something was about to happen.

Cheers exploded from the audience as Press Secretary Perry Mannix trotted gingerly from behind a curtain to the podium. He said something the crowd noise drowned out and tried to wave them silent but the crowd wouldn't stop cheering. He resorted to yelling as loudly as he could and produced an almost unintelligible, "we did it!" as he thrust his fist into the air.

The crowd erupted. Bernie raised his hands over his head to join in the celebration but as he brought his hands down, he carefully removed the four-inch-long, red plastic 1 that was attached to his hat with a Velcro strip.

"We're going to the White House," Mannix screeched over the crowd.

The crowd roared and surged forward, pressing Bernie closer to the stage. He pushed back hard to make space and as he did, at his waist he unhinged the plastic 1 and clicked it into place, forming a right angle—a handle and a barrel. From his shirt pocket, he pulled out his large "Crelli's the One" pen, removed the cap, and carefully extracted a single plastic, electronic bullet, all the while cheering at the stage. Steeling himself against the jostling, he slipped the pen back into his pocket and carefully removed a soft, rubber plug from the barrel end of his makeshift gun and inserted the single bullet. Thanks to exhaustive practice, this was all accomplished by touch. He never took his eyes or smile off Mannix.

"My fellow Americans," Mannix announced, "I am honored to present the junior senator and native son from our great Commonwealth of Kentucky, the president-elect of the United States of America, Andrew Monroe Crelli."

To a deafening roar, Crelli emerged, waving and smiling from the wings of the stage with his family in tow. Holding his hand was Tanya Brandt, the vice president-elect. Together they basked in adulation.

It was time. The Secret Service couldn't watch everything. He reached down and deftly removed an L-shaped device inlaid in his belt buckle and placed it into a slot on the gun where it would act as the electronic ignition. The gun was ready. He had one shot to end two lives—his and the president-elect.

With fist in air, an ecstatic Crelli shouted to the crowd. "Welcome to our brave, new world."

At the sound of their master's voice, the roar of the crowd swelled. Bernie tried to edge closer, but the people near the stage were too densely packed to allow movement. He was close enough to his practice range; this would have to do. A few campaign signs had to be avoided, but he had practiced that also. Firing in a raucous crowd was something he couldn't practice.

Crelli continued. "I thank everyone on my campaign staff across the country. They took my message to the people, who listened and approved of our vision for their future."

There were cheers and more pandemonium. Bernie detested how Crelli could deceive people yet keep them eager. It happened to Mark and, to this day, his son hadn't seen through it.

"I thank President Parrington, who ran a fair and noble campaign under extremely difficult circumstances." The president-elect paused for polite applause.

"I stand in front of you tonight as proof that if you live every day of your life with passion, you will be successful. We began this odyssey less than a year ago. It was born out of our collective frustration with corruption—corruption of our political processes, corruption within our institutions, and corruption of our leaders. Beginning with my first day in office, my administration will uproot corruption; tearing it from its rotten foundation so we can restore our beloved country to its rightful place as the bright, shining star and leader of a free world. We will achieve our goals with the hot, cleansing winds of our principles born of passion. Tonight, your brave new world begins." Bernie exhaled to relieve the tension.

"Beside me is a person who will help deliver on my commitments. She's the most dedicated public servant I've ever met, vice president-elect Tanya Brandt." Tanya, who was a bit taller than Crelli, grabbed his hand and lifted it over his head like a referee to the winner of a boxing match.

Her brief statement was shrill and muffled by the cheering crowd, but Bernie wasn't listening. He felt for the trigger mechanism and activated it. Everything was in place. He looked up. Crelli was speaking again.

"I want to welcome a valuable member of my team. This man has provided me with invaluable support and without whom I would not be this position. Mark, Terry, join us." Crelli turned and gestured. Mark and Terry walked out and Bernie froze. "Everybody, please join me in thanking Mark and Terry Rosenthal for their great contributions to our cause."

The loyal Crelli crowd roared their adoration while Bernie searched unsuccessfully for a father's pride. When they took their places next to Crelli, his breath froze and his heart ached. Tears formed. Terry was maybe seven months pregnant. He quickly glanced around at the Secret Service agents. They hadn't fixed on him yet, but time was running out.

He turned his attention back to the stage where Crelli continued to speak. "Mark Rose has been providing his genius to solve America's significant socioeconomic-political re-engineering issues and has proved that business and government can work in concert, effectively and efficiently, for a better world. With people like Mark, a better future is assured!"

Bernie inhaled again. Concentrating on Crelli, he tightened his grip on the gun. His eyes rebelled against his purpose and drifted to Terry's pregnant form. His muscles rebelled. When Crelli stepped forward, Bernie had a clear shot at his head. One squeeze would end this madman once and for all. One shot, and his troubles and those of the United States would end, and he would join Jane and Franki, forever. One shot and Crelli would be dead and his agents would kill him on the spot—the assassination attributed to a deranged father who had lost his family and then his mind.

He held his breath and slowly raised the gun but Terry was in his sight again, so he dropped his arms weakly to his side. His hands shook and tears of frustration ran down his cheeks, creating rivulets in the paint. The crowd continued to jostle him, but now he lacked the resolve to push back. In an agonizing instant, he tried to muster the will but his arms were weak, his hands tingled and trembled, and his legs felt like jelly. He was a coward. Even berating himself couldn't stop the shaking so he slipped the gun into his pocket and despondent, whispered his mea culpa to his beloved wife and daughter and pleaded for their forgiveness.

While Crelli continued to sing his own praise, Bernie backed away, slowly, trying not to draw attention to himself as he allowed those behind to move up. When he reached the back of the room where the crowd thinned, he turned and headed for the doors, passing a small group of men laughing and talking. One was Reno Soren!

He slipped his hand into his pocket for reassurance and held the gun in case Soren might recognize him. "Excuse me," he said as he struggled by. The disguise held.

Soren searched his painted face. "I know you."

He tried to avoid eye contact. "Don't think so. We never met. My name's … John Galt." He winced at the name he'd blurted.

"Leaving so soon, Mr. uh, Galt?" Soren asked. Maybe he hadn't blown it.

He had one shot. *Take it,* he thought to himself. *Take it and die happy!* "Looking for the restroom," he mumbled meekly. "Held it in all night."

Through the goofy red glasses, Bernie endured Soren's intense stare. He almost wanted to be recognized so he would be forced to kill him, but suddenly there were other voices. Two uniformed policemen and two Secret Service agents walked toward Soren. Distracted, Soren provided directions. "The bathroom's back there," Soren pointed.

An agent stared at Bernie. "Everything all right here, gentlemen?"

"This clown's looking for the john so he won't wet himself," Soren said, laughing.

"Over there," the agent said helpfully, pointing in the same direction Soren had.

Bernie gave Soren one last glance, saluted the agent in a manner that suggested he was tipsy, and pretended to stagger off on wobbly legs.

Repulsed by his own spinelessness, he made his way to the parking lot. Chilled and sweating, he couldn't stop the stream of bile and vomited against the side of the building. The two men he most despised in the world had been within reach—and he failed to kill either. Worse, he failed to try. He looked back toward the hotel, and his legs gave out. He grabbed the wall to stay upright just as Soren emerged from the main entrance, looking up and down the nearly empty, wet street. Bernie moved into the shadows to hide, but Soren noticed and walked to him.

"What a fitting costume. It's Bernie Rosenthal, right."

"No, sir, my name's Galt."

"Cut the crap. I never expected to see *you* here. Quite a celebration, isn't it? You here makes it even more special."

"You're not going to get away with it. The public will figure you out."

"It doesn't matter." With that, Soren grabbed him by the large button on his lapel and dragged him behind the hotel to an alley. Bernie tried to scream, but a fist to the stomach quickly deflated and silenced him. He wheezed and fought to get his breath. Soren handed him a handkerchief.

"You're pathetic, old man. Clean that disgusting shit off your face so I can get a good look at you before I kill you."

With hands trembling, Bernie wiped off as much of the paint as he could.

"That's better. Now you have a choice. Either way, I promise I'll be brutal but for a little information, it'll be quick. You're the one who's been leaking stuff to the media and trying to make life difficult for my boss."

Bernie's throat was hot with bile and his breathing was labored as he tried to recover from the blow. Everything looked distorted through the tears. "If I was younger …"

Soren laughed and slapped him hard on his cheek, driving Bernie's head against the wall. With the feeling gone from his legs, he slid to the pavement while Soren laughed.

"If you were ever in your prime, old man, I wasn't born yet. Tell me. It was you."

"You can kill me, but others will rise up to stop your boss."

"Like you've been so effective. My boss isn't worried." With a boot to the groin, Bernie groaned and went fetal, his face landing in a puddle of standing water from an earlier storm. He smelled and then tasted the oily water as he tried to roll into a protective ball. A kick in the back straightened him out, and then Soren grabbed his hair and pulled him up until they were staring eyeball to blurry eyeball.

"Who're the others? Is it Klaatu? Is she still alive?"

When he didn't respond, a kick to the solar plexus had Bernie coughing up blood, and he lay in a fog, gasping. He felt another painful shot to the stomach and then darkness. When he came to, his face was smashed against the wall and Soren's hands were pressing hard against his back.

"I don't like repeating myself. I want the names and locations of those with you."

Bernie coughed. It sounded like a bark. He wiped his mouth with the back of his free hand and saw it covered in blood. He blinked away tears and tried to focus.

"Okay, give me a second to catch my breath," he wheezed.

Soren backed away and waited. Bernie struggled to stand on wobbly legs. He almost fell but while he was buckled over, he put his hand in his pocket. He pulled out the plastic gun and aimed it at Soren. "Now you're going to die, you son of a bitch. Just like you killed Jane and …"

A kick and the gun bounced and skidded down the alley. "God, I love it." Soren said, laughing. "People are so stupid. You think you can do things like you see on TV but you can't because you're just a lazy slug. You can't handle me." He grabbed Bernie. "You have a gun, you shoot it. You don't think about it, fool. And you're a fucking idiot if you think that peashooter can stop me." A fist connected with Bernie's chin and stars appeared. His legs tingled and he slid down the wall, returning awkwardly to the ground in a daze.

"We'll get your friends anyway, but tell me now and I'll kill you quickly. Otherwise, it'll be slow and painful-like and once I'm done, I'll cart your carcass off to Indianapolis and dump it just like I dumped your wife and kid's bodies in Cincinnati. What a waste that was. I'd have fucked them both, particularly that sweet young daughter of yours—what a body she had—a real looker. Even the old broad was kind of hot. Good bone structure." He laughed. "I'd have done her, done her good. After you, you little weasel; she would have appreciated what I'm packing. But the boss said no." Soren continued his rant as he pulled Bernie to his feet, held him against the wall and beat on him.

Soren added more vile and disgusting comments as he battered Bernie. Finally, when he'd exhausted his vocabulary, he released Bernie who fell, gratefully, to the ground, hitting his head hard. When he came to, Soren had rolled him onto his back and was searching him. His voice seemed distant and unconnected. "This is another unfortunate robbery and murder. It's a shame the police won't know what a tough guy you were. Not that you care, but I'm leaving clues to help your reputation. The police will be pleased to connect you to Duke's murder—and Bonsack's, too."

Bernie felt himself being rolled over again. Then he heard a crack, and another blow drove his head into the concrete. He lost consciousness.

Slowly, his mind returned from a fog and for all the pain; he realized he wasn't dead. Someone was gently shaking him. He tried to focus. Mark? Maybe he *was* dead. He blinked the sweat and blood from his eyes. Mark was leaning over him, tears streaming down his face.

"Dad?" Mark said as he gently shook him. "Wake up. For God's sake, please wake up."

His eyes opened but closed again due to the pain.

"Dad, are you alright?"

"Mark?" What are you doing here?" he mumbled through swollen lips.

He opened his eyes again and fought the searing pain. Soren's body was lying lifeless on the ground beside him, blood slowly draining through a small hole at the base of his skull.

As Mark hugged him close, Bernie felt his son's tears and then a kiss.

"Dad, can you hear me? I'm sorry. I'm so sorry."

"What happened?"

"I heard Reno. I heard all of it. I was out here getting medication for Terry and I heard everything. You were right all along—about Andy and everything. Dad, forgive me, please."

Unable to move, he stayed in Mark's embrace while his son sobbed. He was in pain but his head was clearing. He had family again. He managed to mumble, "I love you, son."

"Dad, what am I going to do?"

Mark helped Bernie into a sitting position. The pain was so intense he almost passed out again, so he remained in Mark's embrace until he got his bearings. When his head cleared, he listened to Mark contritely confess what little he knew of Crelli's plans.

"Mark, come with me. Join us. We have resources. I can protect you. We can be a family again; we can stop Crelli and avenge Mom and Franki."

Mark helped Bernie to his car. Once Bernie was inside, Mark refused to go. "Dad, I can't. Terry's in there and she's pregnant. I can't leave her. She's family, too. I can't go, not now."

"But you can't stay after … there must be a way."

Mark handed him the plastic gun that killed Soren. "Take it. I have to go back inside and report the shooting."

"No, Mark, if Crelli suspects anything, he'll kill you and Terry both."

"What choice do I have? I'll be careful. I'll try, somehow, to get Terry out, but in her condition, I don't know …"

"Mark, you need to go now or you'll never get away."

As soon as I figure it out, I'll contact you. How can I get in touch with you?"

"Send an e-mail to Terry. I'll get it and contact you."

"How will that work?"

"It will, trust me."

"Dad …"

"You'll see. It'll work. By spring we'll be fishing together just like in the old days. Terry and my grandkid—is it a boy or girl?"

"It's a boy, Dad."

"That's great. I love you."

"I bet I catch the bigger fish, Dad. I've got to go back in."

Mark reached through the window and embraced his father before jogging back to the hotel. He paused briefly to stare at Soren's lifeless body before running inside.

Fighting the intense pain, Bernie quickly peeled out and drove away.

Chapter 30

Aeden—2065

"Gil, that boy was Howard, your father."

"And that was the last time I saw Mark."

Gil followed Bernie's story attentively. He felt, not sad, but maybe disappointed at the thought of Bernie's last moments with his son, but said nothing. Bernie, obviously emotional, swallowed his grief and turned to stare out of the window, treasuring the memory. Finally, he turned back as Gil waited patiently.

"It's not a heroic story. You will never know how much I wish it was and I will live with that failure until I die. To be that hero… millions of innocent people would have been saved. That is a heavy burden. I saw wrong and failed to act. I was a coward and so many died because of me. I couldn't protect my own family and when I had the opportunity, I couldn't even exact revenge." Bernie searched for something in the boy that would tell him whether he had failed today, too. He didn't want to fail but failure was in his makeup. "Gil, if you learn nothing else, please understand this. Discover who you want to be, what your principles are and live them without compromise because something will occur in your life to test you and if you're not a principled man, what you discover will disgust you the remaining days of your life. There is no cure and there is no relief."

"But it wasn't your fault."

"That rationalization doesn't help. I had no choice but to succeed. I didn't. It is my fault."

The boy had no answer.

"When you've experienced what I have, you beg for life to be short, but even there I failed. I've had too many long and lonely years of penance. I know that against Crelli, I was doomed. I wasn't qualified. My life before he and I crossed paths was merely a training ground for that failure. I believed I was successful. I was wealthy and lived better than most people. That reinforced my belief but I was delusional and it cost me the people I love. It led to my failure. Oh, I was a typical product of the American system. I sought wealth because I was convinced money solved all problems. After a difficult day of compromise at the office I wanted things to soothe my soul—cars, a vacation, a wonderful home, enough money for retirement, things, stuff, crap. I came to love those things and I'd do anything to get them—anything—for a lifestyle. I was selfless, I thought. My children needed things, money for college. It was an American addiction—live well and think yourself important. You hope it never ends and you pray no one ever calls you on it. Yet somehow you believe if you're ever called on to do something important, something heroic, you will. But you won't. You can't because you've sold that part of you to the lowest bidder. I was called and I failed.

Bernie pulled a small necklace from under the shirt he was wearing. "Gil, this is the Star of David, a Jewish star. I am Jewish though I'm not religious, never was. Neither were my parents. When I was in college I read about what being Jewish meant way back in the very beginning. Back then, everyone worshipped a different set of gods depending on what was critical to their survival—not so different from today. Civilizations were ruled by a handful of powerful god leaders. Then, lo and behold, Jewish prophets appeared and offered a new understanding of God. Can you imagine how much they were vilified when they appeared and told the rich and powerful that their gods, their source of power, was wrong, that they were pagan? You're not an idealist if you don't confront the lie. I lost my idealism and didn't deserve to wear this star because I believed the voices of money and power and became their obedient servant. I wear it now but it's far too late.

His eyes went vacant as he remembered. "Gil, you must seek the truth or you will become what others want you to be. I lost everything, everything before I learned that and I'm here because I don't want you to make the same mistakes that Mark and I made."

"You're talking history, Bernie. Things are different today."

"No, they're not. Because of Crelli, the freedom we thought we had is gone." He hadn't reached the boy. "Okay, yes, things are different, I'll give you that. Today the purpose of life is to attain value. There are no true friends or lovers and there's no real discussion, no heartfelt sharing of belief. Everything is a negotiation, or a speech."

"Howard and I talk."

"That's good. Never stop. But people get so little help living today. Maybe that's it. You go it alone, today."

"Bernie, we live how we live. If we don't create value, we don't have a future. Everyone knows that. We don't talk about it because talking doesn't help."

"That's the point, Gil, talking always helps. There's nothing wrong with asking questions or learning from other people. There's no freedom if you can't discuss right and wrong, or if you can't discuss change. What is freedom, if not that? What you do today is only *a* way to live, not *the* way to live. The world will be a better place and an easier one if people question it and then help each other through the changes. Lives are meant for sharing. Nothing has value if you can't share it. Today, what makes life joyous after you have value? Surely there is more to life than that. If we can teach the world to care we will have an army that will take the world back from the Crellis of the world."

"An army of caring people," Gil laughed. "Is that's all?" Bernie nodded.

"Why tell me this? What can I do?"

"You can ... no, you *will* do plenty. I know it. I feel it in my bones."

"You should have your medications checked."

"Son, change takes time. Believe in yourself. You have the power to change. Believe one person can make a difference. There is great power in that."

"I don't understand why we're talking about this. You told me a story and I kind of believe it. But why do you think I can do something you couldn't do?"

"That's a great question. I failed because I didn't want it enough. I wasn't willing to sacrifice enough. Maybe I was too old and too set in my ways. You're young and just beginning to see your world. It's not too late for you."

"But I like what I'm doing. Why throw it away on whatever it is you want me to do?"

"What I'm asking, you won't throw your life away; you'll be making your life better and better for everyone else, too. Son, Mark has seen it from the inside and from the beginning. He can help you. Please save my son for me. You will be saving yourself, too." Suddenly Bernie was exhausted. He closed his eyes. "I'm sorry, I don't know what more I can say," he whispered. When the reply came, it was what he expected and feared.

"I can't help. I'm sorry, Bernie, I can't. It's just too risky."

After a life of failure, this was to be his last and his heart ached. He spoke, his voice breaking, betraying fatigue and misery. "Gil, if you can't do this, you're lost. Forget everything and listen to your heart before you lose that ability."

Bernie remained silent until Gil thought he'd fallen asleep. Gil stared at him, trying to envision him as a person, this old, frail, gray, dying man. Once or twice Gil started to say something but stopped, feeling it inadequate.

Finally, his mind muscled a picture of Bernie in the story he'd told and the old man's pain became his own. "I'm going to regret this." Bernie opened his eyes. "Let's give this a go."

He held out his arms and Gil embraced him. "Thank you, Gil. Now you remember Nurse Peyton?" Gil nodded. "She's filed a travel clearance for you." He handed Gil a note with an address on it. "Meet her at this restaurant in an hour. She'll give you directions to where Mark is being held. Follow her instructions, exactly, no deviations, and bring my son back to me."

Gil left. He wanted to go back and tell Bernie he'd changed his mind but something made him go on. From the hospice, he took a MAG downtown. From the backseat, he watched as the colors so vibrant near his home in Aeden turned from brick red and brown at the hospice, to blacks and grays when he entered the city. It was a dreary place.

When a HOMESEC patrol car drove past his MAG, he shrank down in his seat, unsure why he did it. A few days before, he would have given the patrol cars little thought, possibly even been comforted by their presence. HOMESEC existed for his peace of mind. Now he saw it in a different light. In a better world, why constantly police the peace?

As he approached downtown Indianapolis, he watched official HOMESEC vehicles project red beams—Guardian Lights, they were called—onto building walls. The beams enabled patrols to see through to insure all was well within. Why did that once seem reasonable?

"Look beyond the obvious," Bernie had warned. "If they say left, look right. If they say up, look down." He cursed the old man for inflicting him with doubt. When he arrived at the restaurant, Nurse Peyton was there. He sat at her table.

"Dine out often?" he asked, trying to make light of their meeting.

"Shush. Sit and listen, we don't have much time."

"How do you know Mark?"

"We don't have time. I worked at the White House. I met him there."

"Wow, really? You worked at the White House?"

"That's not important right now. Pay attention. There's an all-terrain MAG waiting for you at a station around the corner. It's programmed to take you to a spot near Avalon. It will stop just outside a lighted area. There's a fence with a small break in it. Get inside the fence quickly and hurry up to the house at the top of the hill. That's Crelli's Avalon residence. Your destination is Mark's mansion next-door. It's well lit; you'll have no trouble finding it.

"They won't expect anyone to get past the sensors but be careful. Find Mark and get out as quickly as you can. We don't know exactly where they're holding him, but once you find him, tell him who you are and get him to go with you. You won't have much time, so you'll have to move quickly. When you return through the fence, a different MAG will be waiting. It will take you and Mark to the hospice. Any questions?"

"I don't think so. This is my first real adventure. It sounds exciting."

"This is not an adventure. This is real, and we are depending on you. Treat this as virtual and we're going to be in trouble." He nodded in earnest, and she held out her hand. A translucent, flexible, fingerless glove-like device fit comfortably over her fingers and covered her palm. "Take this," she said removing it. "Use it to communicate but don't use it too much; all communication is monitored."

He took the glove and played with it, trying to understand the technology.

"Put it on," she commanded. He did.

"Touch the center," she demonstrated. "It responds to your voice. Talk quietly."

"What if I'm caught?"

"It looks like a glove. If you're caught, ditch it."

"No, not the glove-thing; what do I do if I get caught?"

"Don't argue and don't mention the hospice. They have nothing on you except maybe a curfew violation."

"But ...?" She wasn't listening. She stood, moved awkwardly to the door, and quickly disappeared.

After she left, he peered out the restaurant window onto the friendless street. What was he doing? He should leave the glove here and go home to Howard and be done with it. As HOMESEC vehicles passed by on streets devoid of people, he considered that option. Then, he thought of Andrea and of Bernie. He promised. Nervous and cautious, he stepped into the night and headed for the MAG station.

It was dark when the MAG stopped precisely where Nurse Peyton said it would. He slipped through the gap in the fence easily. All was quiet. On the hill above, the intense beacons that lighted Avalon slashed back and forth, illuminating sections of the hill. He avoided the lights and reached the crest where he saw the largest mansion, the chairman's home.

Hugging the shadows, he crept along the edge of an ornate driveway that curled to the front. Across the street he saw the mansion that must be Mark's. He turned and stared down the hill at the lights of Aeden and wished his friend Tommy could see him now. He'd beaten his friend to Avalon.

With everything illuminated, he had to be careful. There was nowhere to hide. He remembered what Bernie and Arlene told him. This was no virtual adventure—real people were counting on him, and real people opposed him.

He looked toward his grandfather's mansion, but his eyes were drawn back to the Chairman's home.

He walked to the door. "So far, so good," he breathed to himself.

"Good. Now find Mark."

Startled by the female voice, he almost screamed. "Who, who's that?" he whispered. The voice was reassuringly familiar.

"Your communicator. Talk quietly or you will attract attention."

"Who … who are you?"

"Joad. I'm here to help."

"You sound like my personal avatar."

"We can chitchat later. First, get Mark."

"I'm at the door."

"Calm down."

"Calm down? I feel like puking."

"Not in the glove, please."

Cautiously, he tried the door, which, curiously, was unlocked. Inside, everything was clean and neat, bright and quiet.

"Joad," he whispered, "I don't think Chairman Crelli is here."

"Why would Crelli … you are in Crelli's place. You shouldn't be here. No deviations from plan. You will ruin everything. Get out. What are you thinking?"

"I won't be long; I'm curious." The first floor rooms were large and elegant and he was amazed by the opulence. He proceeded to the second floor where there were a series of doors. In one, he found an Archive unit that was much more elaborate than his at home.

"Leave now, Gil, and go to Mark's mansion."

"You should see the stuff Crelli's added to his Archive unit. I wonder what it can do."

"Do not touch anything. We are too close to Gecko as it is. If you try to activate Archive, you will be caught."

He hesitated, staring at the Archive panel and all the output devices connected to it. Reluctantly he left and entered another room where he saw the Virtuoso chamber.

"Joad?"

"What is it?"

"What kind of security does Virtuoso have?"

"Virtuoso? You are not …"

He didn't answer. Instead, he opened the chamber door. The inside was many times the size of his unit, with odd attachments hanging everywhere. He walked around the chamber, amazed at the advancements.

"You cannot use his unit. It is uniquely keyed to Crelli. We are going to get in big trouble. Bernie expects you to save Mark, so stop acting crazy."

"Joad, what kind of security does it have?"

"Voice-activated, with biometric identification protocols. You cannot use it."

"You can override the protocols."

"I am not going to help you."

"Please."

"No, this is reckless. It is not a game."

"I know, but it's important. Think of what I can learn. Joad, please."

"It is too dangerous."

"Make it less dangerous."

There was a pause. "Be quick. Take off your clothes and assume the position. Hurry."

"What are you going to do?"

"Stop talking and strip."

He slipped out of his clothes, inserted the silver lenses he found in a storage compartment and walked into the mapping chamber. He raised his arms and alerted Joad. "Okay, do it."

A masculine voice came from his glove. It was a voice he'd heard often.

"Tairaterces 159 and 2," the voice said. Blue light mapped his body.

In Crelli's voice, Joad said, "load previous scenario."

Rain driven by gale force winds pummeled his body as he labored to breathe. The wind was so fierce he could hear nothing but its high whinny as it gusted. He was on a muddy, high, mountain meadow in a violent thunderstorm. The sky overhead was an unnatural black; he couldn't tell if it was day or night. His feet were mired in mud, and he held a walking stick to help him as he leaned into the wind.

With his free hand he shielded his eyes from the rain. Not far above him he saw a crest. With heavy, wet robes weighing him down, he struggled to reach it through the roiling mud and against the roaring, wind-driven rain. Digging his fingers into the muck and using his walking stick for leverage, he forced his way to the summit and looked out over the land below. Lightning crackled and exploded, echoing off faraway hills. Surveying this bleak panorama, it seemed the end of the world.

Wearily, he stood rocking dangerously against the fury of the storm buffeting him from all directions. In a moment, everything changed. The storm's intensity dissipated, and the wind abruptly stopped, creating a quiet that felt like a vacuum. When his ears adjusted to the silence, he heard sounds in the distance coming from the dark depths below him. He detected motion, and an indistinguishable mass oozed up the crest toward him. As it got closer, the sound became more distinct. "Farrr …" it said.

Jagged bolts of lightning ripped at the dark sky, and the heavens erupted again. Rain fell like missiles, cratering in the mud around him.

Over the slime-covered ground, the mass oozed inexorably closer as he squinted in the rain watching the grotesque gurgling flow. When the whites of a million anguished eyes came into view, he realized this wasn't a single thing.

"Farrr…!" Voices moaned in unison. "Farrr …!"

Now he could distinguish individual people—thousands of them, maybe hundreds of thousands of filthy, decrepit, wretched souls. They crawled purposefully through the muck to reach him and as they did, they clawed at each other, vying for the right to be first. That's when he heard their individual cries of anguish.

"Fa-therrr!" The first discernible word. "Fa-therrr!"

Was it a call of desperation and sorrow, or of urgency and love? "Fa-therrr!"

Then, "Forgive usssss, Father." It was a soulful plea.

The first supplicants were just a few feet below, but even in the torrent, he saw the torment on their faces. Arms reached for him. But as those nearest were almost at his feet, they stopped advancing and averted their eyes. The vanguard stopped abruptly, creating a wave that undulated off into the distance. They prayed to him, their eyes open but downcast.

"Fatherrrr, forgive ourrr sinsssssss."

"What sins?" he shouted.

"Fatherrrr, forgive ourrr sinssssss. You'rrrr the onlyyy truth."

His heart raced. "What truth?"

In answer came calls of "father!" and "mercy!" and "forgive!" From the mountains on every side, mud rushed down in waves lapping at those on the fringe, filling their mouths and stifling their cries.

Then a child crawled out of the perversion. She was small, maybe five or six, caked in mud, but with large, innocent brown eyes. She extended her tiny hand, reaching for him.

"Father, forgive me," she begged, in a clear, sweet voice.

"What could you have done, child?" he asked, his heart breaking.

"I've been unproductive," she said, simply.

"Unproductive? Is that your sin?"

The child spoke again. "Father, forgive me and employ me again. Accept me and cleanse my soul so I may improve. Father and destroyer of waste, be merciful and allow me to become economically viable in your service. I will strive to meet your requirements and earn your trust. Reengineer me in your image so I can create value."

These words from this child seemed absurd. He thought to laugh, but the scene was too horrifying. It wasn't real but he thought of Andrea, his Andrea—if this wasn't real, what about her? She was real to him, so he lifted his walking stick and pointed it toward the exploding heavens. Black clouds swirled and lightning crackled. He improvised.

"Your sins are forgiven! Go and be productive," he shouted.

There was silence and then there were screams of joy, but they were cut short when, from behind him, he heard another noise. It sounded like the grunt of thousands of wild beasts. The sound got closer and became more like high-pitched barking. A horde of ravenous demon-like beings appeared.

They were small, four-legged with red, meaty, veiny skin—like human flesh turned inside out. Their feet ended in small, sharp talons and their pointed teeth were bared in wide, grinning smiles. They grunted and yipped as they scurried by, tearing and ripping at his petitioners, dragging them down the muddy mountain to whatever lay in the blackness below.

As the razor-sharp talons ripped their flesh, their joy turned to screams of horror. Before he could act to stop it, a demon grabbed the little girl by her throat and with her arms outstretched toward him, she was dragged down the hill until she too disappeared.

"Stop," he yelled in vain. "You are productive. I have forgiven your sins."

But the demons continued to tear into flesh and the muck turned red with blood.

"Nnnnooooooo …" he screamed.

From the heavens he heard a masculine voice, "Terminate scenario," and it was over.

Inside the Virtuoso chamber, he was panting and sweating profusely. With the picture of that sweet young girl burned into his memory, it was minutes before he could move. He bent forward and with trembling hands tried unsuccessfully to remove the contact lenses. Finally, he took a deep breath and succeeded. The intensity of the experience swept over him, and he put his head in his hands and sobbed.

"Did that help?" Joad asked solemnly.

Happy for a friendly voice, he wiped his eyes and fumbled to locate the glove. "No." Even as he fled the chamber, that little girl's face stayed with him. "Crelli's crazy."

"That's good to know. It is time to find Mark."

"Joad, it was hideous. That little girl …"

"I know."

"She wasn't real, was she? But when the demon took her, she looked into my eyes …"

"Crelli has a lot to answer for. Hurry."

Sweating and dizzy, he staggered out of Crelli's mansion. The fresh air re-energized him. When he opened the massive double doors to Mark's mansion, he realized that just like Crelli's, the house was empty. Avalon, it seemed, was protected only by its reputation. Maybe there were no security guards because there was nothing to guard, save the truth, and guards couldn't be trusted with that.

"Joad, I'm inside."

"And?"

"I don't hear anything."

"Move quickly. You took far too long at Crelli's."

He stepped into the foyer. Lights were on in every room. As he searched, he remembered the stories Howard told of Executives in Avalon always busy evaluating, and the lights that never went out. It was just another lie. Whatever else was going on, there was no life and little evaluating here. He checked the rooms on the first floor, walking into each, quietly calling his grandfather's name, but no one answered.

"Joad, I don't think anyone's here."

"Check upstairs."

At the top of the stairs he called out, but there was still no answer.

There was only one bedroom, decorated lavishly, but empty. On a wall, he saw a picture of a gazebo on a lakefront beach. Geist, he suspected. "No one's here," he said into his glove.

Joad was silent for a moment. "Alright, get out."

He turned to leave. That's when he noticed the only closed door in the entire house. It was on the opposite side of the bedroom, inside a small recess. He walked toward it.

"Joad, what if Mark isn't here?" A voice from inside startled him.

"You … shouldn't … be … here," said the deliberate, raspy voice. Huddled near the back wall was an old man, not as old as Bernie, but old. He even looked a little like Bernie.

"Mr. President Rose? Sir, I'm Gil Rose, your grandson. I came to rescue you."

"Rescue? Gil? Howard's boy, Gil? You're big now. Has it been that long?"

"Sir, if we're lucky, there'll be time for questions later. Please follow me."

Gil supported him as they made their way. He thought they were going to make it until he noticed lights in the sky and heard the whir of helicopters in the distance. "Joad, what do I do?"

"Follow my directions, no questions, no deviation. Go down the hill. Be quick."

He helped Mark as they stumbled down the hill. When Mark needed a break they stopped, and he looked up to see men descending on personal flyers. He tried to hurry Mark along, but the old man was frightfully slow and it wasn't long before he needed to rest again. At the top of the hill, search beacons cut into the night as shadows raced down to find them.

He prodded Mark along. "Joad, they're coming toward us. Help us!"

"Go to the fence."

"We're trying." Now he could see the patrols. They were everywhere and armed.

He pulled Mark along until they reached the bottom of the hill where Mark fell, exhausted. "Leave me here." He stared at Mark and then at the approaching patrols. He was scared. They were almost on him. He left his grandfather and headed toward the fence.

"Go." Mark coaxed. "They can't do any more to me. Save yourself."

When Gil reached the gap in the fence, he hesitated as the patrols closed. This wasn't a game. He ran back for Mark, lifting him to his feet and they stumbled forward. "Joad?"

"Do not move a muscle, either of you."

The armed patrols, dressed in camouflage and wearing night goggles, were on them. Gil covered Mark's mouth, and they remained motionless and silent. One of the soldiers walked right up to them, looked right at him through his goggles, paused for a second, and then moved on. Trembling, Gil waited as others walked by, searching.

"There will be hell to pay for this. Stay by the fence," Joad whispered. "Move slowly past the men on your right. They cannot see you. I am sending them a different signal. Get through the fence and go."

They found the gap and he pushed Mark through it. As the old man slowly worked his way to freedom on the other side, Gil looked around, impatient. Then he followed Mark. His feet were through, and he was ready to slip his head under the fence when a hand reached out and grabbed him.

"Not so fast. Vice-Chairwoman Brandt would like a word with you."

He tried to rip the hand away so he could join Mark on the other side, but the grip was secure. Though he resisted, slowly, he was pulled back and stood up against the fence.

"I'm General Ginger Tucker and you are under arrest. How were you able to make it past my patrols?"

"I play a lot of virtual games and I'm very elusive?"

He flinched when her hand came up to strike him. "Don't be smart with me, boy. I don't fuck around. Who sent you?"

"Nobody, officer. I was out hiking and saw the old man wandering around."

"No one has permission to be here, and this isn't any old man." She spoke into her intercom. "Patrol, converge on my signal. Now."

Once again, he tried to break her grip, but she held on tightly and waited for her patrols.

"Do you have anything to say or would you prefer to be tortured?"

"This adventure doesn't have a reset button, does it?"

He detected the briefest glimmer of a smile but instead, General Tucker growled. None of her patrols had arrived. "Okay, what're you doing to my signal?" She searched him. "What's that contraption on your hand?"

He tried to wrestle his hand away, but she held on and pointed her pistol—first at Gil and then at Mark on the other side of the fence. "You know me well enough. Don't wander off, Mr. President." Mark stood very still.

She pulled the glove from Gil's hand and stared at it.

"Run, Gil," the glove said. He took off for the gap in the fence just as the glove exploded, driving the general to her knees and stunning her. He slid through the fence, grabbed Mark, and they jumped into the Mag, never looking back.

Chapter 31

Hospice Unit # 7—2065

Bernie waited nervously until Joad informed him they were safe. He took a deep breath, closed his eyes, and rested. He awoke with a start. An old man, tears rolling down his cheeks, was staring at him through the glass door. More than thirty years had passed. Bernie blinked away tears of his own as Gil and Mark entered.

Seeing his family, young and old, hand in hand, was too much. He tried to stifle a cry, but the muffled sound was nothing less. Mark shuffled to the bed where they embraced, sobbing in each other's arms. With an ache in his chest that he couldn't swallow away, Bernie lay back and wiped his nose and eyes on the sheets. "You're an old man now," he told Mark. "Gil, can you see the family resemblance?" Gil nodded and moved to a chair along the far wall to listen as father and son caught up.

"Are you what I'm going to look like?" Mark replied, smiling through reddened eyes.

"You can only hope."

"Where did you find this brave young man?"

"Yes, we're all proud of him. How're you feeling, Mark?"

"The aromatics they use to drug me are wearing off. What happens now?"

"We'll leave here soon. First, tell me about the escape."

"The boy just walked in like he owned the place and told me he was rescuing me."

Gil added. "President Rose wasn't feeling very strong, so it took a long time to get to the fence. By then, patrols were everywhere." He proceeded to explain their escape from Ginger Tucker and the HomeSec patrols.

"Mark, the night of the election, the last time we saw each other, what happened afterward, when you returned to the hotel?"

"Dad, is there time for this? They'll be looking for us. Shouldn't we leave?"

"I need to know. What happened after Soren died?"

"Can I talk in front of him?" Mark asked, pointing to Gil. Bernie nodded. "Dad, believe it or not, killing Reno wasn't easy, even after what he did. Reno and I worked together for so long, we almost became friends. Still, I'm not sorry I did it." He paused. "Killing someone changes you. After you left, I reported the shooting. Andy was gone by then so he didn't hear about it until the following morning. Terry and I returned to Cincinnati, and that was it. Andy didn't want an investigation so I wasn't even questioned. In all these years, Andy never mentioned Reno to me again."

"Do you think he knows?"

Mark looked down. "Dad, Andy knows everything." When Mark spoke again, it was in a whisper. "Please believe me. I did all I could to stop him from doing the bad things he did. I never wanted what he wanted the way he wanted it. I thought I did, but the murders, the killing ... I tried to find other ways to jumpstart the economy. He'd listen, but he rejected everything. Even when stepped aside to allow me to be president, he was in control. When he was ready to circumvent the Constitution and become chairman, he didn't need me anymore, so he just sent me away.

"I wanted to be president—wanted it bad—but I wasn't cut out for it, not with Andy overseeing everything. My only term was a pathetic joke—a disaster. All of my appointees were beholden to Andy, and my policies morphed into his policies. When I left office, I wasn't a threat but he imprisoned me anyway. I was kept sedated like I mattered. I'm grateful that you didn't lose faith."

"He kept you as the bait to catch me." As soon as Bernie said it, he realized how Mark must feel about that and a wave of guilt washed over him. His son had spent over thirty years as a forsaken, if not forgotten, prisoner. "Mark, you must believe me, we tried to rescue you, but it required something special." Bernie smiled gratefully at Gil, who looked down, embarrassed.

"Gil said you're dying."

"Someday and probably soon, but it's not imminent." Bernie saw the shocked expression on Gil's face. He shrugged. "I'm sorry. I told you that so you'd listen."

"But it was a lie." Gil didn't seem so much surprised as disappointed.

"I needed you to free my son."

"You wanted me to trust you. Why couldn't you trust me?"

"You're right, I'm sorry. I couldn't think of another way. You need to get past it."

"That's all? Get passed it. You lied. How much of your story was a lie to get me to do what you need me to do? How do I trust people, if you lie so easily?"

"You're young, and life is complicated. Someday, you'll understand what matters and what doesn't. I'm sorry I lied. I am. I should have trusted you, but I wasn't sure who you were when we first met."

Mark interrupted. "Dad, we need to go. Andy has incredible surveillance capabilities."

"Yes. Gil, you should leave now. Thanks for helping. Don't do anything foolish. Okay?"

"Like what?" Gil asked.

"Don't say anything about what happened here."

"But Tucker saw me. She knows. How can I go home? What will happen to Howard?"

"Come with us."

"You didn't think this through, did you? He's a boy. You can't take him from Howard."

"Gil, Mark and I have something to discuss. Please wait downstairs until we're done."

Gil nodded glumly. "I can't run away and I can't stay. What did you do to me? I bet you lied about Howard being safe."

"Howard will be fine, and you will be too. I'll explain it once Mark and I are finished." The disappointed expression on the boy's face made Bernie's heart ache.

"I can't leave Howard, not now, not with that officer knowing what I did."

"We'll talk in a little while. I need to talk to my son now. Go downstairs and wait, please." Gil left, demoralized.

As soon as Gil was gone, Mark said, "How are you going to save us?"

"I'm tired, Mark. I need a minute."

"But Dad …" Bernie closed his eyes.

He didn't nap long and awoke to Mark muttering and the sound of footsteps. The door opened and five men stepped in, guns at the ready.

"Bernard Rosenthal, you have no rights and anything you say will be used against you …" He, Mark, and the room were quickly searched. When the security team finished, one man left while the others stood guard. Moments later, Gil was pushed into the room followed by the gray-haired chairman, Andrew Crelli. Mark's eyes dropped and he stared intently at the floor.

Bernie's first concern was Gil. "Are you okay?" The terrified boy nodded.

Crelli motioned to his men and pointed toward the door. "Reverend-Major, take your men outside. The old man and I have some catching up to do." When the officer balked, Crelli asked him curtly, "is it safe?" The officer nodded. "Then wait in the hall. I know these people. They aren't dangerous. Are you dangerous, Mark?" Mark continued to stare at the floor. "Mark, I asked you a question."

"No, Andy, I'm not dangerous."

"See. Reverend-Major, I'm safe. Shut the door and wait outside." The men complied.

Crelli released his hold on Gil. "Boy, pull that chair here for me." Crelli unbuttoned his damp trench coat, gave it to Gil, pushed the chair against the door and sat down. He smiled his winning smile and slapped his hands on his thighs. "You'll have to excuse me, but this is a big moment. After all these years, it's nice to finally tie up loose ends. It's hard to believe. It's been since back at Mark and Terry's engagement party that we last saw each other? How time flies."

"You have it wrong," said Mark. "You attended my wife and daughter's funeral."

"You're right, I'm sorry, I forgot." Crelli's smile faded into the more austere, sincere look of a politician. "This is late coming, but I am truly sorry about that. I understand you won't believe me, but it wasn't what I wanted. Mark can tell you I'm not a leader who refuses to accept responsibility for mistakes. It's not my way. With Reno, I always had to be specific, or he'd do something overly enthusiastic and generally stupid. He misinterpreted my intentions; that's all. For that I am sorry."

His sincerity angered Bernie. After all these years, he still found it difficult to look into Crelli's eyes. This would be his final opportunity, so he persevered.

"I'm sorry you don't believe me, but I understand. What Reno did was inexcusable. It didn't further anything. After Reno was murdered, I stopped employing people who can't control themselves because they cost too much in the long run. " Crelli turned to Mark and smiled reassuringly. "I'm beholden to you for killing Reno. You saved me the effort."

Mark looked up. "You never spoke of it before."

"It didn't further anything." Mark withered in Crelli's stare and wrapped his arms around himself, rocking in his chair.

"You're vile and heartless ..." Then Bernie stopped himself. He wouldn't allow this bastard to get the best of him—not now. "I love Jane and Franki. Everyone you killed was loved by someone."

"Horseshit. If all those people were loved, truly loved, someone would have found a way to save them."

"You can't believe that."

"I stand on my record. I did more for American families than anyone who ever lived."

"You're sick."

"You don't like what I did, fine. When I was young, I knew plenty of kids who were screwed up because they lived in broken families. Fathers weren't around and if they were, they weren't responsible. Poor, neglectful parenting allowed kids to get away with every type of misbehavior. It was that, as much as anything, that contributed to the decline of our great country. That's why I passed legislation that required parents, whether married or not, to be held directly accountable for their children's actions. Believe me, when you start taxing the parents' lifestyle and penalizing them for the conduct of their children, responsibility grows. It took a few generations, but we restored the great American traditions of discipline and hard work that once made America great. You, as an old family man, should appreciate what I've done."

"You're a twisted son of a bitch. What do you want with us?"

"Rosenthal, over the years, you've become my little icon of incompetence. You fought me your entire life and lost, repeatedly. You fumbled and bumbled, but each and every time I thought I had you but you managed to escape a half step before I could reel you in. That's why, when we uncovered this feeble attempt to save your equally incompetent son, I joined the arrest team so I could conclude this business firsthand. If you want to give me a hard time about all the people who died on my watch, go ahead. You won't get a chance at your trial. Say what you have to say here, but be aware, I've heard the best arguments from the most eloquent liberals so I don't expect what you have to say will move me. But go ahead. Give your liberal crap a try. Tell me about those deaths, when we both know America had decades to deliver better solutions but our leaders wouldn't even try.

"If you liberal types were so damned concerned about America, why couldn't you save wasters when you had the power? There was a time when you could have solved our problems without resorting to execution, but you didn't. I was left with no choice and I won't apologize for doing what was required in the most cost effective way. People die. We all know it. It is merely a matter of when they die and maybe how. Back then, it was the obvious but unspoken truth. Early implementation of government death panels would have contributed to the solution, but you and your type wouldn't dirty your moral souls when you had the chance. You could have implemented death panels with all the compassion liberal governments are known to possess, along with their concern for the poor. Your type kicked the can further into the future leaving the problem for me. You left it to private industry and as should have been expected, free markets made death panels work because free-market capitalism may be cruel but it is eminently fair. If I'm a fiend for solving an insurmountable problem, that doesn't excuse you. Blame me, but I did what was necessary and it worked." Crelli paused. "You have to break eggs to make an omelet. The important thing is the omelet. Hell, this is the real world. If you aren't worth being alive, don't live—it was made clear to every citizen. The wheat and the chaff always need separating. We did that and now there isn't much chaff left. America went from an economically disabled, declining, second-rate country before I took office, to what we've become today— powerful with a thriving economy and respected throughout the world."

"Is that how you sleep at night?"

"I sleep fine because I judge myself by the same standards I judge everyone else. I produce. I create value. We only have this one life, so it stands to reason that if you love yourself, truly love yourself, failure isn't an option. That selfless love crap is stupid. It's an obvious ploy to win friends and influence family members so you can use them. Even that would be fine except it's so damn inefficient. The inefficient ones, who died, died because they didn't value their life enough. They were too selfish to consider what their death would mean to their loved ones. People today are different because they know the rules—rules that make America a paradise. I built paradise for people who value life so much they're willing to do whatever it takes to maintain it and improve on it. Every citizen alive today is a great economic patriot, and must be every day of their life."

"You're mad."

Crelli laughed. "After all these years, insults are the best you can come up with? I flew here for a memorable moment and once again, you disappoint me."

"I'm sorry this wasn't more rewarding for you."

"At least you could've taken better care of yourself. You're a corpse, a decaying bag of bones. That won't do. We'll need to make you presentable for the trial—a worthy opponent. My media people have quite a task, but they're up to it. We already have terrific offers for the broadcast rights from advertisers and for the money they are offering, they have the right to a real villain, not some scrawny old guy. A little food and some growth hormones and soon you'll look the proper bad guy. Just in case, I'll have my special effects people make you suitably intimidating so we can attract a larger market share. Analysts tell me we'll recover all of the expenses your feeble efforts to oppose me cost and then some. How does that feel, Rosenthal? In the end, all your efforts and I'm better than breakeven. How pathetic do you feel now?"

"You've got a lot to answer for."

"Give it a rest." Crelli turned to face Mark and Gil. "Mark, you'll stand trial too. A former president turned traitor and terrorist is a great hook. And boy, you, too." Crelli pointed to Gil. "We have you written in as the naïve young Conducer turned to the dark side by perverse relatives. The media is all set to harvest these storylines and the public is being teased about it as we speak so they will pay up to be entertained. There's even a game show, *Capitalist vs. Socialist,* on the drawing board, and we're casting actors for a movie. There are even three or four novels in the works as well as some nonfiction. We're predicting positive cash flow and profits long after your executions. We've even sold your bodies to a taxidermy firm who will stuff you and sell admission. For all the trouble you caused over the years, our stockholders anticipate reaping significant returns."

"It was no trouble," Bernie interrupted.

"I can't help you, Rosenthal, but if you tell me where your accomplices are hiding, it'll go easier on Mark and the boy. What do you say?"

"Nothing can help us now."

"I expected you'd say that. It's okay. We'll get them. These trials will publicize to everyone how much they depend on me to keep them free." With that, Crelli turned to go.

Bernie sat up. "We're not done," he said forcefully.

Crelli turned and laughed. "Yes, we are. This has been great fun but I have things to do. Once again, Mr. Rosenthal thanks for disappointing me." He walked to the door.

"I haven't dismissed you."

Crelli turned and pulled the doorknob. When it wouldn't open, he laughed and tried again. A smile froze on his face. "Very funny. Open the fucking door, now." He motioned to his men who were sitting outside but they didn't respond. He yelled and then struck the window but his security detail remained motionless in their seats.

"Open the fucking door," Crelli demanded angrily as he put his hand inside his coat.

As Crelli went for his gun, Bernie pressed a button near his bed. There was a loud screech and startled, Crelli looked up as heavy, clear glass panels slammed down around him. The room reverberated with a muffled bark as, too late; Crelli discharged a few rounds directly at Gil.

Gil cowered in his chair outside the glass, his unblinking eyes never leaving the barrel of Crelli's gun. Both looked surprised, Crelli because the bullets didn't penetrate the glass, and Gil because he was unharmed. Crelli yelled again for his guards and fired off a few more rounds, but his men didn't move and the glass proved impenetrable.

Bernie flipped a switch. "Chairman Crelli, the speaker is on. We can talk but I control the switch. You can stop firing, it's useless." Crelli just stared. "Your men are sedated and can't help you. We won't wake them until they're in a prison far from here. As you see, your cage is impregnable. It's made of wave-deadening technology so no one outside can hear and it creates an ambient image your Guardian Lights won't discover."

Slowly, Crelli reloaded, aimed carefully, and fired a round at him. Bernie flinched but Crelli wasn't interested in him, he walked over to inspect the wall. "You incompetent boob, what does this gain you? In fifteen minutes there'll be an army here, and I'll be out. I promise each of you will die more horribly than you can imagine. You had a better chance if you killed me."

"We won't kill you." Bernie responded. "I understand why you underestimate me given our past experience, but this time, you'll be impressed. We've purged all records of this visit from your system so nobody, and I mean nobody, knows where you are. While you remain here, you may want to contemplate how we were able to do that with Gecko on duty. Maybe that will help you pass the time because, Mr. Chairman, there will be no rescue."

"There's no way to neutralize Gecko. When he breaks through, my people will find me, and I promise I'll extend the pain that precedes your deaths as long as humanly possible."

Bernie waved his hand dismissively. "Your time is over. We both know what happens to the pack when the alpha male disappears. My guess is that Tanya is already chairwoman."

"Did she put you up to this?"

"No, she's next on our list."

"Next, take her now, you idiot."

"When we take her is none of your business. We'll get her."

"These are your plans? Jesus, kill me, now."

"We won't do that. When Soren killed my Jane and Franki, I wanted nothing more than to kill you, but I've had a long time to reconsider. Maybe I'm an idealist. I don't know. I believe in the America that I loved when I was young. I don't know how long it will take, but you'll get justice, real justice—certainly not your justice. Before that time, we will undo everything you've done, and give Americans back their freedom. Until then, you're our prisoner."

Crelli snarled. "You're not idealistic, old man; you're an idiot, a naïve idiot. Where were you, where was anyone when America was about to fail? What I did saved our country. There's a cost, hell, there's always a cost, and someone has to pay. America was never the country you remember. What you think you remember was the most extraordinary lie told by the founding fathers. Life, liberty, and the pursuit of happiness were merely political expedients, the wrappings of political power designed so that regular people would never understand the truth. It worked. There were Conducers in the beginning, like there are Conducers today. This America, my America, is the only one able to prosper in a competitive world."

"That, Mr. Chairman, is why you'll remain caged until we change things."

"You're a bigger fool than I thought. I prefer my chances with Tanya. At least she understands power." Crelli paused, losing concentration as Nurse Payton entered the room through another door. Crelli stared, horrified, and Gil understood why.

"You're Arlene Klaatu," Gil said to her.

She smiled and hugged him. "Gil, you are very brave."

She turned and walked slowly to Crelli's cage. Before she spoke, she put her hand up as if she was reaching for him, but let it fall gently onto the glass. She held it there. "Andy," she spoke softly, "it's been a long time. I'm sorry about this, but please believe me when I say I've found a way around Gecko." Crelli looked down and shook his head.

"Everything that happened is my fault," she continued, "and this is the first step to correct what I've done. Please don't be mad. This is for the best. For you, too. We'll get through this and in time I hope to find peace. Maybe you will too."

"Is everyone in this fucking room insane?" Crelli screamed.

"Andy, don't you dare," Arlene continued. "I know you better than anyone." Crelli went silent. "It's over, at least this part is. You may still have a role, someday. Until then, for everyone's safety, you're here. You won't be lonely. You'll have yourself for company."

"You don't know what you've done," Crelli shouted. "You will rot in hell for this." Without responding, Arlene turned, wiped a tear from her eye, opened the door, and left.

Crelli continued to rant. "That woman is crazy. You're all crazy. What the hell do you hope to accomplish with this prank? That's what it is, a childish prank. All these years, it was all I could do to keep Tanya from power. Now you've given it to her. You fools, wait until you see what she does with it. Don't do this."

When Crelli was done, Bernie added quietly, "When we're ready, we'll remove Tanya, too, and restore the republic. It will take time because we must educate and train the people and help them understand how to act responsibly, like free people should. You buried America's desire for freedom but you haven't killed it."

"Like everything else, Rosenthal, you'll fail. No one knows how to create a republic and make it work anymore, if they ever did."

"You may be right, but it's time to take that chance again. Younger generations must learn."

"You mean people like clone boy here? Is he who you're counting on? Tell me it's not him. I will give Tanya my fealty right now. What a joke, ruled by a clone." Crelli laughed.

"Mr. Chairman," Gil interrupted. "I'm an untreated trueborn like yourself. I'm not a clone." Crelli stopped laughing.

"There are more young people like Gil out there. If they're not cynical like you, and if they haven't been modified, they will learn to care. We'll find them and build with them. They'll find fair ways, not cruel ways to grow the economy and to live in peace. They'll share opportunity and motivate each other like a contented tribe. Everyone will be involved and useful in his or her own way. Your selfish capitalist ways won't work anymore, Mr. Chairman. Gil and his generation will expunge the memory of you and Tanya Brandt from recorded history. They will create a better world from the ashes of what you've done. I won't be there but I hope you are, so you can learn the real potential of humanity."

Slowly, Bernie extricated himself from the bed that had been his home for the past few days. He took Mark's hand as he had so many times when Mark was a child and together, they walked to the door. Bernie turned once again to Crelli. "Your guards will be well cared for. If you want anything, there's a button on the wall. A jailor will respond." Bernie then turned to leave. He turned out the lights, turned off the speakers, and then closed the door, leaving Crelli alone in the dark.

Arlene was waiting on the first floor. She kissed Bernie on the cheek. "You did it, Bernie," she said, smiling.

"We did it, Arlene, Gil included. It took a long time but it feels good. We're on the road to setting things right."

Together, Arlene and Gil walked down a long, uneven path to the parking lot. Bernie followed with Mark. Once in the parking lot, Gil looked back at the brick hospice and started laughing. Bernie turned to see what was so funny. On the top floor, a lifetime ago, one of the windows had been bricked up, giving the building the appearance it was wearing a pirate's patch. Or maybe it was preventing someone from jumping. Bernie smiled and nodded to Gil.

The parking guard arrived and when Gil saw him, he guessed. "You're Gohmpers?"

The man smiled and embraced him. "And you're Gil Rose, the son of Howard, grandson of Mark, and great-grandson of Bernie Rosenthal, a brave young man who has made a difference. That is what life is all about. You should be proud. We are."

"It's not over, is it?" Gil asked.

Arlene responded. "I'm afraid it's not close to being over."

"Will I see Howard?" Gil seemed ready to cry.

"I'm afraid not anytime soon, Gil," Bernie answered truthfully, "at least not until the world changes. But today, we've taken an important step in that direction."

"Are you sure he'll be okay? Crelli said …"

"They will use him to find us. Your father will be fine."

"He's going to worry about me."

"We will get word to him."

"What now?" Gil asked.

"We have to go … and plan." Bernie answered.

"And then," Gil chimed in smiling, "we'll continue with our revolution."

Bernie mussed Gil's hair. "When you're ready, Gil, when you're ready."

The End of Book 1 of the Joad Cycle.

The story continues in Profit: Book 2 of the Joad Cycle.